THE CENTURION'S SERVANT

Hilda Petrie-Coutts

Copyright © Hilda Petrie-Coutts 2012

All Rights Reserved

Scripture quotations are from The Holy Bible NIV.

In this novel both historical and imaginary figures appear in what is a work of fiction in this first novel of an exciting trilogy.

Chapter One

'There was a man who was sent from God---his name was John. He came as a witness concerning that light, so that through him, all men might believe. He himself was not the light---he came only as a witness to the light. The light that gives light to every man was coming into the world.'

John 1 v 6-9.

As though the dark forces holding sway over the earth received knowledge that challenge was about to commence, from One already in the world, the Living Word, Son of God made manifest in flesh, they churned the seas into raging fury, buffeted the moon with racing cloud shapes and moaned angry protest in the night wind that poured over the Judean desert.

It still lacked an hour to dawn, was freezing cold and the youth who raised his handsome face from the hard bed of the wilderness, shivered slightly as he drew on his sandals, listening to the eerie keening that filled his ears.

'Simeon, wake up! Hush!'

He bent over his younger brother, gently shaking his shoulder. The lad stirred, opening dark eyes to stare bemused at the impetuous face above him then gasped as realization dawned. He sat up on his sleeping mat. Of course, they were in the desert beyond Jericho, had broken their journey here last night, bound with thousands of others on similar quest to find the man called John, whom some named Baptist.

Beside them stood the tent where their parents lay in quiet slumber, whilst around them stretched a sleeping multitude come forth from their homes in Jerusalem and its villages, joined by a great throng who had walked the weary way from distant Galilee.

'Look at the stars, David! I've never seen them so bright!' He stared up into the glittering vault above him, marvelling at its immensity then gave a swift shudder. 'There's a certain strangeness to the night,' he murmured.

'Come quickly,' replied the other impatiently. 'Remember we planned to make an early start, to seek out the Holy man for ourselves.'

'But what of our parents,' protested Simeon? 'Surely they will worry, thinking we are lost!' The other shrugged.

'Oh, we'll meet with them again, once they reach Jordan. Come now—hurry!' His face bore impatience.

Simeon belted his tunic, closing his mind to duty. They stepped forward softly, carefully, fearful of disturbing the sleeping forms about them but only an indignant camel coughed protest as they passed.

Now the road was mere rough track stretching bare and mysterious in the moonlight. Gentle as that light was, it outlined all too cruelly the disability of the younger boy, for Simeon had been born with a clubbed foot, which gave him an odd, shambling gait. Yet the lad attempted to match David's easy swinging stride, hesitating only as sound of horses hooves thudded towards them.

'Quickly Simeon—look Romans! Get down behind those rocks!' The two lads lifted their faces again, as the noisy party of riders, swept past them onwards to Jordan.

'Roman swine,' muttered David and shook his fist! 'Come on, Simeon, it will soon be dawn, and we won't stand a chance of seeing anything once the multitude is afoot!'

He pointed to a track that led off the main path, up a hill that was all rocks and huge boulders, interspersed with a few stunted bushes. 'Up there,' he ordered.

They puffed and panted their way up the steep slope, then paused, realizing the danger of proceeding further in the dim light. David turned, standing silhouetted against the sky, tall and slim as a young sapling. He reached down a hand to help his younger brother up onto the narrow shaly ledge on which he was standing.

'I'm sorry if I'm holding you back, David. This twisted leg of mine makes the going slow, so if you want to go on by yourself!' There was no self-pity on Simeon's dark skinned face as he spoke.

'What foolish words are these? Would I leave a brother?'

He slipped an arm about the other's shoulders. 'Perhaps, Simeon, this man John, may have the power of healing. If so, it will have been well worth the journey here. Come, it is only a few more feet to the summit and see, the sky is brightening.'

They managed to surmount the rocky buttress and at that moment the sky was suffused with peach light, dousing the stars, as the sun shot red gold above the horizon. They dropped their eyes before its brilliance to where below them the waters of the Jordan glittered like blood between the green banks. Pockets of cotton wool mist, hung in hollows, soon to yield to the intense heat of the sun. Small groups of men were already assembled below down there, on that amazingly verdant strip of land bordering the river, where graceful willows blended with tamarisk and wild olives and tall reeds spiked the water.

'Where is he then, the man John,' wondered Simeon?

'Look,' whispered David. 'Look down there to your right. Can that be the Prophet?'

'Oh, yes, I see the man you mean. What's he doing?'

The boys shaded their eyes, staring below to where a tall figure had detached itself from the sparse cover of the trees and stood head bowed in meditation or prayer.

'Let's climb further down. Follow me Simeon—and keep quiet!'

They slithered their way downwards, David forcibly containing his impatience, as he helped his brother. At last, they found themselves on a narrow slab of rock, behind which lay the entrance to a small cave. David ventured inside, prodding with a stick amongst the stones and dry grass, in case a snake might harbour there. It was safe. Only a small lizard darted frantically away.

'This is a good place, Simeon. The mouth of the cave will give shelter from the heat of the sun and we are only about forty feet above the river from here. Now, where did he go, the man we saw?'

'Isn't that him there, lying face downwards on the ground?' Even as he spoke, the man rose to his feet and raised outstretched arms to the sky. The slight breeze which had arisen lifted the heavy masses of his uncombed hair and beard. The muscles of his shoulders bunched hard, as he turned and shook an angry fist, in the direction of the approach path over the hill.

'Yes Lord, they will come soon, the curious, those who come to scorn your Holy word and to mock your prophet! Yet will I reason with them, adjure them in your sacred name to amend their ways, baptise them, that they may symbolically die to sin and be reborn, cleansed into new hope of redemption. Fill me with your Holy Spirit, Lord! Hold the mantle of your authority close about me, that I may deal with this generation of vipers!' And he uttered a great cry.

David nudged Simeon, face startled. 'He sounds angry, doesn't he? Why does he call the people snakes? I had thought him to be a kindly man!'

'Yet with such ire spoke the prophets of old,' breathed Simeon. He, broke off, chewing his lip, brows wrinkling in concentration, then slid to the edge of the slab of rock and peered down. David placed a restraining hand on his shoulder, fearful that he should slip.

'David, is it possible..?' Simeon broke off, hardly daring to frame the thought that had just formed in his mind.

'Is what possible?'

'Why, that this John could be the promised one, the Messiah, he of whom it is foretold, that he will come to set his people free?' Simeon's voice quivered with excitement, as he shot the question at his brother.

'Others have already wondered that,' replied David. 'Little is known of John, save that he preaches the word of God, in a way such as has not been heard since the days of our ancestors and fears no man! Some say that he has offended Herod Antipas, has taken exception to the Tetrarch's marriage to his brother's wife as being thing which is against Holy law!'

So deep in conversation were the boys, that they had taken their eyes off the prophet.

'The peace of God be with you!' The deep voice came from above their heads and they swung about in confusion. How had he managed to climb up here, without their having seen him? How much had he heard? Little did they know that John possessed the agility of a mountain goat, born of long years eking a precarious existence in the wilderness, living amongst the wild beasts, many of which he considered nobler than the generation of men, whom he had been required of God to minister to and so prepare the way of another.

He stared down gravely at the boys from eyes that were smoky brown, and red rimmed from the desert sand.

'Master!' they bowed and returned his gaze, then lowered their eyes before him. They felt as though this stranger had stripped their souls bare of subterfuge. Possibly, their discomfort lasted only a couple of minutes, to them it seemed interminable. Then the stranger smiled, as though satisfied by his wordless examination.

'Have you come far,' he inquired?

'From Jerusalem,' replied David, recovering his composure. 'We are come to listen to the one we have heard spoken of as a prophet, who speaks the word of God.'

'It is you, isn't it,' broke in Simeon, his face bright with excitement. 'You are John—the Baptist?'

'Yes, my son.' John rested his hand on the boy's shoulder. His downward glance took in the clubbed foot, then rested back on Simeon's face searchingly. 'How are you called?'

'I am Simeon, son of Ezra, the weaver.'

'And you, my son?' John turned to the other boy.

'David. We are brothers.'

John signed to them to be seated then dropped to the ground beside them. 'So, you have come to find me. Now that you have, what would you have me do for you?' He watched their faces broodingly. 'Have you come because you repent of your sins, to accept baptism?'

David flushed slightly. He wanted no direct involvement. He darted a sideways glance at his brother, as for once his ready tongue stuck against the roof of his mouth. Simeon came to his rescue.

'We have heard so much, Master. All of the world speaks of you—well all Judea,' he corrected himself truthfully. 'David and I were curious. Repentance, surely that is for those who have committed real sins? I mean like murder and adultery.'

'How old are you, Simeon?'

'Almost fifteen years!'

'So, and you, David?'

'Sixteen. Master, we are sorry to have disturbed you at your prayers. We thought only to find a quiet place to watch. The other members of our family will be here soon, together with the rest of the multitude.'

John rose and left the cave. He climbed swiftly to the summit and glanced keenly ahead, shading his eyes from the now brilliant rays of the sun. They were coming as they had been over the last months, coming in their hordes, expecting what—to see a spectacle, to jeer at one touched by the desert sun? Yes, there would be many such—but also, those drawn by the chance that here was a leader who would enable them to throw off the Roman yoke. Others there would be seeking prophecy and then some precious few coming humbly in repentance for their sins. He had perhaps half an hour before they reached Jordan's banks, time enough. He returned to the boys.

Some two hours later, the sun poured liquid gold over the bronzed desert and a shimmering heat haze rose above the rock filled wilderness that stretched for miles. Only here, on the fertile banks of the river was there comparative cool and shade. Somewhere between three and four thousand people, were now assembled beside the Jordan, the lucky ones gathered under the shade of wild olives---the more affluent sitting in the open confines of their tents. The vast majority though, stood faces tense, listening to the words of the dominant figure, standing poised on a pinnacle of rock above the river, making use of this natural stage to address the enormous crowd.

Two Roman soldiers hot and uncomfortable in their metal breastplates and heavy helmets stood noting all with watchful eyes, their pose arrogant, faces scornful.

'Well, Flavius, is he religious fanatic or yet another political rabble raiser?' The speaker made a disparaging gesture, towards the Baptist, whose voice thundered with amazing volume, reaching almost every ear. His fellow soldier shrugged.

'Gaius, I really don't know. In a way, I feel he is neither. Certainly he makes me feel most uneasy.'

'Huh—well, when we return to Jerusalem, Tribune Marcus is expecting our report as to whether he presents danger to peace in the area.' He scowled. 'I will be glad when our tour of duty is over in this foul country. Of course, you expect resentment from those in an occupied land, until the inhabitants learn it is their own best interests to accept that under the guardianship of Rome, they will obtain the most stable form of government.' He paused, and raised a wineskin to his lips, then handed it to his companion. 'So, what do you think yourself? Is he dangerous?'

'Not in the normal sense. Look at the crowd—not exactly inflamed, are they? It's more a sense of amazement at his words, tinged with fear.' Flavius looked slightly uneasy.

'Fear of what, do you suppose?'

'Fear of their god,' explained Flavius. 'The Jews have only one, you know. They call him Jehovah!'

'Only one god,' exclaimed Gaius scornfully! 'Why, we have so many! So have the Greeks and all civilized nations.' He paused reflectively and spat. 'Come to think of it, I've never seen a statue to the Jewish god. The Emperor hasn't forbidden them statues, has he?'

'No!' Flavius snorted. 'Their god is supposedly invisible and they are not permitted to worship before a statue in the universal way.' He lifted his helmet for a minute, running his fingers through his short cropped hair. 'As I've heard, they trace their ancestry back through the centuries to a certain Abraham. They're an ancient race, once very warlike.'

'Really, well I wish this John the Baptist would preach in their temple in Jerusalem instead of insisting on his people coming out into the desert! Here! What's happening now?'

The two uniformed Roman soldiers, pushed forward, to get a better view of what was transpiring ahead. Crowds were falling to their knees, heads pressed against the ground. John leapt down into the water. He raised his arms high, wide then threw back his shaggy head, as he burst into impassioned prayer.

'Father, look graciously upon your repentant people. Restrain the terror of your wrath, cleave not the heavens with the lightening of your sword, but pour the healing of your love on those who now come before you, humbly confessing their sins!'

As the soldiers watched in amazement, streams of people descended into the water, many weeping openly and beating their breasts. John bent over them, ministering to the never ending, undulating file of humanity. As the water closed briefly over one form after the other, the soldiers shook their heads in disbelief.

'Well, I've never seen anything to match this! You can't even say its hysteria. What's happening to them, Gaius? I mean, I just don't understand!' Flavius florid face expressed bewilderment. 'Here, Gaius—

where do you think you are going? Come back!'

He followed still protesting behind his companion, who was pressing forward to the bank of the river itself.

'What should we do to be saved,' people were calling? John raised his head from those thronging in the water, and stared above him to those on the bank. The soldiers were close enough now to see the weird light in those dark eyes, eyes that blazed the sincerity of his message.

'The man with two tunics should share with him who has none and the one who has food, should do the same!'

Two more men leapt into the water, raising clasped hands to John in mute despair! 'Tax collectors,' murmured the crowd. 'Those two are tax collectors! Surely the Baptist will have no dealing with them!'

'Teacher,' said the two despised ones, finding their voice. 'What should we do?'

John looked at them with compassion. He knew what courage it must have taken for them to appear before this crowd. Tax collectors in the employ of the hated Romans were detested and scorned by all.

'Don't collect more than you are required to,' he told them.

They abased themselves in the water before him. Gaius with Flavius close in tow, now stood on the bank immediately over John. He stared down at the Baptist, an unfathomable expression on his face.

'And what should we do?' inquired Gaius.

'Don't extort money and don't accuse people falsely! Be content with your pay!'

The two Romans peered down sombrely at the teacher, their expressions tinged with guilt. It was as though the whole of their lives had been spread in a tapestry before John, every evil action manifest. But his attention was distracted from them, as two bands of white robed priests approached the water, the crowds still milling forward, parting in their midst, to allow these others through.

'Who are these,' managed Flavius, thick lipped?

'Pharisees and Sadducees—now we should see something!' and Gaius trained his eyes upon them in sardonic amusement.

John's face went dark with anger, as he stared at the newcomers. 'You brood of vipers,' he greeted them. 'Who warned you to flee from the coming wrath?'

'We demand to know who you are! Are you the Christ?'

'No—I am not the Christ.'

'Then who are you? Are you Elijah?'

'I am not!'

'Are you—that prophet?'

'No!' John's face was turned steadily towards them, his eyes blazing. They persisted, looking at him with a kind of insolence.

'Who are you? Give us an answer to those who sent us. What do you say about yourself?' interrogated the Sadducees implacably. John raised a hand for silence, for many were murmuring in anger, at the haughty priests. When he replied, it was in the words of Isaiah, the prophet.

'I am the voice of one calling in the wilderness make straight the way of the Lord!'

Some Pharisees now pushed forward.

'Why then, do you baptise, if you are not the Christ, nor Elijah, nor the prophet?' They smoothed their fringed robes, as they awaited his answer. John looked at them and through them. Then he raised his eyes to heaven. His voice when he spoke was low, but it was heard by the whole multitude.

'I baptise with water,' John replied. 'But among you, stands one you do not yet know. He is the one who comes after me, the thongs of whose sandals, I am not worthy to untie. He will baptise you with the Holy Spirit and with fire! His winnowing fork is in his hand, to clear his threshing floor, and to gather up the wheat into his barn—but he will burn up the chaff with unquenchable fire!'

He jerked his head in mark of dismissal to the two indignant priestly groups and resumed his ministry to those many people still crowding down into the water.

'Well,' muttered Flavius. 'What do you make of all that?'

'That someone else is to come soon. Someone as I understand it that will be of supreme importance to the Jewish nation.' Gaius rubbed his chin reflectively. 'Much as I want to return to Jerusalem, I feel we should remain here for a few more days, until we find out whether this fellow is just talking wildly or from definite knowledge. Judea is seething like a hornet's nest at present. Tribune Marcus says that even Prefect Pontius Pilate is uneasy. Any sign of insurrection has to be stamped out ruthlessly before the Jews find a leader who will mobilize them against us.'

Flavius chuckled. 'Look at them! What could such as these do against the might of Rome!' He slapped his thigh and cast a last disparaging glance at the Baptist, waist deep in the swirling water, and at the dripping men and women who clambered from the Jordan, hands clasped, ecstatic looks on their faces.

Together the two soldiers pushed their way out of the milling throng, exclaiming in distaste at the fringe of crippled and diseased who had somehow managed the journey in the hope that through John they might find healing.

High above the heads of the crowd, watching and hearing all from the vantage point of their cave, David and Simeon sat munching a meal of bread, goat's cheese and grapes. David spat the seeds out towards the soldiers below them, staring angrily at the hated intruders. The sun glinted on their armour and the hilts of their swords. He half rose, grasping a stone, his intention plain, but Simeon restrained him.

'Don't be a fool, David!'

'I could get him right between the eyes from here!' But giving a sigh of frustration he dropped the missile. 'Well, if John is right, someone is coming soon who will lead us!' His hazel eyes shone with enthusiasm at the thought, but Simeon shook his head reflectively.

'No, David. John's message is one of repentance and peace. How can you think in such terms, when only short hours ago, you were baptised!'

'Because I believe the promised one will come to lead his people! We have the word of all the prophets for that!' He slapped Simeon lightly on the shoulder and grinned. 'Stop worrying brother. I would never do anything to put you in danger!'

'You think I am a coward?' Simeon's face registered hurt and annoyance.

'Would I dishonour you by such a thought?' He leaned forward again. 'Look, Simeon, is not that our father?' He indicated a grey bearded, hawk nosed, elderly man, wearing a grey and cinnamon striped robe, who was drawing near to the river bank. There had been a lull in proceedings. Those who had responded in their hearts to John's call to repentance had already submitted themselves to the cleansing rite of baptism. Hundreds of others pointed fingers of scorn at the penitents, for it was unheard of for members of the Jewish race to accept baptism, which was the rite extended to Gentiles seeking admission to the Jewish faith, and who were expected to submit, to what was regarded as a ceremony of humiliation, of being ritually cleansed.

What would their father do? The boys watched anxiously. They themselves had accepted baptism at John's hands, shortly after sunrise, before there were any witnesses present. Ezra was a God fearing man, honest, respected by all who knew him. For the first time, his sons began to wonder what had caused him to join the multitude of the curious. But their thoughts were distracted by the attitude of the Baptist.

For John had risen to full height and was staring fixedly at a tall, slim figure, who had detached himself from the crowd, which had drawn back slightly at this point, many seating themselves and eating of whatever food they had brought with them.

The newcomer drew closer to John. The boys could not see his face as his back was to them, but the sun poured over his dark hair, polishing it to bright chestnut. He stood on the bank now, immediately over John. He appeared to be proffering himself for baptism, but John it seemed was remonstrating. They managed to pick up the words.

'I need to be baptised by you and do you come to me?'

John's face expressed troubled amazement.

This exchange aroused immediate interest amongst the crowd. David heard those below him muttering, that this was 'Jesus, out of Nazareth!' Jesus—who was he then?

Jesus raised a reassuring hand to John. They heard the words, clearly spoken. 'Let it be so now. It is proper for us to do this, to fulfil all righteousness.'

John bowed his head in prayer, then raising his face to Jesus, turned upon him a most tender expression and welcomed him down into the water. The boys rose to their feet, drawn by an instinct they could not name. They did not know they were trembling. They could not take their eyes from the figure that rose now, wet from the water and climbed back up onto the grass.

Before he could make a move to bend, to retrieve his white robe, the water clinging to his form seemed transfixed by the sunlight into shining aureole. A slight moan of awe rose from the crowd, for the light intensified—whilst from the heavens, a snow white dove descended, seeming to light upon Jesus, then they could see it no more, for all light fused into one, as a voice from heaven was heard, like a sigh, touching every heart.

'This is my Son, whom I love. With Him, I am well pleased!'

For a few minutes, every tongue was stilled. Men glanced at their neighbours, asking mutely if they had experienced the same knowledge. Still shaking, Simeon slipped a hand into David's.

'I believe we have seen him. This Jesus, he is the Messiah!'

'You are right! He has come! Oh, Simeon, Simeon! Do you realize what this means?'

'Not quite, brother, only I do not think it is what you are looking to. Did you see the radiance of his expression just now? To me that glance spoke of pure love. Love for all mankind!' The words had been uttered between lips trembling with emotion. Never had David seen his brother so moved. 'This is a man of peace.'

David snorted in impatience then peered down below him in frustration, for the figure of Jesus had disappeared in the crowd. He caught Simeon by the arm.

'Come on! We're going down there. I want to find him. Now careful where you put your feet.' Together they clambered down, the heat hitting them like a physical force, once they left the cool confine of the cave. They pushed their way through the dense crowd, until they reached the bank of the Jordan. John glanced up, saw them and turned his rare smile upon them.

'Where is he, Master? Where is the Holy One,' asked Simeon softly?

John smiled gently. 'He has retreated to speak with his Father. This, my son, was the very Son of God!' He raised a hand over them in blessing and turned away.

'David! Simeon! All day I have worried over you. Your mother has been distraught! Where have you been?' Ezra forced iron strong fingers upon each young shoulder, as he wheeled his sons about, propelling them back from the river to where he had set up his tent. Naomi had indeed been overcome by worry. She and her husband had woken to find their sons gone. They had searched around their camp, but to no avail. It had been Ezra, who had guessed that it was their youthful spirit of adventure, that had caused the boys to make an early start and they would be reunited with their sons at Jordan. Nevertheless, with so many converging on the area, there were dangers to be considered. Wherever there were crowds of the unwary, robbers could be found, desperate men who would slit a throat as easily as snip the purse from your belt.

Then there were the Roman soldiery careless of human life if they thought any less than respectful of the Might that was Rome. Ezra knew his elder son, bore a deep resentment towards the occupying force that his parents, together with all others, should have to pay taxes to the hated foreigners. He had even caught him in recent conversation with a member of the Zealots, the group of fanatical Nationalists, who advocated violent struggle as being the only way to rid Palestine of Roman rule.

'Mother, your pardon, we should not have worried you—we were watching from up there on the hill.' David lowered his head in contrition.

'There's a small cave,' explained Simeon. 'We were able to see and hear everything. Why, we even met John this morning early, talked privately with the Holy man.'

He smiled apologetically at Naomi, whose eyes were bright with unshed tears, so relieved was she to have her sons safe back. Any seeing the quiet beauty of this dark skinned woman, with her almost regal bearing, would realize it was from her, rather than their father, that the boys had inherited their good looks and Simeon her colouring. She scolded gently, whilst exacting a promise, that they would never repeat the offence.

That night, Ezra, together with his sons and the other men of their party, sat around a camp fire, while the women were safe within tents—discussing the events of the day. They intended to stay tomorrow, making their return on the third day.

They discussed the burning question, by what authority did John baptise? If that authority were indeed of Jehovah, then they were living in an amazing time, for the prophets had only emerged during times of crisis. Then there had been John's statement, that though he himself was not the expected One, the Messiah that he was there to prepare the way for the long awaited Saviour of their race.

'Is it true, that John named one Jesus of Nazareth as Messiah,' asked Reuban, cousin to Ezra? His narrow, pock marked face bore shades of tiredness. He had a wracking cough and it was only the slender hope that John was the awaited one that had given him the resolution, to make the long journey from Jerusalem. He had been present, when sadly John had denied what all had hoped for.

'My friends, perhaps I can lay before you, events that happened some thirty years ago, and which I feel give explanation of all that is being discussed here tonight!'

All turned to look at the elderly man, who sat stroking his straggly bead, waiting courteously to be invited to proceed. The boys nudged each other. This was Simon, at whose feet they had learned the law. He was highly respected as living a blameless life and had spent many years service in the Temple.

The other men leaned forward, eager to hear his words.

He cleared his throat and began.

'As I have said, the events I am about to tell you of date back about thirty years and concern two babies, boys born within six months of each other. Their mothers were cousins.

You all saw those two children today, in the glory of their manhood. Yes, my friends, I speak of John named the Baptist and of Jesus of Nazareth.' He was silent for a moment, watching their faces. It was obvious he held their complete attention now, for all sat forward hanging on his lips.

'I am now in my seventieth year, but in spite of that fact those events I would speak of are still fresh in my mind. I see them as pictures unfolding before my eyes.' He paused. 'For many years, I had the honour of giving service in the temple, as had one Zechariah, a man well on in years. His wife had always longed for a son, but was barren, which was great sorrow to the couple. However, they were old and accepted that this was the will of the Lord.' Glances of sympathy greeted his words. It was an ill thing for a man not to have a son to carry on his name. Then 'Get on with it, Simon,' interrupted a stranger in their midst. He was frowned upon for his discourtesy. Simon continued.

'One day, when lots had been drawn as was the custom, to see who would have the honour to go into the Temple to burn incense, Zechariah went in alone, with all of us praying and attending to our duties outside. I followed him. I should not have done so, but thought that one day the honour might fall on me and wished to be able to emulate the venerable old priest. I peered into the sacred place—and stood transfixed! There, to the right of the altar, brilliant with light, stood an angel!' Amazement greeted his words, but none doubted.

'He was in conversation with Zechariah, telling him that his wife Elizabeth should conceive a man child, who would be filled with the Holy Spirit, even from birth! He would bring great joy to his parents and would bring many people back to the Lord, to prepare the way for him. No wine was ever to pass his lips. He was to prepare his people for the coming of the awaited one.'

Men looked at each other significantly at these words, as Simon continued, 'But Zechariah doubted the angel's words. The angel accordingly struck him with dumbness, until the matters prophesied should come to pass. Well, I was full of fear and shrank back amongst the others as Zechariah came stumbling out white and trembling and making signs that he could not speak. All guessed he had seen a vision!'

Simon's audience uttered a moan of awe as the old man smiled and continued, 'I kept my council about all I had seen and heard. And wonder of wonders, Elizabeth bore a child in her old age and called him John, the name laid on him by the angel, whose own name was Gabriel. Her friends and relatives were surprised at the name, for none in the family were called John—but Zechariah wrote the name on a tablet, confirming that it was his wish. Well, immediately, his lips were unsealed. He commenced giving praise to the Lord and to prophesy of the child—"And you, my child, will be called a prophet of the Most High, for you will go before the Lord to prepare the way for him!"

'So,' breathed Ezra, 'It was ordained even before his birth that John was to be a prophet! Speak on, Simon. You mentioned two babies?'

'The next I would speak of is Jesus of Nazareth, the young man whom John today named Messiah!'

'Go on, go on,' cried his audience, faces tense.

'Elizabeth had a young cousin, named Mary. When Elizabeth was almost six months pregnant, so before John's birth, the maid Mary had a visitation from an angel, who explained that she also was to bear a child, whom she should call Jesus. "He will be great," the angel said, "And will be called the Son of the Most High and his kingdom will never end!" Mary hurried to Zechariah's house, quite a journey and told these things to Elizabeth, from whose lips I later heard them. Mary stayed with Elizabeth for three months. She was a virgin, espoused to a carpenter of the house of David, whose name was Joseph. Her child was conceived not of man, but of the Holy Spirit! All praise to the Most High, to whom all things are possible!' There was another murmur of awe and his listeners exchanged further glances of amazement.

'What happened next,' inquired Ezra?

'Caesar Augustus—he who was Emperor before Tiberius, decreed that the whole Roman world should have a census taken at that time,' he paused rudely interrupted by a man who cursed and spat.

'Taxes—bloody Roman taxes! That's what a census is all about!' He was shouted down by those eager to hear more. Simon fixed his own indignant gaze on the fellow, stroked his beard and continued, 'Well, accordingly, Mary had to travel with her espoused husband Joseph from their home in Nazareth, to Joseph's place of birth in Bethlehem. Jesus was born there—in a stable, the only accommodation to be found in that over-crowded town, which was milling with the hundreds come there to register for the census.' The irate man who had previously interrupted now grumbled volubly again, but Simon persevered.

'The little new born babe was wrapped in swaddling robes, and laid in a straw filled manger for his cradle. Shepherds watching their sheep on a hillside above Bethlehem had a visitation from angels, praising God in the Highest and proclaiming the new born babe in the stable, to be—the Messiah! I later heard this from the lips of one of them!'

Another moan of awe and exultation went up from the small circle of men. It was echoed in the tent by Naomi, who was also listening, eyes shining. She leaned nearer to the opening.

'I actually saw Jesus, as a child of some twelve years old,' Simon continued. 'It was when his parents visited Jerusalem for Passover. The lad became separated from them in the crowds. They had travelled a full day's journey on their way home, before they realized Jesus was not with their party and so had to start the long way back, searching for him.

Three whole days later, to their amazement they found him in the temple courts, sitting amongst the learned teachers there, listening to them and asking them questions! And all of the teachers and priests were astounded at the boy's wisdom and understanding. I have taught many youngsters, but never have I come across one like Jesus of Nazareth. It was as though, he was teaching me! His parents were distressed, understandably I suppose, and remonstrated with him for causing them such anxiety. I shall never forget his words!'

'What did he say,' asked Reuban?

'Why, he said, "Why were you searching for me? Didn't you know I had to be in my Father's house?" But he went home with them and behaved with all obedience. I have heard little of either John or Jesus until recently—but have always known in my heart, that the world would never be the same again, following the birth of these two.'

'So then, this Jesus of Nazareth, really could be the long awaited one? It is possible that he is the Messiah?' Ezra spoke quietly, hardly daring to acknowledge in his own mind the full import of this revelation. 'What is it then, my son?' Ezra turned towards his younger son, who had gently touched his sleeve.

'May I speak, my father?' Ezra nodded.

'Jesus is indeed the Messiah! John himself named him to me as the Son of God!' None could doubt the boy's words, spoken with a fervour and sincerity that touched all who sat listening.

'Well said, young Simeon.' Old Simon smiled at the youngster. 'Strangely enough, another of your name, a righteous, elderly man, also called Simeon, named Jesus as the Christ, when Joseph and Mary took their infant son to the temple courts at Jerusalem, to be consecrated to the Lord, as you know is required by holy law, for all first born males.

I remember now how Simeon, to whom knowledge had been revealed by the Holy Spirit, took the baby in his arms and blessed him, and gave praise to the Lord, saying—"Sovereign Lord, as you have promised, now dismiss your servant in peace, for my eyes have seen your salvation, which you have prepared in the sight of all people, a light for revelation to the Gentiles and for glory to your people, Israel."

I remember how the child's parents marvelled at these words, and how Simeon blessed them also, prophesying great matters lying ahead, as the destiny of their son.'

'Did this Simeon say anything else,' inquired David, who was hanging upon every word that was said.

'Not that I remember. But there was an elderly prophetess present at that meeting, a widow. One who had spent all her life, fasting and praying in the Temple and she also gave thanks to God, for the birth of Jesus, proclaiming him to all who passed by. Let me see, yes, her name was Anna, the daughter of Phanuel, of the house of Asher.' Simon paused, and bent his head, obviously deep in thought.

'Well, what more do we need,' exclaimed David triumphantly! 'The King is among us! The one our nation has been waiting for, to lead us against the tyranny of Rome, to set his people free!' He sprang to his feet, brandishing his clenched fists to the sky in jubilation.

Ezra glanced in appalled confusion, at this wilful elder son of his, who was shouting these words in a loud voice, within hearing of any who might pass by. They could all be arrested, if any reported the young hothead's speech to the Romans. They could all end up sold into slavery—or worse.

'The hour is late. Get to your bed, David—you too, Simeon!' The men glanced around themselves uneasily and quietly dispersed.

The two boys lay close to each other on their sleeping mats, near the tent. David tossed in the excitement of a nightmare. Simeon breathed gently, at peace.

Chapter Two

David stirred. He rubbed his eyes—then struggled against the hand that suddenly clamped down over his mouth! Bewildered, he glanced up into the stern, bearded face of the man who held him in a pincer like grasp.

'Not a sound boy or you die!' The voice was low, sibilant, the eyes that glared into his own, cruel, darkly hooded. 'Get to your feet. Follow me.' He removed his hand, allowing David to see the curved knife, which glinted in the dying light of the fire.

'I will come.' David rose to his feet. He reached for his robe and pulled it about him. Below him, his brother Simeon slept, peacefully.

'Walk! Come, hurry, hurry! Over to that outcrop of rocks.'

David felt tentacles of fear slide over him, but forced himself to walk quietly forward as instructed. Above his head, the velvet blackness of the desert sky was spangled with a million stars. It was freezing cold and he wished he had dared to stop, to draw on his sandals, for already his feet were cut, as he stumbled in the semi darkness.

His captor gave him a push, and he fell sprawling into a cave. About a dozen men were assembled there. The far interior of the cave was dappled with shadows, cast by the flickering light of a lantern, set on a ledge. David took a deep breath and glanced about him, hands pressed hard on his knees. Who were they, this group of hard faced men, who hid themselves in this way? Were they robbers, bandits? If so, what could they want with a lad like him?

'Well, what have we here? Who is this young man, Matthias? The speaker beckoned to David to rise. He had an air of authority about him, which set him apart as leader of this secretive band. Instinctively, David knew this was no mere robber. He inclined his head and stood quietly before the man, showing no sign of the fear, which was tightening the back of his throat.

Matthias chuckled. He glanced around him, before answering, and saw what he sought. He reached forward and snatched a wineskin from the hands of one who had been drinking. He threw back his head and gulped the sharp wine in great mouthfuls, letting small dribbles run from the corners of his mouth. His leader watched him impassively then as Matthias continued to drink, he moved. In a bound, he was at Matthias side and his fist had sent the wineskin flying out of the cave. The man swore, but did not retaliate.

'When I address you, reply to me.' His eyes burned down and Matthias wilted before the ferocity of that stare.

'Your pardon, Barabbas, I meant no discourtesy!' He jerked his head towards David. 'This is a young cockerel, whom I heard crowing an interesting song tonight! He was shouting to a crowd of about fifty down by the river bank that—now how did he put it? Ah, yes, the king is among us, who will lead us against the tyranny of Rome, and set his people free!' Matthias had recovered his composure, used to his leader's peremptory behaviour.

'So?' Barabbas viewed David with greater interest.

'Come, sit down boy. Someone get a fresh wineskin, a drink for our young guest.' He gestured for David to join him on the pile of mats at the side of the cave, where the embers of a small fire glowed. The boy drew gratefully nearer to the warmth. The wine was strong and set courage surging through his veins.

'Now,' encouraged Barabbas. 'Tell us about yourself, boy. First of all, who are you?'

'My name is David, son of Ezra the weaver. I am from Jerusalem.'

'So what are you doing here, in the desert?' Barabbas considered him curiously. 'I suppose you followed with the crowds pouring out here to listen to the Baptist. Yet you do not seem the type.'

'I did come to see John and am more than glad that I came today!'

'Why today in particular? What was special about today?' Barabbas squatted on his haunches, his face close to David's.

'I saw the promised one. I saw the Messiah!' There was no doubting the sincerity of the lad's announcement. Various exclamations came from the group of men, all of whom were now listening intently to the conversation. Barabbas ran his hands over his long hair and curly beard, in almost absent minded gesture, as he shot out his next question.

'So—you think John to be the Messiah?'

'Not so, Master. But John it was who identified the Holy One!'

'John publicly announced someone as Messiah? Who was it boy? What was his name?' and Barabbas drew in his breath.

David opened his mouth to answer then clamped it shut again. Who were these men anyway, who met secretly in the night and had stolen him from his camp? How could he trust them, with his so precious knowledge, the identity of the Messiah? What if they meant harm to the Holy One?

'Well, his name, boy, his name?' Barabbas thrust his face even closer to David's, his eyes boring into the boys own, as though to prise the information he sought, through the power of his gaze.

'I do not know.' David forced the lie out between lips grown dry.

'Do not play games with me. His name fool or I will silence you forever!' Suddenly one brawny arm encircled David's shoulders, his knife against the boy's throat. 'So, have you nothing to say?'

'Only this,' gasped David. 'I would protect the Holy One with my life! How do I know that I can trust you?' The knife bit against his skin, but the eyes that glared back into Barabbas own, were fearless, contemptuous of danger.

'Wait, Barabbas!' The shout came from the back of the cave, where a man moved out of the shadows and approached them.

'Simon?' Barabbas looked up.

'It may be that I can be of help in this matter. I have met this lad before!' The dancing flame of the flickering lantern illumined his strong, bearded, dark skinned face and tall, muscular form. As he drew nearer still, points of reflected light shone in his intelligent, deep set eyes. Barabbas stared back at him.

'I am always willing to listen, to the son of one of the honoured founders of our movement.' he replied and waited, face inscrutable.

Simon smiled towards David, whose eyes widened, as he produced a sudden answering smile.

'Do you remember me, David? We met in Jerusalem!'

'Of course I remember you,' breathed David! 'We spoke outside my father's shop, the shop of Ezra the weaver. You told me you were a member of the Zealots and I asked how old I would have to be to join your company! Then my father came and you disappeared!'

David's face was flushed with excitement now, for he suddenly realized into whose hands he had fallen. 'I looked around for you, for days afterwards,' he blurted out.

'So, you wish to be one of us, lad?' Barabbas looked at him keenly. 'You vouch for this youth, Simon?'

'I do. He is just the sort of enthusiastic stripling we need to recruit! He has a hatred of all Romans.' He smiled at David reassuringly.

'I do indeed hate them for what they are doing to our people! It galls me to see my father and the rest of our nation forced to pay extortionate taxes to Tiberius.' He paused, and continued in passionate tones, 'Now the Messiah has come, I believe that under his leadership, we will achieve victory and drive the Roman swine out of our land!'

Barabbas slapped him on the shoulder. 'Well said! How strange it is, that having waited here on Jordan's banks for weeks in hope that John would announce the Messiah, we leave for a few days, only to find on our return, we missed the event.' He smiled approvingly at Matthias. 'You did well to bring this young man here tonight, Matthias.'

He turned David once more.

'Now, I ask you the name of the Messiah, David?'

'Jesus—Jesus of Nazareth,' David had no reservation in revealing the name now. He did it joyfully. It was repeated from lip to lip, right around the cave, as men explored it on their tongues.

'Listen David, I want you to tell me everything that happened between John and this Jesus.' Barabbas eyes were burning with a fierce joy.

'Jesus offered himself for baptism, but at first John did not want to baptise him, until Jesus insisted. John said that Jesus should be baptising him instead. When Jesus rose from the water, dripping wet, the sun shone on him, but the light I saw was more than the dazzle of sunlight. It blazed all about him and a white dove flew down and lighted on him, and I heard a voice, deep and compelling, saying--This is my Son whom I love. With Him I am well pleased.'

'Did anyone else hear this voice,' demanded Barabbas, looking shaken.

'I would say that the whole multitude heard, in their hearts!' David's face was glowing. Barabbas stared down at his feet. At last he looked up again.

'Thank you, David. Where is this Jesus now?'

'I wish I could answer that. My brother Simeon and I both asked the Baptist, where the Holy One had gone and he merely said that Jesus had retired to speak with his father.' He shook his head sadly. 'It was impossible to see which way he went, with so many hundreds still milling about the river banks.'

'Well lad, you had better return to your family, before they miss you. If they've already discovered your absence, I suggest you say you went looking for the Messiah.' He smiled at David's look of discomfiture, for the youth had already been planning to throw in his lot with his new friends. 'It is better so, but we will meet again, of that you may be sure!'

'Come on then,' grunted Matthias. 'Let me take you back and then I may be able to get some sleep this night.' The glance he threw on his erstwhile prisoner was certainly kinder now. Simon rose with David. He said he would walk back with them. They were just leaving the secret world of the cave, when the night exploded into noise. There was shouting, raucous voices and screams, terrible screams. David's blood ran cold. He was suddenly filled with the most terrible fear.

'Don't worry lad,' encouraged Matthias. 'With so many crowding into this wild place, there are bound to be incidents. Nevertheless, we will go carefully, circle round and keep to the shadows. Those sounds came from the direction where your people are encamped.' He shot out a huge fist and restrained David, who was about to run forward.

'I said we would go carefully.'

'Matthias speaks wisely David. It was probably only a drunken brawl, men throwing dice or a quarrel over a woman.' Simon smiled reassuringly. The sounds had stopped now, only the clop clopping of horses hooves could be heard, receding into the distance.

'Romans,' snorted Matthias and spat. 'I noticed a party of them down by the river, a couple of hours after we arrived back here, keeping an eye on John no doubt!'

'I saw soldiers this morning,' breathed David. 'Two in particular were watching John closely. They left the river bank shortly before John baptised Jesus.' A knot of anxiety was coiling about his entrails. He wanted to rush ahead, but knew he must behave with discipline if the Zealots were to take him seriously as a future recruit. The sound of horses had disappeared now, but other sounds arose, a wailing, the traditional mourning cries of the Jewish people. Suddenly David broke away from the other two. Intuitively he knew that tragedy had come to his family.

He stood amongst the wreckage of his father's tent, staring down in stupefaction at the dead face of Naomi, his gentle mother, cradled in the arms of Ezra, his father. Both were smothered in blood. Ezra raised his dying eyes to his elder son.

'David, you must fly—or they will kill you too!'

David sank to his knees, tearing his robe and trying to staunch the blood that was welling from his father's chest. Ezra coughed as blood tinged foam bubbled from his mouth. He managed to sit up a little, to focus his last thoughts on this dearly loved son of his, this wilful boy, who had brought death to his family.

'Listen—my son, listen carefully, for I have little time. An informer heard your words about a king being among us, who would destroy the tyranny of Rome. One of our own people betrayed your words to the Roman soldiers.

They came looking for the son of Ezra, who had spoken so, to arrest him. Your young brother said—aghh!' He coughed violently and now a stream of blood trickled down his chin. He rallied and continued, 'Don't interrupt. Let me speak,' for David was about to cry out in his despair. 'Simeon told the soldiers that it was he who had spoken against Rome. I tried to prevent their taking him, but they struck him across the head. It was too much! I drew my knife—and one of the soldiers raised his sword. Your dear mother, Naomi, with whom I shall soon be reunited, rushed forward and took the blow that was meant for me.' He paused. There were tears welling slowly in his eyes. 'I sprang at the beast. His friend came at me from behind. They have taken your brother to their Tribune.'

'Father! Father, don't try to speak further. Lie down. Oh, my father and my mother! I have killed you!'

'No, David, but you must flee. Keep away from Jerusalem. I lay it on your heart though, to save your young brother, if it is possible. Now bend your head. I want to give you my blessing.' The coughing brought more blood. Someone bent over the group.

David heard a gentle voice saying-

'My name is James. I am a disciple of the Baptist.' He detached Naomi from Ezra's arms and helped him into a half sitting position. It was important that the dying man bless his son. He had no need to guide David downwards. He had voluntarily thrown himself into his father's lap, weeping uncontrollably.

'May the blessing of the Almighty, Our Sovereign Lord, the God of Abraham, of Isaac and of Jacob be with you now and always. May you ever live in His ways! I bless you David, my first born, son of my heart. Take this bag of gold from my belt and go. Go as fast as you can from this place. Others will do for me what must be done. I-----' Ezra choked and turned his head to look towards Naomi. Then his spirit sped to seek hers.

James placed a gentle hand on David's head, then bent and raised him firmly to his feet. He fumbled at Ezra's belt and withdrew the heavy money bag. He pushed it into David's hands.

'Take this my son, and obey your father. It is dangerous for you to remain here. As far as I know, the Romans have all gone, but they have spies. My friends and I will see that your parents have proper burial. Have no fear for that.'

'I will be revenged on those that have done this deed!' The stars were dimming into dawn. The silent circle of men, who surrounded the scene, now recommenced their keening. David glanced wildly around.

'Yes, you mourn now! But where were all of you, when those animals were murdering my parents, taking my brother! Do you call yourselves men? You are cowards! I spit on you!'

'No, David. Do not blame them, nor think of revenge. Violence breeds violence.' James bent his lips to David's ear. 'Get to Nazareth,' he murmured. Even as he spoke, a hand darted forward and David felt himself dragged away. Matthias had moved with the speed of a serpent. David struggled, but was dealt a buffet over the head, which stunned him. And so it was that two of Ezra's sons were borne unconscious from the

Jordan, Simeon on the back of a Roman's soldier's horse and David over the broad shoulders of Matthias the Zealot.

Barabbas stared down at David's unconscious form, as he weighed the heavy bag of gold in his hand.

'Did you have to hit him so hard, Matthias?' He walked to the mouth of the cave. It would soon be dawn. He was torn with indecision. On the one hand, he wished to remain, so he might discover the whereabouts of the Messiah, but there again, it seemed more than likely that the Romans would return, probably anxious to learn more of this new Jewish leader.

'Simon. What I want you to do is this. Take this lad with you and make your way to Nazareth. I will meet you there within the month. If this Jesus has already left the area, as he may well have done, then it seems likely that he will have returned to his home. Find out what his actions are, if he seems to be gathering people to him.' He glanced once more at David. He had already decided that the boy should join his band, which was excellent reason for accepting this bag of gold as initiation fee, for all money was held in common, not but that he would have kept it in any case. David held an idealized vision of Barabbas and his men. They were prepared to rob, even to murder to obtain the means to mobilize the Jews against Rome.

David groaned and attempted to sit up. Simon dropped to his knees beside him. One of the men, Benjamin, handed a wineskin down.

'Give him a drink Simon. To have both parents murdered by those Roman swine, is thing hard to take!' He looked pityingly at the boy, as did the other men, offering encouraging comments as David struggled to his feet.

He looked about him bewildered, then realization flooded back and he shrieked out in mixture of fury and anguish. Simon placed a hand over his mouth. The boy calmed.

'How did I get here?' He caught sight of Matthias. 'It was you, wasn't it? You hit me! If you hadn't brought me here in the first place, my parents would still be alive!'

Matthias frowned.

'Say rather, that your own unbridled tongue brought this on yourself. Let it be a lesson, though a hard one, to keep your council.' He stared at

David, then with expression of rough kindliness, took the smaller of the two daggers from his belt and proffered it to him. 'Here boy, take this and learn to use it, that you may be revenged on those sons of dogs who did this to your family. You are one of us now!'

One of them! How marvellous that would have seemed just an hour ago, but now nothing mattered, but that he had brought death to his parents. His brother—Simeon! He had almost forgotten the fate of Simeon, who with such bravery had taken responsibility for David's words. Where was he now? What would the Romans do with him?

'My brother, they have taken him to their tribune. I heard the soldiers mention their tribune's name, Tribune Marcus! I must get to Jerusalem and save Simeon.'

Barabbas stepped forward now and held up his hand. He looked at David authoritatively.

'No, David. It is too early for that. You would be recognized by neighbours, so called friends and be betrayed to the soldiers. That will not help your brother. There are many of our people in Jerusalem. They will find out what has happened to Simeon and we will deal with this for you. I now give you, your first commission as one of my men. You are to go with Simon to Nazareth, to look for the man whom you saw John baptise. You saw his face and can identify him.'

He saw David's eyes upon Ezra's purse, which he still held in his hands.

'That is my father's purse! Give it to me!' His eyes glinted with fury.

'Quietly, lad! We hold all gold in common, but I will not send you off penniless. Here, take these few coins.' He emptied the gold into a bigger bag and tossed five pieces of gold back into Ezra's purse, which he returned to David. 'Go now, before the sun rises. Simon will instruct you what to do and will train you to be useful member of our party. Now off with you!'

The anger drained from David's face, to be replaced by white, strained look. He turned mutely, to follow Simon, accepting the pack which Benjamin offered him, a water skin and piece of dried meat.

'Wait,' called Barabbas. 'Your feet are bare. Put these on!'

He tossed a pair of worn sandals to David, who refused them. Simon snatched them up and put them in his pack. The lad would be glad of them soon!

They travelled fast, keeping away from the route taken by those coming out from Jerusalem. Simon said they had to go due north. It was incredibly hot by day, a heat haze shimmering before their eyes. Simon spoke little, concentrating on the road ahead. David seemed to have withdrawn into a world of his own, a world of bitterness and loneliness. Night fell and they camped between two huge rocks, rationing their water supply. Simon said that the next day would bring them near a spring. Simon soon fell asleep, exhausted. David sat looking up at the glittering stars in the immensity of the night sky. How many times had he looked up at them in the past, with his father! Where was Ezra now—and Naomi? He knew that there was another world after this one. What was it like? With so many who had lived and died since the first man, Adam, how would you find your own family, amongst the millions who would be there?

David heard the steady sound of Simon's breathing. What would he not do for the gift of repose, to be able to close his eyes and know that the burden of guilt had been lifted from him! But this could never happen. He had been responsible for his parent's death. He thought back to his baptism at John's hands, just two days ago, it seemed more like a century now. Although part of him had resisted acknowledging sin at that time and in showing repentance, there had nevertheless been a sense of inner cleanliness, a feeling of joy and peace, though mixed still with ambition to drive the Romans out of Palestine with whatever violence that might take. Then the excitement of hearing John name Jesus, as the Son of God. All knew this was the term reserved for the Messiah.

He threshed about restlessly. If Jesus were Messiah, then surely he would gather all men to him, mobilize them to rid the country of these invaders! Perhaps Jesus would become the leader of the Zealot party and of all others who hated the dominance of Rome. Lead them in battle to victory! Help him to avenge his parents. Yet, what had Simeon said— 'This is a man of peace, David.'

Peace? How could there be peace, whilst Palestine was under foreign occupation. Simeon was a sentimentalist! But where was he now, this much loved brother? What had they done to him?

The turmoil in his mind exploded into action. He sprang to his feet, and ran wildly into the desert, not caring where he went. The moon had risen now. Some eighty feet away a hyena growled, lifting evil head above his prey. Every sound carried in that barren wilderness, and David was sobbing as he ran. Further off, could be heard the roar of lions and the scream of a night bird.

Why had it happened? Why had his father, this good man, been killed? What reason was there for his mother to have died, she who had been all goodness and gentleness?

'There cannot be a God, if he allows such things to happen! I do not believe there is a God!' He screamed the words out, face contorted.

The pain that shot through his heel was a white hot agony! He gasped as he stumbled to the ground. Realization dawned, as he saw the snake gliding away in waving motion. He had been bitten, was alone in the wilderness, facing almost certain death. His hand seized a rock and he threw it with furious effort at the disappearing reptile. Then he collapsed, as he felt death creeping up through his veins.

'Lie still and be quiet. Are you a man or a girl, that you make so much noise! You are not to move—not to shout—not to twitch even a muscle. I am going to cut your foot, try to draw the venom out. If you struggle, you will only make the poison work it's way through your veins the more quickly. If you lie quite still and let me do what must be done then there is a chance.'

David heard the words, through the pain and the panic and made an effort to lie still. He felt the cut of the knife and realized that Simon had bent his head over his foot, was trying to suck the venom out of the wound on his heel.

'Thank you—Simon,' he muttered between lips that had started to chatter with cold.

'Never mind trying to thank me. Just lie still, absolutely still!' He hissed the words out urgently, not wanting to take his lips away from the wound.

For a whole week, the boy raged in fever. Simon had borne him back to the slight shelter of the rocks, had tried to make him comfortable. On the third day, the wound on his heel looked very angry, was suppurating. The man had shaken his head, feeling there was very little hope. He had made a fire, great effort being needed to find anything to burn, in this barren place. He held his knife in the small blaze then applied it relentlessly to the boy's foot, ignoring the wail of pain. All night, he dampened the burning forehead, with what little water was left, pouring a few drops between the cracked lips.

At sunrise, David still lived, and the inflammation surrounding the charred skin seemed no worse at the least. But both water-skins were now empty. There was no alternative. He must carry David on his back to the spring, half a day's march away. Well, the sooner he started the better, before the heat of the sun made travelling too difficult.

When Simon made camp by the spring, he was trembling from the endurance that had been needed. It was almost evening. He had not taken into account, the extra time that had been necessary to carry the dead weight of the now delirious youngster. For three days more, David hung between life and death. It was obvious he had lost a great deal of weight. Simon himself looked gaunt from worry and lack of sleep. He had only left David for brief periods, when hunting for small game to eat, bringing a bird down with his sling. Then there were berries and wild fruit amongst the sparse vegetation surrounding the spring that bubbled out between the rocks.

Simon was bending over David and shaking his head. The lad could not last much longer, that he knew. He cursed under his breath. At first his concern had been to keep the boy alive in order to carry out his leader's commission, but a feeling of responsibility had developed for David and a grudging respect for the lad's fighting spirit, which had refused to yield to death. A week of fighting to keep him alive, was it to be for nothing?

A shadow fell across David's form. Simon swung about, looking up and reaching for his knife.

'Peace be with you,' said a quiet voice and Simon relaxed beneath the compassionate stare of the tall, slim figure, who leaned down over the sick youth. His eyes met the searching gaze of the stranger, who was now looking at him interrogatively. He turned away, unable to sustain contact with the intensity of the glance from those gold flecked eyes, for more than a few seconds. He felt as though not only his face, but also his secret thoughts had been examined. The stranger dropped to his knees beside David.

'A serpent?' he inquired, gesturing towards the inflamed heel.

'Yes—but how could you know that,? muttered Simon. He looked at the stranger uncertainly. 'Who are you? Where have you come from?'

The stranger did not answer him. 'David, son of Ezra, arise,' said the quiet voice. To Simon's utter amazement, the boy stirred and sat up. He looked up wonderingly into the dark eyes, those strange almost luminous eyes that held a golden light, eyes such as he had never seen, and breathed recognition.

'Master—Lord, 'he murmured. Then under Simon's astonished stare, David rose unsteadily to his feet. Simon glanced down at the damaged heel, the red and purple contusion and the swelling, had disappeared. He shivered with a sudden fear. What was this? This stranger had bid the youth to rise and he had done so, had returned from the realms of unconsciousness, from near death, and now stood on a foot that seemed completely healed! It wasn't possible, but it had happened and he had seen it! The stranger smiled fleetingly.

'Fear not,' he said gently to Simon. 'Give glory to God!

Seek me in Nazareth.' They watched silently, as he lifted a hand in farewell, the slight breeze stirring his dark chestnut hair and beard. He passed beyond their sight, behind a rocky rise.

Suddenly a light dawned in Simon's mind. His hand clamped down lightly on David's shoulder, for the boy still stood looking in the direction which the stranger had taken. 'David, tell me lad. Was this the Messiah?'

'Yes, Simon. This was Jesus of Nazareth, the Holy One.

He healed me. I know that for many days, my spirit was almost in the land of shadows, for I could see my body stretched in pain with you ministering to me. How can I ever thank you for that care, Simon! But I know I would have died, if the Lord Jesus had not healed me.' The lad's eyes were filled with tears of happiness. Gone was the anger and hatred that had blazed there a week ago. This was a new David, one who had been reborn.

Simon stared at David, his mind struggling to accept events beyond reason.

'David, I knew that no mere man could have healed you just by a word, not even the most accomplished physician could have done so! This truly was the Son of God, who stood beside us.' Then Simon did something which he had not done since early boyhood. He sank spontaneously to his knees, and gave praise and thanks to Almighty God.

David knelt next to him, praying quietly. As the boy prayed, he knew that the burden of guilt for his parent's death had been lifted from his shoulders. Simon reached out and gave the boy a hug, his dark skinned face glowing with a surge of emotion.

The lonely heart of David responded to this spontaneous show of affection. A bonding of brotherhood had just taken place between these two, drawn together by the miraculous event which had just occurred.

'Perhaps we should follow after him now,' suggested Simon. 'We should have asked him to stay, to have offered him food. Indeed, he carried no pack with him, nor any weapon, not even a knife. I am very quick to notice such matters,' he added.

'No, Simon. We will not follow him.' The youngster spoke with authority, a new maturity. 'If the master had wanted us with him, he would have said so. He wished to be alone and that is why he said—'Seek me in Nazareth'. However, Simon, I do know of one who would be very glad of something to eat!' He placed his hands over his stomach, with a wry grimace. 'I am famished!'

'Of course! You have not eaten in days!' A grin broke over Simon's swarthy face. 'However, before a single morsel of food passes your lips, you will put these on and that is an order.' He produced the worn sandals that Barabbas had tossed to the boy a week ago, and which Simon had kept for him. 'Pride is not worth a serpent's sting,' he said quietly.

Night fell. Again the sky was black velvet, crested with stars. A faint wind moaned across the wilderness, its freezing breath searching out all slightest forms of shelter, pouring in whirling eddies between rocks and huge boulders, flicking sand at the straggled desert plants, which somehow managed to sustain the lack of water and the extremes of temperature by day and night, blending sighing plaint with the cry of One who stood alone, calling out to Almighty God to minister to him. The Living Word, Son of God made flesh, born as man to bring message from the Father, made final commitment, praying, head bowed, on the heights of a hill. Then the light of God shone about him and angels came to minister to him.

While the world slept, the Lord Jesus stepped forward, to light a flame of love and hope in men's hearts that would never be extinguished.

Chapter Three

Simeon, younger son of Ezra, sat huddled in a corner of the guard room. His face was distorted by grief and tears coursed unchecked from eyes red with weeping.

It was two days now since he had recovered consciousness from the blow that had mercifully prevented his witnessing his parent's death. At first, when his senses had started to return, the pain in his head almost blotted out memory, for it was like a hammer beating, a red hot hammer sending waves of sickness surging down into his stomach. Gradually his mind cleared, as he realized he was strapped to the back of a horse, hands and feet bound. He started to retch. The sounds of his vomiting brought a curse from the rider who sat before him. Flavius jerked his horse to a stop and dismounted. He threw the lad roughly to the ground, staring at him contemptuously.

'If you must vomit, do it on the ground, not all over my horse!' He gave the boy a kick. Other riders had eased their beasts to a halt. They turned their heads, looking to see what was delaying Flavius. One of them leapt from his horse and bent over Simeon. He stared at the boy with compassion.

'No need to kick him Flavius, it will only make him vomit more. Here lad,' He took a water flask from his pack and held it to the boy's lips. 'Take a sip and then rinse your mouth! That's right. Now drink a little.' He recapped his flask and smiled at the scowling Flavius. 'You want him in a fit state to testify to Tribune Marcus, don't you?'

Flavius snorted. 'That is the purpose of taking him to Jerusalem. As for his health, well I imagine he will soon be carrion, like his parents!' He sneered at the dawning horror in the boy's eyes. 'The Tribune has a swift answer to those who plan insurrection!' He drew a hand across his throat suggestively.

'My parents—what of my parents!' suddenly Simeon's face drained of all colour. He looked up beseechingly at the ring of Romans who surrounded him, then managing to stagger to his feet, despite his bound limbs, fixed Flavius with a look of burning intensity.

'Have you dared to harm my parents?'

Flavius chuckled. 'They are dead—father, mother—both!'

He stepped back instinctively, before the hatred in the boy's face, the blaze of pain and fury that spoke plainly what he would do, were he at liberty and armed. 'When you first admitted to shouting insurrection, I hardly believed it of one who seemed so meek and mild, so girl like,' he scoffed. 'However, I see that you have the same streak of fanaticism as those who spawned you!'

'You killed my father and my mother—Naomi, my gentle mother!' Simeon did not know how to deal with the horror of it. His eyes dilated in shock.

'Nay boy, it was I who killed your mother. But it was an accident! 'The speaker was Gaius. 'She took the blow meant for your father!' He leaned down from his horse and spoke quietly. 'Flavius here stunned you. Your father drew a knife and would have killed Flavius. I drew my sword, intending to fend him off. Your mother, thinking I meant to kill him, ran forward straight into my sword before I could deflect the blow. Your father leapt at me and Flavius slew him! There had been no intention to kill either of them, merely to arrest you, to discover the truth of words you were alleged to have made, regarding a 'King of the Jews' who would lead them against Rome.'

Gaius glanced away from Simeon, not wanting to meet the accusation in the young face. He had no idea, why he should have felt led to make either explanation or excuse, but something about the lad, caused him to reflect on motives that normally received no question. He preferred to make war on men, to conduct himself with honour, not to waste time and effort on the futile struggles of a few Jewish fanatics.

Flavius put an end to any further discussion by slipping a cloth between Simeon's teeth, securing it behind his head. They would soon be approaching Jericho, where they would be able to freshen up and breakfast. He threw Simeon unceremoniously back across his horse, before remounting. The sun was already beating down relentlessly on the narrow, rough track that served for road across the wilderness, to the ancient oasis town that beckoned before them, with its gently stirring palm trees and white buildings. Soon the horses were clattering along streets that were said to be centuries old.

They rested at Jericho a short while, before undertaking the next blistering twenty five miles to Jerusalem. So it was, that only forty-eight hours after Simeon had been immersed under Jordan's waters and baptised of John, he was returned to Jerusalem which he had left with such excitement and high hopes, now in disgrace and orphaned.

Simeon raised his head. He had been oblivious to the laughter of the soldiers who sat on the far side of the room, some playing dice, some making bawdy jokes. Tears still welled slowly into his eyes, as he stared at the tall, autocratic figure, who had thrown the door open. The men leapt to their feet, coming to attention. It was Tribune Marcus, admired and feared by the Legion. His word was life or death and he was immediately responsible only to Governor, Pontius Pilate. His eyes raked the men, singling out Gaius and Flavius.

'You two—come here!' His expression was grim, as he stared at them. Flavius cleared his throat uncertainly, his florid face paling slightly beneath that searching glance, his throat suddenly dry. Gaius however, sustained his commander's glare without visible trepidation, only by a slight drawing in of his leathery cheek muscles was any reaction shown.

'So, you two whom I entrusted with the mission of keeping a delicate eye on the situation on the Jordan, having been told that it was of the utmost importance not to inflame the Jews—what do you do? Kill two honest citizens, friends and neighbours of Micah the jeweller, who dwells on Joachim Street and supplies jewels to the gracious Lady Claudia, wife to our honoured Prefect Pontius Pilate! Yes, well may you look so! I've just had Pilate demanding to know what kind of idiots I command!' The red plumes on Marcus helmet, seemed to quiver with the same controlled rage that leant such ire to the flashing dark eyes that darted dangerously beneath his thick black brows. Usually, relations between himself and the Governor were of the most cordial and that was the way he intended to keep them.

Marcus was an ambitious man. He knew that Prefect Pontius Pilate was a man to watch, even though there were those of the opinion that Emperor Tiberius would not have sent him to this particularly remote trouble spot, if he considered him suitable for future high political office. Marcus also highly esteemed Pilate's wife, the Lady Claudia, and not only because of her rumoured membership of the late Emperor's family, rather he had a soft spot in his otherwise implacable heart for the beautiful, patrician woman, who carried with her an air of spirituality, a rare quality in those of the house of Caesar. She was held in affection by all the tough soldiers based both here in Jerusalem, at the Antonia fortress and at her more permanent home on the coast, at Caesarea.

Simeon straightened up, as the Tribune's words penetrated his brain. Was it possible that Marcus was reproving the men who had murdered his parents?

'Sir, may I speak,' he said uncertainly, then gathering confidence, stepped forward. He raised his hands, and tried to dash away his tears, with as much dignity as he could muster. One of the men leapt forward, sword extended between the lad and Marcus. The Tribune contemptuously signed to the man to draw back, taking in the distressed youngster, with his tear stained face and clubbed foot.

'Surely this cannot be the firebrand who occasioned this upset!' His eyes swept over the lad in disbelief. 'Tell me lad,' he continued in kindlier tones. 'Are you David, the son of Ezra?'

'No! My name is Simeon. I was the son of Ezra. Now my father is dead and my mother, killed by your men!' He stared accusingly towards Gaius and Flavius.

'Not was, but still the son of Ezra. From what I have heard, your father fought to save you—died for your sake. Be proud of him, boy and of your mother!' Marcus spoke harshly, more to penetrate the cocoon of misery and self pity which Simeon had wrapped around himself than because he wanted to inflict hurt. He smiled faintly at the flash of anger in the boy's eyes. That was better. Now they could talk.

'So tell me, where is your brother David? No, don't bother to deny that you have a brother. I have been speaking with Micah the jeweller, who has told me all about your family. He said that David was the hothead, you, the quiet one. I also know that David went with your parents to Jordan, but was not in the vicinity, when my men so mishandled matters. So tell me, where is David? I do not want to harm him, merely to ask him a few questions about—the Messiah?' He watched Simeon's face closely, saw the look of apprehension.

'David and I became separated at the Jordan. I do not know where he is, unless your men have killed him also!' The best form of defence was attack.

'Well, let that be for now. Tell me Simeon, were you or your family badly treated in any way before the unfortunate happenings at the Jordan? Have you suffered at all under Roman rule, apart from the natural reluctance of your people to paying taxes? Have the Jews not gained immeasurably from the stability of government they now enjoy, plus the fact that they have complete religious freedom!'

Simeon raised sorrowful young eyes, to his haughty interrogator. 'Perhaps all we really lack, is our freedom as a nation,' he replied

'So then, you think that your Messiah will prove to be the leader you need to incite your people against Rome?' He placed his hands on his hips, as he stared at the boy. He sensed intuitively, that Simeon would not lie.

'The Holy One is a man of peace,' replied Simeon softly

'How can you know that? Obviously only if you have met him! So what is his name? Where is he?' Marcus eyes raked the lad's face. Simeon did not flinch under that stare. He looked straight ahead, making no reply.

'Answer me!' Marcus raised his hand and slapped the boy across the face, 'His name?' He scowled angrily, as Simeon held his peace. 'Do you realize boy, that for this insolence, I could have you whipped to death!' Still Simeon was silent. Marcus signed to two of his men, who leapt forward, and ripped the boy's tunic from his slim dark, shoulders, whilst another lifted the dreaded flagellum, the many thonged, metal tipped whip, from a hook on the wall.

Simeon's eyes widened with fear, but still he did not speak.

'Hum! You have more courage than I had imagined!' He nodded to the soldiers. 'Loose him.' He turned towards his men.

'Learn from this, the type of people you are dealing with.

The Jew is a strange creature. He has all the weaknesses of other men, but in matters relating to his religion he is fanatical. My advisors tell me, that for centuries prophets have arisen in this ancient race, predicting the advent of a great spiritual leader, the Messiah! They hold themselves to be a nation apart singled out by the God they worship to be his chosen people. As I understand it, from listening to their teachers, their God always protected them in battle, until they disobeyed his command to keep themselves apart. For on occasion, they intermarried with women from tribes they had conquered, some indeed following gods of other nations. Accordingly their God removed his protection from them at these times and they were overcome in battle.' He paused and continued reflectively. 'Today, they are dispersed into many lands. But whether here in Palestine or elsewhere, they await this Messiah, that word signifies Christos in the Greek—the Anointed One, in our own language.'

One of the legionaries cleared his throat, daring a question.

'The man whom John the Baptist is supposed to have named—would he be a member of the house of Herod?' The man asked his question respectfully.

'It would be logical to expect so, but no! He is not from their corrupt royal house.' Marcus viewed his men with a slight smile about his lips. He turned and looked full at Simeon. 'His name is Jesus of Nazareth!' If he wanted any confirmation of the news which a collaborator had brought him, then the look on the lad's face provided it. He nodded. 'I understand he is a carpenter from an area where we had much insurrection of recent years. Nazareth is only a few miles from Sephoris where we had to deal most severely with rebellion almost twenty years ago now. We crucified thousands there at the time!'

'Are we going to find this man, arrest him, Tribune?'

'Not so. If there is going to be an uprising, then I want to get all ringleaders. Douse the flames, once and for all! No spark must remain to rekindle rebellion.' There came the sound of horse's hooves clattering in the courtyard below and Marcus paused, signing to one of his men to investigate.

'It's Centurion Claudius, sir! He asks leave to attend you.'

'Claudius! A thousand welcomes!' Tribune Marcus opened his arms in greeting to the sturdy figure that stood on the threshold. It was the Centurion commanding the garrison at Capernaum, but more than this, Claudius was an old and trusted friend, the eldest son of a wealthy Roman landowner, who as a result of a bitter dispute with his father had spent the last twenty years as a soldier of Rome. He had been offered chance of advancement, but had not taken it, not so far. Marcus had increased Claudius authority to cover the whole area around the Sea of Galilee.

A smile broke out on the rugged features of the newcomer, who as he stepped forward, was warmly clasped by Marcus. For a few moments, the two men clapped each other on the shoulders. 'Wine—wine for

Centurion Claudius,' called the Tribune. A servant moved deftly at Marcus bidding, filling two silver goblets.

'To the Emperor,' intoned Marcus.

'Emperor Tiberius,' rejoined Claudius, as together they raised their goblets to their irascible Emperor, now in his sixty-eighth year and growing it was said, daily more suspicious and unpredictable. But he was Caesar, was worshipped almost as god. It was fourteen years now, since Tiberius, adopted son of the late Emperor Augustus, had ascended the throne; but whereas under the wise and benign rule of Augustus Caesar, reforms had abounded following years of civil war within the empire, and men had breathed more easily, now there was tension in high places, its effects percolating down through the political and military hierarchy. The ill fortune which attended his Germanic wars, had not improved Tiberius temper. His rages and swift disposal of all who offended him, made him much feared and treated circumspectly, even in this remote part of the Roman Empire.

'Come, my friend, we will go to my quarters, where we can be private,' said Marcus. He noticed Simeon, still standing straight and still in his torn robe. The boy watched him apprehensively. Marcus scowled, unsure what to do with him. Suddenly he brightened. He turned to Claudius.

'I would ask a favour of you, my friend.'

'You have but to name it?'

'Could you do with an extra servant? For reasons I will speak of in private, I wish to get this lad out of Jerusalem, and to keep him under supervision.' Marcus watched Claudius face expectantly.

'A small request and one I gladly accede to.' He walked over to the young Jew and his bright blue eyes, bored down into the Simeon's brown ones.

'How are you named, lad?'

'Simeon, sir—son of Ezra,' returned the youngster softly.

He immediately felt trust for this stranger of another race, but why, he could not say.

'Will you come willingly with me to Capernaum,' Claudius inquired? Simeon heard him in disbelief. Romans did not ask, they ordered. A

Centurion such as this man had the power of life and death. But he had asked!

'I will,' replied Simeon and meant it.

'Good,' replied Claudius. He smiled at the boy then followed Marcus out of the room. Two hours later, cleansed and refreshed after the deft ministrations of quiet slaves, the two officers reclined on couches, facing each other, as they finished their repast.

Marcus bit deeply into a peach, its juices seeping from the corners of his mouth. Claudius watched him in amusement. Suddenly they were boys again in Rome, meeting daily at the school where they were taught to read and write and learn simple mathematics, progressing into Latin and Greek literature. Once following a beating for inattention, they had escaped their pedagogues, the slaves who both helped to teach and conduct them daily to and from school. They had climbed the wall of a friend's garden, and hidden amongst the abundant undergrowth and had sat eating stolen peaches, whilst fountains splashed occasional drops on their heads. How sweet that stolen fruit had tasted, and the juice had run down Marcus face then, as it did now.

'Do you remember our schooldays,' asked Claudius?

'Do I not---the peaches?'

'Yes and the beating when we were found! It was the second in one day!' Claudius ran his dark skinned hand through his crisply curling hair, already slightly silvering at the temples.' We never dreamed then, that one day we would become part of an Imperial army and fight our way across the known world!' He snapped off a small bunch of purple grapes, spitting the seeds out reflectively. Suddenly he sat upright on the couch and looked at Marcus from eyes grown curious.

'So my friend, why did you send for me--trouble?'

'Well, it could be trouble. The Messiah, the Holy One the Jews have been expecting, has arrived on the scene. John the Baptist has apparently identified one Jesus of Nazareth as the awaited one. Of course he may turn out to be yet another teacher who will collect a following and then disappear into obscurity, or again, he may ally himself with the Zealots and the marauding bands of cave dwellers who cause sporadic unrest in one area after another.'

'Do you know anything about this Jesus yet?'

'No. Only his name and that he is a carpenter—and that he has disappeared!'

Claudius blue eyes snapped with interest.

'When did John name him?'

'Three days back—since I sent word for you to come. I was already concerned at the numbers pouring out of Jerusalem to see John in the desert, wanted to discuss this with you and then this news about the Messiah!'

'You say he is from Nazareth, this Messiah, well that is my territory, not too far south from Capernaum where I am based. It is providential that you got in touch with me and amazing that you should have done so before this news broke!' He looked at Marcus interrogatively. 'So my friend, what is the connection with the lad Simeon, whom you want me to take back with me? Is he involved with this Jesus of Nazareth?'

'Only to the extent that I believe he has seen the man and can identify him. But it is more than that. I sent some of my men to keep a discreet eye on the Baptist. They heard that this lad, or his brother who has disappeared, had not only seen the Messiah but had been boasting that this new leader was going to overthrow Rome. Now it was probably only boyish enthusiasm mixed with religious fervour, engendered by John's teaching, but those idiot soldiers of mine, slew the lad's parents and brought him here. Even this would not have been so bad, but the couple who were killed were seemingly sober citizens, and friends of the jeweller whom the Lady Claudia patronizes. Hence today, I've had Pontius Pilate on my back, for he holds his lady wife in high respect, and she is much distressed by the happening.'

Claudius nodded understandingly.

'So you want the lad quietly out of the way, until the dust settles and to watch him in case he should have direct connection with this Jesus. No problem there, Marcus. Have you told Pilate that John has announced the Messiah?'

'Yes. He wants the matter handled very carefully. He knows a report was sent to the Emperor of the lack of diplomacy he displayed when he first arrived in Jerusalem, the business of the standards!'

'Yes, I remember hearing how under cover of darkness, he placed the Roman eagle on top the walls and also that the standard was erected on most public buildings. Surely he must have known about the Jewish laws against graven images? The fury that erupted amongst the Jews—their high officials and nobility was such that he had to back down, lower the eagle. That was bad for our morale and will have proved most unpleasing to the Emperor. He is already smarting from his reversals in Germany.'

Claudius chewed his lip thoughtfully. 'We will have to see that this Messiah business is handled very tactfully.'

'I suggest that you leave for Capernaum at dawn tomorrow.

Keep an eye open for young Simeon's brother, David. He is two years older and a firebrand. I have a feeling that he will appear near the Messiah. Find out if you are able, any information on the background of Jesus, how he is regarded by those who know him.' Marcus yawned and stretched. He clapped and waited as the silent slaves removed the remains of their meal, then strode over to the window. The night wind was cool, wafting its clean breath from the mountains, over the brooding tranquillity of a city settling itself to sleep. A myriad lamps gave soft outline to Jerusalem's shape, which sprawled to the west of the fortress, whilst directly behind it, soared the enormous temple to the Jewish God, rebuilt by the late King Herod of gleaming white marble, heavily gilded in gold. Work on its surrounding buildings was still ongoing. The Jewish police guards watching the temple could be seen by the light of flaring torches. Their protective patrol went on day and night. Over all gleamed heaven's canopy of stars.

Marcus gave an involuntary shudder, as he turned from his silent survey. Why this particular city, produced vibrations of unease, within his tough soldier's breast, he did not know. But he did know how to distract such feelings.

'Well Claudius—fancy a girl for the night?' Without waiting for a reply, he gave a short order. Minutes later, a veiled figure stood in the doorway, the soft turquoise silk which draped the supple curves of the woman's body gave promise of voluptuous beauty, lightly concealed. Marcus nodded to her. She dropped her veil, revealing a bold, young face, seductively painted, framed by the abundant tresses of her hennaed hair. She smiled respectfully at Marcus, but at his direction knelt before Claudius.

'No—no. It is most kind, Marcus and I am grateful for the courtesy, but

I prefer to sleep alone.' He gestured the girl towards the door. Marcus watched the incident amused.

'Was she not to your liking? She is of a type that used to appeal to you?'

'I have taken a wife, Marcus.'

'You have? Why this is wonderful news, I never thought you would marry again. Why, it must be at least twenty years, since Daphne's death. Marcus dark eyes sparkled. 'This is cause for a toast!' He poured the wine himself. 'What is her name?'

'Miriam,' replied Claudius, accepting the goblet.

'Well, here is to a long and happy life and may all the gods shower you with their blessing.' He seated himself, not noticing that Claudius himself did not drink, although his lips touched the goblet. 'Miriam,' he mused. 'Surely that is a Jewish name?'

'My wife is of the Jewish race. She is an orphan, well as good as. Her mother is dead and her father is a leper, which is I suppose what you would call a living death. It is many years since he was driven from the city walls. There is a colony of these unfortunates in the hills behind Capernaum.'

Marcus watched his friend incredulously. 'You married a girl from such a background—but why?'

Claudius smiled gently. 'If you could see Miriam, you would know why!' There was an expression of happiness on his rugged face, such as Marcus had never discerned there before.

'I take it that she is very beautiful!'

'Yes, but it is more than that. She has an inner beauty, a serenity and she loves me.'

'I thought Jewish women, were not allowed to marry outside their faith?'

'There were difficulties, but they have been resolved,' Claudius said carefully.

'Then what more can I say—except to wish you all happiness old friend. Mind you, I suppose you must be held in much respect by the

Jews in Capernaum. After all, you caused their new synagogue to be built. Excellent strategy that. Keep them happy within their faith and they are far less likely to indulge in rebellion.' He thought he understood the reason for Claudius choice. The two men talked longer, before retiring.

It was a week later. Simeon stood on the shingle, listening to wave-lets breaking on the shore. It was so quiet at this hour; silver water, silver grey sky, flushing now to peach, until the Sea of Galilee, shimmered gold under the rays   of the risen sun. Several fishing boats were drawing in to land their catch at Capernaum's little harbour, some half a mile from where he stood. Behind him, the terraced gardens of Centurion Claudius splendid villa swept down to the sea.

In front, was a glorious view of the surrounding hills and of Mount Hermon crested with snow. It was breathtakingly beautiful here after Jerusalem's stuffy streets.

With a glance over his shoulder to check no-one was looking, Simeon slipped out of his new tunic and kicked his sandals off. The water sent cool shock waves through his skin, as he threshed about enjoying a sport that was not impeded by his club foot and in which he enjoyed total freedom.

It was while lapped in the crystal waters of this inland sea, just two days ago, that Simeon lifted his grief to the mighty God of Israel. He had prayed that the demon of revenge that had enveloped his young heart should be lifted from him, and he should be given grace to accept the pain of his parents' death, and that the murderous feelings towards those responsible should be wiped from his mind. And the mighty Jehovah heard this young son, who called to him. When Simeon stepped from the water, all anger had drained from him, the only feeling remaining, loving memory of his parents and pity for those who had killed them.

As he swam now, his thoughts were of John, and of his baptism at Jordan. He raised his head, glancing towards the peak of distant Mount Hermon, some thirty miles north, at whose base it was said, was a cave from which the river Jordan had its source—the same Jordan that flowed through Galilee's sea, and after leaving it sped on for over sixty miles, to empty its lower reaches into the toxic waters of the Dead Sea. One river, linking baptism into new life, with an unknown future!

'Simeon—Simeon! The master is calling for you!'

A young Negro slave boy, in a scarlet tunic, waved to him from the top of the steps which led down to the beach.

'I'm coming, Mencius.' He scrambled into his clothes.

'Why—you are almost as dark skinned as I am,' said the Negro lad in amusement.

'I suppose I am,' said Simeon. 'You will find many degrees of skin colouring amongst the Jewish race. Some are very fair, like your mistress, the Lady Miriam, many of a swarthy complexion, whilst others are dark skinned like me. However, I believe it is not the shade of our skin, or caste of features that is important, it is what we are like inside, whether as people we are good or evil, the way we treat others.'

He smiled self consciously at the other boy as he climbed the steep slope back to the house, hurrying between banks cascading with purple bougainvillea and scarlet hibiscus. He paused in the paved courtyard, bordering the villa, where a fountain splashed.

A young slave girl was singing softly, as she swept beneath the stone seats and around the bases of the many statues portraying foreign gods. Simeon drew in his breath as he looked at her. Her long, darkly curling hair, reached her trim waist, her dusky face had the bloom of a fresh peach, and the large dark eyes shifted with embarrassment before the fixedness of Simeon's stare.

'Good morning,' he breathed, thinking she was surely the loveliest girl he had ever seen. So it was that in that brief moment, Simeon was to give his heart, to one whom he would love for his lifelong. Maybe she had some inkling of the havoc she had caused in his breast, for she gave him a shy smile.

'Simeon—Simeon!' came a stentorian roar. It was Centurion Claudius calling and he must go.

'What is your name,' he asked softly?

'Sarah!' And the sound held music! A wonderful name, he thought, for was it not the name of Abraham's wife, the name of the mother of his race. He was disturbed from his reverie by a strident voice.

'Simeon—where have you been? Did I not send for you an hour ago?' Centurion Claudius drew his brows together in impatient scowl. 'Make yourself ready lad, for you accompany me to Nazareth!'

'Your pardon, sir—I did but go for a swim. The morning was so beautiful!'

'Beautiful? Not more so, than any other! However, if the water has wakened you and made you sufficiently alert to attend me...!'

His grumbling tirade was interrupted by a gurgle of laughter.

Lady Miriam knew that her husband's bark was worse than his bite. She reached a placating hand to him. 'I do not think it was really an hour ago that I dispatched Mencius to find Simeon. Perhaps it could have been ten minutes?'

Claudius walked over to the window of the atrium, where Miriam stood framed against the sunlight. Her black hair gleamed like ebony where the veil was drawn back and her green eyes were pools of mischief against her camellia cream skin. He scooped his much loved young wife up in a bear hug.

'Are you sure you want to ride with me? It will be hot and dusty and the roads you know are never safe in this area. I would prefer it that you remain at home.'

'Nowhere am I safer than at my husband's side!' The look she cast on him was one of determination. 'I want to go.'

'Then it will be in a litter and veiled.' He accepted her kiss and set her down. He turned to Simeon. 'Well lad, I have appointed you as my body servant, so buckle this breastplate for me and then get my helmet. I take it that you can ride lad?'

'Why yes.' Simeon blushed as he lied. He could hardly contain his excitement that they were to journey to Nazareth.

Would Jesus be there? His enthusiasm almost waned, as a fear caught his mind. Suppose Claudius planned to arrest Jesus? But then, was it not more likely, that it was merely curiosity that drew the Centurion to Nazareth? He had already heard it mentioned in many quarters, that Claudius was well disposed to the Jews, had built a wonderful new synagogue for them, here at Capernaum.

How many times, before they reached Nazareth, did Simeon regret the lie that he could ride. He had hoped that the inelegant manner in which he had mounted would be excused on account of his club foot. But he knew from the amused glance that Claudius would occasionally direct to him, that he was now aware that this was the first time the boy had been astride a horse.

They rested at Tiberias. Simeon's thighs were so stiff, that he could hardly dismount. One of the seasoned soldiers of the guard of twenty men, who accompanied the party, helped the lad. He gave him a small jar of ointment, telling him to use it for his saddle sores. If the soldiers were surprised at their Centurion's choice of a lame Jewish lad as body servant, they made no comment. Perhaps it was Simeon's cheerful attitude which called forth a small respect from the men and an ironic smile from Claudius.

'Well Julius, any unrest here at Tiberias,' inquired Claudius? He had just toasted the Emperor with the young Centurion who was stationed at this busy garrison town, and had for some years, served under Claudius command.

'None sir,' replied the officer,' In fact, the whole area has been amazingly quiet of late!' He looked at Claudius appraisingly. 'What is the purpose of the visit you are making to Nazareth? Have you heard of anything untoward happening there?'

Before Claudius could answer, there came a soft trill of laughter from Miriam, who sat with the two men in the secluded garden adjoining Julius house.

'Some of my relatives are from Nazareth, so although my husband is on a routine visit, I hope also to show him some of the places of my girlhood.' Julius nodded, satisfied. This of course explained why Claudius had brought his new young wife which was relatively unconventional. Still, with one as beautiful and charming as the Lady Miriam, it was not surprising that Claudius preferred to keep her close to him.

'You must stay the night here. I will have a room prepared. Your men can be accommodated at the garrison.'

Later that evening, Claudius slipped an arm around his wife, drawing her close, as they enjoyed the cool of the evening, as a breeze swept across the waters of Galilee. They leaned from the balcony of their room, breathing in the heavy scent of jasmine in the garden below.

'Why did you tell Julius that you had relatives in Nazareth?'

'Because my grandparents were from Nazareth—and also, because I know why you have an interest in the place, and thought it perhaps better that Julius knew nothing of this!'

'What was that? What is it that you think you know of my objective in visiting Nazareth?' Claudius pulled her gently back from the balcony and led her to the bedchamber. He indicated that she should seat herself then stood looking down on her. 'Well, Miriam, explain!'

'The Messiah! Your new servant, Simeon, told me that the Baptist had named Jesus of Nazareth as Messiah. Oh my Lord, my dearest Lord,' She slipped to her knees and took his right hand in both of hers. 'You have been so graciously kind to our people. All Capernaum respects you for building our wonderful new synagogue, to replace the crumbling building we once had. I know of your personal interest in our faith, that you have regard for our ways and for our God. Then you have raised me up to place of honour as your wife, when you could so easily have taken me as slave.'

'It is a decision that will gladden me to the end of my days!' He raised her and seated her next to him on the bed. 'So tell me Miriam, what does the advent of the Messiah mean to you?' He smiled as he tried to phrase his question carefully. 'Do the teachings handed down by your holy men, your prophets indicate that the Messiah will be a military leader, a warrior prince?'

Miriam looked at him with eyes grown serious.

'I do not know the honest answer to this question. Many of our people look for a warrior king, but many more understand the Messiah to be a holy one, a great teacher, who will bring revival of our faith. As a girl, I did not receive the education given to boys in the mysteries of our religion. Jewish girls are trained in domestic matters mostly, to equip them for wifehood.'

She was silent for a moment, then continued. 'Why do you not ask Simeon to give you the references in scripture to the promised coming of the Messiah? He is a boy of good family, well reared and with great interest in religion.'

'I may do that. He is a strange lad, brave too. Did I tell you that he risked a beating from Marcus, rather than betray the Messiah's identity?' Claudius sat thinking. 'He also seems to have made an amazing recovery from the grief of losing his parents, an acceptance. Well, Miriam sweet wife, promise me one thing, you will never try in any way to interfere with my official duties. However kindly I may be disposed towards your people for your sake, I am nevertheless the official arm of Rome in this area. My first, my only loyalty, is to my Emperor.'

Later that night, whilst Miriam's dark, shining tresses, cloaked her fair young shoulders in sleep, her breath fanning softly between lips bruised from kissing, Claudius lay brooding on his pillow. His mind was full of all he had ever heard of the Jewish God.

Why was he so drawn to the religion of an ancient race and to this unseen God, who strictly forbade his people to build statues to him, who claimed to be the one and only true God, who had always been, who was and who always would be, who had created the universe, created man in his image and had announced through his prophets, that He would send his Anointed One.

He thought of the deep reverence in which his wife held her mighty God and of the selfless bravery shown by an orphan lad to try to protect the Anointed One sent of this same God. He had to meet this Jesus. Perhaps then, there would be an answer to his questions and to the deep spiritual need which he had never acknowledged.

He blew out the lamp, and slept.

Chapter Four

The woman rose from the spring, adjusting the heavy pitcher on her shoulder. It was the third trip she had made for water this morning and she breathed heavily, as she walked down the uneven slope. Already the sun's rays burned fiercely and it was hot, despite the swirling wind that moaned fitfully from the wooded hills behind her. The spring was the only source of water supply for Nazareth, and Mary had made this journey for many years, the once sprightly steps of girlhood, giving way to the measured tread of middle age.

She hesitated for a moment, glancing down, where far below in the gully, under the cliff on which Nazareth was built, the road snaked away, rising ever upwards towards Jerusalem.

Would it be today that her beloved eldest son, Jesus, would return from his journey to lower Jordan? Eventually, she knew he must take this route. But only a caravan wound its way along the busy road, heavily laden camels swaying under their load of silks and spices.

Perhaps it was thoughts of that rich cargo that brought to mind events spanning the thirty one years since Jesus birth, in a rough stable in Bethlehem. The sheer normality of all that separated the present from the wondrous happenings of her late girlhood, sometimes made her pause to consider whether her memories were not just a dream.

She remembered the fabulous gifts brought to her tiny son, by the Magi, the wise men that had travelled from far countries in search of this child, who was born to be King of the Jews. They had followed his star from the East—that star of unusual brightness, flooding the whole heavens with radiant light—light to announce the birth of one who was to be the Light of the World!

Yes, they had been real, those gifts. She remembered how she had sat cradling her baby, watching incredulously as those marvellously apparelled strangers, dark skinned, venerable in appearance, had knelt before her infant son in adoration, placing their treasures as gifts at his feet.

'Gold, a casket full of gold and jewels and those gem encrusted vessels, containing frankincense and myrrh. Yes, the gifts were real,' she murmured now, 'But how much more wonderful, the gift of the tiny boy child, his birth forecast over long centuries by ancient prophets. But what did it all mean?' She had wondered it then, as she did at present and still found no answer.

As she had learned afterwards, those wise men had first visited King Herod in his palace, explaining there that they had come in search of the new child born to be king. They had followed his star from the East and wished to worship him. Herod in agitation and fury at this unexpected news, asked the Magi to return to him once they had found and identified the child, so that he also could visit and worship this new king.

But murder was in the heart of this most evil monarch, who although he had done much for his people by providing wonderful new buildings, mostly for his own glorification, had also a record of unbridled lust and viciousness, murdering even those nearest to him in his own family when he felt threatened by them. Treachery was his middle name, unbridled in his passions, unbelievably cruel by nature. The Magi had not returned to him.

Bethlehem! Mary knelt, letting the pitcher down carefully, so that no precious drop should be spilt. She loosed the veil from her head and let the wind take her hair. It had been darkly glossy then, black as the raven's wing. Now silver streaks added their framing grace to the beautiful planes of her face, while faint lines surrounded gentle eyes, that had once widened in amaze, when the angel had saluted her,

"Greetings to you, who are highly favoured—the Lord is with you...!"

So long ago that had been, whilst she was but a slip of a girl here in Nazareth, and affianced to Joseph. The angel had explained that the Holy Spirit would come upon her and the power of the Most High, overshadow her. She, a virgin was to conceive and give birth to a son—a Holy One, who would be called the Son of the Most High, whose kingdom would have no end!

Memories flooded her mind. The amazement she had felt, to find her elderly cousin Elizabeth, whom she greatly respected, and to whom she had gone for advice, was also to bear a son, her first child, in her old age. She still remembered the joy she felt for her cousin, when the angel had made this known to her. She could still feel Elizabeth's arms about her, the mound of the older woman's six month pregnancy verifying the angel's words, as she shared her wondering joy of her own pregnancy—

and Elizabeth's words!

'Blessed are you among women, and blessed is the child you will bear.'

She had stayed three months with Elizabeth and her ageing husband, the priest Zechariah, before returning to Nazareth. Their son John had been born, a serious, dark eyed baby, his very birth a miracle, who whilst still a youth, disappeared into the desert, living alone to prepare himself for the ministry which lay ahead. His parents died before they could see him in the full strength of his young manhood. Now this same John, called the Baptist, was fulfilling prophecy made of him by the Angel Gabriel—and that long dead prophet, Isaiah, as he now called all of Israel to repentance.

It was to see John that her son Jesus, had left with others of their village, over two weeks ago. Some of his friends had returned, but of Jesus there was as yet no sign. No one wanted to talk to her of what had happened at Jordan and she was sure something unusual had occurred, for her normally friendly neighbours, seemed if not exactly to avoid her well certainly to have become more distant. She shook her head in perplexity.

Her eyes sped back to the caravan and her thoughts returned to Bethlehem, and that journey made there with Joseph, long ago, in the last days of her pregnancy. There had been no option but to travel at this time, to register in Bethlehem the town of David, for the purpose of the census ordered by Emperor Augustus. Joseph like Mary was of the line of David—and all the Roman world had been instructed to register in their own place for taxation.

When at the point of exhaustion, she had almost fallen off the back of the donkey into Joseph's strong carpenter's arms she had known her infant's birth was imminent. She was past caring that there was no room left in the last inn they had wearily tried. At least the stable cave was warm, with the heat generated from the oxen and donkeys—the pile of straw, relatively clean.

Joseph had taken one last wondering look at the unusually bright star, immediately overhead, on which all had been commenting, and which seemed to be filling the night sky with its radiance. It had blazed with all the brilliance of a comet, yet it was not one. Men had never seen a star like this before, nor would again.

Then Joseph had prepared an old wooden manger to act as cradle, for the small man child, Son of God, nestling in Mary's arms. The Living Word, son of the Creator of the Universe, cooing softly at his mother's breast. Such exquisite joy to have held him so! Much of it was like a dream now. Those quiet shepherds who had slipped into the stable, out of the night—and knelt before her little one and then reverently left.

They had eventually found better accommodation. It was later, much later that they had received the visit of the Magi with their precious gifts—all these things, so amazing. Before that, they had made that quick visit to Jerusalem, to present baby Jesus in the Temple, to consecrate their first born son to the Lord, according to the law of Moses and she remembered the prophecies made in the temple, by old Simeon and the Prophetess Anna, regarding the glorious future of the tiny child, whose eyes shimmered in the flaring Temple lights, then back to Bethlehem to complete the census formalities.

Her acceptance when dear solid Joseph, told her to prepare for a journey to far off Egypt, having been warned in a dream vision from God to flee, as Herod was searching to find and kill the child. No time to return to Nazareth, to collect their possessions. The Magi's gifts had provided the necessary money for the journey and so it was, that a woman and her baby, seated on a small donkey, had been led safely out of Judea by a man obedient to the Almighty's command.

It had not been until they returned from Egypt two years later, after Joseph had been told in a dream by an angel, that it was safe to do so, that they were appalled to learn, that soon after they had escaped to Egypt, all male children in Bethlehem under two years of age, had been slaughtered at Herod's orders. The cruel ruler was now dead and his son Archelaus, equally wicked and unpredictable, ruling as Tetrarch in Judea, other parts of Palestine divided by the Emperor between Herod's other sons, Antipas and Phillip.

They had decided to settle back in Nazareth. Joseph had been a skilled carpenter and his busy shop provided a good living for his ever increasing family. Mary sighed, as she remembered the births of Joseph's children. First there had been James, followed by Joses, Judas and Simon and the two little girls. Then her thoughts returned to Jesus, conceived of the Holy Spirit, a child apart—a man apart.

She missed Joseph so much. He had been kind, such a good man. She had felt desolate after his death and had it not been for Jesus taking over management of the carpenter's shop, times would have been very difficult indeed.

Even as a stripling, Jesus had shown the same skill as his guardian. Before many weeks, clients were returning with their orders. Once Jesus had felled his trees and sawn them into manageable lengths, his young half brothers aided by the ageing donkey, had helped to drag timber down from the slopes above Nazareth. He had always shown an enormous patience with the younger ones, gentleness tinged with authority.

Now the family was scattered. The girls married to local craftsmen. James had left months before, to join the disciples of John the Baptist, Simon to become a stonemason and only Joses and Judas continued to work in the shop, with its living quarters behind. As for Jesus, he had made it known to his mother that he was now to embark on his father's work and Mary knew that he had referred to God. This trip to Jordan, had been the start of his new life, but he had promised to return, and so she waited, day by day.

Perhaps tomorrow! Mary lifted the pitcher and walked on.

Joses and Judas raised their heads from the yoke they were finishing, as they had heard the clank of armour. A Roman Centurion stood framed in the doorway, flanked by uniformed soldiers. The young carpenters eyed the Centurion apprehensively. Judas dropped his plane.

'Greetings,' said Claudius smoothly. 'I have been told that this is the house of Jesus the carpenter. Is either of you Jesus?

'No,' replied Joses, his mouth suddenly dry with apprehension, 'Our brother has left home.'

'Ah—and when did he leave?'

'Almost three weeks ago. Why do you seek him, Lord?'

'I merely wish to ask him a few questions.'

'Question, about what,' Mary had heard the strange voice and now came through from the inner room. Her eyes widened as she saw the Centurion.' I am Jesus mother,' she added.

'So—you are named Mary then? According to our records, you had a husband, Joseph?'

'Yes, sir, my husband died several years ago. But tell me, why is a

Roman officer looking for my son?' Mary watched him steadily, no sign of fear on her beautiful face. Claudius warmed to her, sensing a strength and control. He smiled.

'Tell me of your son Jesus? Why has he left home?'

'To see John the Baptist,' she replied evenly, 'like so many other hundreds of our people!' Mary had just seen the veiled figure of a woman in the doorway. She glanced towards her curiously. 'Would you like some refreshments, you and your lady,' she asked courteously?

Claudius ushered Miriam into the workshop and they both followed Mary through into the inner room, seating themselves on a cushioned bench at her invitation. She poured wine and placed a plate of honey cakes before them, then seated herself.

'Why do you seek my son?' Mary looked into Claudius bright blue eyes, fighting to keep fear at bay. Miriam leaned forward. She had dropped her veil and Mary saw the concern in the eyes of one who reminded her of herself as a girl, the same shaped eyes and mouth.

Miriam smiled. 'I am Jewish,' she murmured. 'Please answer my husband's questions. He wishes no harm to your son.'

'You are aware that Jesus has been named Messiah?' Claudius shot the question at Mary, seeing that she had relaxed. The shock of his words caused her to pale.

'The Messiah!' she had always known that one day the announcement would be made, yet dreaded the time of its coming. Now she rallied, and turned serene eyes on the Centurion. 'Do you mock me,' she inquired?

'No, Mary. In fact I will let you hear it, from the lips of one of your own race.' He rose and called for Simeon. His young servant came in at his command and stood waiting attentively. 'Simeon, this lady is the mother of Jesus. Tell her what occurred at Jordan.'

Miriam leaned forward towards Simeon. She looked at him meaningfully. 'Tell her everything,' she murmured.

So Mary learned from the lips of this lame, dark skinned youth, the news that John had proclaimed her son as the Messiah, the Anointed One. The loop of time between the angel's prediction of the birth of the Son of God and John's recent acknowledgement of Jesus Messiahship had closed. The shining light of God was now to illumine a dark world, for those who had the eyes to see and Mary, who had waited for this sign, now murmured a prayer of exultation.

She started to talk to Claudius and Miriam, told them of all that had happened so many years ago in Bethlehem, of the truth and honesty, the tenderness of Jesus, how he had studied the scriptures since early boyhood, spending time with the leader of the synagogue, learning, always learning, when other lads were only too happy at the close of school to hurry to their play. She told of how he had sustained his family on Joseph's death, how his greatest joy was to teach in the synagogue.

'You must not fear that he will become a military leader,' she said softly. 'He will seek only to lead men to God.'

Back in Capernaum again, Claudius sat late into the night, pondering on all he had recently learned. Mary's story of a stable birth, a virgin having conceived as foretold by an angel, worshipping shepherds, adoration of a tiny babe by visiting potentates, all of this he would normally have regarded as a tissue of lies, or the outpourings of one deranged had it not been for that quality in Mary, which defied disbelief. If then, her words were true, what did all of this portend?

What effect on the finely balanced political scene, would the emergence of a Jewish Messiah bring? He had a growing curiosity to meet Jesus for himself, together with an unease of spirit. Could it really be that the Jewish God, Jehovah, was indeed the only true God? And if he came to believe this, how could he reconcile this knowledge, with his allegiance to the Emperor and Rome!

A few days after Claudius had returned to Jerusalem, two other visitors wandered around the busy village of Nazareth, questioning all who would spend time with them. What was known of a carpenter named Jesus? Many there were who mentioned him as an excellent craftsman, but it was when speaking to the elders of the synagogue that they met a spirit of opposition. One of the elders had just returned from the area of Jordan, where John was baptising. The holy man had made an outrageous statement it seemed, that their Jesus, Jesus the carpenter, was the Lamb of God!

How could this be when all knew him to be one of themselves, a good and honest man it was true, but the long waited Messiah? The holy man was obviously mistaken! The desert sun had disturbed him. The news had apparently percolated through the whole village, and there was a feeling of resentment growing towards their missing carpenter.

Simon the Zealot and David, son of Ezra, were puzzled. It might have been expected that the township would have been delighted, to have one of its sons named as the long awaited Messiah. Instead of which, there was this resentment smouldering amongst Jesus friends and neighbours.

'Do you think we dare visit his family?' asked David.

'Why not—at worst they can only refuse to see us,' replied Simon. He was feeling bitterly disappointed, that there appeared to be no following for Jesus, amongst his fellow townsmen. Could the whole thing have been a mistake?

While speaking with Mary and her two sons, they experienced a sense of exhilaration. Why Mary had broken her thirty years silence regarding the early wonders attending Jesus birth, she was not sure, but once having shared these with Claudius and Miriam, it was like having a floodgate released. All her love for her son, her belief in the high spiritual office to which he had been born, now gushed forth. As David and Simeon stared into those beautiful eyes, they were swept along on the tide of her exultation. But Simon ventured a chastening question.

'Was it wise, think you lady, to have mentioned all these things to the Centurion?'

'I felt at peace speaking with him. His wife is a lovely Jewish girl called Miriam, and his body servant, Simeon, a dark skinned, handsome lad, with a club foot, had actually been present when John proclaimed Jesus as Messiah.'

'My brother! You are talking of my brother, Simon!' David's face was bright with joy. 'I had feared him dead—or a prisoner in Jerusalem. Where did you say this Centurion came from?'

'From Capernaum—he is in charge of the garrison there.' Mary smiled reassuringly at David. 'I promise you, that your brother looked well and was certainly in no fear of Claudius.'

'Mother,' asked Joses thoughtfully. 'Do you suppose that Jesus will remember that he is invited, to our cousin's wedding, in six weeks time?' Mary gave a delighted chuckle. Of course, whatever else happened, she knew that Jesus would not overlook an occasion so important in their family, for was not their cousin Jacob marrying the lovely Ruth, who although not bringing a rich dowry to the family, was exceedingly lovely and of a sweet nature! Jesus had always had a kindness towards Jacob.

Simon checked the date of the wedding, before leaving. He had friends in Nazareth, whom he wished to contact, members of his own party. He had left meeting them to last, because he wanted to form his own opinion of the character of Jesus, before speaking with the Zealots.

Certainly he would always remember Mary's expression of amazement and joy, when David described how Jesus had brought him back from near death in the desert. Simon's own spirits had lifted as David spoke, for he relived his own feelings of awe, at the miracle of healing Jesus had wrought. What a wonderful leader he would make; one to inspire men, to gather them to him in their thousands, to drive the Romans out of the land. One tolerated men such as Barabbas, because it needed men of this type, cruel, relentless to form a platform for the military strength that would be needed to oust the invaders. He thought back to the leaders of the Zealot movement, Judas the Galilean, his father and the Pharisee, Zadduk.

The Zealots had stolen singly out of Nazareth, walking casually through darkening streets, to melt into the hillside.

They met in a cave at the base of one of the wooded slopes, men with the feverish light of rebellion in their eyes. Galileans had ever been a turbulent race, broad of speech, swift to anger, unusually sensitive to criticism, and always waiting, seeking, for the Messiah who would arise to be their rallying point, the spark to set the whole of Palestine alight.

Simeon smiled satisfaction, as he took a rough count of heads, almost two hundred. They all cried greetings to Simon, held in respect for his father's sake, despite his youth and because he had already proved himself many times. Simon struck his left fist into his right cupped palm, the Zealot symbol and the cave resounded to the crack of two hundred fists, reciprocating the greeting.

'My brothers,' he called, as soon as he could be heard, 'I have come to you, from Jordan by Jericho, from whence Barabbas sends you his greetings. We have kept watch on the Baptist, these many months, waiting for him to announce the Messiah, whose advent he has been so long forecasting.

Well, as many of you now know, he has named him. Jesus the carpenter is Messiah. Let me present to you a new recruit. This lad, David, son of Ezra—his parents were murdered by the Romans a few weeks back. He was present when John baptised Jesus, and proclaimed him as the awaited one.' He paused, as several men called out contemptuously, that

Jesus might be a good carpenter, but he had never shown any sign of leadership.

'He is an excellent preacher,' said the more sober voice of an older man. 'But Simon, I fear he lacks the fire of a leader!'

'Jesus is not a man of war.' It was David who spoke, 'But he really is the Son of God. Through the power of the Almighty One, this Jesus brought me back from certain death, following a serpent's sting in the desert. He healed me with a word!'

The men listened incredulously. Could he be speaking of the man they all knew? He who was skilled carpenter, who had a gift for bringing the scriptures to life, but who nevertheless was a quiet man, who had never courted a woman, never raised his fists in anger and never heard to curse Rome! To have cured a boy from near death, with just a word, indicated power—that could be used to destroy, as well as to heal. The power they had all been waiting for! They passed the wineskins amongst them. A volley of voices was raised.

'Jesus! Jesus of Nazareth! Jesus is the Messiah!'

Later they dispersed to their homes, to watch and wait for Jesus return. Already in their minds, they had transported him to position of leader— the one who would lead them to victory!

Five weeks later, Simon and David son of Ezra, stepped ashore at Capernaum. A fisherman friend in the movement had brought them and now they waved farewell, as his boat set its sails for Bethsaida, a few miles along the coast. They had waited fruitlessly in Nazareth, watching hopefully each day, for the return of Jesus. Then they heard the rumour that a new teacher was preaching along the shores of Galilee. Could it be? They had spent the previous night dreaming, whilst the stars glittered like jewels above their heads and the moon silvered the wake left in the calm waters, as the boat left Tiberias far behind, drawing steadily towards Capernaum.

The sun was pleasantly warm on their heads, as they clambered up the shore. Simon knew Capernaum well. Although a busy little fishing village, with most making their livelihood from the rich harvest to be garnered from the waters of Lake Tiberias, as the Romans had renamed Galilee, there would not normally be crowds of people, converging on the beach at this early hour.

Two boats were moored close by, their owners tired after a night's fishing, but busily mending and cleaning their nets, before going home for a meal and to rest. One of them was a giant of a man, curly haired, rough bearded. He nodded to Simon and David before continuing his conversation with one who bore a resemblance to him, but lacked his stature.

'Good morning,' called Simon to the black bearded fisherman. 'Have you had a good catch?'

The giant Galilean scowled at Simon, and shook his head.

'No, my friend, my brother Andrew and I fished all night and hardly caught a thing—not worth lifting the nets for!' He stared at Simon. 'Who are you,' he demanded. 'By your tongue, you're not from these parts?'

'My name is Simon. I'm from Jerusalem, as is my young friend here. This is David.'

'Simon?' The bearded fisherman laughed and turned to his brother. 'Hear that, Andrew? Same name as me! That's worth a drink! Wait awhile.' He groped under the nets and produced a wineskin. He offered it to his namesake with a smile, indicating that he should pass it to David. He scooped his arm towards his two partners, sitting a few yards away.

'Meet James and John, sons of Zebedee,' he said. Then he called to John who had looked up. 'Here are two from Jerusalem—the tall one is Simon, the lad David.'

'David, son of Ezra,' said the lad easily, 'Greetings, my masters! Have any of you seen one called Jesus of Nazareth? We had heard that he was preaching in these parts.'

John stood up and stretched, glancing inquisitively at the newcomers from eyes dark as a storm cloud. David almost sensed that he was committing every detail of their appearance to memory. Although a young man, his hair was white at the temples adding an austere touch to his strong features. James seemed to be a few years older, black haired, hook nosed, a sensitive mouth belying a choleric temperament. He also bent a curious eye on the Judeans.

'Greetings to you both,' said John. His voice held a rich timbre. 'I saw you come ashore from the boat of Akim the Sumerian. What seek you with Jesus, the Holy One?'

'To hear him preach,' replied Simon the Zealot. 'Why do you name him Holy One?'

'You may judge whether the term is applicable for yourself soon,' answered John. 'See, he is coming up over the brow of the hill.'

Simon and David swung around expectantly. They glanced up at the grassy slope, to the right of the quay, as a great shout went up from the townsfolk assembled along the shore.

'He is coming! The Rabbi Jesus comes!'

The crowds who had been idling on the beach, scrambled urgently to their feet and started forwards, to join with the throng of people coming down the grassy cliffs. In the midst of them, walked a tall, white clad figure, the wind lifting his dark, chestnut hair. David gasped in excitement.

It was Jesus of Nazareth!

Chapter Five

Centurion Claudius stood on the flat roof of his villa, shading his hand over his eyes. He just heard the sound of shouting coming from the shore and glanced to see what was disturbing the normal quiet of the morning. Crowds were converging on the beach a few hundred yards from the steps of his terraced garden.

He went down to the lower hall and rapped out an order. A trumpet blast alerted the men in the garrison, quarter of a mile back on the outskirts of the town. Within minutes, a long column of soldiers, helmets and shields gleaming in the sunlight, were making their way towards the villa, while his house guards assembled along the perimeter of the gardens. Satisfied, Claudius clambered back up the steps leading onto the roof.

'What is wrong, my Lord?' Miriam had heard the commotion and joined him, holding one of the carved balusters as she leaned over.

'I don't know yet—some sort of disturbance. There must be over a thousand people down there. Can you make out what they're shouting?' He scowled in concentration.

'No. Yes, I can.' She turned to him in excitement. 'Claudius, they are shouting Jesus! Rabbi Jesus!'

Claudius smothered an oath. Surely it couldn't be—the Messiah? He called to Simeon. 'Send a man to tell the troops coming from the garrison to station themselves quietly behind the house, and to keep a low profile. They are to take no action without my direct orders!'

Simon the fisherman rowed slightly out from the shore, bemused at receiving this request from the teacher. He wasn't sure whether to feel disgruntled at being kept from his bed, or flattered that the Rabbi Jesus had selected his boat from which to preach for this was the reason that they were putting away from the shore, so that Jesus could teach the crowds without being crushed. Yesterday, only a very few people had attended the teacher, today the crowd was massive and still growing Obviously the townsfolk had thought that Jesus was attempting to leave them, but when they saw him motion to Simon to stop the boat they realized his intention. Their pushing and shoving ceased, as they stared towards the boat in expectation.

Jesus raised his hands to the people and addressed them, then seated himself with a gesture of thanks towards Simon. As he began to teach the people, Simon listened enthralled. Never before had he heard words like these. He had attended many times, to the long, dry discourses of the Pharisees with their meticulous regard to every fine detail of the law, but they only left a man painfully aware of his own inadequacies, without hope for the future—but this! His eyes burned with an unaccustomed ardour, as he devoured every word that fell from Jesus lips.

For almost two hours Jesus taught the people, answering the questions thrown at him from the shore. Some of the elders of the synagogue had attached themselves to the crowd and realized his faultless knowledge of scripture, but that he had a new teaching, a way of answering one question with another that made them consider attitudes and values in a way that they had never done before. Also, he taught by a series of stories, parables, letting a simple tale give emphasis to a deeper truth. The elders and scribe began to feel uneasy, threatened. When they attempted to remonstrate, the people shouted them down. Never had a visiting Rabbi commanded such respect, such a following.

James and John, sons of Zebedee sat in their own boat. They also had put out from the shore. Although John was attentive to every word spoken, his eyes also roved the multitude, watching their faces, gauging their reactions. The expressions which he saw were of something approaching awe. Even mothers placed hands lightly over their children's mouths, that Jesus words should not be lost.

At last, Jesus raised hands in blessing over the crowd, and turned with a smile towards Simon. 'Put out into deep water, and let down the nets for a catch,' said the firm voice. Simon almost snorted in disbelief at these words. What—let their nets down in bright sunlight? Whoever could expect to catch fish in such a manner! He exchanged a look with his brother Andrew, who shrugged his shoulders and nodded.

'Master, we've worked all night and caught nothing. But because you say so, I will let down the nets!' He signalled his intention to his partners in the other boat, ignoring their amused smiles as they followed behind intent on enjoying Simon's anticipated discomfiture. Jesus was a wonderful teacher, but obviously no fisherman!

As they approached deep water, Simon and Andrew started to let down their nets. In minutes, the strain on the nets indicated a heavy catch. Simon choked back a coarse swear word as he began to draw in the nets, the weight of the enormous catch of fish such that their boat began to sink.

'John, James! Quickly, quickly----take up the strain, or we sink!' Frantically the sons of Zebedee worked with Simon and Andrew, both boats now dangerously low in the water with the weight of the tremendous catch of silvery, struggling fish! Somehow they managed to get the boats ashore. Willing helpers ran forward to help drag the boats up on the beach, to help with the huge catch. Simon stared at Jesus in awe and sank to his knees.

'Go away from me Lord! I am a sinful man!' For he and all his companions were astonished at the catch of fish they had taken. No ordinary man could have provided knowledge of this happening, which went against all that Simon had learned in a lifetime of fishing. He knew as they all did, that what had just happened verged on the miraculous.

As he continued to kneel before Jesus, Simon raised his eyes fearfully. For the first time, he looked full into the eyes of the Holy One, eyes that seemed to shimmer with golden light, surely a reflection of the sun!

'Don't be afraid,' said the deep voice. 'From now on, you will no longer catch fish, but men!' He led them from the shore, those four fishermen, towards a more precious catch. Simon preceded Jesus through the crowds, who fell back before them, and up along the narrow streets of the town. The houses were built in blocks, constructed of granite, roofed with woven reeds, overlaid with palm branches, covered with marl, a crumbly mix of clay and sand.

'Will you honour my house, Lord?' Simon led him inside closely followed by the others. He was just about to shut the door against the curious, when someone laid firm hands on it. Simon pulled it open again, staring irefully, to see who was being so importunate. His eyes lighted on Simon the Zealot, accompanied by David.

'Simon, my friend,' said the Zealot smoothly. 'Forgive this intrusion, but I humbly ask to see the Holy One. We have already met once,' he added.

A voice from within commanded, 'Let them come!'

They entered, Simon with confidence, David in deepest humility. Then confidence fled. Simon and David felt the gaze of Jesus sweep over them. Simon started to tremble, could not control the shaking of his limbs. The tall fisherman called to his wife and his mother-in-law to provide food for his guests. They seated themselves on thick piles of mats. Gradually, the Zealot's spasm passed, but what remained, was an inner knowledge that he was in the presence of one who bore the Spirit of the Living God.

'Simon, son of John,' said Jesus, looking thoughtfully at the fisherman, 'You will be called Cephas!'

'Cephas—that is Peter, is it not, Lord----a rock! Yes, I like it.' He smiled expansively, and tried the name on his tongue, 'Peter—Simon Peter!'

'We go to Cana, will start tomorrow,' said Jesus.

'Why to Cana, Lord,' asked Andrew respectfully.

'There is to be a wedding,' said Jesus.

The soldiers had returned to their garrison, but the house guards remained on duty in the garden that night, for crowds still milled around the shore, even though it was said that the teacher had gone. But his name was on everyone's lips. His new teaching, with authority, like nothing man had ever heard before. Could it be that he really was the Messiah?

Simeon stood in front of Centurion Claudius, whilst his master continued to ply him with questions. He had allowed the lad to leave the villa and to mingle with the crowds that morning, to learn what message Jesus had for the people.

He had come back late, eyes shining, face bright with happiness. Claudius interrogated him for two hours. Simeon repeated faithfully every word that Jesus had said and Claudius had dismissed the lad and now sat quietly crouched on a seat, elbows on knees, head bent, hands clasped over his eyes. He knew, believed! His lips murmured in prayer.

It was already dusk. Mary, with her sons Joses, Simon and Judas, waited outside the house of Ruth, the bride to be. Her future bridegroom, Jacob, had already entered with a few male friends, to escort Ruth back to his own house. A shout went up, torches were lit and the bride was carried to the house, shoulder high beneath a white, embroidered canopy, followed by her bride maidens. Soon the procession was wending its way along darkening streets, the bride's long curling, auburn hair, reflecting the red gold of the flaring torches. She was dressed in flowing white, jewels glinting at ears and throat, her face covered by a filmy veil.

She was beautiful, and sat serenely erect, aware that this was her hour. Flutes and tambourines, announced her passage, whilst the bride maidens held small lamps on high.

Mary and her sons followed close behind the principals, for they were related to the groom and joined in the shouts extolling the virtue and loveliness of the bride. Soon the noisy, dancing throng arrived outside Jacob's house, where all was in readiness. Mary glanced around a little sadly. She was so sure that Jesus would have arrived. Then a quiet voice behind her, made her gasp in relief.

'Oh, my son, you have come! What happiness!' Her arms went about him, then she drew back, puzzled. It was Jesus, her first born, but she sensed a difference. What was it? A tremor ran through her for now she knew. This was no longer Jesus son of Mary, but Jesus Son of the Living God and she dropped her eyes in sudden humility.

These were his disciples he said, and Mary rallied, murmuring greeting to Peter and Andrew, to James and John sons of Zebedee and Simon the Zealot. There was also a quiet lad in the party, David son of Ezra. Jacob the bridegroom swung round as he saw Jesus and his party.

'Welcome—your friends also,' he called to Jesus, his face flushed with happiness. The whole procession made their way into the house to celebrate. Tomorrow the wedding feast would take place, but tonight, the bride would sleep on her own for her last night as a virgin in a chamber specially prepared for her and her bride maidens.

There had been festivities all morning, dancing, singing, the house filled to overflowing with guests—more than had been anticipated. Wine had been flowing unceasingly. Now, as evening fell, the bride at last appeared followed by her bride maidens, as a great shout went up and the rabbi prepared to make the special prayers and to give his blessing She seated herself under the embroidered canopy, still veiled, inclining her head to the guests. Jacob came to sit next to her, beneath the canopy and the feast began, all dipping into the delicious food which had taken all day to prepare. Toast after toast was drunk—then one of the servants approached the master of the feast, his face grave. But the man whose official function it was to arrange the feast had his back to the servant and did not hear the frightened words---

'The wine has all gone!'

But Mary heard. This would bring disgrace to Jacob sully the start of his marriage. She would lay the matter before her son, before Jesus. She rose from the table and went to find him, where he stood silently watching at the back of the room. She had to push such was the crush in that confined space.

He looked down at her.

'They have no more wine,' she blurted anxiously.

'Dear woman, why do you involve me,' Jesus replied? 'My time is not yet come.' But his eyes were gentle, as Mary looked at him pleadingly. He smiled relenting.

She turned quietly to the worried servants and said to them-

'Do whatever he tells you!'

Jesus disciples had also heard Mary's words. They watched, curious to see what their master could do to remedy the grave situation. Where could wine be had at this time—and in sufficient quantity to serve so large a gathering? Nearby, in the entrance hall stood six enormous, stone water jars, used for ceremonial washing, each holding about a hundred litres. Jesus called to the servants.

'Fill the jars with water.' So they started to fill the jars to the brim splashing water as they struggled at their task.

'Now draw some out, and take it to the master of the banquet!'

Mary and the disciples watched the man's face expectantly as he tasted the sparkling red wine, which minutes before had been plain water. A delighted expression spread across his face. He smiled across at the bridegroom and motioned him to his side.

'Everyone brings out the choice wine first and then after the guests have had too much to drink, the cheaper wine, but you have saved the best until now!'

She had hoped that Jesus would in some way save the situation, but now as the shock of realization hit her, that Jesus had done the impossible, turned one substance into another, water into wine, she felt waves of faintness steal over her to be replaced by wondering joy. Her eyes flooded with tears, as she stammered her thanks. His disciples had fallen to their knees, mumbling forth words of praise from trembling lips. Quickly he raised them. He did not want it known. But the servants knew, and one day, the whole world would learn of this the first miracle of Jesus ministry, in the little town of Cana.

Meanwhile, the disciples followed him out into the night, faces white with awe at this the glory of God, revealed in His Son.

Jesus was returning to Capernaum. Initially, Mary had felt dismayed when he explained that he intended to stay there. Although she knew deep inside, that their lives must now be separate, she had still nurtured hope that he would have lived within the confines of Nazareth. She and her sons were to accompany him to Capernaum, to see where he was going to start his ministry. The sons of Zebedee had invited the Nazorenes to stay in their house.

As for Jesus, Peter had cleared a small room, next to the large communal room. Here the master could stay—a quiet place to withdraw to. It was bare, apart from a sleeping mat, a rug and a small chest bearing a water jug and a basin. They had arrived late in the evening, unnoticed by the townsfolk. Peter ushered his master into the small room somewhat awkwardly. It seemed such an inadequate place to house such an august visitor, but the master had smiled thanks and lifted a hand in blessing as Peter withdrew.

Jesus knelt, praying into the night and the Spirit was on him as he communed with his Father.

It was the Sabbath, the seventh day of the week sacred to the Lord God. On it, the Jews did no work. Here in Capernaum, they made their way to the splendid new synagogue, built for them by Centurion Claudius. Surely the Almighty must have touched the heart of this gentile, a Roman known to be strict, but just.

The congregation recited the Shema---

"Hear, Oh Israel, Jehovah our God, is one Jehovah;

And thou shalt love Jehovah thy God, with all thy heart,

And with all thy soul, and with all thy mind!"

The prayers went on, a time of silent prayer then all who had managed to get a place in the synagogue caught their breath in anticipation as the hazaan lifted one of the sacred scrolls from the chest and handed it to Jesus of Nazareth to read from. Jesus inclined his head to the attendant, found the place he sought in the scroll and started to read.

All eyes were upon the gracious figure that stood at the reading desk. As he spoke, the words took on a new and vibrant meaning. The elders who had allowed this new rabbi to teach, at the insistence of the Master of the synagogue, became enrapt in his words. He closed the scroll, which the hazaan replaced in its niche, and was now teaching. There was complete silence in that building. The Spirit of the Most High was upon the hearts of his people through the teaching, the message of His Son.

Then there was sudden confusion as a man leapt wildly to his feet, brandishing his fists at Jesus. He commenced to rage and foam at his mouth, his face contorting eyes ferocious with mixture of fright and anger.

'What do you want with us, Jesus of Nazareth? Have you come to destroy us? I know who you are—the Holy One of God!' All tried to draw back from the deranged man, for it was obvious that he was possessed of an evil spirit. There was fear on their faces.

'Be quiet,' said Jesus sternly. 'Come out of him!'

The man convulsed, the evil spirit which possessed the man shook him violently, and came out of him with a shriek! The man came back to his right mind. The look of love he turned on Jesus, said more than any words of gratitude. The people were all so amazed that they asked each other-

'What is this? He even gives orders to evil spirits—and they obey him!'

As they poured out of the synagogue, those who were crowding about the building, frustrated at not having found space for admittance, cried out to the worshippers asking what had been the cause of the noise they had heard within. The news of what had transpired spread like wildfire, and an immense crowd followed Jesus and his disciples back to Peter's house.

Peter's wife greeted him with the news that his mother-in-law was in bed with a fever. Peter looked at Jesus with trusting eyes.

'Master, if it be thy will,' he said? Jesus smiled. He followed Peter to the sick woman's bed, and bent over her, touching her hand. Immediately the woman was well and smiling her gratitude. Within minutes she was up and bustling around, waiting on him and the others. Peter's eyes shone. The emotions filling his heart were almost too much for his simple fisherman's mind to contend with. He exchanged glances with the others, raising his hands in automatic gesture of praise.

There was heard a barrage of voices outside the house, calling on Jesus name, nor did the sound get less. Jesus rose to his feet and opened the door. The pressure of people was such that they almost cascaded into the house. But then, as he raised his hands, they fell back before him.

It was sunset and the rose and magenta of the evening sky made glorious backcloth to the white robed figure that walked among his people. They brought all their sick relatives to him. Word of what had occurred in the synagogue that morning, had spread to every area of the town. Cries of wonder arose, as the sufferers were healed from all manner of diseases. The disciples tried to form a screen around him, fearing that he would be crushed, but still they came, and a spirit of awe was upon the crowd.

There were also amongst the people those possessed of demons. These afflicted ones, were made to roar and scream in fright by the demons that controlled them. They had knowledge of who Jesus was, and attempted to shout this out. But this Jesus would no way permit. At his words, and before the stern look in his eyes, the demons were cast forth and many people, who had been under control of these evil spirits, were wonderfully released from their power. The peace of God was in their hearts. The joy of those related to the once possessed man, was beyond comprehension, for this healing was to bring peace and happiness into their lives too.

Simeon stood before Centurion Claudius. He looked tired, but seemed feverishly happy. The Centurion gestured to the boy to sit.

'Bring him wine,' he said to Mencius, then dismissed the black slave. He watched Simeon pensively. Already Miriam had described the events in the synagogue earlier that day and Simeon had been dispatched to mingle with the crowds, to see what else would happen. Now, late at night, he had returned with a story of wondrous events, miraculous cures performed by the Rabbi Jesus and witnessed by hundreds.

'How have the people responded, the truth boy? Do any seek to persuade him to take leadership over them?' His bright blue eyes bored into Simeon's dark ones. Simeon shook his head. How could he explain about the Holy One in a way that this gentile could accept?

'The spirit of our God is upon him,' he replied.

'That I believe, but does your God wish Jesus to lead a revolt against Rome?' Claudius was lacerating his own mind as he questioned the lad, for now he absolutely believed that Jesus was the Son of God, but his twenty years of training as a Roman officer was a discipline that bruised his soul. He had his duty to man, to a man in Rome, an Emperor called Tiberius, whom Rome revered as one of their gods. What if his heart was yielding to the yet unknown Jesus, what if a cry was rising from deep within, for help to blot out the pain of the years, the confusion of life, the emptiness. True there was now the inestimable joy of his beautiful young wife, but in spite of his love for Miriam, Claudius knew he craved for something more.

'You may retire, Simeon. Tomorrow, I wish that you bring more news to me.'

He walked heavily upstairs to his bedchamber. Miriam sat up in bed, her long hair cloaking her loveliness. His eyes darkened with a mixture of tenderness and desire.

'Do you really believe Jesus to be Messiah?' she asked softly, as much later he lay quiet beside her.

'Miriam, yes—yes I do! Almost I wish I did not, for I believe him to be a most wonderful man, if it be that one can describe him as mere man!'

'You fear for his future,' inquired Miriam intuitively?

'Yes, my dear. His people will not allow him, just to be a great preacher and healer. They are looking for a political leader, one with charisma, and he will seem a natural choice!'

He stroked her hair absently, as he spoke.

'Suppose he is totally opposed to violence?'

'Then all may be well. But Miriam, I have a sense of foreboding! Bah, I am becoming fanciful.'

Miriam sighed. 'I wish our son could look forward to birth in a land where there is no future strife!' Her words made Claudius sit up startled.

'What did you just say—about our son?'

'I was waiting time to tell you, my Lord. You are to be a father!' Claudius held her close, as they slept in each other's arms.

Jesus rose before sunrise. He walked through the sleeping streets of Capernaum, up onto the lonely heights of a hill. He knelt there, amongst the damp grasses and wild flowers, crying aloud to his Father to be with him and guide him, on the road that lay ahead. And as he prayed, he became one with the Father. The power of God fell upon him.

He stood up. It was dawn. He looked down upon the world, that he, the Living Word, had created with his Father, and seeing it thus in the rays of the risen sun, knew it to be very fair. Snow crested peaks of distant mountains were touched with flame, the hills were rose gold, dappled with blue shadows; white mist hung over Galilee's silver sea—a bird sang—and it was day.

He heard their voices, breathless, querulous. 'Where is Jesus? Why did he leave without telling us?' It was John who guessed that he had probably climbed this, the nearest hill. John was perhaps the most spiritual of the disciples. He had sensed that Jesus would have needed to retire to a quiet place and where more appropriate than here?

As he stood, silhouetted against the skyline, the sun's rays turned his white robes to gold, his hair and beard to glowing copper. Then he moved to meet them. The radiance of dawn had passed, but the golden light still shimmered in his eyes. He looked at them and they lowered their gaze, ashamed of their grumbling.

'Everyone is looking for you!'

He nodded. He asked that they bring his mother and brothers. They would start to make their way to Nazareth. David, the youngest and fleetest was sent.

'Let us go somewhere else,' Jesus was saying, 'to nearby villages, so that I can preach there also. That is why I have come.' And so began a ministry that was to take them the length and breadth of Galilee, as Jesus preached in the synagogues, healed the sick and comforted the broken hearted and drove out demons.

Simon the Zealot kept in constant touch with members of his party, who were now on fire with enthusiasm, Jesus was proving to be the answer to their wildest dreams of the long awaited Messiah! Maybe he showed no sign of wishing to speak against Rome, to fight, but what did that matter! He would be the figurehead and behind him, they would mobilize all the Jews in Palestine.

He was back in his native Nazareth, and went into the synagogue to preach, as was his custom. Maybe he was already aware of the sly comments in the streets by erstwhile neighbours. They had heard about the miracles, the wondrous healings, but he knew the hearts of men, the seething jealousies that so easily arise, the small sharp wounds made by that so agile weapon, the tongue. His mother and brothers would be accepted again, but Jesus they would not accept. He had done the unforgivable, raised himself to lofty position above them, when they all remembered him as local boy who had become their carpenter.

He stood at the reading desk and received the scroll of the attendant. It was that of the prophet Isaiah. Unrolling it, he found the place where it is written-

"The Spirit of the Lord is upon me, because he has anointed me to preach good news to the poor. He has sent me to proclaim freedom for the prisoners and recovery of sight to the blind, to release the oppressed, to proclaim the year of the Lord's favour."

He rolled up the scroll and gave it back to the attendant.

The eyes of everyone were fastened on him.

'Today this scripture is fulfilled in your hearing!'

The townspeople of Nazareth were amazed at the gracious words he spoke. This was a different Jesus, with power, a new authority. The words that flowed from his lips were not the stilted language of the Scribes and Pharisees. He spoke of repentance, the love of God who was Almighty Father, caring for his children, waiting for them to turn to him, to confess their sins and receive his forgiveness. They should care for each other, show love and tenderness, so that their Father in heaven, should return that same love to them, a hundredfold.

They listened in amazement. But wasn't this Joseph's son? His disciples felt uneasy, as they heard the murmuring. It was the first time that any had shown less than the deepest respect for their master.

'Where did he get these things,' the people asked? 'What's this wisdom that's been given to him that he even does miracles? Isn't this the carpenter? Is this not Mary's son and the brother of James, Joses, Jude and Simon? Aren't his sisters here with us?' And they took offence at him.

Jesus looked at them sadly and shook his head.

'Only in his home town, among his relatives and in his own house, is a prophet without honour.' His eyes travelled to Joses, Jude and Simon who were sitting with those who criticized him. They glanced down, shame faced. But they would have to live in this place once Jesus was on his travels again, and they would need work from their fellow townsmen.

Peter, Andrew and John, flanked themselves behind him, as he left the synagogue. To their concern, their master quoted several passages of scripture which cut the Nazorenes' hearts to the quick, with its sharp analysis of their meanness of spirit. It took only this small spark to ignite their volatile tempers.

Simon the Zealot had placed his men amongst the congregation and also with those who were loitering outside. They were ready for any confrontation which might take place, for Simon had already gauged the uncertain temper of this crowd. Suddenly, those in the synagogue turned as one man upon Jesus. They hustled him out of the building, furious that he knew their cold hearts.

'Throw him over the cliff! Kill him!'

The cry was taken up by those outside, as well as those pouring out of the synagogue. Jesus disciples tried to keep at his side, but were pushed away by the sheer weight of numbers, as the murderous intent of the crowd became more obvious. They surged forward to the cliff face of the hill on which Nazareth was built.

Then the Zealots acted, tripping men up, jostling them as though by accident. Confusion reigned.

Jesus walked through the midst of the crowd—and went on his way.

Chapter Six

Centurion Claudius had ridden off on a routine trip into the hills taking twenty of his men with him. Simeon had been left behind to watch for the return of Jesus. He was feeling unwell this morning, responding with only an absent-minded smile to a few teasing remarks made by the pretty slave girl Sarah. His head was aching as he slipped out into the garden, hoping that the fresh breeze blowing off the lake would clear the pain throbbing at his temples.

'Hsst! Over here Simeon! Other side of the wall!'

Surely he must be dreaming? Simeon turned his head. That was David's voice! He hurried across to the containing stone wall to the right of the garden and clambered over—and it was his brother! He gave a cry of joy as they fell into each other's arms. It really was David, he was alive! David hugged him.

'Simeon! Oh, my brother! How I have longed for this moment!' David had tears in his eyes. Simeon's own eyes were damp too.

'David, I feared you dead! I never thought to see you again, he said brokenly. Where have you been, all these weeks?' He crouched next to David, beneath the covering shade of a fig tree. 'You know about our parent's death?' Simeon's eyes filled with tears, as he asked this, for seeing his brother had brought that awful night of Ezra and Naomi's murder back into his mind all too vividly.

'Yes. Yes I know. We must speak of it.' Then David quietly recounted all that had happened that fateful evening, explaining his meeting with the Zealots, receiving the blessing of their dying father, joining the nationalists, being sent with Simon into the desert, the serpent's sting and recall from near death by Jesus of Nazareth. He paused for a few minutes, as though mentally reviewing everything that had happened.

'Jesus healed you? You met him?' Simeon's face was bright with awe, as he latched on to this salient point.

'Not only that, Simeon I am now one of his followers, as is Simon the Zealot. We are just back from Nazareth. The Master is resting a few miles away from the town, but he will be in Capernaum later this very day.'

Simeon stared at David, looking at him objectively then, realizing that this was a different David. All the old enthusiasm was there, but tempered by a new gentleness of spirit. Simeon nodded, deep in thought. Even from listening to Jesus on the fringe of the crowd a few weeks ago, he had realized that none could hear the words of the Holy One and remain untouched by them. But David was surely most wonderfully privileged to follow the Messiah and a small stab of an emotion akin to jealousy shot through his mind, to be replaced by repentant happiness that such thing had happened to his brother. But something was niggling at the back of his mind. Jesus was glorious prince of peace, so why include a member of the Zealots in his following? All knew that the Zealots were warmongers, fanatical nationalists! He thought of Claudius many probing questions and he shuddered. Surely it wasn't possible? If only this headache would ease, so that he could think clearly.

'I knew that you were here as servant to the Roman Centurion,' David continued. 'I learned this of Mary, the Mother of Jesus, when I first visited Nazareth, but this has been the first opportunity I have had to come to you. Never again shall you wait upon a detested Roman—never again shall my brother be used as a slave!' David's eyes flashed with all the old fire.

'But I am not a slave. Centurion Claudius has appointed me as his body servant, a position of trust. He and his lady, have shown me every kindness, in fact,' he hesitated, 'He almost treats me like a son! Listen David, his wife Miriam is of our race and Claudius himself caused Capernaum's new synagogue to be built. He is showing tremendous interest in our religion, questions me repeatedly about Jesus. I know he believes him to be the Messiah!'

'And you are taken in by all this? You can actually accept one of the Roman murderers in place of your own father? I do not believe it!' There was contempt in David's voice.

Simeon flushed. 'You are receiving the grace of walking with the Holy One, my brother. I have only heard him speak once, but enough to know that his teaching is of love and kindness to all men—to all men, David. That means Roman as well as Jew!' He paused. 'There are good men amongst the Romans as well as murderers, just as among our own people, there are those whose hearts are full of hate.' He placed a hand to his forehead, which was now throbbing unmercifully.

David hung his head silently, pricked to the heart. He knew that Simeon spoke truth—knew that his own sentiments were not worthy of the one he followed.

'Perhaps you should know...' He hesitated.

'Know what?' Simeon watched his brother keenly, as the other snatched some figs from the tree and started to munch them. David looked unsure of himself. Simeon stood up. 'Know what,' he prodded?

'Well, I heard that your Centurion is to lose his life this day! One of his slaves mentioned to a member of the Zealots, that he rides to Magdala this morning with only a small party. Too good a chance to be missed! So you see, brother, you had better come with me now in case you should be suspected of involvement. Besides, your new Centurion may not be so much to your liking!'

Simeon's thoughts raced, Claudius to be assassinated? He pictured Lady Miriam's distress, realized the void that would remain in his own heart for the blue eyed Roman. What should he do?

'Where is this to take place,' he questioned, keeping his voice calm. David smiled, satisfied that Simeon was coming to his senses.

'It will be in the gully between the hills, ten miles from Magdala. There is a cliff that overhangs the stream there. He will have to cross the stream at that point. Men will be on the cliff above.' He looked encouragingly at Simeon. 'Well, are you coming with me now?'

'There are matters which I must attend to first,' Simeon replied guardedly. 'Where will you be, later in the day?'

'At the house of Simon Peter, the fisherman!'

'Does the Messiah know any of this,' asked Simeon, although he already knew the answer to this question.

'Of course not,' replied David, looking slightly shamefaced. 'He would have nothing to do with anything of this sort!' Suddenly he lowered his head, considering for the first time, the ugliness of the deed the Zealots planned and that they had not even tried to make Simon party to it for fear that he had turned soft through following the teacher, at least, this was what he had heard them saying. Into his mind, came the Law of Moses, received of God. 'Thou shall not kill'! Well, it was too late to do anything now!

But it wasn't. Swiftly Simeon promised to see his brother later, embraced him and hurried back to the house. He called for one of the house guards.

'Saddle a horse for me,' he commanded, with new authority and hearing that note, the man obeyed, helping the lad into the saddle. Simeon rode like the wind, his face beaded with sweat, the pain in his head almost blinding him to where he was going. But there was only one path and the horse flew along it, enjoying the light weight of his rider. Simeon tried to remember how long a start the Centurion's party had. It must have been at least an hour. There were now strange aches in his limbs, dryness in his throat.

The path divided and instinctively he took the higher fork which took him up on the side of a hill. Below him in the distance, lay the town of Magdala. The white buildings seemed to shimmer in front of his eyes. Then minutes later he caught sight of the Romans—saw the scarlet plumes of Claudius helmet. He kicked his horse's flanks, shouting wildly. There below him, was the stream. Claudius had almost reached it and the overhang, which bore death to him. Why did they not turn?

Claudius reigned in his horse, listening. He thought he had heard shouting! Then he spied the lad, sweeping down the slope towards him, and heard those words of warning!

'Claudius—Beware the stream! Do not cross!' Claudius reaction was instant. He wheeled his horse about, shouting to his men to do likewise. As he turned his horse, a spear streaked whistling down, missing him by inches, followed by a swift shower of arrows and one of his men fell wounded.

'After them,' shouted Claudius. But his men were too late. The Zealots had fast ponies and struck high up into the hills, pursued by the Romans. Their ponies were dragged into a cave they often used, dense branches of thorn bushes pulled swiftly in front, to mask the entrance, as their foes searched in vain.

Sullenly the Romans withdrew to where their Centurion was cradling the lad Simeon in his arms. They all dismounted, looking down at the still figure that had saved all their lives. How had he known? There would be questions to be asked, but what mattered was, that but for him, their commander would now lie dead, and they also would have been dead, or disgraced.

'The boy is in a faint,' said Claudius. 'We will return to Capernaum.' He laid Simeon across his horse and the silent party set forth.

It was two days later and Simeon was dangerously ill. Claudius had called in his own doctor. The youth was lying still on his bed, a deathly pallor to the dark skin and there seemed to be a strange rigidity to his limbs. The doctor advised the Centurion to ensure that all members of his household kept away. There was sickness of this sort in the town. It was catching. Nor was there any cure, the young man probably only had a few hours.

Claudius looked down at Simeon pityingly. In spite of the doctor's words, he leaned over him and stroked his forehead.

Why had Simeon saved the life of an enemy—why had he exposed those of his own race to possible death, in order to save that enemy? But were they really enemies? His heart told him no. He had always longed for a son, was going to be blessed with one, for Miriam now bore a child under her heart and anyone less like the son of his dreams, than this Jewish lad with his dark skin and club foot, was hard to imagine. Yet all the ice around Claudius heart cracked, as he bent over the boy. He knew that he loved young Simeon. If he lived, would adopt him as son of his house, after any children that Miriam would bear. He must not die!

'There is but one chance,' said the doctor slowly. He looked dispassionately at Claudius, to see what reaction his words would have. 'Jesus of Nazareth is back in Capernaum. It would take a miracle to save this lad. No medicine of mine will serve. Do you wish me to ask the Rabbi Jesus to come?'

Claudius thought swiftly. Of course, Jesus could heal Simeon! He knew this without doubt. But would he wish to heal the servant of an enemy? Again he knew the answer.

'Call the elders of the synagogue here,' he commanded. They came. He instructed them to ask Jesus to heal the boy, to go quickly. They hurried away from the house, eager to do the bidding of their benefactor. As they sped on their way, Claudius came to another decision. It was not fitting that the Messiah should come to his house, for his followers might possibly take offence at such a visit, nor was it necessary that the teacher should come. He called some friends of his, who were visiting with Miriam. They smiled at him inquiringly.

'Go to Jesus of Nazareth, and speak these words to him,' he said. The elders were already with Jesus, pleading with him earnestly to come and heal the servant of the Centurion. His eyes softened as he listened to their urgent voices.

'This man deserves to have you do this, because he loves our nation and has built our synagogue.'

So Jesus went with them. Perhaps he pondered on the strangeness of Jews making supplication on behalf of an enemy leader. Certainly the white clad figure walked swiftly amongst the attendant crowd, shading his eyes, as they pointed towards the beautiful marble villa, a quarter of a mile away, by the side of the lake.

Other people were hurrying towards them from the villa. He was only a few hundred yards from the house, when the people scurrying to meet him, stood awkwardly in front of Jesus. An elderly Jewish friend of Claudius elected himself as spokesman. He bowed. 'Lord,' he began then paused, for striding rapidly towards them, was Centurion Claudius himself. The soldier stood before Jesus, glancing deep into those shimmering gold eyes that seemed to penetrate his very soul. And Claudius bowed low, standing before one whom he knew to be the Son of God.

'Lord,' he said. 'My servant lies at home paralyzed and in terrible suffering.'

'I will come to him,' said Jesus.

'Lord, I do not deserve to have you come under my roof. But just say the word, and my servant will be healed. For I myself am a man under authority, with soldiers under me. I tell this one—"Go!" and he goes; and that one "Come" and he comes. I say to my servant—"Do this" and he does it.' He stood to attention in front of Jesus, waiting for his answer, but already knowing it.

When Jesus had heard Claudius statement, he was astonished. He said to those following him-'I tell you the truth, I've not found anyone in Israel with such great faith! I say to you, that many will come from the East and the West, and will take their places at the feast with Abraham, Isaac and Jacob in the kingdom of Heaven. But the subjects of the kingdom, will be thrown into the darkness, where there will be weeping and gnashing of teeth!'

Then Jesus said to the Centurion—'Go! It will be done, just as you believed it would.' Claudius bowed, his eyes speaking for him. Then he turned on his heel, and marched back to his house. As he reached the door, the doctor came hurrying to meet him. 'He is healed! The boy is completely healed! See, he is coming to you!'

And there came Simeon. He was stumbling, although his face was beaming with health. Claudius glanced down at the boy's legs—the deformed foot had straightened! The lad was adjusting his stride to a normal one. Claudius ignored the curious glances of those around him. He opened his arms and swung the lad up into his mighty clasp. 'Come to your father, my son,' he cried, and led him to Miriam.

David had experienced great concern, when Simeon failed to contact him following the morning of their meeting. What had happened? Then word had reached him that the Centurion and his men, had returned to the villa, with Simeon slung over the Centurion's horse. David had wandered along the sea shore, torn with anxiety. What had Simeon been doing away from the villa, in the company of Claudius and what had Claudius done with him? He blamed himself bitterly for telling Simeon of the Zealot's plan. He should have understood that a sensitive lad like Simeon might not approve of murder, even of a Roman. As he walked through the wet shingle, he suddenly knew that neither did he.

David was being exposed to two very different forms of teaching—that of the Holy One, with his emphasis on love, repentance and healing and on the ideology of the Zealots, based on violent struggle to rid Palestine of the Romans.

It was impossible to walk with a foot in both camps. He thought of his parents, killed by those same Romans, and then he remembered his healing by the Lord in the desert and all he had learned from Jesus during the weeks he had walked quietly at his side. He had watched the sick being healed, deformed limbs straightened, the blind receiving sight, the deaf their hearing and the demon possessed release. And always the word was of love, love for Almighty God, and love for his fellow men.

If Jesus was indeed the Son of God, as the disciples now firmly believed, then obviously it was God's wish that men should care for each other. But how could you love a Roman? The Jews were the chosen race, God's own people! Should they love the enemies of their race? Was this not thing impossible? How could you have kindly feelings towards those who raped, pillaged, burned, and exacted extortionate taxes?

'Hallo, David!' It was Simon, who had sensed earlier that David was worried about something, and had been following him.

'Oh—it's you, Simon!'

'What's troubling you, David?' His swarthy face was concerned, as he slipped an arm around his friend's shoulders. He treated David as a young brother, and was very protective towards him.

'Simon—do you hate the Romans?'

'Detest them!'

'But, you are one of Jesus disciples and he tells us to love all men!' Simon smiled. He saw the boy's difficulty.

'Would it help you, to think of men as individuals, rather than belonging to any special race,' he said gently.

'But you are still a Zealot, Simon? All those men you meet in the different villages, they all want one thing, don't they, to kill Romans and to drive them out of our country! They also want to make Jesus their leader only we both know this can never be! Well?' David's face contorted with conflicting thoughts.

'David, we neither of us know what the future holds. We can only do what our hearts dictate in the present. We both love Jesus of Nazareth. Know him to be the Messiah, and wish to protect him from all harm. Yes, the Zealots do wish to make him their leader, but there are worse problems—the Pharisees and the Sadducees! I have heard that they are converging on Capernaum from as far away as Jerusalem. They will wish to question Jesus about his new teaching, try to catch him out with clever questions. They are the religious force of Israel, conformists, jealous of their absolute control on all matters of the law.'

'The master will know how to deal with them,' replied David confidently and smiled, 'Even as he does with us! He knows all out hearts, Simon, the problems, worries, doubts about right and wrong.' He was silent for a moment. Then he started to tell Simon about his meeting with Simeon, the news about the planned assassination, which Simon had not been party to and the fact that a very much still alive Centurion had returned, with his brother thrown seemingly unconscious across his horse.

'I will find out what I can for you. We have a woman in that household, who is well disposed towards the Zealots, Rahab the cook. Her son is a

Zealot. In the meanwhile, come back with me. I don't know why, but I have a feeling that all will be well with your brother. The Centurion has a reputation for being a just man.'

David had followed closely behind Jesus, when he was requested to heal the Centurion's servant, by the elders. His heart was thumping when the Lord had started towards the villa. News had come from Rahab that morning that Simeon lay paralyzed, in high fever. He had seen the Centurion bow before the Messiah, heard his amazing statement, that he knew Jesus could heal his servant merely by a command—was not worthy that the teacher should enter his house. He had looked into the frank, blue eyes and had known that this was one Roman he could not hate. He also knew that Simeon had been healed. Tears of joy ran down his cheeks. 'Glory be to God,' he murmured. The Master turned his head and smiled at him.

Shortly afterwards, a man came running from the Centurion's villa, to shout to the crowd that the young man Simeon had indeed been healed.

Jesus was walking ahead of the people, by the sea-shore. He paused by the side of a tax collectors booth. Inside sat Matthew Levi, son of Alpheus, detested as were all of his kind, who collaborated with the Romans by collecting their iniquitous taxes and as they had no doubt, feathering his own nest at the same time. You only had to look at that fine house of his. Where did the money for that come from? It was obvious, wasn't it!

They halted beside him, puzzled. Jesus was staring down into Matthew's dark, narrow face, with its high forehead and shrewd eyes. The man pulled at his beard, in slight confusion at the teacher's penetrating stare. Then he rose to his feet, smoothing his embroidered robe, adjusting his sash of office. He had heard all the stories concerning Jesus, had wondered on his pillow last night about the teacher and the miracles of healing, which were causing thousands to converge on the town, to say nothing of the many religious dignitaries assembling in Capernaum.

What had Matthew Levi to do with one such as Jesus of Nazareth! Sufficient for him, the lovely young prostitutes, who slept in his arms, and his drinking partners, some of them the spendthrift sons of the best families, who enjoyed squandering their families' wealth on debauched living, in which Matthew was only too happy to assist them! He bowed before Jesus, glad to lower his eyes, before that dispassionate gaze, which stripped his soul bare.

'Follow me,' said Jesus. It was a command. And Matthew obeyed. Left the booth, everything, and followed him.

That night Mathew held a feast at his home for Jesus and his disciples. He had invited other tax collectors and collaborators, as well as many outcasts from society; those with a drink problem, gamblers and women of easy virtue. He wondered what Jesus reaction would be, when he discovered the quality of his fellow guests, had invited them almost as act of bravado. Accept me, accept my friends!

Jesus seated himself at Matthew's side at the head of the table. Wine flowed, the women were scantily dressed and noisy toasts were drunk to the teacher. Then gradually those at the table became silent, wine cups were set aside, the salacious remarks ceased and women arranged their costumes as decorously as they were able.

Because of the heat of the night, Matthew had left the door wide open. Phillip, one of the Lord's new disciples, rose from the table to get a breath of fresh night air. Simon Peter joined him. Both were slightly bewildered at their master's choice of companions. As they stood there, a party of Pharisees who had been peering in through the open door, in open disapproval at the wine flushed men and painted women, now called out disparaging remarks about Jesus fellow guests.

'You there!' hissed one of the Pharisees to Peter. 'You are one of the Rabbi Jesus disciples, are you not?'

'I am—and proud to be so,' replied Peter, hands on hips, staring at the priest belligerently. Much as he disapproved of his master's companions that night, he would in no way allow others to criticize his Lord.

'Then tell us fellow, explain why he eats with tax collectors and—er, sinners?'

Peter's fingers curled into fists. He was itching to wipe the sanctimonious expression from his questioner's face. His thick, black eyebrows met in almost straight line across his broad forehead and his eyes flashed dangerously.

Jesus had heard the remarks, as he had been meant to. He rose to his feet, and went to face these representatives of the religious establishment. He stood looking at them. They dropped their eyes before his searching gaze. Then he spoke.

'It is not the healthy who need a doctor, but the sick. I have not come to call the righteous, but sinners!' They walked away, discomforted.

Jesus signed to his disciples to return to their seats. Then he began to talk to those lost ones and the words he spoke fell like balm on their souls. It was a message of love and forgiveness. What they had been, when they sat down at this table was the past, it was no longer the present and would not be the future. Each man and woman who heard him examined their own life, the hurt and emptiness that had caused them to take refuge in their own particular addiction.

His message broke through the thick crust of despair that had eroded their spirits for so long. A young woman in a scarlet, clinging robe, sparkling with sequins, suddenly began to sob.

'Forgive me,' she murmured brokenly, tears streaking her heavily painted face. 'Oh—forgive me!' As if a dam had been released, people started to weep. The sound of sobbing, reverberated through the room, then one by one, they rose to their feet. Jesus stood by the door. As each person drew level with him, he spoke a word of comfort and forgiveness and they walked out into a night of stars and a new future.

At last only Matthew remained. He stood before Jesus, humbled, uncertain.

'You asked me to follow you, Lord. And follow you I will, if you truly want such as me?' Suddenly he looked down at himself, at the gold embroidered robe, jewelled slippers. 'Wait!' He ran out of the room. When he returned, he was wearing a plain, homespun tunic and leather sandals.

'I am ready, Master,' he said. He walked at Jesus side, to join the other disciples. They smiled at him in welcome. Well, he certainly looked more like one of them now. Peter slapped him on the back. A group of followers had been waiting in the shadows. They came forward, looking at Jesus questioningly. He beckoned them to follow him. They climbed a mountain.

About fifty men had accompanied Jesus onto the mountain. The moon was full, huge. It pooled its silvery light down on the Sea of Galilee, far below. They had stumbled up the mountainside behind Jesus, panting, hauling themselves up on rocks, feeling no tiredness just sense of exhilaration. Tiny moths rose from the rough grass and dew damp wild flowers.

Jesus signed to them to stop and seat themselves. He was going further up to pray. As he prayed, he laid their names before his Father. He needed twelve—twelve special disciples, who would accompany him on his travels—whom he would train to carry his message, his 'Way' once he was no longer with them. The choice had to be a good one, for these twelve men, apostles, would have the responsibility of spreading the news of God's new covenant with man, throughout the whole world.

Dawn flushed the sky. The men looked up expectantly as the white robed figure descended, and called out twelve names.

'Simon Peter! Andrew! James and John, sons of Thunder! Phillip. Bartholomew. Matthew! Simon the Zealot! Thomas! James, son of Alpheus! Judas, son of James! Judas Iscariot!' and his gaze locked with each in turn.

They followed him down to a level place. Coming to meet them was a huge crowd of people, some from as far away as Jerusalem and Judea. Jesus looked at them pityingly. There were mothers carrying sick children, elderly people in rags, cripples limping painfully, people with skin diseases and from whom their fellows shrank, men covered in suppurating sores which stank. Everywhere it seemed was pain and misery. He banished a slight feeling of despair, raised his strong carpenter's hands in blessing, the power of his love and healing enveloping them as they pushed forward, to touch him. The power was a tangible thing. You could almost feel it throbbing from him in waves.

And so Jesus walked among them, healing their infirmities, casting out evil spirits, bringing health and cleansing to his people, as others watched in awed amazement! After some hours, he gestured for them to be seated and signed to his disciples.

They sat at his feet, as he commenced to preach to the people.

'Blessed are you that are poor, for yours is the Kingdom of God! Blessed are you who hunger now, for you will be satisfied! Blessed are you who weep now, for you will laugh!

Blessed are you when men hate you, when they exclude and insult you and reject your name as evil, because of the Son of Man.

Rejoice in that day and leap for joy, for great is your reward in heaven—for that is how their fathers treated the prophets!'

He continued his voice resonating, managing to reach even those furthest from him. Simon the Zealot exchanged a look with David, for Jesus was saying, with a slight glance at them, 'But I tell you who hear me, love your enemies and do good to those who hate you! Bless those who curse you, pray for those who ill-treat you. If someone strikes you on one cheek, turn to him the other also.' David flushed scarlet, listening shame facedly to the Holy One's words.

'If you love only those who love you, what credit is that to you? Even sinners love those who love them!'

The minds of all who sat there, groped with such different concept.

'But love your enemies, do good to them, and lend without expecting to get anything back. Then your reward will be great, and you will be sons of the Most High, because he is kind to the ungrateful and wicked. Be merciful, just as your Father is merciful.' He raised his arms high, wide.

'Forgive, and you will be forgiven!'

The twelve gathered around him. He had just announced that they were to accompany him on a visit to Jerusalem, for the Feast of Passover. They pooled their resources. Judas Iscariot was elected to be the purse bearer. David's face was bright with excitement, which soon faded. Simon told him it was too dangerous for him to come. He might be recognized. Sadly he stood in the door of Peter's house, waving goodbye. He had never felt so alone.

Chapter Seven

Miriam sat on a stool letting her toes dabble in a film of moisture, tracing the bright blue floral design on the mosaic floor. The bathroom's misty air was fragrant with the new, exotic perfume Claudius had given her. She lifted her arms gracefully and let Sarah slip the jade silk tunic over her head. A silver girdle was fastened under her firm young breasts, another similar girdle at her waist, catching up the excessive length of the tunic.

'Sarah, I will wear the pearl and emerald pendant, my lord loves and the silver and green sandals.' She followed Sarah through to her bedchamber, humming happily as Sarah ministered to her. Her dark glossy hair was swept up in Grecian style, caught with jewelled combs, surmounted by a fine green veil frosted with silver thread. She outlined her slanting green eyes with kohl and lightly touched her lips with coral salve.

'You look so beautiful, my lady,' breathed Sarah, and sighed softly, as she looked down at her own plain tunic.

Miriam heard that sigh and was touched, for she guessed the cause. Miriam had recently appointed Sarah as her personal maid, removing her from the general household duties which the young slave girl had previously performed. She was a lovely child, just into her teens, with flashing black eyes, dusky skin and hair that fell below her waist in a riot of dark curls. She was a Samaritan, a people whose divergence from traditional Jewish faith centuries before had caused great rift between them.

Miriam bent over a carved rosewood chest and lifted out two tunics, one a rich orange and the other violet. She held them out to the younger girl.

'See Sarah, these are for you. I have so many for my Lord is always very generous!'

'Lady Miriam, you are so kind. I—Oh,' and tears sprang to her eyes, as she murmured incoherent thanks.

'Well, you may go now and try them on! I am sure that Simeon will admire you in them.'

She dismissed the blushing slave girl then sat down, head bowed in thought. Simeon! She had been amazed, when her husband had announced that the quiet, dark skinned lad was now his adopted son, legally his heir after any sons she should bear him. But if it was her husband's wish, then it was pleasing to her. Like all Jewish women she regarded her husband as head of the family, the decision maker, to be deferred to in all matters pertaining to the marriage. But also, like women the world over, she exerted her own influence on the relationship, her submission and supportiveness, earning her the respect of her husband, whilst her opinions blended with his own.

Simeon was barely three years younger than Miriam, and so she regarded him now more as brother than son—but held him in genuine affection. Then there was the matter of his miraculous healing, making him the living symbol to her of her faith in the Messiah.

Miriam sighed. She sometimes felt great heaviness of heart, regarding her religion. She had put herself beyond the pale with all the most devout Jews in Capernaum, through her marriage to a gentile. Even though they tolerated Claudius for his courtesy towards their local Pharisees and Rabbis and his well balanced sense of justice, nevertheless, they would never forget, that she a daughter of the house of Reuban, had married outside her faith.

Then her thoughts stole towards the Holy One. Although her husband was a gentile, Jesus had unhesitatingly healed a member of Claudius household. Did this mean that the Anointed One of God could be opening the fold of his love towards those of other races who came towards him in faith?

She shook her head, glimpsing faintly at truths as yet beyond her understanding, and wandered over to the window, still deep in thought. In the meadow to the west of the villa, Claudius was still training Simeon to balance and throw the javelin, for which the lad seemed to have little aptitude, although he showed a dogged determination to succeed. Her eyes travelled to Simeon's feet, his graceful movements, impossible but a few days ago. That the Holy One had healed not only the fever and paralysis, but also straightened the club foot, which had crippled the boy since birth, was most wonderful, awe inspiring event.

As she watched, she saw Claudius glance behind him, and break away from Simeon and the small band of soldiers, who had been watching events and shouting encouragement to the boy. Ah, that was why—a rider bearing down on them! He wheeled his horse to snorting halt before the Centurion, and proffered him a letter.

'Miriam! I am bidden to Jerusalem by Tribune Marcus, for the Week of the Passover. I am taking sixty men my dear and you!'

Miriam's eyes sparkled with excitement. Jerusalem! She had never been there before. 'My Lord, I am so happy that I am to come with you!'

'Tribune Marcus has expressly invited you, wants to meet you. We were boys together in Rome, my dear. We fought side by side in many a campaign, however, our paths have diverged recently. Marcus is an ambitious man and as a tribune, has his foot on the ladder to success. But there will always be the bonding of true friendship between us.'

'How does he know about me? Is he aware that I am Jewish?' There was a slightly apprehensive look on Miriam's lovely face.

'He knows all about you, dear wife, because I told him of our marriage when I was last in Jerusalem and I must say that I had not expected to return there so very soon. Well, get your slaves to pack what you will need. I imagine we will be away for two to three weeks.'

'When do we leave,' she asked?

'Immediately!'

Claudius saluted Tribune Marcus. A guard had been posted to await his arrival with orders to conduct him directly to the Tribune. He was standing now, in the luxurious apartment in the Antonia Fortress which was private to Marcus.

'So, you have brought her, your lady wife! Will you not present me?' Marcus eyes were sweeping curiously over the veiled figure at Claudius side. Miriam turned towards her husband inquiringly and removed her veil. Marcus exclamation of admiration was not feigned.

'Lady Miriam, you are all this dear friend of mine told me and more! A hundred welcomes to you and my thanks that you undertook the long journey from Capernaum, to visit Jerusalem.' He gestured towards a couch, banked with striped cushions. 'Will you not be seated?'

Just as she was about to accede to his invitation, the door to his chamber opened to admit a tall, autocratic figure, whose white tunic was draped by a crimson robe. He wore a heavy gold chain about his neck, supporting a massive jewelled medallion. But it was his face that drew Miriam's attention. The eyes were dark, restless, under high arching brows, his mouth beneath the flaring nostrils, full lipped, petulant. His short cropped hair gleamed wetly black with perfumed oil. Instinctively, she drew closer to her husband, who snapped to attention.

'Ah, Marcus! I have just seen a deputation, treasurers to the Temple. Some fool had brought them to my apartment instead of directing them to you! They have come to collect the High Priest's vestments. I told them in no uncertain terms, to wait in the guardroom below! If I had my way, Caiaphas blue robe, with its gold bells and pomegranates, would be torn to shreds with its owner. I cannot stand that man! I consider him to be....! Ah, my pardon!' he became aware of Miriam and Claudius, and bit off the rest of his sentence.

'Prefect, may I introduce a trusted friend of mine, Centurion Claudius and his wife, the Lady Miriam. Claudius is based at Capernaum. I have brought him here for the Passover, and to bring me up to date with happenings in Galilee—the Messiah business!'

'A good thought, Marcus!' Pontius Pilate's eyes scanned Claudius briefly.

'I have heard many things of you Centurion and know that you refused promotion, although one of our most experienced officers, and one of the bravest. I am also aware that your father is one of the wealthiest and most highly esteemed senators of Rome. Take my advice, and heal whatever quarrel exists between you. I cannot imagine why you prefer to vegetate in a small fishing community, rather than accepting a cohort at Caesarea! Want to change your mind?'

Claudius bowed deeply. His blue eyes held a fathomless expression, as he shook his head.

'Prefect,' he began quietly. 'I have spent over twenty years fighting for my Emperor, would give my life for him and for Rome whenever it should be required! But until then, with your permission Prefect, I enjoy my duties at Capernaum—and I am newly married!' He glanced fondly towards Miriam. Pontius Pilate burst into a gale of laughter.

'An honest man! A rare breed.' His gaze slid over Miriam's loveliness, and she wished she were veiled, also that there had been time to have changed from her travelling garments and to have bathed, before meeting these two dignitaries. But in a tunic of her favourite green, with her abundant tresses swept high on jade combs, she looked very fair. Pilate smiled as he considered Miriam. 'Well, Centurion, if she were mine, I would probably also forgo the pleasures of Caesarea in preference for rural domesticity! Greetings, lady—you are welcome. My wife, the Lady Claudia, is weary for feminine companionship. When you have rested, Marcus will have you conducted to her rooms in the palace. Oh, your husband may accompany you there,' he added, as a look of apprehension crossed her face.

'You do not live here, sir,' she inquired?

'At the Antonia Fortress? No! I have a suite of rooms here but usually reside at Herod's palace. It is not so cramped for Claudia—nor so noisy! Obviously, this is a fortress, and heavily manned, to keep peace in the Jewish temple and Jerusalem generally.'

'Why is the High Priest's robe here, instead of in the Temple?' Miriam asked the question daringly, her curiosity greater than her usual decorum. Pilate glanced down at her, amused.

'Well may you ask, Lady! It has been custom, these many years now, to allow his official, ceremonial garments into his possession only immediately before and during major Jewish feasts. It is a way of demonstrating curtailment of the powers of his office. This Caiaphas is a crafty wolf, a venomous snake with an unctuous smile. I have no liking for him, nor those who surround him.' He took Miriam by the arm, and led her to the window, the shutters of which were wide open.

'Look down there. Well, what do you see?'

'More people than I have ever seen assembled together before, my Lord! Oh, how beautiful the Temple is, so dazzling white and crested with gold! I knew it would be glorious, but never dreamed it to look thus. Even the courtyard surrounding it is enormous in size, why, there must be thousands of people milling around down there.' Miriam glanced below her fascinated, the three men standing beside her, listening to her breathless remarks in amusement.

'Now raise your eyes, Miriam, to the tops of the porticoes which enclose the Temple precincts, do you see my men?'

It was Marcus who proudly spoke, as his arm made circular movement.

She glanced up as instructed. Hundreds of armed legionaries lined the porticoes on guard, the sun gleaming on their helmets and armour. She felt a shiver run down her spine at this demonstration of might, but rallied, and turned a light smile on Marcus.

'Why Tribune, how carefully you guard my people,' she sighed!

He frowned. 'I know you are of the Jewish race, Lady. But you are now a Roman wife!' Miriam looked down, chastened.

'You are also a Roman citizen,' added Pilate. 'Always remember, Lady Miriam that your first duty is to Rome.'

'I will never forget this, I love my husband, gentlemen, and my life and duty belong to him, for all time!' Pontius Pilate looked at her approvingly.

'Well said, lady! I would that some of our Roman matrons held to the same principal!'

Miriam had been taken to her chamber and Tribune Marcus sat quietly with Claudius, in the window seat, overlooking the Temple. They were in the tallest of the fortresses four towers, so built that it commanded complete view over the whole area of the huge platform on which the temple had been constructed, recently rebuilt by the late King Herod the Great. Part of the work was still being completed some forty six years after the project was started.

'So tell me, Claudius my friend, what news do you have for me of Jesus of Nazareth, the Messiah? His fame has reached Jerusalem, you know. There is wild talk of miraculous healings and that he is gathering thousands around him. What have you to report of him?' Marcus regarded Claudius gravely.

'Marcus, the miracles, the healings are real! Jesus of Nazareth is no mere man. He is indeed the Son of God!' Claudius face was earnest, his blue eyes troubled.

Marcus frowned. 'Son of God—of the Jewish God, you mean, their Jehovah?'

'Yes, Marcus. But before I continue, Prefect Pontius Pilate—is he likely to return here?'

'Most unlikely, he will probably remain in the Citadel, Herod's palace, for the rest of the day. As you know he spends most of his time on the coast at Caesarea, only coming to Jerusalem with extra troops at Passover and the other major feast days. He detests everything to do with the Jewish religion, yet has learned much about it. Other Prefects in the past have shown sensitivity for the faith of this strange and volatile people, but not Pilate! He almost goes out of his way to antagonize the priests! And as for Caiaphas—well you heard him!' Marcus grinned. 'I almost forgot, I must go down and officially release the sacred robes to the temple treasurers. Want to come with me? The chest they are laid in has seals attached, which have to be inspected in front of me by the treasurers, to check we haven't tampered with the garments! Come on!'

Having dealt with the sombre, black bearded Levites, accompanied by four temple guards and Jonathan their dignified Commander, the two men returned to the upper chamber. Marcus dismissed his attendants and nodded to Claudius.

'Well, continue with your views on the Messiah. Have you seen him for yourself?'

'Yes.'

'Have you seen him perform a miracle, a healing?'

'I have.'

'Oh, come now, Claudius, I am being serious!' Marcus gave his friend an indignant glance. 'You surely do not mean it!'

'Marcus, do you remember a young Jewish lad, with a clubbed foot, whose parents were slain by our men, out in the wilderness where John the Baptist was preaching? You asked me to care for him?'

'Of course I do! I gave him to you as a servant. What of him?' Marcus looked up curiously.

'He is here, in the fortress. May I send for him?'

'Why, yes of course, if you want to!' Marcus dark brows shot together in puzzled surprise. Claudius rose and went to the door. He dispatched a guard. He returned to his seat.

'Do you recall what Simeon looked like?'

'Yes. I shall never forget the look on the lad's face, when I threatened him with the flagellum. You know, Claudius, I have killed hundreds of men in battle—so have you and I've ordered men to be tortured or beaten, to extract information. Haven't liked doing it particularly—but it is part of the job, isn't it! Yet somehow, that young lad's face stayed with me. There was a courage and dignity mixed with the fear and something else, which I cannot name.' He paused, deep in thought. There was a tap at the door.

'Come in,' cried Tribune Marcus.

'You sent for me, father,' said Simeon, looking at Claudius.

'Let me present my adopted son to you,' smiled Centurion Claudius. 'Simeon, you remember Tribune Marcus.' The boy bowed his face expressionless.

'But this cannot be the same boy,' said Marcus slowly, as Simeon walked across the tiled floor towards them. 'Simeon, son of Ezra, was lame, had a clubbed foot. I remember this well. You lad, have two sound feet yet you look the same. What trick is this, Claudius?'

'Not trick, Marcus my friend! Simeon, son of Ezra, was healed by Jesus of Nazareth of a paralyzing fever, when he was at death's door. I myself asked the teacher to heal the lad. Not only was he instantly healed, but his foot was made whole as well!' Claudius fixed his compelling stare on Marcus, who rose to his feet in amazement, pulling the lad to him, running his hands over the once deformed foot and ankle.

'Why, it's thing impossible. Look at me boy! Yes—yes, I would remember those eyes anywhere.'

Marcus stood back from Simeon, and folded his arms across his breast. 'So, you had better tell me everything, Claudius. First of all, how was this healing accomplished, what means did the teacher use?'

'Well, Marcus, there is no way to explain it, other than to tell you the truth, and of the sequence of events that led up to this miracle.' Claudius began to swiftly outline Jesus arrival in Capernaum, his calling various fishermen and others to follow him, to become his disciples; how he had begun to teach the people, and to heal them of all manner of diseases and mental afflictions.

'I myself was not present at any of these healings, but I instructed Simeon to attend, to keep me in touch with all Jesus was saying and doing. Also, my wife Miriam had attended the synagogue one Sabbath. Jesus was teaching on that occasion. There was a madman present, one afflicted of demons. Jesus commanded the demon to leave the man, and he became as normal as you or I! No ordinary man has this power, Marcus!' Claudius blue eyes were filled with awe as he spoke and Marcus realized that his friend completely believed what he was saying.

'So, Claudius, you are telling me, that you personally went out to speak to Jesus of Nazareth and asked him to order that Simeon be healed of paralysis! Not that he should come to your villa and lay hands on the boy?' He stared darkly at the other. 'Tell me, Claudius, how was it that a hard headed Centurion, should have believed this possible?'

'If you like, it was a spirit of faith that came upon my heart. I just never doubted!'

'So, you consider that it was through your faith, that Jesus would heal Simeon that it was brought about?'

'I am not sure! I certainly had complete faith that Jesus would heal the lad, yet had another led the teacher to Simeon, I equally believe that Jesus would have healed him!'

Marcus started to pace the room restlessly. 'Look, I am perfectly willing to believe that Jesus is a kind, compassionate human being, with a wondrous power of healing. I also believe that he will be manipulated, by all those incendiary elements in Jewish society who wish to see us driven from Palestine. For the moment, I suspend judgement and will advise Pilate that there is no immediate danger—but I warn you, Claudius, should it be necessary I will take whatever action may be required to maintain order in this unruly land!' Then his expression softened, as he looked at Simeon objectively for the first time.

'Now—what was it you were telling me before about Simeon, that you have adopted him?' If he thought the dark skinned Jewish lad, a strange choice of son, he let no trace of these thoughts show on his face. The boy had courage and had saved Claudius life, nor was there any faking the look of affection Simeon turned on his adoptive father.

'I have other news, personal news, that delights my heart,' said Claudius. 'Not only have I adopted Simeon, and I know you will arrange the necessary documents for him to receive Roman citizenship, but my dear wife is with child! Simeon of course realizes, that his position within my family is such that he will inherit only after heirs of Miriam's body.'

Marcus caught Claudius to him in an iron embrace.

'Well old friend, the last time we drank to your new wife and now to the joy of a child conceived, as well as to a new son!' He snapped his fingers and the door opened. He pointed to a wine flask and waited as the deft Syrian slave poured wine and brought it on a silver tray. 'To you, to your family and to a happy future!' toasted Marcus.

'To you, my comrade, may I one day have the joy of congratulating you on marriage!'

'No! Not for me, Claudius. I lack patience for the scene domestic— prefer my freedom. Besides, can you imagine any woman putting up with me?' He burst into ironic laughter.

'What is that noise,' asked Simeon. He walked over to the window, from whence the sound of shouting, angry voices, was rising to them.

'Well, what is happening down there,' demanded Marcus, instantly at his side.

'It seems to be coming from the Eastern Portico. Look, my Lord, where the cattle and sheep are tethered for sale and the money changers have their tables. The people crowding there are all falling back. Someone is addressing them and sounds very angry!' Suddenly Simeon's face paled and he tried to block Marcus view of the portico. 'It really is nothing,' he said hastily.

'Let me see,' said Claudius firmly pushing the boy aside. 'I don't believe it. But it is! Marcus, the tall man in white, with chestnut hair, before whom they are cringing away, I would stake my life, that it is Jesus of Nazareth!'

'How can you be sure, from this distance? I cannot make out the colour of the man's hair, nor any other detail of his appearance—beyond that he seems to be brandishing a whip! I thought your Messiah was a man of peace. This man is threatening the people.' He came to a decision. 'There are steps from this tower that lead onto the portico roofs. Come with me, you two, we will hear for ourselves what is going on!'

It must have taken about eight minutes for them to hurry along the top of the huge portico, one of the enormous porched areas which entirely surrounded the Temple precincts. It was from the lofty heights of these flat topped roofs, surmounting the hundreds of huge pillars which supported them, that the troops of the garrison were now stationed in constant vigilance in case of uprising. Many times in the past, the people had been inflamed by hotheads, or merely taken umbrage at the Roman presence.

'I think this was roughly the place, beneath which the trouble was taking place,' said the Tribune. As he spoke, a flock of white doves suddenly rose up in the air, circling above their heads, before seeking freedom. The shouting was in the Aramaic tongue of which Marcus and Claudius both had a good grasp.

'Get these out of here! How dare you turn my Father's house into a market?'

Pandemonium broke out below them. Sheep and cattle had been loosed and were blundering in fright amongst the people, seeking escape. And still the voice rang out, shouting in anger, with authority! Then they heard the sound of crashing tables and cries of anguish, as the money changers groped among the people's feet for their gold.

Then they saw Jesus, for he had stepped away from the covered area of the porticoes, beneath which a few Jews had become accustomed to selling animals for sacrifice, and making an unfair profit. Even a pair of doves, could prove a crippling expense for a poor person to cope with and this was the cheapest acceptable sacrifice.

He was still holding a whip made of cords as the crowd fell back before him, grumbling and amazed. About a dozen men now joined him— friends of his it would seem. Then the mood of the crowd changed, for someone had announced his name. This was the young Rabbi from Galilee, Jesus of Nazareth, the worker of miracles it was said, whom some named Son of God—the Anointed One. Suddenly they realized that he had just spoken of the temple as 'My Father's House' and they craned their necks to get a better view of him. Surely he couldn't have meant— why, but that was blasphemy! Unless, unless of course, it could be true, that he could indeed be the Messiah!

A group of Jerusalem's most influential citizens pushed their way towards Jesus, among them members of the Pharisees.

'So you are Jesus of Nazareth! By what authority do you come to Jerusalem, to the sacred Temple and behave thus, to disrupt proceedings on the Eve of Passover?'

Jesus looked at them with eyes that still darted lightening, and before that shimmering golden gaze, men dropped their eyes uneasily.

'What miraculous sign can you show us, to prove your authority to do all this?'

He turned to the last caller. He transferred the whip to his left hand, and placed his right across his breast.

'Destroy this temple, and I will raise it again in three days!' The man who had shouted out gave a guffaw of laughter. He had not understood Jesus gesture, as he indicated his own body as being the temple he spoke of.

It has taken forty-six years so far, to rebuild this Temple and you are going to raise it in three days!' The bantering voice faltered to a stop, as Jesus looked directly at him. The man turned and endeavored to disappear in the crowd, suddenly frightened at what he hardly knew.

The Messiah had dropped the whip and raised his arms on high, face turned upwards as his lips moved in prayer. So it was that Tribune Marcus had his first real glimpse of the man who was to bear the sorrows of the world on his shoulders, Jesus Christ, the Son of God.

Then Jesus began to teach the people, and the words he spoke, held them enthralled. It was a message of love and forgiveness, words such as had never been heard before in the Temple courts. Not the harsh, dry element of the Torah, the law, but containing the one ingredient men had forgotten, God's love.

People thronged about him in the Court of the Gentiles, asking questions, some seeking healing. The last sounds of the bellowing cattle had disappeared, even the money changers were now silent, as men and women searched their souls, seeing themselves for the first time as their Almighty Father saw them, and they were appalled at what they found. Jesus words now fell on receptive ears, spreading the healing balm of his love, as he showed them a different and better way to live.

For about an hour he spoke, then began to make his way out. People surged about him, some begging him to stay, whilst others who had been on the fringe of the huge crowd merely curious about what was going on.

He had gone. Claudius and Simeon followed Marcus back into the fortress, all of them deep in thought Suddenly Marcus gave a dry chuckle.

'I would love to see the High Priest's face, when he learns that Jesus has driven the sheep and cattle out of the Temple grounds and forced out the money changers! It wanted doing too. It is said that Caiaphas demanded a tax from all such dealings, so it is his own private revenue that will suffer now!' He looked at Claudius soberly. 'As for Jesus of Nazareth himself? I can find nothing wrong in him. Providing he continues as we saw him just now he offers no threat to Rome, nor do I see him allowing himself to be set up as a military leader. That would be against all he preaches. No, Claudius my friend, I do not think Jesus need worry about our reaction to him and his teaching, which seems harmless, if impractical in a real world. No, his problems will arise within the ranks of the Jewish priesthood.'

Claudius drew in a deep sigh of relief. He had not realized, how much the safety and welfare of Jesus, had now come to mean to him. He was a soldier of Rome—of the Emperor. Yet in his heart, he was drawing close to the ranks of those who followed the Messiah.

Chapter Eight

'Are you ready, Miriam? The Governor has sent a litter for you—we are invited to dine with Pilate and his lady. This is honour indeed and it behoves us not to be late!'

Miriam smiled as she heard her husband's slightly truculent tones and rose from Sarah's ministrations to greet him. He stopped talking as he saw her and drew in his breath sharply, for Miriam was looking extremely lovely. She was wearing a shining, white, silk tunic, worked in gold thread, purchased for her from an Eastern caravan many months ago, and laid carefully aside until suitably important occasion should present itself to wear such a garment. A white veil sewn with tiny gold stars clouded her black hair. As she moved, delicate gold bells on the end of her long, embroidered girdle, tinkled musically. She wore no jewellery, nor did she need it.

'Wife,' said Claudius huskily, 'You are beautiful!' Miriam smiled, happy at his praise. Then her face grew serious.

'I am grateful that I please my lord.' She smoothed the folds of her tunic, and continued softly. 'Yet sometimes I feel a little guilty to be thus attired, when so many of my people are very poor. Oh Claudius, I had almost forgotten what it is like to be poor until I saw the hundreds of unfortunates upon the road, and those crowding outside the city walls! I will always remember my own impoverished state as a servant in Azor's household—lucky even to be there instead of starving, when my poor father was driven out of Capernaum and up into the hills, when he could no longer hide his leprosy. Poor father,' she said with a sigh, 'First he lost my mother through a fever and then, after working so hard for many years in Azor's vineyard, to contact that loathsome disease.'

'You were twelve when this happened, didn't you say,' probed Claudius gently.

'Yes. I remember I cried and screamed, asking that I could go with my father into the hills, where the other untouchables live. But my father blessed me before leaving. He instructed me to stay, told me it was his last command to me as a father that I should work as a servant in Azor's house. I should be obedient and work hard.'

Claudius took her in his arms and gently kissed her.

'But do you not see, dear wife, how sometimes good may come out of evil? Azor is one of the elders of the synagogue at Capernaum. If you not been working in his house and had I not been invited there to meet with the other Elders to discuss the final touches to the new building I had financed for them, well, you would not have brought wine to me, our eyes would not have met—and you would not now be my dearest wife!'

His blue eyes smiled down into hers, as they had done at that first meeting, and now she rose on tiptoe for his kiss.

'Well, I mustn't crush your costume, Miriam, nor is there time to dally now.' Four slaves clad in scarlet tunics, lifted her litter onto their shoulders. She glanced about her nervously, as they left the Antonia Fortress behind, and wound their way through the streets of the Upper City, crowded as it was with the great influx of people who had arrived for Passover. Every inn was packed to capacity, each dwelling that could accommodate relatives from the far flung corners of Palestine, was crammed, even to the roof tops. Many there were who peered malevolently at the lovely Jewish woman, borne behind the handsome Roman Centurion. There were cries of 'Roman whore!'

Claudius glanced around him angrily, glad that he had availed himself of ten armed auxiliaries who flanked Miriam's litter.

At last, they entered the vast dining hall in Herod's magnificent palace. Miriam caught her breath as she gazed about her. Huge, soaring, marble columns rose to the high ceiling, their bases panelled in gold, black and crimson. At the top of the reception hall, was an ornate throne on a twelve stepped dais. This throne had once been occupied by Herod the Great, who had built this one of his many palaces, although his greatest achievement was the rebuilding of Jerusalem's great Temple. On his death, his puppet kingdom had been split between his three sons. Archelaus had received Judea, Samaria and Idumea and had sat on this throne for ten years, but his excesses had been such that the people had sent delegations to Emperor Augustus, complaining of his cruelty and evil life style. Augustus had banished him and placed Judea under direct Roman rule. Prefects now succeeded one another, until Pontius Pilate was presently appointed.

The Governor was not sitting on the ornate throne, but at a long table, heavy with food and banked by couches. Hence his brooding eyes surveyed his companions at table and those many others, who sat at similar tables at right angles to his. It was a glittering gathering. Here were assembled visiting Roman notables, wealthy worldly Jews, brushing shoulders with Greeks, Arabs and representatives of bordering states, all gathering at Jerusalem at this special time.

At Pilate's side sat his wife, the Lady Claudia, who was said to be related to Rome's royal house. She was gowned after the Grecian fashion, in a fine pleated tunic, sewn with jewels. Her blonde tresses were styled in upswept, glossy curls and gems glittered at ears, throat and delicate wrists. To Pilate's left sat Tribune Marcus. He saw Centurion Claudius enter with his wife and whispered to Pilate. The Prefect glanced down the long length of the hall the more easily as his table was set on a platform. He gave an order to a slave standing behind him, who in his turn gave orders to another.

'The Prefect requests that you join him at his table, sir!'

Claudius swallowed. This was honour indeed. He followed the slave, with Miriam at his side. Pilate surveyed Miriam approvingly. She was lovelier than he had thought. His Centurion was a lucky man. There was movement at the table, as room was made for Miriam next to Claudia, before whom Miriam had inclined gracefully, Centurion Claudius being seated next to Marcus. Miriam knew herself to be trembling slightly. Never in her wildest dreams, had she imagined being present in such a gathering. Claudia placed a reassuring hand on her arm.

'Welcome, Lady Miriam, pray relax, for I sense you are apprehensive.' Her eyes, which could glare in haughty command, were sympathetic to the young Jewish woman.

'My lady, I am,' replied Miriam truthfully.

'There is no need to be,' smiled Claudia.

'She was certainly not nervous earlier today, when she questioned Marcus and me in the Antonia,' exclaimed Pilate. 'This is the lady I told you of, Claudia. I know you sometimes find it difficult to find feminine company to your liking, and so....' he paused.

He didn't finish his sentence, suddenly distracted as his eyes lit on another party of people who had just arrived. He rose to his feet. It was Herod Antipas, ruler of Galilee and Peraea. At his side was his new wife, the woman who had been married to his half brother, Phillip, and was granddaughter to Herod the Great. Behind them walked Salome, Herodias daughter by her former marriage. All Jewish Palestine had been outraged at the sin committed by Herod Antipas marrying Herodias. It was against Holy Law—yes and putting aside his blameless former wife, an Arabian Princess. Even now, John the Baptist was daily denouncing Antipas for his behaviour in the most scathing terms.

Pilate's eyes flickered over Herodias, as he stepped forward to greet the royal party. He had heard much of her beauty. What he saw, was a voluptuous woman, clothed in cloth of gold, a barbaric gold collar of huge pendant rubies, covering her throat and half exposed breasts. Her eyes were hard, ambitions. Pilate decided he did not like her. He glanced at the thirteen years old daughter, Salome. She was a younger version of her mother. Although the young face lacked the hardness, the eyes she turned boldly on Pilate, were shrewd beyond her years. As for Antipas, Pilate had met him before. On the surface, a charming, handsome man, but with a mind like a serpent, swayed by his passions, unimaginably cruel, but seeking peaceful coexistence with his neighbours and more importantly with Rome.

Tetrarch Phillip and his wife were now announced. Phillip was the ruler of the northern territories of Batanaea, Gaulanitis and Trachonitis. Pilate had been advised that this was one ruler Rome did not have to worry about, for he used wisdom and fairness in governing his people. His wife Salome was a quiet woman, who carried herself modestly.

Miriam had watched the new arrivals in amazement, never thinking to see members of Palestine's ruling house, face to face. She wished she were anywhere else, rather than here in this ornate palace, and yearned for home. The newcomers were found places at the top table.

'Phillip and Antipas always stay in the Palace, when they visit Jerusalem for the Jewish feasts,' whispered Claudia.

'I do not feel easy in the presence of Herod Antipas and that new wife of his looks terrifying! Do you get feelings about people, Miriam? I do! That woman reeks of cruelty.'

'My Lady, I have the same feelings towards her,' murmured Miriam softly. 'Will you have to see her often during her stay?'

'No, Miriam, only tonight as a gesture, protocol!'

As the night wore on, Pilate's guests drank far more than was good for them. Herodias strident laughter was heard repeatedly as potent wine, dark as her rubies, passed her lips.

Pilate was in conversation with Tribune Marcus and Claudius, pointedly ignoring the two royal parties as far as possible. His whole training had been as a soldier. Although ambitious, he had little patience with the political intrigues of a nation whose leaders he did not trust, and ruling religious body, the Sanhedrin, led by High Priest Caiaphas, he openly detested.

Herod Antipas cleared his throat and announced that he had brought some dancers of proven excellence. He asked leave to have them admitted, that they might entertain the company, they were a gift for Pilate. Pilate nodded.

There was a booming of a great gong and the centre of the hall, below the tables, flooded with almost naked dancers, men and women, their bodies painted black and gold in the likeness of snakes. To the sound of pipes, they writhed, hissed and linked together, in lascivious coupling. Claudia rose to her feet, outraged.

'My Lord,' she said to Pilate, her voice like ice. 'This entertainment is not to my liking. I shall retire. Come Miriam!' People fell back before them, as the two women took their departure. Another woman moved hesitantly towards them.

'May I come with you,' she asked softly? 'My name is Joanna, wife of Chuza. My husband is an officer in Herod Antipas household. I do not like this—!'

'Of course—come,' said Claudia firmly.

Miriam heaved a great sigh of relief, as they left the great hall, with its crowd of drunken, sexually excited men and women. Attendants preceded them to Lady Claudia's chambers, where they seated themselves on a couch, beneath an open window. How good it felt to feel the night breeze wafting down on them, the clean dazzle of stars instead of the revolting scene of fornication they had left below. But even here, they could still hear the rhythm of the drums and shouts of dancers and spectators.

Miriam put her hand to her throbbing temples.

'You are faint?' Claudia looked at her in concern.

'I am with child this three month,' said Miriam softly.

'So, how happy I am for you! It is your first? Pray the gods it may be a son, to delight your husband!' Then she smiled at Miriam's expression.' Forgive me—I forget that you Jews worship only one god.'

'Yes, Lady Claudia, we do—the One and only true God, Jehovah. I have most earnestly prayed to him for a son, but then, if I have a daughter at least my husband already has a son. He adopted a youth of my race very recently. His name is Simeon.'

How very unusual to adopt a son, when he has only recently married,' breathed Claudia, her curiosity awakened, 'tell me how this came to pass?'

And so it was, that the Prefect's wife and Joanna, wife of Chuza, came to hear of the Messiah, of his teaching of love, his call to repentance and the forgiveness of Almighty God to all who so came before him. Again and again, they questioned Miriam concerning the miracles, particularly Simeon's healing. Before she left that night, to be carried back to the Antonia Fortress in her litter, Miriam had lit flames of faith in two women's hearts. Joanna, with her lovely violet eyes shining in wonder, was to become one of a small band of women who were to devote their love and resources, to caring for the needs of Jesus and his apostles. As for the wife of Pilate, locked into a political system which she abhorred, she was to carry her secret knowledge and belief in the Son of God, to the end of her days.

It was the third day of Passover week. Simeon asked permission as he had done every day so far, to mingle with the crowds in the Temple courts, so that he could hear Jesus teach. None knew at what hour the Rabbi Jesus would come, but thousands packed the Court of the Gentiles, in the hope that they would see him.

Repeatedly now, Jesus would be challenged by members of the Pharisees, angered at the following that Jesus was attracting here in their own sacred precincts, the Temple itself. Nor were they alone in their growing dislike. The Saducees were also painfully aware of his presence, and were furious that this wandering Galilean had dared to drive the money changers and sellers of sacrificial animals out of their accustomed places under the colonnades.

None knew where he stayed. It was rumoured that he left the city at night, to camp on one of the hillsides overlooking Jerusalem. But with thousands camping outside the city walls, because there was simply no place to accommodate so great a multitude, it would have been impossible for the Temple police to have attempted to arrest him. In any case, the temper of the people was such, that there might well have been insurrection, if any tried to harm their current hero. But crowds could be fickle and the members of the Sanhedrin, the council of the Sadducees and Pharisees, were content to wait their time.

Not all of the Pharisees were antagonistic towards the new teacher. A small core of those who had been listening to his teachings viewed his advent with growing interest. The Pharisees, permanently at odds with the ruling religious group, the Sadducees, who held that only the law of Moses held in the Torah was of supreme importance, denigrating the Prophets and religious writings held so dear by the Pharisees, now looked to see if he could be of use to them. Jesus spoke of the resurrection of the dead, an individual accountability for sin, rather than a collective one. Although he swept through the minutiae of theological thistles with which they increasingly lacerated their souls, the constrictions which closed out all liberal attitudes, nevertheless, there was in the very freshness of his teaching which drew them—and in especial one man, Nicodemus.

'I never seem to see my family now,' grumbled Claudius good-humouredly. 'What with Miriam spending most of her day at the palace with the Lady Claudia and her other friend Joanna and you away from morning to sunset, I may as well have left you both at Capernaum. Alright, Simeon, you may go, but just remember I want you back in the Antonia before sunset!'

The Holy One had come later to the temple today. The multitude crowding the court of the Gentiles was vast. Although many gentiles were there, in this one court where they could move with impunity the majority were Jews, men wearing the white, fringed prayer shawls, phylacteries on their foreheads, tiny boxes containing Holy writ, together with veiled women. Many children were there too, curbed to good behaviour by the solemn attitude of their elders.

Suddenly there was a shout—'He comes! Rabbi Jesus comes!' Simeon caught his breath in excitement, and pushed his way through the solid mass of people until he was close to the dynamic figure that raised his hands in greeting and blessing.

For two hours Simeon listened, frowning when anyone heckled or criticized as at first happened. The Saducees had their spies everywhere, and those who for a few coins would try to disrupt the teaching of any rabbi not approved of by the priesthood.

At last evening stroked dramatic paintbrush across the sky. The great mass of the Temple was outlined in flaming tendrils of scarlet and smouldering magenta. Jesus turned to leave. Simeon hesitated. He also should leave to return to the fortress, but with sudden determination he fought his way through the surrounding worshippers, to follow the Holy One. Nor was he the only one to take unpremeditated decision to remain in the teacher's wake. For Nicodemus, an outstanding Pharisee, who was much intrigued by Jesus, and the tremendous impact he was having on all who heard him, also found himself being swept by the crowd out of the Golden Gate of the Temple, and down the path leading to the Kidron Valley.

Dense black shadows, dappled the Mount of Olives, as a sobbing breeze faintly bore the murmuring of his disciples, who kept a discreet distance from their Master, who knelt nearby in prayer. They were chatting to a young lad made known to them, as the younger brother of David, son of Ezra. Their interest was intense, to learn that this boy, Simeon, was that Centurion's servant who had been healed in Capernaum. But their faces were grave when he said he was now the adopted son of the Roman.

Peter the fisherman, stood looking down on Simeon, great fists pressed into his waist, eyes flashing dangerously.

'So, you are staying in the Antonia Fortress! That honeycomb crawling with Roman hornets—and you come here, in the night! Why? Are you here to spy boy, because if so----!' He didn't finish his sentence, but his face did this for him.

'I came here, because I love the Lord Jesus, know him to be the Son of God,' replied Simeon. The moon pooled its light palely down, as it fought free of scudding cloud. It silvered the bark of the gnarled olive tree beneath which Simeon sat, and threw his earnest young face into relief against the brooding darkness of the hillside. Peter saw truth shining out of Simeon's eyes and relaxed.

'Your pardon, young man, but I had to be sure. I take it that you know that your brother is or was a member of the Zealots?'

'Yes. Where is he now, sir? I had hoped he would have come with you?'

'No. Simon thought it wiser to leave him behind at Capernaum, as he is still sought by the Romans.'

'I am sure I can get the order against him rescinded,' said Simeon confidently.

'Then try to do this as soon as possible, for your brother was much distressed not to come with us!' It was John, son of Zebedee who spoke. His wise eyes swept over Simeon.

'Tell me, Simeon, do you intend to stay with Centurion Claudius and become a Roman, or return to your people? Perhaps become a follower of the Lord?' Simeon returned John's gaze evenly.

'I cannot answer that at this moment, master. My heart leads me to say I will come with you now, never return to Claudius villa. But he has shown great kindness to me, is also well disposed to our people. If I hurt him by deserting him, I do not know how he will react. Of course, his wife is Jewish, the Lady Miriam. It is possible he would understand my wishing to join you, but...?' His voice trailed off uncertainly. Andrew, Peter's brother, nodded understandingly and glanced at the others.

'Let your heart be at peace, Simeon,' said John quietly, 'you will always be one of the Lord Jesus followers, whether it is openly with us, or quietly within your home situation. But sooner or later, I foresee that you will be one who spreads the Lord's teachings around the world.' The disciples looked at John, surprised, but not questioning. John sometimes seemed to pierce the mists of the future, a gift developed of the Messiah, even as the rest of them were reaping spiritual gifts in preparation for a vast ministry, at which they did not even glimpse at this time.

A twig crackled and there was movement discernible in the shadows beyond the group.

'Who is there,' demanded Peter, instantly alert.

'Shalom. Greetings, my friends,' said a cultured voice.

'My name is Nicodemus. I am a Pharisee of the Temple. I am here in a private capacity to speak with your master, the Rabbi Jesus.' He loosed the cloak, which concealed his priestly robes, and stood serenely before the group of Galileans, who now surrounded him. It was Peter who took it upon himself to interrupt the Lord at his devotions, standing before the kneeling figure, with deference.

'Your pardon, Lord! There is a man come, a Pharisee. His name is Nicodemus, a member of the Jewish Ruling Council. Do you wish to see him, or shall I send him on his way?' Jesus rose to his feet. He placed a calming hand on Peter's shoulder, and inclined his head. Peter went off to collect Nicodemus, regarding the Pharisee from suspicious eyes beneath his beetling brows, but if Jesus wanted to see him!

Nicodemus bowed courteously before Jesus, his eyes studying what he could see of the rabbi's face by the ghostly fingers of light stealing between the olive branches. As he stood there, he became aware of a sense of power throbbing palpably from the nucleus of the Galilean's presence. As he met the eyes of Jesus, eyes such as he had never seen before, eyes searching out his very soul, he felt his limbs begin to tremble.

Words tumbled from his lips. He had meant to make a long, impressive address to enhance his status, instead he heard himself saying-

'Rabbi, we know you are a teacher who has come from God—for no-one could perform the miraculous signs you are doing, if God were not with him!' Nicodemus steadied himself against the bark of a tree, as he uttered this. Then the Holy One began to speak with him, his words flowing like healing balm, searching out the hidden pain in Nicodemus mind. For years the Pharisee had made meticulous catalogue of all the finer points of the law, seeking, grinding down and adapting the essence of scripture to meet present need. 'Thou shalt not...which may also mean...and therefore...and in which case...!' And what had it produced, this lifetime of conformity, truncated precision, leaving his soul an arid desert, a place of desolation, for Nicodemus knew the lifeless state of his inner self, concealed it behind an aura of sophistication, which disintegrated before the Truth.

And now the Way, the Truth, was made gloriously manifest to him, in these simple words, which held the answer to the destiny of mankind.

'I tell you the truth no-one can see the Kingdom of God, unless he is born again!'

The meaning flashed across the Pharisees brain. But it meant a letting go of all he had spent a lifetime striving for—a death to self and he floundered against the knowledge, seeking refuge in urbanity.

'How can a man be born when he is old?' Nicodemus pressed his lips into smile. 'Surely he cannot enter a second time into his mother's womb to be born!'

Jesus eyes held him pivoted a split second in eternity, unable to struggle, to evade the issue. The words blazed pattern into his brain, and try as he might, Nicodemus thoughts would never again follow the path of his past. 'To be born again, to be born again!' The words would continuously illumine the darkest corners of his soul, as they would with all those who heard them, in the tortuous centuries ahead.

'I tell you the truth no-one can enter the Kingdom of God, unless he is born of water and the Spirit.'

'But,' began Nicodemus...

'Flesh gives birth to flesh, but the Spirit gives birth to spirit. You should not be surprised at my saying 'You must be born again!' The wind rose in sudden gust, the branches of the olive trees soughing about him, as Jesus continued. 'The wind blows wherever it pleases. You hear its sound, but you cannot tell where it comes from, or where it is going. So it is with everyone born of the Spirit.'

'How can this be,' asked Nicodemus, pretending lack of understanding, anything rather than accept what could no longer be denied. But the Holy One cut through his subterfuge with blunt repartee.

'You—are Israel's teacher,' said Jesus, 'and you do not understand these things?' Nicodemus was caught on the raw, but before he could protest, Jesus continued-'I tell you the truth, we speak of what we know, and we testify to what we have seen, but still you people do not accept our testimony. I have spoken to you of earthly things, and you do not believe.

How then will you believe if I speak of heavenly things?'

His voice rose, blending with the warm night wind, reaching his disciples, who had crept closer to hear the conversation.

'No-one has ever gone into Heaven, except the one who came from Heaven—the Son of Man. Just as Moses lifted up the snake in the desert, so the Son of Man must be lifted up, so that whoever believes in him may have eternal life!'

Nicodemus trudged back to the Temple, head bowed in thought. At his side walked Simeon, equally pensive, but with a light shining within. They splashed through the shallows of the Kidron Brook, feet seeking purchase on the slippery fording stones. Simeon steadied the Priest as he almost lost his footing.

'Thank you, young sir,' said the Pharisee with a smile. 'The Galileans told me you are of the family of one of the Roman Centurions. Does he approve of your seeking the company of the Rabbi Jesus?'

'I should have been back in the fortress before nightfall,' said Simeon contritely.

'Well, the Temple courts are locked at this time of night, but you may safely enter with me, and I will escort you as far as the Fortress.'

Claudius was furious. He had imagined all sorts of ills having come to the boy, who now stood, verbally repentant, but inwardly unconcerned of that Claudius was sure; for Simeon had a strange look about him, an air of exultation, as though he was possessed of some great inward joy. He seemed to be partly remote from the tongue lashing which the Centurion now unleashed on him, bowing his head in acceptance of the harsh words which he knew masked concern.

'Get to your bed, Simeon! You are confined to the fortress until we leave.'

Tears started to the lad's eyes at this, but he made no protest. He left the room silently. Claudius threw himself down on a chair, head in hands, chest heaving with suppressed emotion, for he knew why he had felt such inordinate anger.

He, Claudius, would have followed Jesus out into the night had he been able, would have liked to have bared his soul before the Holy One. But it could not be! There was his duty to the Emperor, to Rome. A Roman officer could not be seen to attend one who might eventually be swept to head insurrection against Rome, even though he knew that this Jesus of Nazareth was truly the son of the mighty Jewish God, said to be the only true God.

He sprang to his feet, and stared restlessly out of the shutter. The Temple courts were bare, empty of the huge crowds that filled them during the day. The temple itself, gleamed golden and remote, etched mysteriously against the sky by the lights of the guards flaring torches. On the porticoes, soldiers in smaller numbers than by day kept watchful vigil.

Suddenly he shuddered, caught in the grips of a waking nightmare. It was as though the whole temple area was suddenly under siege, there was the noise of battle, fire, falling masonry and terrible screams.

He shook himself. A few more days and he would be back in Capernaum and it could not come too soon. He went to his chamber, in search of Miriam. But even after their lovemaking, Claudius could not relax. It was almost dawn, before he finally slept.

Chapter Nine

Miriam sang as she walked in the garden. She had slipped out just as dawn spread its silken net of rippling gold across the Sea of Galilee. She paused now as she snapped off a blossom of scarlet hibiscus and tucked it into her dark hair.

The scent of roses and honeysuckle blended with the heavier fragrance of jasmine in this wild part of the garden, a secret grotto which she loved best. She sank down on the marble seat, concealed from prying eyes by the riot of flowering shrubs, as she dreamed about the young life forming beneath her heart.

'So wife, you steal from my bed before I rise now? Is this some custom learned in Jerusalem?'

She looked up startled. She had not heard Claudius follow her. She blushed and laughed. 'Dear Lord, it was the joy of the morning that brought me out here and sweet relief to have left Jerusalem far behind.'

Claudius snorted. He would never understand women. He had thought she would have enjoyed her stay in the Jew's holy city.

'Why, we've been back from Jerusalem for a few weeks now and you still feel relief to be home! You do not miss your visits to the palace, your friendship with the Lady Claudia and the Lady Joanna?' His blue eyes watched her curiously.

'I must admit that I miss Joanna, would love to see her again. But I know this is unlikely as her husband is chamberlain to Herod Antipas, her life inextricably linked with that of the court.' Her face was sad.

'Well, Herod is back at his palace in Tiberias now, only a few miles along the coast. It may be possible for you to accompany me when I visit the Centurion who is based near the city. You've met him, remember?' He slipped his arm about her, as she rose to return to the villa with him. 'The palace is not too far from the garrison, and-----!'

He broke off, glancing below the gardens, to the shore, where he noticed Simeon rising dripping from the sea, accompanied by a taller lad. He shaded his eyes against the brilliant early sunshine. The other young man was not of his household, and it was odd that a stranger should be so near the villa.

'Wait here, Miriam,' he said shortly. He walked swiftly down the pathway that dropped in tiers of steps to the seashore. The two boys looked up, startled.

'Why, my son, you are early up this morning,' said Claudius easily, smiling at Simeon. 'Who is your companion?' Then as he looked at the other lad, he knew. Although the stranger was lighter skinned, more strongly built, his features revealed the kinship between the lads.

'You are David are you not,' said Claudius probingly, 'Simeon's brother!'

'I am.' David returned the Centurion's stare, calmly. 'Greetings, Centurion. I was just enjoying a swim with Simeon. I will go now.'

'Not so fast,' rapped out Claudius. 'I request you accompany me to my villa.' It was an order. David glanced along the seashore, assessing his chances of dashing off, but he could see men posted around the house, and nodded reluctantly.

They had finished breakfast, and Miriam smiled encouragingly at David. Her husband had not ceased to interrogate the youth since the beginning of the meal, wonder being that he had managed to eat anything.

'So David, you are now a full time follower of Jesus of Nazareth. How was it then, that you did not accompany the Rabbi to Jerusalem, for the Passover?'

It was Simeon who answered. He looked at David protectively. 'How could David go—the soldiers in Jerusalem might have arrested him?'

'I wanted to go above all things,' added David, 'but my friend Simon, who is one of the Lord Jesus disciples, advised against it. So I have been staying with Zebedee the fisherman, learning to mend nets and how to sail a boat. He will be waiting for me and I must go soon.'

'When do you expect Jesus of Nazareth to return,' asked Claudius? David hesitated, unwilling to discuss such details with a Roman, even though he was beginning to have a grudging liking for the man who had adopted his brother. But then, Jesus would be back within days, and it was unlikely that this news could bring harm to the master.

'Word is that he has been preaching in Judea, and is now returning through Samaria. I will be much relieved to see him safely back, after John's fate!' David's face showed signs of horror, at the news he had meant to share with Simeon that morning, before their conversation had been so abruptly interrupted.

'John—not the Baptist?' asked Simeon, his young face tense. 'What has happened, David?' That day he had spent with the Baptist, his baptism, the immersion of Jesus by John, when the holy man had announced Jesus as Messiah, his parent's deaths, the whole had left indelible imprint on Simeon's mind.

'The Prophet was executed by Herod's order,' said David briefly. He glanced at the Lady Miriam, whom he knew to be with child. He did not want to distress her with the details.

'John the Baptist is dead,' cried Miriam, 'But why? What had he done, that Herod should have killed him.' Her lovely face was deeply troubled. She had never met John, but knew him to be held in reverence by all devout Jews. As for Simeon, he had gone pale with shock.

'Can't you guess why, Miriam,' asked Claudius? 'Remember how Lady Joanna mentioned the rage of Herod's new wife Herodias, because John was publicly denouncing them for breaking the Jewish law, by his marrying his brother's wife, while Phillip was still alive!' He paused and glanced at David curiously. 'Of course, I already knew that John had been arrested a few months ago, and was being held at the fortress palace of Machaerus, but I had not heard of his death!' His brows met in a straight line as he growled, 'It would seem that your information speeds more accurately than my own, David.'

David shook his head sadly. 'I only heard the news myself in the early hours. A slave from Herod's palace was sent to Capernaum with an order for the smoked fish which Herod loves, prefers even to those smoked in Magdala and he gave the news to a friend of Zebedee. Herod is worried about the effect the news will have here in Galilee where the Baptist is held in reverence, and so the news was supposed to be suppressed. John was only executed three days ago and Herod Antipas left Machaerus the next day! They say he feared to remain in the fortress there in case the shade of John should come to haunt him!'

'So!' Claudius changed the subject, seeing the obvious distress of both

Miriam and Simeon. 'David, you mentioned a friend called Simon, who is one of the Rabbi Jesus disciples. This would be Simon the Zealot?'

'You know of him,' muttered David in confusion. He looked at Simeon. Had his brother disclosed matters told in confidence?

'My dear lad, it is my duty to know all that goes on in this area, especially people involved with a figure as controversial as Jesus, whom John named Messiah!' Claudius looked at Simeon reprovingly. 'As for you, my son, had you had sufficient sense to have made your brother's presence in Capernaum known to me while we were in Jerusalem, it would have presented the perfect opportunity to have approached Tribune Marcus, to have the order of arrest against David rescinded. Well, I will enclose a message to this effect when next I send dispatches to Jerusalem.'

Simeon flushed uncomfortably. He felt he had fallen in Claudius estimation because he had not mentioned knowledge of his brother's whereabouts, although this was not so.

'So, David, you are welcome to visit my house again whenever you wish to see Simeon. I have the deepest respect for your master, the Holy One—after all he healed your brother at the request of one he might have considered as an enemy.' Claudius eyes were remote, his thoughts turned inwards.

'The love of Jesus extends to all men,' said David gently. 'Farewell Centurion Claudius. Lady Miriam!' He bowed. 'Simeon—I hope to see you again soon.'

He was gone. Claudius looked at his wife's troubled face. He slipped a hand into the folds of his tunic and produced a pouch. He held it out to her. 'For you, wife!' he said watching her face as the shimmering necklace lay revealed. She gasped in delight. 'Go and try it on!' The diversion had worked, he thought. But Miriam's eyes were troubled, as she slipped the shining jewels about her throat in the privacy of the bedroom. She breathed a faint sigh. Below in the atrium, the Centurion was making plans.

'Now you, Simeon, come with me! I have a visit to make in Capernaum.'

Chuza paced his bedchamber, face working with concern and anger, concern for his wife's condition, and anger, that although he had access to the best physicians in the land, none of them were able to bring her relief. Nor did they seem to be able to offer a reasonable diagnosis of what ailed her.

He turned back to the bed, staring in perplexity at Joanna's face, deathly white against the pillows. Her eyes were closed, but every few minutes a tremor crossed her features, leaving him uncertain as to whether she was actually asleep or not.

He bent forward, placing a gentle hand on her shoulder.

'Joanna?' She opened her eyes, those lovely violet eyes, and they dilated in terror! She sat up. Limbs rigid, she let loose scream after scream. Chuza stepped back from her appalled. He called to the Arab physician, sitting on a chair at the back of the room.

'Do something! Anything! She mustn't be allowed to scream like this—why, Herod will hear her!'

The physician rose, bowed and swiftly mixed a potion. He uttered a sibilant command to the young woman. The chords of her neck strained as she would scream again, but she turned wild eyes upon the doctor who fixed her with hypnotic stare, then as she calmed slightly, set the cup to her lips, managing to get most of the draught down her throat. Within minutes, her head slumped to one side as she slipped into drugged slumber.

'My thanks, physician,' sighed Chuza in relief. 'How long will she sleep?'

'It is strong, my lord, so maybe twelve hours. But it is no answer. Yet sleep often brings healing in its train.' He pushed back a strand of grey hair that had escaped his embroidered turban then stroked his grey beard gravely.

'You are Herod's own chief physician, wise above all others, yet you cannot bring my wife out of whatever overcomes her?' Chuza's dark eyes were pools of frustration, his usual bland, official smile completely missing from his full lips. He stood there, one of the richest men in Herod's kingdom, yet unable with all his wealth, to buy health for the woman whom he prized so highly for her looks and breeding, having been born of one of the many wives of Herod the Great. As far as it was possible he loved Joanna, was proud of her grace and the respect in which all held her, even Herod Antipas.

Sensing movement behind him, he turned his head away from the still form on the pillows.

'Ah, Chuza! I thought I heard screams? Is your wife still—unwell?' She stood there, regarding him with a mocking smile on her painted lips, eyes bent curiously on the inert figure in the bed. Salome glittered with every step she lightly took, from jewelled diadem at brow, to pearls wound in her waist length hair, diamonds and rubies shining at ears, throat and almost naked young bosom. Her tunic drifted gossamer fine, in sapphire silk. At thirteen she already had the power to quicken a man's pulse and stir desire to ungovernable extent, as she had demonstrated so recently at Machaerus, Herod's palace in the Judean desert.

'What think you caused your lady's illness? As I remember, it was when she saw the king present the head of John the Baptist to me on a salver that her seizures started. But I am sure that as loyal subject of Herod, she must have whole-heartedly applauded action which rid the earth of a madman, a fanatic, who cast aspersions on my mother's union with the king! ' She wandered to the marble and gilt table, surmounted by a bronze mirror, where Joanna's toilet articles lay and her open jewel casket. With impudent grace, Salome extracted a heavy gold chain, with intricate link and held it about her own throat.

'Do you not think it suits me, Lord Chuza? I am sure the Lady Joanna would wish me to have it!' She turned her heavily kohled eyes upon the chamberlain. 'Will you fasten it for me, sir?' He did so, the veins at his forehead knotting, for the chain was a recent gift to his wife, but Salome's power and influence with his master Herod, had been too terribly demonstrated for him to make protest. As he bent over her neck, the smell of her heavy musk perfume filled his nostrils and his breath quickened. Then she was gone, her mocking laughter growing fainter as she sought more interesting company.

A week later, Joanna was still heavily drugged, only now the physician had fresh worries. The potion he was using could bring addiction to the sufferer, for it was an infusion of poppy with another subtle ingredient. He voiced his concern to Chuza.

'Look Physician, you must have knowledge of what is causing these attacks! How say you, is this madness?'

Chuza forced the words out. He was weary of the stress the situation was causing him. The danger was that Salome would use innuendo as a lever to replace him as chamberlain, with another courtier favoured of her mother. All knew that his wife was very religious and had shown a keen interest in the Baptist's teaching. If Salome could bring Herod to believe that Joanna's illness was directly attributable to overwhelming distress at John's execution thus criticizing Herod's action, then it might be considered, that Chuza also criticized his monarch and this would be treason.

'Lord Chuza, in my opinion, it is an evil spirit that has possessed your wife, indeed more than one. Without the drug, she will continue to scream and behave with violence, yet with constant use of the drug she may be so weakened as to die!' The old man faced Chuza calmly. He had spoken the truth as he knew it. He watched Chuza's face, reading the man's thoughts, that an overdose would put an end to a dangerous situation.

There was a knock at the door, which was now kept locked. Chuza opened it. A slave came in, bowed and said, 'Centurion Claudius and his lady desire to see the Lady Joanna.'

Chuza looked at the slave in surprise, Centurion Claudius? Of course, the officer in charge of the small garrison at Capernaum, who had sat at Pontius Pilate's table with his wife, Miriam at Herod's palace in Jerusalem! Joanna had become very fond of the lovely Galilean girl and the two of them had spent much time together in Jerusalem. He was about to tell the slave that his wife was too ill for visitors then, blind instinct made him decide otherwise.

'Bring them here,' he said incisively.

Miriam and Claudius stared in dismay at the frail figure on the bed. It was obvious that she had lost much weight, and dark shadows marked her eye sockets. Chuza dismissed the slave, and gave brief account to the couple of all that had transpired in the last few weeks.

'I fear that my wife is not long for this world,' he said. 'This man is the finest physician in the kingdom, and he can do nothing but drug her senses. He has told me but now, that it is an evil spirit that possesses Joanna.'

Miriam leaned over Joanna, and stroked her damp forehead compassionately. Then she swung around and looked encouragingly at Chuza. 'There is one person who can heal your wife, Lord Chuza—Jesus of Nazareth!'

Chuza looked at her, startled. He had of course, heard of the miracle worker from Galilee and that men were muttering that either he was a blasphemer or perhaps the long awaited Messiah. As he considered the position, Chuza realized that he believed the controversial rabbi, might indeed be able to heal his wife, but wouldn't it be equally dangerous to be discovered dealing with one who might be thought a possible enemy of the state? What would Herod's reaction be if he heard that Chuza had contacted Jesus? Miriam with a woman's instinct sensed his dilemma.

'My Lord Chuza,' she said quietly. 'Why not allow your lady to spend a few weeks with Claudius and myself at our villa? It is not as luxurious as this palace, but I can promise that your wife will be comfortable. If she should come in contact with the Holy One, by accident—well!'

Chuza's face brightened. He liked the idea. After all, the two women were friends. He smiled at the Centurion, who had kept silent so far.

'Be assured of my deep gratitude Centurion, if you are indeed willing to invite my wife to enjoy the solitude of your villa, which may prove beneficial to her condition. My physician will supply you with the drug needed for her sedation and I will have her clothes packed immediately!' He summoned Joanna's slaves. Before Claudius could protest, silken garments were being hastily folded into a chest. Chuza looked down at Joanna. Even in her weakened state, she was still very beautiful, and he felt a pang in his heart. He walked to the dressing table. 'Pack those,' he instructed the slave, indicating the toilet articles. He glanced at the jewel casket, containing a fortune in gold and gems. Chuza loved wealth, was worldly and ambitious, but he still cared in his own way, for his wife.

'Lady Miriam,' he said. 'I place my wife's jewellery in your hands, to be given to her if she recovers and if not, to use as you will.'

Joanna was being carried quietly out of the palace, whilst Herod and his family were at dinner that night. The little fishing boat set sail immediately, bearing Joanna away from the corruption of the Court, into an unknown future.

He was back! The news swept through Galilee and thousands converged on Capernaum. But Jesus had received word of John the Baptist's cruel death, to please the whim of Queen Herodias. His own brother James brought him the news of how John's disciples had collected the decapitated form of their dear master for burial.

He retired to the wilderness to pray, deeply distressed at the happening which had marred the joy of his homecoming. The disciples anchored the boat and splashed ashore. David had managed to find place among them, and now plied Simon the Zealot with questions about all that had occurred in Judea and Samaria. Jesus had asked to be alone. He frequently withdrew from them to pray to his heavenly Father, usually preferring to climb the nearest hill, a place apart.

David glanced shoreward. A stiff breeze was spanking the sea, seeming to help speed the myriad of small boats towards them, bearing the crowds who had decided to follow Jesus to this remote place. In those boats were countless sick and disabled people brought by desperate relatives, in the knowledge that if they could only manage to touch the fringed cloak of the master, they would receive healing!

More people were approaching them on foot, pouring out of the surrounding towns, down trodden people seeking hope; the poor; those crippled mentally and physically; people searching a meaning to their existence. Mingling with these, were the ever watchful Scribes and Pharisees—also members of the ascetic Essene sect, who lived within their own communities in the desert, and who awaited a Messiah, temporal lord, as well as a Messianic High Priest and in addition to all these, a large sprinkling of the Zealots, waiting opportunity as always to pronounce Jesus publicly as Messiah and so provide spark for national uprising.

The disciples watched as the people approached nearer. The Holy One had managed a few hours of quiet retreat, but the crowds were almost upon them. Peter and John ascended the hill, scrambling amongst the loose stone. He heard their voices long before they reached him, and was already on his feet, shading his eyes against the sun, as he saw the thousands streaming towards his disciples. It must have taken much endurance and faith to have travelled overland in the heat of the day, as many of the disabled had done. His eyes were filled with compassion, tenderness beyond the understanding of men.

David, son of Ezra looked about him uneasily. This was the first time he had encountered such a huge crowd seeking the Holy One, for he had not accompanied the disciples during Jesus ministry in Judea and Samaria. A slight feeling of panic arose in his breast, as he heard the voice of the multitude, crying out for Jesus, imploring help. The noise was rising from all sides. How would his beloved Master be able to contend with need on such an enormous scale? Then Jesus was amongst them. The ranks of the crowd parted like the waves of the sea, when it had fallen back to Moses advance. A spirit of awe descended on the people as hundreds were healed. They fell on their knees before him, giving thanks to God, cries of pain now replaced by tears of joy.

A small boy smiled up at David.

'My mother, the Holy One has healed her!'

As he knelt beside the boy, his own love flooding towards him, David looked up at the middle aged woman, who was raising her hands in praise.

'You have been healed, Lady?'

'I had a disease of the spine, could not walk upright. Now look!' She stood exultantly on tip-toe. 'There is no more pain—no pain! I did but touch his robe as he passed by!'

David gave the little boy a hug and released him. Everywhere people were crying with happiness and still, Jesus walked among them, pausing now to deal with those possessed of evil spirits.

Suddenly he became aware of a commotion behind him. He turned. Phillip and John were remonstrating with a woman. She was using the foulest language which David had ever heard, and which would have been more at home in any barracks, than on the lips of the beautiful woman dressed in a crimson tunic, trimmed with silver. As David watched appalled, her face contorted with rage as she fought to get nearer to Jesus. She screamed and spat, tearing her robe. Then she calmed slightly, gathering herself like a panther, as her hands rose, nails pointed upwards towards the throat of the quiet figure that had turned and now looked full at her.

He raised his hand and spoke a word of authority. The woman fell to the ground, writhing and vomiting. Seven times the Holy One addressed the demons possessing the body of Mary called the Magdalene and as they fled, leaving her crumpled, seemingly lifeless on the ground, David felt a great chill.

'Its cold,' he murmured to Phillip.

'It always is, when demons are coming out,' said Phillip softly. 'But it is done now. This was a bad case, but no demons can withstand the Son of Man!'

'Why do you name Jesus so?' inquired David 'We all know him to be the Son of God!'

'For obvious reasons, David—if he is ever officially proclaimed the Messiah, the Son of God, then both the Sadducees and the Roman authorities will act, arrest him for treason. The Lord knows this and has to show great care not to allow any to address him as Messiah publicly. He always refers to himself now as the Son of Man.'

Peter bent over the still form of Mary Magdalene. He had glimpsed her many times in the past as she had flaunted her way through the streets of Capernaum, richly clad, hip length black, waving hair unveiled. She lived in Magdala it was said, but spent much time in Tiberias. She was a prostitute much used by the nobility of Herod's court. The young woman took his hand now as she opened her eyes and looked about her, confused, puzzled.

'Where am I,' she whispered? Suddenly past and present fused. The once innocent young girl, who had lived far south in Judea with her sister Martha and brother Lazarus, had left home with a rich merchant, filled with a spirit of adventure and deeply in love with one who had discarded her in Tiberias. This same girl, who became possessed with deep loathing for all men on account of the one who had betrayed her, resorted to prostitution, enjoying the power her beauty gave her over men, smashing through any gentler feelings they evinced in her. Hating them, degrading herself, inspecting the broken facets of her personality every morning, but driven to repeat the process every night, seeking through sheer exhaustion to achieve sleep. But there were evil faces in her dreams, goading her on whenever she weakened to slight feelings of repentance. If life could ever be said to be a living hell, then the demons who inhabited Mary Magdalene, had made it so for this their willing daughter.

'Will you stand up, lady,' said Peter. 'You are healed.' He helped her up. She became aware of her torn clothing and looked about her, bewildered. It was not true to say she did not know what had happened, for she did. She had felt irresistible urge to mock the Holy One, had been overcome by deepest hostility towards him, his purity, the fact that he knew her demons, knew that she—they—had no power over him!

She burst into tears, suddenly convicted by knowledge of the enormity of her past sins and the realization that they had been forgiven by the quiet man who stood close by, who was not mere man, but Son of the Living God. He had made it possible for her to start again, to throw aside the tattered garment of her past—to be born again.

Peter left her sitting on a rock, looking pale, but with a light of pure love shining in her eyes, a love that had nothing to do with physical emotion, intense, spiritual joy, that she would now spread to all she came in contact with.

The afternoon was late, the people listening to Jesus, who was teaching them through parables, feeding their souls now that he had healed their bodies. But bodies also need sustenance, and Jesus knew he must deal with the peoples' physical needs. He called to Phillip.

'Where shall we buy bread for these people to eat,' he asked and watched Phillips shocked expression, as his disciple pondered the impossibility of feeding approximately five thousand people stranded in the middle of the bare countryside. Even if there were shops nearby, the cost on their slender communal purse would be prohibitively heavy. Jesus restrained a smile as he read Phillip's busy thoughts, for he already knew in his own mind what he was about to do.

The little boy who had spoken to David earlier had heard Jesus question about food. He tugged at David's arm, bending his face earnestly upon him.

'I have some food, sir,' he cried. 'Look, in this basket!' 'What does the boy say,' asked Andrew, who was standing next to David.

'He has some food in his basket,' replied David, keeping a straight face so as not to hurt the little lad's feelings.

In the meanwhile, Phillip had worked out a sum in his mind. 'Eight month's wages would not buy enough bread for each to have a bite!' He exclaimed this with a dolorous expression, nor saw the slight crinkling at the corner of the Holy One's mouth. He looked towards Andrew, who was holding a basket aloft, while he propelled a small boy towards Jesus with the other hand.

'Here is a boy, with five small barley loaves and two small fish, but how far will they go amongst so many?' But with flash of spiritual insight, Andrew already knew how far they would go, could go, around the whole world if necessary. Jesus nodded. Here it was the faith he had been waiting for.

Andrew reached Jesus with the basket and the child. He stood back, as

Jesus placed an arm about the little one and accepted the gift of his supper.

'Make the people sit down,' Jesus said. It was a flat, grassy area and the disciples arranged the crowd of five thousand, into groups of about fifty. Then Jesus lifted up the five small loaves and gave thanks. As he said the grace, the crowd leaned forward puzzled, was it a joke? Then he started to break the bread, and the disciples came to him time and time again, carrying great loads of bread in their cloaks, to distribute amongst the crowds, who reached out eager hands amidst a continuous murmur of awe. Trip after trip the disciples made, and then repeated the process as their master broke the fish. No one was sure how long the feeding of five thousand took only that every single person was fed and that the disciples gathered up twelve basketfuls of leftovers, that nothing should be wasted.

The disciples were almost too amazed to speak. The immensity of the miracle, had taken even them by surprise. They were jubilant, bubbling with excitement. Surely now, when he had done what no man had ever done before, that which no ordinary man could possibly do—surely now, Jesus would announce his true identity to the people.

The people themselves were now muttering among themselves, as a feverish mood of expectancy swept through them. The wondrous healings, now this miracle of feeding five thousand people with five loaves and two little fishes! Surely it meant only one thing!

A cry went up from one person to another. 'Surely this is the Prophet who is to come into the world!' The Zealots heard that cry and it was what they had been waiting for! Barabbas was amongst those in the crowd, who raised the exuberant cry, 'Jesus! Jesus is the Messiah—Jesus for King!'

A party of Zealots pushed their way through the excited throng, intending to seize Jesus and officially announce him publicly as Messiah. Jesus, knowing that they intended to make him king by force, spoke swiftly to his disciples. They formed a guard in front of him, shoulder to shoulder and in the melee Jesus slipped away in the twilight, withdrawing again to the mountain, to be by himself.

The disciples drew breath of relief that he had managed to get away. They themselves now drew apart from the crowd, and made for the lake. The situation had become dangerous, and perhaps they began to have glimmerings at the back of their minds as to what might happen, if they didn't protect the Holy One from the obvious ambition of the Zealots, to create an earthly monarch of the Son of God.

Chapter Ten

The disciples had waited anxiously for their master to appear. The moon had risen, glimpsed through drifting cloud and the waves were lifting glistening flanks against the boat. At last they pulled away from the shore and as the weather grew rougher took decision to make for Capernaum, which was what Jesus had told them to do. But they had been loath to leave without him.

'My stomach is heaving within me,' said David plaintively. 'Nor do we seem to be making any headway!'

'If you want to be sick, lean over the side,' instructed Peter brusquely. 'Mind you don't fall in!'

But David shook his head, plainly terrified of the huge waves now buffeting the boat. Simon the Zealot, also no seaman, was showing like signs of uneasiness. The wind was rising, the roar of it filling their ears, as the small craft juddered before its escalating fury, the disciples faces and clothing soaked with rain and spray.

Mathew turned to John anxiously.

'Are we going to sink?'

'Courage,' replied John. 'This is but a fledgling of a storm!' It was almost four in the morning. They had battled unceasingly against the enormous waves, each one of which seemed intent on swamping them and now the moon was covered with scudding cloud. David huddled miserably in the bottom of the boat. He knew he was going to die and tried hard not to cry out, so great his fear. Peter, Andrew, James and John, had no time for the lad. As experienced sailors it was their responsibility to save the boat, and as for the others, they were frightened for their own skins.

'What is that light,' Simon whispered suddenly between trembling lips, 'Look! Something is approaching on the waters—it has the shape of a man. It's a ghost! It's a ghost I tell you!' The others had seen it now. A sickening fear gripped them, fear greater than that of drowning. Then they heard the familiar voice.

'Take courage! It is I! Don't be afraid!'

It was Jesus. He was walking to them on the tops of the waves. Surely it was a dream! Peter was the first to respond. If it was the Holy One, what now had they to fear? But was it really Jesus, or some evil spirit of the night, taking his shape.

'Lord, if it's you, tell me to come to you on the water!'

'Come!' The words came floating towards Peter.

Then in spite of the size of the waves that were still tossing the boat, Peter put first one leg and then the other out of the boat. He took a deep breath and fixed his eyes on Jesus and started to walk on the water. Then a wave caught him sideways and his eyes left the Holy One. He began to sink. The water was up to his neck! The wind was all about him now, as desperately he tried to lift his eyes from the waves, but fear held him in its grip.

'Lord, save me!' Immediately Jesus reached out his hand and lifted him.

'You of little faith,' he said reprovingly. 'Why did you doubt!' But the look of tenderness in his eyes softened the reproof. Hand in hand, they walked the storm waves, until they reached the boat, where willing helpers waited in amazement. As they clambered into the boat, Jesus raised his hands to the waves. The wind calmed down, the sea became as smooth as a garden pool. The disciples fell to their knees in the boat and cried out tremblingly------'Master, truly you are the Son of God!'

Joanna had only been there for a week, but already Miriam was sick with tiredness. She had installed the lovely wife of Herod's chamberlain, in a room next to the bedroom she shared with Claudius. He had protested and did so increasingly.

'Look you, wife, I have every respect for your friendship with Joanna, honour you for what you are trying to do. But you must realize that she is not the same woman you met in Jerusalem. Her mind is deranged and she may become dangerous, and you dear Miriam are carrying our child! Have some thought for the baby, even if you have none for your own safety!'

Miriam sighed, and pushed her hair wearily out of her eyes. She knew that what Claudius said was true, but she had to try. She was the only lifeline the sick woman had. In an attempt to prevent Joanna's too great dependency on the drug which quietened her, she had been cutting the dosage. The result was that Joanna only slept fitfully, and when she awoke, screamed and clawed at the air. She was obviously in the grip of some terrible fear which consumed all rational thought.

It was almost dawn. Joanna lay white and still against the pillow. Miriam slumped almost as white, on a chair. Claudius stared down at her in mixture of love and exasperation. He had not realized the strength of will possessed by his young wife, and knew himself powerless against it. There was a quiet tap at the door. It was Simeon.

'Forgive me, sir,' he said the Claudius, 'but I heard the lady Joanna screaming, and wanted to see if I could help in any way.' He looked at Miriam with commiseration. 'You look exhausted,' he said bluntly. 'You cannot be allowed to continue like this.'

Claudius looked at him in surprise. He had never heard young Simeon speak with such authority before. Perhaps Miriam would heed their joint voices. She didn't.

Simeon went below with the Centurion to the atrium.

'Look sir, I have a suggestion to make. Let me go to my brother, and make arrangement for the Holy One to see Lady Joanna.'

'You do not need my permission for that lad! But from what I hear, Jesus is moving around a lot. Wherever he goes, he is almost mobbed by crowds. How can we ever get Joanna near him? She is far too unstable to take, even in a litter. Nor can I expect the Holy One to come under a Roman roof? Oh yes, I know he would do so unhesitatingly. But it is not fitting for him to.'

'Leave it to me,' said Simeon confidently. 'I know something can be arranged.' He smiled at Claudius and stole out of the house and along the beach, until he reached the town. He knew where Peter's house was, and knocked timidly on the door. Dawn had not yet broken and Peter groaned at the noise. For it was not unusual. There were always those seeking the Holy One early. Not only was Jesus getting hardly any sleep, but nor was he being allowed time to eat. His mother and brothers had heard of the problem, and had come with the intention of taking care of him, but his ministry was more important than his human needs.

Peter's face relented, when he saw who knocked. He called to David, who lay on a pallet on the floor.

'Wake up, lad. It's your brother.'

'Simeon! What brings you here? Is there trouble?' David clasped his brother fondly, as he fired the question.

'I need help—help for Claudius and Miriam!' Peter and David listened, as Simeon explained the dilemma and who Joanna was. 'From what I have gleaned, Lady Joanna was present at that fatal banquet, when as all have heard, Princess Salome danced before Herod. As reward for her performance, which is said to have inflamed the senses of all men present, on her mother's advice, she demanded the head of John the Baptist.' He paused and swallowed. Even though he had not been there himself, Simeon's vivid imagination clothed the facts with inner vision.

'So Joanna actually saw the Baptist's head presented to Salome on a platter,' said Peter. 'That was surely enough to unhinge any sensitive mind, but from what you have described of her condition, it sounds as though an evil spirit born of her fear and of the wickedness present at that debauched gathering, had entered this unfortunate young woman!' Peter shook his head, overcome by grief at the terrible end that John had met. The wonder was, he thought, that God had not struck down the perpetrators, for the Lord will not be mocked.

'Lady Miriam has brought her here, to her villa. She rests next to Claudius and Miriam's own bedchamber. Miriam has hardly slept since her arrival. Joanna's screams are terrible! The whole household is suffering from lack of sleep. Claudius fears for his lady's health, for she is with child.'

'I will ask the Holy One to visit the villa,' said Peter slowly. 'But it will have to be accomplished at night, for the crowds watch his every move and thousands would surround the villa and there is no knowing what the garrison would do.'

'May I make a suggestion,' said David thoughtfully, 'Look, Simeon—it still lacks well over an hour to daylight! Run back along the beach, get the Lady Joanna down onto the shore but sufficiently away from the villa, and then if the Holy One is willing---!'

'I am,' said a quiet voice.

They all looked up startled. How long had Jesus been standing at the door, waiting to be invited into this situation. His face was showing signs of tiredness, yet there was the usual radiance to the smile he bent on Simeon, who now fell to his knees worshipping his Lord and murmuring thanks for his own healing, a few weeks back.

If the house guards were surprised at the little party who carried the wife of Herod's chamberlain, out of the villa, through the garden and down the steps to the beach while it was still night, they made no sign of it. They were merely thankful to be spared her intermittent screams for a while.

Claudius and Simeon carried the sick woman between them, with Miriam and the maid Sarah in tow. The pebbles crunched wetly underfoot, a drift of sea mist preventing their seeing more than a foot or two in front of them, despite the lamp which Sarah carried. Suddenly Joanna's limp figure stiffened. She went into spasm, letting forth a most terrible scream. So unexpectedly did it happen that the men almost dropped her.

Then there came a quiet, authoritative voice.

'Set her down. Stand back.'

The men obeyed, fearing that Joanna might fall without support, but not questioning the command. It was the first time Joanna had stood unaided since her illness. She swayed, arms flailing about her in fear, frightful shapes blurred through her mind, and there was blood—blood everywhere and fleering faces.

Then the mist lifted and the figure of Jesus stood immediately before her. The evil spirit within her made her scream aloud with fear, seeking to flee. Sarah's hand shook so that she almost dropped the lamp. Miriam snatched it from her. She held it on high, illumining the woman and the gracious figure of the Son of God, who raised his hands and prayed, rebuking the evil spirit. Joanna became still, and they thought it was finished, but the evil thing within her, had a craftiness thinking to pretend to having been banished.

'You spirit of fear,' said Jesus, with authority, 'I command you come out of her!' The spirit shrieked, the young woman's body fell into convulsion. She lay on the shore like one dead. Then the Holy One bent and took her limp hand. 'Arise,' he said. Then to their wondering eyes, Joanna rose shakily to her feet. She raised her hands together in prayer.

'My Lord—and my God,' she whispered. As she said this, the sky brightened, the sea glimmered like leaded silver, then dawn flushed the sky and the hills were a glory.

Joanna now became aware of the people around her, of Miriam and Claudius, young Simeon and Sarah and of the smiling faces of the disciples who had accompanied Jesus. But she had eyes only for the Messiah whom she would now follow, helping to spread his message of love to all men.

'Again Lord, I thank you,' said Claudius. He looked as though he would say more. But bowing his head, he turned and walked blindly along the shore, tears filling his eyes. Miriam followed him, taking his hand. She knew the conflict taking place within his breast, could not resolve it only wait in the confidence born of faith, that one day Claudius would find the strength to openly acknowledge his belief in the Holy One.

'May I come with you,' asked Joanna of the disciples?

'Come,' said John. 'You may stay with my family, until you decide where you want to go.' He led her away with them. Simeon ran after Miriam, telling her what was happening. She gave a gasp of dismay. How could she have left Joanna's side?

'She will be alright,' said Simeon. 'I heard Peter say, that she would be company for another young woman who was recently delivered of seven evil spirits, Mary of Magdala and another girl so delivered called Susannah.

'But, she may need me,' breathed Miriam.

'You will see her again soon, but you need to rest yourself! Father,' he touched Claudius arm. 'Lady Miriam should be abed.'

Centurion Claudius reacted immediately. He lifted Miriam in his arms, and bore her home. She slept for twenty-four hours. When she awoke, it was to her husband's kiss. She slipped out of bed, and they embraced again. She was filled with a feeling of overwhelming happiness as she realized that their ordeal was over, Joanna was healed, could lead a normal life again. They stared out of the window towards the white walled houses of Capernaum, clustered around the high pillared synagogue. The sun poured like honey over the roof-tops and long buildings where the fish were prepared. A faint reek of smoke came from the curing tower. The sea was blue as a fresh hyacinth and gulls swooped around the harbour, diving on the scraps thrown out by women who gutted the fish. It all looked so peaceful, so normal. Yet out there, on the hillsides, beyond the town, the Zealots gathered, waiting their time to set the whole region afire.

Claudius gave his wife a quick squeeze.

'Well Miriam, I shall be out most of today. You are to rest! Do you hear me?'

'My Lord, I should think all of Capernaum can hear you,' she laughed. Claudius loud voice was a joke between them, born as it was of over twenty years bellowing orders in the thick of battle and on the parade ground.

'I will send that maid of yours to you, where is she? Sarah!' There was no answer to his command. Miriam, who was leaning over the balcony that looked onto the garden and sea, gave an exclamation of amusement.

'Look Claudius---but hush!' She pointed below her, where walking between an archway of purple bougainvillea, two young people were staring into each other's eyes, holding hands. They stopped and he seemed to be murmuring something to her. Then he lifted her hand to his lips and kissed it. The young girl broke away from him, with a gurgle of laughter and flurried into the house.

'We will have to find you another maid soon,' surmised Claudius with a smile. 'Well, I commend his choice. She is a lovely child.' He walked downstairs, casting a quizzical look at the flushed Samaritan girl who hurried past him.

'Father, may I speak with you,' asked Simeon. He stood before Claudius in the atrium, eyes shining his face solemn.

'Certainly, Simeon.' the Centurion ran a hand through his hair. 'Well, what is it?'

'I—well, I want to get married, sir!' There, it was out. Simeon's dark face glowed with a mixture of embarrassment and emotion. He looked absurdly young, standing there.

'Sarah?'

'Yes, sir, you approve then?' He breathed a sigh of relief.

'Not so fast, Simeon—now just how old are you?'

'Fifteen—almost a man,' Simeon stated.

'Just so! How old is Sarah?' Claudius kept his face suitably grave.

'Fourteen, sir.'

'Hum. Well, what I suggest is this—that you take a few months to consider matters then if you are of the same mind, you become betrothed, perhaps a year from then you may contemplate marriage. It is a very serious matter, Simeon, choosing a wife. This masculine flesh of ours has its own desires, which are suitably channelled in marriage, but the actual selection of a wife is no light matter. Now you have only known Sarah for a few scant weeks!'

'Forgive me, sir,' interrupted Simeon, 'but how long was it from the time that you first met the Lady Miriam, that you knew that you loved her?'

'Why, that is beside the point since I am a mature man, have travelled the world and was married once before.'

'How long, sir?'

'Immediately I looked into her eyes,' replied Claudius, not knowing why the truth left his lips in this unseemly fashion. Simeon nodded seriously.

'Father, in the same way, I also knew on the day I first saw Sarah, as she was sweeping the courtyard and we exchanged some few words, that she would become my wife and we would spend the rest of our lives together.'

'Well,' replied Claudius quietly, 'I give consent and blessing to your future union, but nevertheless, I ask that you are first betrothed for a year. This is in any case customary under Jewish practice. During this year, Miriam and I will treat Sarah as a daughter, and you will respect her virginity. Is this understood?' His blue eyes stared relentlessly into Simeon's, who swallowed his disappointment at the length of waiting, but knew this to be fair and reasonable.

'Why, sir, I thank you with all my heart, as I know Sarah will. When may we become betrothed? May it be today?' His pleading face was turned on Claudius, who shook his head.

'Simeon, have you no thought for Sarah? She will want to be suitable attired, and if I know Miriam, she will insist on preparing on a feast for you both. After all, it is an occasion, when my son becomes betrothed!'

'It is indeed,' cried a merry voice, and Miriam entered the atrium, leading Sarah by the hand. The Samaritan girls cheeks were red as poppies with confusion, but the glance she sped at Simeon spoke its own tale. She bowed before the Centurion, whom she held in awe and flushed further under his stare, for Claudius was examining her objectively for the first time. She was shorter than Miriam by a heads breadth, sweetly curved already looking unusually mature for so young a girl. But Claudius knew that girls ripened early in this hot clime, were usually betrothed before they were thirteen. Her waist length hair was a riot of curls, which no brush could completely tame and her dark eyes were heavily fringed by lashes, which fanned her dusky cheeks as she looked down bashfully under his stare.

'Sarah—Simeon has asked to take you to wife! How do you say, girl— is it your own wish, to marry him?'

She nodded then whispered softly, 'I wish it with all my heart.'

'Well, so be it.' He looked about him. 'Mencius, come here, boy! 'The Negro slave came forward, a smile on his lips, for he had been listening fascinated to the conversation, hidden behind a pillar.

Ah---Mencius! Go and fetch me a file.' He tapped the table impatiently until Mencius returned, then taking Sarah's slender wrist he carefully filed through the slave bracelet which she wore.

'Sarah,' he said solemnly, 'I formally release you. You are no longer a slave, but a freedwoman. I will have a document of manumission drawn up.' He drew her to him, and saluted her lightly on the cheek. 'Go with Miriam now and arrange for a date of formal betrothal. Simeon, you may kiss her, and then come with me. We ride into Capernaum.'

They tethered their horses outside an inn, then Claudius set off, not through the rich area of the town where lay the villas of the few wealthy Jews he knew, mostly collaborators, but through the humbler streets. Simeon realized that they were heading in the direction of Peter the fisherman's house. Claudius brisk steps faltered. He seemed unable to decide whether to go forward or not.

Then there came a shout, 'Simeon, here!' David waved to them in greeting, from the rooftop of a neighbouring house. It was that of the Zebedee family.

'Wait—I'm coming down.' He was as good as his word. 'I am so glad to see you! Centurion Claudius, greetings sir! Simeon!' he clapped his brothers shoulders. 'What brings you here?'

'I wish to see the Lady Joanna,' said Claudius. Simeon glanced at him. What was it that made him feel, that this was not the sole purpose of the expedition. Yet it was logical! But he watched as Claudius eyes strayed towards the door of Peter's house.

'Jesus has gone for a while,' said David, seeing the overt glance.

'Oh, for how long,' questioned Simeon in dismay.

'I can only tell you, what Simon the Zealot told me,' said David, glancing slightly uneasily at the Centurion. How could one trust a Roman, even this man? 'Well, the Holy One called the twelve together and gave them power and authority to drive out all demons, and to cure diseases, as he sent them out to preach the Kingdom of God and to heal the sick.'

'What,' said Simeon! 'He gave this authority, his authority, to them? Did Simon say anything else?'

'Yes. He told them to "Take nothing for the journey, no staff, no bags, no bread and no extra tunic. Whatever house you enter, stay there until you leave that town. If people do not welcome you, shake the dust off your feet when you leave their town, as a testimony against them!" So you see, I am once more alone, but no, that is not true for many of us in Capernaum are meeting to discuss the Holy One's teachings so that we may more fully understand.' David's face held a fervour that touched Claudius, who had stood silent during this exchange.

He had heard David described as a young firebrand, but could see in him the same gentleness of spirit, mixed with a glowing ardour, that was evinced in his brother Simeon, and which he was to find was typical of all who followed the Holy One. It was as though a lamp of joy had been lit within, shining out through the eyes and whole personality.

Then David recalled the Centurion's question about Joanna.

'But you asked for the Lady Joanna. If you will follow me, I will bring you to her. She is staying in the house of Mary of Magdala. Why there she is—Mary, that is!' he gestured to a tall, beautiful woman who walked towards them. She was simply garbed in a cream tunic, a veil covering the glorious hair of which she was so proud. But nothing could disguise the exquisite planes of her face, now devoid of the heavy cosmetics which used to reveal her trade a few days ago, now a lifetime away.

She smiled in greeting to David, then turned as a man who had been following her, calling out her name, now managed to draw level. She turned round to him. The men did not hear what suggestion he made to Mary, called Magdalene, but they did see her reaction. She fetched him a buffet on the ear that sent him into the gutter.

'I could do with her amongst my guards,' marvelled Claudius, with a broad smile upon his lips. 'I wonder what the fellow said to the lady to so distress her!'

David hesitated. Then he whispered quietly, for Mary was turning towards them again, and he certainly did not wish to experience the same fate, as the well dressed citizen, who was trying to restore both his dignity and stained clothing, for everything collected in that noisome gutter.

'Mary was a lady who dispensed her charms liberally.'

'You mean, a prostitute,' asked Claudius bluntly?

'Yes, but is so no longer. Jesus cast seven devils out of her and forgave her sins, and she has changed completely, is another person,' declared David.

'Has been reborn,' murmured Simeon, remembering Jesus teaching of Nicodemus.

'Yes. She now has a problem though. There are many who remember her erstwhile activities, and come to her as they used, only now Mary either blisters them with her tongue, or takes stronger action!' His voice tailed off, as Mary reached them.

'Greetings, David,' she said lightly, as though nothing untoward had happened. 'Lady Joanna is asking for you. I think she wants to get word to, well,' she fixed Claudius uniform with a surprised glance 'I suppose it might be word to you, Centurion. I take it you are Centurion Claudius?'

Claudius looked at her bemused. He had never been spoken to before by a woman, in this brusque manner Women were quiet creatures, who bowed before you, were soothing. They did not address a man as an equal. Yet there was something engagingly fresh in her manner.

'Yes, Lady Mary,' said Claudius, giving her the courtesy title. 'I have come here to contact the Lady Joanna.'

'Mary will do, Mary of Magdala, though once of Bethany,' she added wistfully. 'Joanna is in my house, so if you like to follow me, you and...?' She glanced at Simeon curiously. 'Ah, I see the resemblance! David, this is your brother.'

She led them back the way she had come, the streets clearing swiftly, as people saw the Centurion's uniform. There were some mutterings and Simeon felt uneasy on Claudius account.

The home they entered was simply though comfortably furnished. Mary had taken this little house to retreat to, when life in Tiberias and Magdala became too hectic. She had made a good living in the past, entertaining Herod's guests in the palace, as well as any visiting rich citizen who was able to reward her substantially for use of her body. Even here in Capernaum, many had seen Mary coming home in the early hours, swaying from the heavy drinking which blotted out reality, and shouting bawdy songs, until she collapsed into her doorway.

She beckoned the men inside, and opened the shutters. A low couch piled with cushions took up one wall, in front of it a chest, which could also serve as a table. There were two chairs. Embroidered rugs were strewn on the stone floor.

A voice could be heard singing in the room beyond. Mary knocked then opened the door. They heard her in brief conversation, then Lady Joanna appeared. She was simply dressed, in a plain white tunic, her hair braided. Although her beautiful violet eyes were still deeply shadowed from the suffering she had endured, the crazed look of fear had completely disappeared. Instead, her face bore an expression of deep peace, her whole manner tranquil, composed.

'Lady Joanna, greetings.' Centurion Claudius bowed and then smiled gravely. 'Dear lady, I do not need to ask how you are, it is all too marvellously evident.'

'Centurion Claudius, dear friend, it is only today that I have been told of all that you and your lady did for me, that I owe my life and my sanity to you both!' She took his hands and smiled up at him. 'I would surely have died in Tiberias, had you not carried me to Capernaum and brought me to the Lord Jesus.'

'She slept all of yesterday,' explained Mary.

'As did my wife,' said Claudius. 'Miriam is anxious to see you, Joanna. You must know that you have a home with us, for as long as you wish. Perhaps eventually, you may decide that you want to return home to the Lord Chuza and your life at Herod's court?'

'No, Claudius,' she interrupted gently. 'I shall never be returning to the court, nor to my husband. I have finished with that corrupt atmosphere forever. From now onwards, I shall be a humble follower of the Lord Jesus, spend my life trying to live in the manner he teaches.'

Claudius listened to her in shocked surprise. She didn't realize what she was saying! Lady Joanna was a member of the nobility. She had been brought up in a palace, had never known deprivation of any kind. How could someone of this type, possibly hope to cope with the pressures of an impecunious existence, mixing with the common people and furthermore, if she really meant to follow Jesus and his disciples, then to lead a nomadic, and definitely a dangerous life. No. It was unthinkable. But was it? The serene young woman standing before him had a light shining out of her eyes that set her apart as one whose life had been touched by the presence of the Holy One. He sensed the difference, the strength in her.

'You mean it, don't you? Where will you stay?'

'Here with Mary to start with, if she will have me.' She turned to the Magdalene, who nodded corroboration. 'But first, Centurion Claudius, I want to visit my dear friend Miriam, for I do long to see her again and to thank her.'

'This will be a great delight to Miriam. Lady, I will take you now. Our horses are close by. You shall sit behind me, for it is but a short ride. Come Simeon, my son. What of you, David?'

'I must return to Zebedee,' replied David. He watched as minutes later, the three disappeared in the direction of the villa. He still could not come to terms, with his own brother, living with an enemy and calling him father! But it was on the whispered news Simeon had conveyed to him, that his young brother was to take a wife that David mused, as he wandered down to the seashore where old Zebedee sat mending nets.

'Where have you been, you young idler,' scolded Zebedee. 'Your eyes are full of dreams. Your thoughts are turned on some maiden, well?' He stroked his full grey beard as he spoke and turned his shrewd fisherman's eyes on David.

'Her name is Sarah,' replied David, 'and I have never met her!'

'So, what riddle is this?'

'My brother Simeon is to become betrothed to a Samaritan girl and her name is Sarah.'

'Why, but these are happy tidings, David. Sarah, a good name, the name of Abraham's wife! However, a pity she is a Samaritan! How old is your brother?'

'Fifteen. He had his birthday a week ago.'

'And you, David---how old are you?'

He smiled as David threw out his chest, and said, 'Almost seventeen!' their conversation was interrupted at this point, as a shadow fell across the shingle where they sat. They looked up and David saw again, the strong, cruel features, of a man he would never forget—Barabbas!

He had not seen him since the night of his parent's death, on the one and only occasion on which their paths had crossed. The intense black eyes bored down on him, and automatically he sprang to his feet.

'Barabbas!'

'Yes, David, son of Ezra, Barabbas!' he clapped David across the shoulders, merely nodding to Zebedee, as he said, 'Let us walk along the shore, for I feel we have much to discuss.' David desperately wished to refuse, wanted no further connection with the Zealot chief. He had made his decision after long discussions with Simon. He was now a follower of Jesus of Nazareth, and had put aside all his pretensions to the Zealot brotherhood.

'So, David, you carried out your first commission extremely well it would seem. I asked you together with Simon, to discover the whereabouts of the Messiah and here you are closely involved with Jesus disciples! Excellent, I had hoped to have seen Simon, but have been informed that he has left Capernaum, would you know where he has gone?'

David stopped walking and faced Barabbas squarely.

'Barabbas, there is something which I must say to you. A member of your band kidnapped me on the night of my father's murder, indeed, had it not been for your intervention in my affairs, I would have been present to make my own answer to the Romans, and that would have prevented my parent's death!' His eyes met those of the Zealot chieftain, without a trace of fear. There was a new strength in him, a maturity.

Barabbas recognized it and changed his tactics accordingly. He appeared to consider, then replied in even tones, 'If you believe my men were in any way responsible for your parents deaths, then I regret this—but would suggest to you, young man, that without my intervention, you would probably also be dead now!'

'You took my money and then sent me off with Simon, merely because it suited you and because I could identify the Messiah.' David's words were chosen to sting, and they did. Barabbas eyes narrowed angrily. He bared his teeth in a smile and David felt he resembled nothing so much as a leopard about to spring. But Barabbas was used to controlling men, knew the psychology involved in dealing with a young idealist such as David.

'So, David, you have been greatly privileged to be able to associate with the Messiah. Many would envy you this, to be able to listen at all times to the teachings of the Holy One, to be present at his secret councils. His fame has spread in these few short months right across our land, from Judea to the furthermost territories of Tetrarch Phillip! Soon, the whole region will be ready to rise and carry him in triumph through to Jerusalem, proclaim him our King! How wonderful it will be for you David, to be at the Messiah's side when he leads us to victory against Rome, for we will shed every last drop of Jewish blood to drive the invaders into the sea!'

Almost in spite of himself David felt the words of the Zealot leader infuse his senses. His dormant hatred of Rome quivered through his brain, like the chords of a throbbing harp. Once more he saw Naomi's dead face and his father's glazing eyes, then a curtain of light shut off the memories. He heard again the words spoken on the mount by Jesus—"Love your enemies, do good to those who hate you, bless those who curse you!" He looked full on Barabbas, and uttered the words out loud.

'Love your enemies—do good to those who hate you! Bless those who curse you! Pray for those who ill treat you. If someone strikes you on one cheek, turn to him the other also!'

'What nonsense is this?' exclaimed Barabbas scathingly! 'These are the words of a madman! Who can love an enemy? Whence had you this ridiculous philosophy, boy?'

'These are the words of the Son of God,' replied David quietly. 'He has come from the Father to bring peace to our world—not the sword.'

'How can there be peace, when our land is under Roman rule! When our citizens are murdered on the whim of a power crazed Emperor, who names himself god! When Roman soldiers can burn and pillage our towns, rape our women and sell our people as slaves! When we are taxed beyond our ability to pay, in order to finance the great circuses held in Rome, where human beings are fed to wild animals for the pleasure of the masses! Where is your loyalty to our land, David, to our people? The Romans put your parents to the sword! Six of them, raped my young wife. I found her in a pool of blood. As I bent over her to hold her to me, she whispered her shame and seized the dagger from my belt and plunged it into her breast, killing herself and our unborn child! His voice broke.

'Tell me, David, son of Ezra—should I forgive the Romans?'

David's eyes filled with pity, as Barabbas revealed the tragedy of his wife's death, for it explained so much about the man, his burning hatred of Rome. He placed a comforting hand on the Zealot's arm. It was shrugged off.

'Barabbas, what can I say, except that my heart bleeds for you, a thing like that—such terrible hurt for any man to sustain, I understand your hatred, because I myself have dealt with this same destructive force for reasons which you know of. When I left your camp with Simon, I went screaming into the night, so full of hate that I even cried out that there was no God, I blasphemed! Then a serpent stung me. For a week, I lay between life and death with Simon caring for me. My life force was ebbing away. Then something happened, Barabbas.'

'So, what was it?' The Zealot's interest was aroused. He had heard the story of David's healing, but only absorbed in clinical fashion, that here was excellent propaganda to confirm Jesus Messiahship, had even vaguely wondered whether it was fabrication, cleverly put forward by Simon and David, for there were no witnesses. If it were, then he heartily approved it. But as he looked at David's face, he knew that this lad would never lie, could not.

'Tell me, what was it that happened, David, son of Ezra?'

'The Holy One bent over me. He called me to arise, knew my name. I was healed from that moment. Simon will tell you, that I was all but dead, my heel putrefying. But Barabbas, it was not simply that my flesh had been healed, so had my soul. All my venomous hatred towards those who had killed my parents had left me.'

'So, you immediately loved all Romans, accepted their presence in our land, our people's subjection?' Barabbas scanned his face in scornful disbelief.

'No, not that either. For some months, I struggled internally, with my feelings of aggression towards those who represent Rome. There was still a natural instinct to want to struggle, take arms if necessary. But it is not the answer, Barabbas. Violence only breeds violence!' He paused and looked Barabbas keenly in the eyes.

'Tell me, Barabbas, have you taken life yourself, killed any in revenge for your wife's death?' The Zealots face darkened with the surge of blood under the skin, his pupils dilated, as he screamed---

'Yes—I have killed many for this reason, David, son of Ezra, and will kill many more. I have plunged my dagger into their guts, and left them screaming for the release of death and have joyed in their agony! Does that afflict that lily white soul of yours, lad? Do you shrink from me?' The malevolence in his glance, juddered through David's soul, in its tearing, rending cruelty. Yet at the back of all this hate, was the deeply wounded spirit of another human being desperate for healing, and finding it nowhere, lashing out in ever deepening assault on those he held to blame, lacerating his own soul more and more in the process. Suddenly he shot a great hand out and seized the front of David's tunic, almost lifting him off his feet and shaking him like a dog with a rat. Calmly, David raised both of his hands and with quick movement, pressed upon a certain point in the Zealot's arm. With a curse, Barabbas let go, exclaiming at the numbing pain the pressure on the nerve had caused.

'How learned you that trick, boy?'

'From Simon, amongst other things, now calm yourself, Barabbas! To lose control of our feelings only exposes our weaknesses.' David straightened his tunic.

Again curses broke from Barabbas lips. It was humiliating to be taught the basics of understanding and controlling men by this unbearded stripling, yet now he viewed David with a grudging respect mixed with exasperation. What was this new strength that the boy had acquired, an ability to distance himself from natural aggression, yet with no slightest sign of cowardice.

'Barabbas, I have learned much from the teachings of the Holy One. Some of it seems almost impossible to put into practice, when listened to from the bastion of selfishness, behind which all human beings hide. To put ourselves first is our prime motive, to take what we want from life, to wreak vengeance on those who destroy or take what is ours, to impose our will on others. It is only when we start to empty ourselves of self, that we are then able to really understand the words of Jesus, who is the Living Word of God and to walk in His ways.'

Doubt, an almost softening towards belief, followed by despairing anger, flooded across Barabbas face. He raised his great fists, to the blue Galilean sky and screamed an oath of defiance. Then he stared at David.

'How say you boy, if placed before you, bound and at your mercy, those Roman fiends who murdered your parents, what would you do, Huh! Would you love your enemy boy?'

His probing words brought mental picture of faceless soldiers, dripping blood, before David's inner vision! Then came memory of a night on a nearby mountain, the moon silvering the scene with gentle radiance, as the Holy One taught his disciples and all those others who sat around, listening to the Son of God.

'Do not judge and you will not be judged. Do not condemn, and you will not be condemned, forgive—and you will be forgiven!' He quoted the words softly, and Barabbas dropped his hands to his sides, shaking his great head helplessly.

'I see that it is impossible to reason with you, David. But one day you may have to make a real choice, not mere play on words. Until then, I will leave you. Ah, yes, there is one thing more though! I hear that your younger brother has been adopted as his son, by the Roman Centurion, who lives nearby. It would no doubt explain your lack of animosity towards the enemy. Tell your brother and those whom he now holds as kin, to beware how he associates with scum! We almost removed this particular Centurion from the face of the earth a few weeks back, will not make a mistake the next time. His so called relatives had better beware!'

Before David could remonstrate, Barabbas had turned on his heel, and a mocking-----'Farewell, David, son of Ezra,' floated on the air.

Chapter Eleven

Simon the Zealot's dark skinned face stared unseeingly into the distance, where a scant mile ahead, the lights of a small village glimmered in the brief, violet twilight. At his side, tramped the one man amongst the twelve whom he held in contempt, Judas named Iscariot. Why, he asked himself, of all the disciples had the Holy One instructed Judas to accompany him? But Judas seemed impervious to the lack of communication shown by his companion. He chattered much of the power that would be shared by all of them should Jesus be declared King—and of money!

At last, Simon could stand it no longer. He stopped in his tracks, and stared at Judas coldly. Had the man so little understanding of the teaching of Jesus—that it was of a deep reverence for God, of love and caring, a putting of others before self.

'Judas, what does being a disciple of the Holy One actually mean to you?'

'What does it mean? That is a strange question, my brother! For so many years our people have struggled under the Roman yoke—have suffered humiliation, slavery, death! But at the back of each bruised heart, one thought has given glimmer of hope, that one day, one glorious day the Messiah would arise, to lead our people against Rome! I see in Jesus of Nazareth the leader who will unite us in this holy struggle.'

'But the Holy One always teaches of peace!'

'Oh, I know—I know! But that is only a blind, it must be. He has power over men Simon, power to heal, power to draw them to him like a magnet. I believe that he only bides time until his fame encompasses the whole land, before declaring himself King! Once he does Simon, then your party the Zealots, will mobilize behind him and so will mine!' Saying this, Judas Iscariot produced a sicar from within his robe, a short, curved dagger, the dull glint of it just discernible in the half light.

'So it's true,' exclaimed Simon. 'You are a dagger man, a Sicarii!' He stared in amazement as Judas made darting, thrusting movements around him at incredible speed. Faster and faster his hand flew and Simeon stood immobile, knowing that death had kissed him about fifty times. Then with a low chuckle, Judas sheathed his evil weapon.

'Yes, Simon. I am a Sicarii, and proud of it! Many times, I have dipped my blade in the heart of a collaborator. We have a list Simon, a long, long list of those who grow fat at the hands of their Roman masters, feeding like maggots on the wounded flesh of Israel. Oh, I know that members of your party look on the Sicarii as fanatics, but you need us, oh how you need us to cleanse our land of the filth that defiles our nation!

'And you really believe, that Jesus would consent to head a rebellion that would bring even greater hardship and suffering to our people? You have walked with him these many weeks, Judas, you know his heart. Yes, he grieves for his children, for their pain in the terrible exploitation that has taken place. But you are mistaken, if you believe he has come to lead an army. His Kingdom is a heavenly one, Judas!' The note of conviction in Simon's voice in no way disturbed his companion, for Judas chuckled again.

'Well, let us see that this Kingdom of Heaven is born on earth,' he said. 'I am surprised at you, Simon. You are a Zealot, born of a much respected father. Your own reputation as a freedom fighter and organizer makes you welcome in every household where men are not frightened to stand for what they believe in. What's happened to you man? I was delighted to find that you were to be my partner on this first commission entrusted to us by the master. I thought that we would share much in common! I now ask you one simple question. Simon, are you still a Zealot?'

Before Simon could answer, a figure bounded down between them, from an overhanging shelf of rock.

'You, dagger man, do not have the right to ask this question—but I do!' Simon looked at the figure in near disbelief. It couldn't be, but it was. Barabbas!

'Barabbas!' How long had the Zealot chieftain crouched above their heads? How much had he overheard?

'Am I the devil that you put on such a long face, Simon? But come, it was wrong of me to surprise you in such a way. Nay friend, you will not need that!' He moved like lightning, sending the dagger which had leapt to the fanatic's hand spinning into the undergrowth. The man's howl of anguish was more for the loss of his dagger, than of pain. With a curse, he started to grope for his weapon. Barabbas slipped an arm about Simon's shoulders.

'That will keep him occupied long enough for us to talk. He will not leave that spot until he has found his toy!'

'But beware him once he finds it, Barabbas.' Simon knew that his heart was thudding, for soon he was going to have to declare his new allegiance to Barabbas.

'Pshaw! Should I fear such a creature? One who creeps around in the dark! He is of unbalanced mind like all Sicarii. I am the more surprised that the Messiah has included one of this murdering crew amongst his disciples.' Barabbas drew them behind a grove of stunted trees then threw himself on the ground. Simon dropped beside him.

'I had heard that you were in Galilee again Barabbas, so why have you waited this long to contact me?' Simon could hardly make out his companion's features now in the gathering darkness.

'Out of diplomacy—I had no wish to intrude into the closed community of disciples the Messiah has attracted about him. You are of sufficient stature not to need me to advise you how to act. I depend on you Simon, as do the rest of your colleagues, to alert us when the time is right for us to rise. We have complete and utter trust in you, my young friend. Even the way in which you diplomatically parried the questions of Judas, makes me more secure in that trust. Your father, together with Zadduk, was the founder of our movement. Under his son, the whole nation will come to bless his name, and yours!'

Barabbas had a mind that analyzed situations at amazing speed, sifting every grain of information, noting each least inflection of the voice, sensing apprehension in another like a physical smell, and Simon was apprehensive and Barabbas knew why. The unbelievable was happening. Simon, so very strong in the Zealot movement was becoming infected with whatever spiritual malaise it was, that could turn tough fighting man, into a pacifist. What immense power was it that Jesus of Nazareth held over men that could so change a man's heart, his allegiance?

But Barabbas knew enough about men to realize that if he accused Simon of shifting his loyalty from the Zealots, that this would merely cause resentment and deepen a rift between them. Barabbas own loyalty to the party was born of a deep seated spirit of revenge, whereas Simon like that young fool David, was an idealist. It was to that idealism that he now appealed and Simon weakened before the knowledge that many thousands of Zealots were looking to his leadership.

'The Holy One shows no sign as yet of seeking kingship or military might. The world has never seen his like before, Barabbas. Yes, his heart tears in anguish for the conditions in our land. His compassion is for the homeless, the beggars who almost outnumber those in work, is infinite. No sick person ever comes to him seeking healing in vain. He works among those afflicted in mind and spirit until he almost drops from fatigue. But he is but a single man and for this reason, he has given power to the twelve to go out in his name, to heal the sick and exorcise demons!'

'You mean that he has given this authority—to you, Simon?' Barabbas shot his great head forward in amazement. 'I had heard that the disciples were going out to the villages by twos, but I thought this was merely to preach!' This put an even more complicated complexion on the situation. If Simon had been invested with healing powers, then he would be an even more important link with the Messiah.

'Barabbas, I can promise you only one thing. Should Jesus ever decide to declare himself officially not only Messiah, the Son of God—but a military leader, if he ever sets up a banner, calls men to fight against Rome, then you and my comrades will hear from me immediately. But I must warn you, Barabbas, that I truly never expect this to happen.' He rose to his feet, as did Barabbas. Suddenly Barabbas clapped his arms about Simon and hugged him, in an unusual show of emotion.

'Dear lad, I can only repeat, that I have complete trust in you. The changed world that Jesus wants, to me it sounds like an impossibility. You cannot change the evil that lies within men's hearts with soft words. Yet, if such thing could be, then Jesus of Nazareth will have achieved something that no one else ever has, since the beginning of time.' He walked Simon back along the path, seeking Judas. They found the man sitting calmly beside the path, where they had left him.

'You found your sicar then?' inquired Barabbas mockingly.

'Yes! It would no have been produced in the first place had you announced your arrival less precipitately,' replied Judas in aggrieved tones. 'I have heard much of you, Barabbas. Do you accompany us to the village?'

'No. I fear I must deprive you of my presence, but you can always look for me behind the next bush or rock, beside a stream as you bend to drink. So take good care of this friend of mine, of Simon the Zealot. He is very precious to our party!'

He was gone, his movements so swift, so sure, that no twig crackled under his departing feet. Only a mocking laugh marked his passage.

The two men walked in silence now, each caught in the turmoil of their own thoughts. At last the lights of the village shone in front of them, and a pack of barking dogs announced their presence. They had obeyed the Master's instructions and brought no food with them and Simon at least had brought no money, but Judas had a hidden purse strapped underneath his tunic next to his dagger. Both men were very weary and hungry and slightly concerned at the greeting they were likely to receive, coming like beggars out of the night.

Although lights shone from all of the small houses, none were abroad after dark except at the end of the narrow street, where the sounds of revelry came from an inn. Then three men surrounded them, darting out of the shadows.

'Alms—alms for the poor,' they intoned, skinny arms outstretched, rags flapping about emaciated forms, as a sudden wind arose, moaning down from a gully in the hills. One of the men looked Judas in the face, and he shrank back in distaste as he saw the leonine cast of feature that betokened leprosy.

'He is a leper!' Judas sprang back involuntarily, but not so Simon. He looked at the man confidently and walked towards him.

'Unclean—unclean,' warned the leper, drawing back amazed. But Simon still advanced and placing a hand on the man's arm, he looked him straight in the eyes.

'Have you heard of Jesus of Nazareth,' he asked gently.

'Why yes, my master. He is the miracle worker and teacher. We have heard much of him, of the wonders he performs.' The leper tried to extricate himself from the stranger's grasp. If he were found touching one not similarly afflicted he could be stoned to death.

'I am one of the Lord Jesus disciples,' said Simon. 'Do you believe that Jesus has the power to cure you of leprosy?'

The man's features formed themselves into an expression of hope. He drew a quavering breath. 'I do,' he said simply.

'Then by the power vested in me, by Jesus of Nazareth—be made whole.' As Simon spoke, he felt power surging through his body, flooding outwards, a stream of living water wrought of his faith in the Son of God. And as Judas looked on in wonder, he saw the man's distorted face eaten by the hungry evil that was leprosy, realign itself. The mutilated stumps of fingers seemed to quiver, to move and now the man leapt in joy, clapping those same hands in an ecstasy beyond words. The handsome face that stared wonderingly back at him, had tears flooding down cheeks as smooth as a child's.

'Go and wash yourself. Tomorrow, show yourself to the priests and give praise to God our Father, in whose name the Lord Jesus brings healing,' said Simon. The other lepers had fallen to their knees in awe. They were shaking with fear—and a dawning hope, for they also were lepers.

'Lord—lord!' they called to Simon, not daring to put their prayer into words. He smiled down at them, and kneeling put a hand on the shoulders of each.

'Call me not Lord, my friends. I am but a humble servant of Jesus of Nazareth, but in his name I ask you to repent of your sins.'

'We do—yes, we do,' whispered the lepers, tears pouring down their deformed cheeks. 'Of your mercy we ask for healing, will find and follow the Holy One, all of our days.'

'Then in the name of Jesus of Nazareth, be made clean!' As he spoke the words, again Simon felt the Holy Spirit of God, pouring anointing through him, using him as a channel to heal the two men who knelt so humbly in the dusty road. Simon rose and looked down on them in complete confidence, and it happened as before, ugly, distorted faces blurred, as their structure was reformed before his eyes, limbs reshaping in the same manner. They looked at each other, crying aloud at the miracle of their healing. Then they staggered about on feet that now had toes, learning new balance.

'Go with your friend, bathe and forget not to present yourselves before the priests for examination in the morning, according to the Law.

'All praise and honour to Almighty God and to his Prophet, the Lord Jesus,' murmured one man brokenly. 'Pray, what is your name, master?'

'Simon,' he said.

'Simon, called the Zealot?' It was the first man to be healed, who looked at the disciple. 'Even hidden away in the hills, we have heard much of the Holy One, and the names of his disciples. But I once saw you, Simon, before I was stricken with leprosy and when you were but a youth. It was a few years ago, at a meeting of the Zealots in Capernaum. Yes, Simon, I also was once a Zealot.'

Simon stared keenly at the man, looking at him objectively for the first time in the dim lighting of the quiet street. He knew so many hundreds of party members, had met more men than he could ever remember, yet the face of this man, stirred a hidden chord in his memory.

'My name is Nathan. I once owned a small vineyard and was forced to sell it to pay the heavy taxes levied on me. I then worked as a manager for Azor, he who is an elder in the synagogue in Capernaum.'

'And who is a Roman collaborator,' breathed Judas Iscariot. He was about to add that Azor's name was on the Sicarii's assassination list, but caution made him hold his peace.

'Some have named him so,' said Nathan quietly. 'One thing only will I say in his favour, he took my daughter Miriam into his home as a servant when I was driven out of the town, when the priests declared me unclean. That was almost six years ago otherwise, she would have had to beg her bread and she might have fallen prey to all kinds of evil.' Nathan dashed a tear from his eye, as he murmured, 'My dear wife is dead these many years. I tried to bring up Miriam myself. Life was good although a struggle while I still had my vineyard. Azor offered me a low price for it, but I had to let it go to pay the Roman tax. It was then that I worked for Azor in his large vineyard, but I knew he had taken advantage of my critical situation. I often wonder about Miriam. She was twelve when I was cast out, must be almost eighteen now.'

'Tell me, my friend, how did your daughter Miriam look?'

'Why, like any other ill-nourished twelve year old girl. Skinny, hair black as the raven's wing, but unusual eyes, green as the fresh leaves on a fig tree.' He smiled sadly, as he recalled the young girl who had wept so bitterly and attempted to hang onto him, as he did the hardest thing any parent can do, turned his back on his child.

'I have been living in Capernaum and I think I can give you news of your daughter. There is a Centurion based in the town, whose name is Claudius. He is an honourable man, if any Roman can be named such, that is! Well, he recently married a young girl. She is said to have worked as a maid-servant in the house of Azor. Her name is Miriam and it is said, that she is beautiful as she is good and from what has been mentioned to me, by a young friend she has eyes the colour of jade.'

Simon watched Nathan's face light up with joy. She was alive and well. What if she were married to a Roman, distressing though such news was! Suddenly, Nathan realized that he would be able to see her again. He raised his hands in praise, as he breathed a prayer of gratitude to the mighty God of Israel, to whom all things were possible. His two comrades joined him in his prayers. None of them looked at Judas, whose eyes had narrowed, as he stored away the information he had just learned about the Centurion's wife.

'Shalom! Greetings my friends! Forgive that I intrude, but I must confess to having seen and overheard, all that has just passed from my window.' They swung around in surprise, and saw one dressed in the robes of a Pharisee standing in the doorway of the adjacent house. 'My name is Eleazar. I am a Pharisee. Will you honour my humble house by entering and allowing me to offer you hospitality?'

Simon and Judas remembered the instructions of Jesus, that whatsoever house they entered when they arrived in a village, they were to remain there for the duration of their stay and the idea of staying under the roof of a Pharisee certainly did not appeal. But Eleazar smiled, and held the door open. The lepers had disappeared into the shadows, so slightly hesitantly the two disciples bowed their thanks and entered.

They gratefully accepted the customary courtesy of being able to cleanse themselves, the cool water deliciously refreshing after the long walk along the hot, dusty road. Then they reclined, shoulder to shoulder, on a couch, facing Eleazar. An elderly woman brought food to the table then quietly withdrew. Eleazar said a blessing, and broke the bread. They dipped into the mutton stew, gradually warming to their host, as they relaxed. He was an elderly man, with an inner serenity, which came across to them in his gentle words. Although Jesus spoke in scathing terms about the majority of the Pharisees, nevertheless, there were still many like this man, who were godly men, spending their lives teaching the local people, interpreting scripture and also, as Eleazar mentioned of his own duties, teaching the village boys in school. Young boys received their education from the age of five until early manhood, which was reached at the onset of puberty at thirteen. This instruction of the scriptures to Israel's young male population, ascertaining that they had committed most of the Hebrew text by heart, was of supreme importance in keeping the practice of the law a living force, deep rooted in their hearts and channelling unadulterated love and respect for Almighty God, whose name, Jehovah, was almost too sacred to be mentioned.

'How many boys do you teach,' inquired Simon?

'Over a hundred, but surely you are not really interested in my humble activities, whereas I must admit to enormous curiosity about your master and his teachings. I saw you with my own eyes bring healing to three lepers, by the power of Jesus name! Whence cometh this power, my friends? Is it of God, or of Beelzebub?' He lowered his voice as he spoke, as though almost ashamed.

'You, Eleazar, are a learned man, to whom the education of our young is entrusted. How is it that such as you, can phrase such terrible thought! Can good come of evil, light to the soul out of darkness, healing and forgiveness of sins from the devil? Surely it doesn't need a simple man, without your deep knowledge garnered over the years, to show you truth that shines like a beacon flame! Have you not heard, that Jesus of Nazareth is he of whom John the Baptist forecast, "One more powerful than I will come, the thongs of whose sandals I am not worthy to untie! He will baptise you with the Holy Spirit and with fire!" It is of this power of the Holy Spirit, endued of Almighty God, that Jesus brings forgiveness and healing to our people and now sends us his disciples, out to bring healing in his name.' Simon's face was alight with the passion of his message and his faith. Eleazar nodded slowly.

'Forgive me. Forgive me Simon that I doubted. You must understand that others in recent times have attempted healing, by spells and incantations. I once heard of a wandering Egyptian, who charged great sums for so called cures of those unfortunates, whose demented minds locked their bodies into physical illness, that these people then lapsed back into their previous state after a period of time.' Eleazar's face was grave, as he explained his reason for doubting. Then a smile spread gently across his features as he said, 'Since the news of the wondrous healing power of Jesus of Nazareth came to my ears, I have wanted to believe but because of the responsibility I bear as a Pharisee, I had to be sure. What I saw with my own eyes on the street tonight, confirms my hopes that Jesus might indeed be the one spoken of by the Prophet Isaiah.'

'To what prophecy do you refer, Rabbi?' asked Judas, leaning forward. Then Eleazar quoted from the prophet.

'As Isaiah said--"In the future, He will honour Galilee of the Gentiles, by way of the sea, along the Jordan! The people in darkness have seen a great light, for to us a child is born, to us a child is given, and the government will be on his shoulders, and he will be called Wonderful Councillor, Mighty God, Everlasting Father, and Prince of Peace. He will reign on David's throne and over his kingdom, establishing and upholding it, with justice and righteousness, from that time on and forever." He paused and added musingly, 'Long have I pondered on these words and others spoken by Isaiah!'

'Speak on, oh learned one,' breathed Judas, as belief dawned in his eyes and a blaze of ambition, that was to consume his soul. But it was on Simon, that Eleazar bent his gaze.

'You my son, have already studied this prophecy, and others, have you not' he probed gently. 'Tell me Simon, do you consider that your Master is indeed the Messiah long awaited by his people, as foretold by our holy men down the ages?'

'Yes, I believe that he is,' said Simon quietly, 'But not that he is a military leader, in the sense that the Jews have envisaged the promised one. No, Eleazar, I am a Zealot, who have fought and dreamed for Israel's freedom from the hand of the Roman oppressors. I took up position at Jesus side, from the time he was acclaimed of John and now realize that Jesus of Nazareth leads his people towards a spiritual kingdom, not an earthly one! If we follow his teachings, then we are indeed free. If despite all that the Romans can do to us a man is free within his own soul of cruelty and hatred and if he can accept without bitterness, the worst that this world can do to him, then the heavenly kingdom of God is already born within his own heart! After death, the next life will be an extension of that pure love and selflessness, in the presence of the majesty of the Living God, before whose throne, we will all prostrate ourselves, singing praises with all the angels and the prophets.'

Simon's eyes had filled with that strange light of confidence and joy, as these words poured from his lips. Eleazar rose instinctively to his feet, and raised his hands in blessing over the head of the younger man.

'May the blessings of the Most High, be upon your Master, His Son, and upon you his servant, Simon.' A flash of jealousy, stabbed across

Judas face, as he sat still and silent, his thoughts on a very different plane.

The sun had risen. Already the street was full of curious villagers. The story of the lepers healing, had passed from door to door, and the people had poured outside to see for themselves the two disciples of Jesus of Nazareth, who had wrought these wonders. Some of the men of the village had already attended the huge gatherings that attended Jesus passage wherever he went, they knew of his teachings, his miracles, but now it seemed, the Holy One had passed some of his power to his disciples.

An old man, crippled with arthritis, hobbled behind the crowd that had assembled outside Eleazar's house.

'All honour be to Jesus and his disciples,' people called hopefully. Their voices became louder, querulous, until eventually the door opened, and Eleazar appeared. They fell silent before his reproving gaze but seeing the forms of the two disciples behind him, they strained their voices again.

'Peace upon you,' said Judas, unctuously, and pushed forward, between the people, joying in the respectful way, they fell back before him. At last, Judas drew level with the old cripple. His glance took in the twisted limbs, bowed back, and knotted fingers, which he raised beseechingly to Judas.

'Of your mercy, disciple of the Holy One, I humbly pray your blessing and that these tortured limbs of mine might be released!' His wavering cry was heard by those around him, who looked expectantly at Judas. The dagger man revelled in the situation, the knowledge that it lay within his power to cure the wretch before him. In this moment, Judas forgot all that he had learned of Jesus teaching of humility, that it was of faith in the Holy Spirit of God, born of love, reflected from the Father, by way of the Son, bringing His healing of love to His people. Judas spoke from his own prideful heart and from his ambition.

'You there, old man!' he sucked in his breath, 'Stand up, be straight!' He looked confidently at the bowed form before him. But nothing happened. So again, this time with a tinge of uncertainty in his voice, he called out, 'Old man, stand straight! Be healed of your affliction!'

All eyes were on the elderly arthritic, known to all those in the village. His condition had worsened over the years and all knew the pain he bore in the most mundane of life's matters. No doctor could cure this condition, or alleviate the symptoms in any slightest degree. So now they looked on, knowing that only a genuine miracle could relieve old Jacob's misery. But nothing was happening! Judas face flamed darkly red, under his bronzed skin, his eyes hardened, and now the look he cast on the old supplicant, anything but kindly.

Simon had followed closely behind Judas, and had overheard the whole episode. He stood hesitant then pushed forward, to stand at Judas side.

'How are you named, my father,' he asked gently, to old Jacob?

'Jacob, once the tent maker to this town—and you, my son, are also disciple of Jesus of Nazareth?' The weary eyes were turned forlornly upon him.

'Jacob, do you repent of your sins?' The man inclined his head. 'I do, most humbly,' his voice broke on a sob.

'Then in the name of Jesus of Nazareth, receive your healing!' At this before the wondering gaze of all who pressed around, Jacob straightened his back, seemed to grow physically before their eyes as contorted back and limbs straightened. Bony deformity blurred and was gone. All pain had left him and the joy that flooded through his soul was almost too intense to express. Then his lips moved in prayer, as he fell on his knees, eyes streaming with tears.

'Glory be to Almighty God and to his Holy One, the Lord Jesus.' He rose to his feet, and placed a hand on Simon's shoulder, which he could not have reached, only minutes ago. 'Peace be upon you, my son and an old man's blessings!' Then his eyes lighted upon Judas, who stood sullenly looking on. 'Blessings on you also, disciple of the Holy One,' he said, and Judas relaxed slightly, vindicated by Jacob's inclusion of him in the miracle.

Simon and Judas, travelled to several villages in the course of the next two weeks, and in each township, Judas became increasingly bitter, more disillusioned. For whereas Simon healed all who came to him for help, always casting out demons and bringing relief to the maimed and diseased, through the name of Jesus, Judas was to be disappointed, time and time again. True, Simon kept a watchful eye upon him, and those who presented themselves for healing, unobtrusively sharing in the ministry so that few realized that it was only through the younger of the two men, that their healing came.

But Judas knew, and a strong dislike of Simon, verging on hatred was born before they returned to their Master at Capernaum.

Chapter Twelve

Centurion Claudius tucked a gentle hand under his wife's chin, lifting her face as he stared earnestly into her eyes. The early signs of motherhood only enhanced her beauty and Claudius thought to that moment in four months time, when he would hold in his arms the little life which nestled soft now beneath Miriam's heart. For years he had dreamed of having a son of his own. His first wife had died childless, almost twenty years ago. There had been one small lump under her breast, nothing of any account. He had marched off on a campaign, leading his cohort. When he returned home, his wife was dead, already buried!

The shock of it had stayed with Claudius over the years. He swore he would never love or marry again, fulfilled his natural needs, as many soldiers did, with any woman of easy virtue who took his fancy. Then he had looked into Miriam's eyes, as she had poured wine for him at a reception in Azor's house. She had been plainly, indeed very modestly dressed, her hair veiled, but when he gazed into those slanting green eyes, something had stirred deep in his soul, as it had in hers. They had married within two months of that meeting.

'I love you, wife! I wish I did not have to leave you at this time, but I must go to Tiberias. There are matters which I have to discuss with Centurion Julius Quintus.'

'Do you take Simeon with you? He would enjoy the trip!'

No,' he shook his head slowly. 'I would like to, but I prefer he should remain here with you. There is so much unrest in the area. I will feel happier knowing that Simeon is here to look after you.' he kissed her gently. 'I will call at the palace. The Lady Joanna has entrusted me with a letter for the Chamberlain, and I do not think Chuza is going to be exactly delighted to learn that his wife is seeking a divorce, that she intends to devote the rest of her life to following the Holy One.' He lifted his helmet from the table where he had placed it, and firmly clamped it on. The red plumes matched with the scarlet cloak that fell from his shoulders, and his armour gleamed from the burnishing given it by his slaves.

'You always look so remote in your uniform. Oh, Claudius, will the time ever come, when you will no longer be a man of war?'

'One day, sweet wife! I cannot imagine what I will find to do if I have no men to command, grow vegetables perhaps? No, I do not see myself as a gardener. I have it. I will become a philosopher and immerse myself in a library.' His blue eyes were full of merriment. 'Perhaps you will find other occupation for me, to prevent my getting bored! No, be careful, Miriam. You will bruise yourself against my armour,' for she had thrown herself into his arms, green eyes challenging him.

'Do you really think I would give you time to read books or to get bored, my dear Lord? This is but our first son, which I carry. There will be many more and daughters! Now go, that you may return the sooner!' She loosed him and called to Sarah, who although she was no longer a servant, still liked to attend Miriam, for a strong bond of affection had grown between the two girls.

'Promise me one thing, Miriam and now I am being deadly serious! You are not to leave the villa while I am away. Even if you go into the garden, have Simeon and some of the house-guards about you. Do you promise me?' She heard the note of authority in his voice, and nodded.

'I promise, Claudius, now goodbye my dearest love!' She watched from the balcony, as he led his men away from the villa, and sighed. If only Claudius were a private citizen, his time his own. She had enough wisdom to know that you should not seek to change the one you love, that change, any change, comes from that person's heart. She knew that Tribune Marcus had told Claudius, that he would be allowed to retire at any time he chose with a very handsome pension and property, in recompense for his lifetime service to Rome. He would be in a position where he would be comfortably off for the rest of his life, and would always be treated with honour. But to Claudius, the army was a way of life, command of men his lifeblood.

Claudius sat with Julius Quintus and Centurions Tacitus and Urbanus. The wine was cool on his throat. They were sitting in the courtyard of the small fort at Tiberias, where the main force controlling the area was stationed. As senior centurion, Claudius should really have taken up residence at Tiberias, but Capernaum was only a short distance away. Unlike Tiberias, it had an almost completely Jewish community, thus giving Claudius a much closer contact with the pulsing unrest of the Galileans. This newly built town of Tiberias where the palace of Herod

Antipas gleaming dazzling white in the sunshine, its huge marble pillars soaring high against the blue sky, was peopled mainly by Gentiles. Here, Roman and Greek culture met; there was a huge circus seating thousands, where the games were held; a theatre, whence dramas of the Greeks unfolded to a cosmopolitan audience; a gymnasium and gaming halls, and close by, hot sulphur baths. Tiberias was the new capital, built little over ten years ago on the ruins of an old town. Antipas had made the mistake of building over the remains of an ancient graveyard, which made his new city unclean in the eyes of the Jews, and all who were devout, shunned the place. Antipas had accordingly brought gentiles in to people his beautiful city, building temples to the Greek and Roman gods in diplomatic gesture to the might of Rome.

The Roman soldiers enjoyed their posting at this particular garrison. Here they almost felt at home, for it had more the character of a Roman city than a town set amongst the curious nation who worshipped an unseen God, and who denied themselves the pleasures of ordinary men. This much was known of them, that they closely followed a strict code of conduct given by their God to a famous leader and prophet named Moses. Also, that they were forever mounting one insurrection after another, even though they knew that this would only end in crucifixion for hundreds and the sacking of offending villages.

Claudius had called a meeting of his fellow officers, who took this opportunity to question him about recent events.

'So, Claudius, you really feel we have nothing to fear, from this Jesus of Nazareth? Seemingly thousands are gathering about him, wherever he goes. True I have heard nothing but good of the man, but it only takes a spark, doesn't it. So far we have been lucky there has been comparative peace in the area. Do you think it will last?' Centurion Julius Quintus stared broodingly at Claudius. Much as he respected his senior's knowledge of the Jews and his military reputation, which was legendary, nevertheless he felt very uneasy about the reports of the new rabbi's following.

'Julius, as soon as I feel there is the slightest cause for alarm I will act, but for the time being we have positively nothing to fear from the holy man. If anything, he is acting as a distraction from others who would seek to ferment unrest. His teaching is of peace, if someone strikes you, to turn the other cheek!'

'But that is impossible to any man of courage,' exclaimed Urbanus in contempt! 'Well, if the Jews are heeding this teaching, so much the better for us! Long may he flourish!' he gave a mocking laugh. 'How say you, Tacitus?'

His fellow Centurion looked at him thoughtfully.

'You know, Urbanus, I think it might indeed take a great deal of courage to—how did you put it, Claudius, turn the other cheek. I know I would not be capable of it, would you?'

Centurion Claudius did not reply. Instead he rose to his feet.

'Well my friends, I have a commission to the palace. I will call back later.' He saluted them, and departed. Why he wondered, had he felt angry at Urbanus scathing criticism of Jesus. He had only spoken words Claudius himself would have used in similar circumstances. Would he be able to turn the other cheek, if it were ever necessary? He shook his head and mounted his horse, still deep in thought. He proceeded slowly through the crowded streets, followed by his escort on foot. The palace grounds were ablaze with flowers of every hue, and palm trees hung still under the blazing sun, no slightest breeze stirring their branches, only the splashing of countless fountains lent an impression of freshness to the sultry day. But inside, the palace was marbled coolness, and Claudius waited patiently in the high domed reception hall, whilst a slave went in search of the chamberlain, the Lord Chuza.

'Centurion Claudius, my friend, how good it is to see you. Come let me order refreshments for you.' Chuza's proud face bore a satisfied smile. If the Roman Centurion had chosen to visit him, then surely this could mean only one thing that his wife was better, would soon be returning to him. If it were otherwise, then surely Claudius would merely have sent a message.

'We will go to my private chambers, Centurion. Slave, bring wine, food!'

Claudius remained silent, holding his helmet. They were in the smaller room, hung with rich tapestries, the floor spread with wolf skins and rugs woven in intricate designs. Chuza gestured towards one of the gold framed couches.

'Be seated, my friend. Ah—slave, put that tray down. Bring chilled wine!'

'I have a letter for you, from the Lady Joanna.'

'A letter, why but this is most wonderful! She must be much recovered, to have written a letter. When you carried her out of the palace, heavily sedated, I must confess that I feared I might never see her again.'

Chuza's face was grave, as he remembered his last glimpse of his wife and how he had actually breathed a deep sigh of relief, when she was out of the palace. No grounds then for Princess Salome to spread gossip, in an attempt to taint him with any imagined disloyalty following his wife's collapse from the shock of seeing John the Baptist's head, brought openly on a platter, for Salome's pleasure. For her wild screams of dementia formed an unconscious reproach to the cruelty of the princess and of her mother, who had demanded the execution, through the lips of her daughter. Queen Herodias was an enemy to be feared. She had a reputation for extreme cruelty if she thought any were less than respectful to her position as wife to Herod Antipas.

John had only escaped her rage for a few scant weeks, when he had criticized her morally unacceptable marriage to her husband's brother. At first he had been imprisoned in heavy chains in the palace fortress of Machaerus, and Herodias had amused herself by descending to the black, dank dungeon, and taunting him by the light of a flaring torch, then leaving him again in stygian darkness, with only her harsh laughter, to mark her passage to the airy brightness of the world above. From this fortress, she had been able to oversee in the far distance, the very point on the Jordan, where John in his temerity, had denounced her marriage to Antipas.

Chuza knew his own position was delicate in the extreme, as Herodias aided by her daughter Salome, would strike out with the speed of a cobra, at any who sought however slightly to undermine the royal marriage. For this reason, Herodias was trying to persuade Antipas to replace most of his previous officials, with others of her own choosing. But Antipas held Chuza in high regard and had much respect for Joanna, in whose veins ran royal blood.

The slave poured their wine, then withdrew, following a peremptory gesture from the chamberlain.

'Your health, my friend!' he savoured the wine on his tongue, while he broke the seal on the scroll. 'Excuse me,' he murmured. Claudius watched his face change, from self assured expectancy to bewilderment, then to a gathering anger.

'Centurion,' he spluttered, rising to his feet. 'Do you know the contents of this letter?' His face had darkened with rage and a pulse beat at his temple.

'I do not know exactly what it contains, but have a shrewd idea. Lady Joanna told my wife of her plans for the future, and forgive me that I mention it, that those plans envisage leading a separate existence from the pressures of the court.'

'Rather that she has decided to remove herself from her husband, you mean! How dare she treat me thus! I will have her brought back in chains, imprisoned for this insolence! How think you, the members of the court will view me, the High Chamberlain, who is unable to control his wife!' He walked back and forth, his face working in fury.

'Calm yourself, my Lord Chuza. Let me tell you of those events which have taken place, since your wife left Tiberias, sick unto death.' Claudius tones were ice cool, impersonal in the extreme, and this seemed to help restore Chuza to less choleric humour. He threw himself down on the couch next to Claudius.

'Well, say on, Centurion.' He poured more wine, spilling it in his haste. Claudius then quietly covered all that had recently happened; he told of Miriam's devoted care of Joanna, of fraught, sleepless nights shattered by the sick woman's screams, as Miriam tried to wean her away from the addiction to the heavy opiate. When he spoke of Jesus of Nazareth, Chuza's face became scowling mask, but then the man relaxed, listening in puzzled silence as he heard of his wife's miraculous healing.

'There has been much talk of this new Holy Man. Antipas has even speculated, that Jesus might be John the Baptist, raised from the dead, others have suggested that Elijah has appeared, according to prophecy or perhaps one of the other ancient prophets, long dead.' He turned his dark, cruel eyes on Claudius. 'How say you, soldier of Rome is this Jesus of the stature of a prophet, of the Messiah?'

'He is the kindest man I have ever come across. His teaching is of love and caring. He has never turned away any who came to him for healing nor has he any political leanings, never incites the people in any way, but always teaches them to endure their lot with patience. As you point out, I am not a Jew, chamberlain. My duty to my Emperor is to maintain peace in this troubled area. If I had any slightest worry about the effect that Jesus teaching was having on the mass of people who follow him, then I would have to act. But he seems to be helping, rather than hindering those in authority.' Claudius had spoken with detachment, trying to protect the man he now revered, as Son of God.

Chuza nodded thoughtfully. 'Well said, Centurion. I will pass your comments on to Herod, for I know he has been in two minds whether to arrest Jesus. But to return to the problem of my wife, is this just some strange feminine whim, wrought of gratitude to the teacher that she says she intends to follow him in company with other women, who revere his teaching. What will people say? Has she thought of that? She will be looked on, as a......!' He bit off the word that almost left his lips. He continued, 'I have no option, Claudius. I must publicly divorce her as being of unsound mind. This will free me of the stigma and allow her to live her own life. But I never, never want to see her again, or even hear her name mentioned!'

Claudius rose. He felt certain sympathy for Chuza, who certainly had been placed in a most invidious position, but he was a good judge of men, and this one would always place his own neck, before any affection or duty to another human being. He had shown very little interest in Joanna's fate, once he realized she would not be returning.

'What actual message then, shall I bear back to Lady Joanna?'

'Tell her I accede to her request and that, no, let me think!' He sprang to his feet, face working in mixture of anger and hurt pride. 'Centurion Claudius, I ask of your courtesy, that you return to the palace later, say tomorrow morning. By that time I will have discussed the divorce with Herod, and will be able to furnish written proof to that foolish woman, that she no longer has the honour of being the wife of Lord Chuza. All her properties are forfeit to me, naturally, yet will I be generous, lest any speak against me. She has a house in Jerusalem. This she may keep. Her jewellery, she already has. That is the essence of what I will write, and that I ask that you will deliver to her.'

'My Lord Chuza,' and Claudius bowed, 'I had indeed hoped to have left Tiberias tonight, but will come tomorrow, as you request.'

He turned on his heel, and started towards the door. Chuza clapped his hands, summoning a slave to conduct the Centurion. He felt he had behaved churlishly, to a man who had put himself to much trouble on his behalf already. Well, tomorrow he would produce a suitable gift, that none should criticize his treatment of an officer, highly regarded by Pontius Pilate.

Claudius returned to the fortress, where he was warmly welcomed back, by his fellow officers. The evening passed pleasantly enough, the younger men prevailing on Claudius, to regale them with accounts of the many campaigns he had fought in. They listened enthralled, as had Claudius himself when a young soldier to his seniors, those men whose exploits were now legendary, as he realized his own were becoming.

He felt restless as he lay on his bed that night. The sultry heat of the day had given way to an oppressive sensation of approaching storm. He yawned as he heard the crash of thunder reverberating through the fortress walls, lightning flashes bright behind his closed eyelids. Just another of those sudden fierce storms, that swept across the lake. His thoughts were all of Miriam, well his return was but an extra day away, their reunion would be the sweeter.

Miriam stepped out of the bath, and sighed as Esther, her new maid, wrapped a towel about her. She had hoped that Claudius might have returned, but had known that this was extremely unlikely. Usually even short trips, could last over two or three days, as much administrative work had to be attended to.

She placed her hands over the small mound in her stomach. Already the baby made small movements, and like all mothers, Miriam joyed to feel the quickening of this precious new life.

'May it be a fine, strong son, my lady,' said the slave girl. She was not beautiful like Sarah, having a broad face and slightly flat features, but she was attentive and quick to learn. Her parents had fallen into debt, and had had to sell themselves and their children into slavery. Esther was thirteen, small for her age and skinny, and Miriam thought back to her own early girlhood, when she had been left as a servant in Azor's household, when her father had been driven out of the town, to join the leper colony in the hills. Life was hard, but at least young Esther had come to a good home.

She girded up her tunic now and went to her chamber. There was a tap at the door, and Sarah stood there.

'Shall I sleep in here with you tonight, Miriam?'

The young girl had blossomed since her betrothal to Simeon, and now no longer wore the despised slave bracelet. She held Miriam in deep affection, and was particularly protective towards her.

'No, Sarah, it is a kind thought, but I will be alright! Have you any idea of how many nights I have had to spend alone? It is the lot of a soldier's wife.' She looked considerately at Sarah. 'What think you Simeon will decide to make of his future? I know he has no liking for the military life. Claudius could easily enlist him in one of the Legions in another land, for of course as a Jew, Simeon could not take up arms against his own people, but as I think my husband has come to realize, war is not for Simeon. Yet a man must occupy himself, must work.'

Sarah tossed her mass of dark curls. 'Of course he must work, wants to. My lady, if I tell you what he aspires to be, you will not tell the Centurion, for Simeon will wish to discuss it with him personally, would be angry if he knew I had told you!'

'What does he want to be, Sarah, I won't tell?' Miriam smiled, frankly curious.

'A physician! Do you think Centurion Claudius would have him placed in a school of medicine?'

'But that would mean his leaving Capernaum. I know little of such matters, but I believe it takes many years training to become a physician. You know, Sarah, I can just imagine him as a doctor and a good one. Have no fear, I know Claudius will approve his wish, and help him to accomplish it.'

'Even if I have to part with Simeon for a while and hard as this would be, I could face it, knowing that by supporting him in his resolve, we would achieve ultimate happiness together. But perhaps, it might be possible for me to accompany him, to which ever city he goes to for his training?' Sarah looked wistfully at Miriam, who caught her to her in a swift hug.

'Leave it to Claudius, my dear and pray about it,' she said softly, 'now, goodnight child. Was it not Jesus who said, 'Do not worry about tomorrow, for tomorrow will worry about itself?'

She walked to the window. The night sky was heavy with burgeoning clouds, showing only a slight glint of stars. A strong wind had arisen, and Miriam realized that one of the violent storms, that sometimes tore across the surface of the lake, churning its silver waters into raging fury was about to erupt. As though in confirmation a flash of lightning sliced the waters and a clap of thunder vibrated between the hills. She shivered slightly and closed the casement, neglecting to lock it. She slipped between the sheets, and tried to turn her thoughts from the violence of nature, towards the tiny life within her.

A crash of thunder, which sounded almost immediately overhead, made her sit up suddenly. She sensed, rather than saw, the figure advancing towards the bed. Why, it must be Claudius returned after all. She opened her mouth to call a welcome, when a hand clamped down over her mouth, whilst a knee forced her thighs apart. She struggled furiously the fingers were about her throat, choking her. The smell of acrid sweat filled her nostrils. She gagged, retched as the hands relaxed, and a voice asked-

'You are Miriam—the Roman's whore?'

Her voice was merest whisper. 'I am the Centurion's wife and you will die for this!'

The hands went back to her throat. She thrashed about, but there was a roaring in her ears. Before the world went black, she felt her attacker enter her. Then she went limp. He expended his passion, laughing and cursing as he did so.

With a final grunt, he heaved himself off and stared as a flash of lightning from the open window, illumined the still form of the woman he had raped. Then his hand rose, but in that moment, the door burst open, and Simeon stood on the threshold.

'One of the house-guards....,' he started then froze in horror, at what he saw by the light of the lamp he carried. Before he could act, the man plunged the dagger into the woman's breast then leapt for the window. But Simeon was upon him, throwing him to the floor in rage too great to contain. Backwards and forwards they wrestled, until Simeon caught him by the shoulders and banged his head up and down on the marble floor. Then he loosed the man, as a white hot agony entered his back. The dagger bit deep, but there was not much force to the blow. But the fiend was on his feet and laughed as the blackness of the night closed around him.

Simeon crawled to the door, crying out for the guards.

'Help! Help—after the murderer!'

The room was full of people now. Guards rushed to the window, onto the balcony. One of them blanched at the sight on the bed—then Sarah was there. Her eyes went to the bleeding youth on the floor, but it was to that still shape on the bed, that she now ran. There was blood everywhere, from the wound in the young woman's breast and lower down. Sarah cried out in horror.

'Get out—get out!' she cried to the guards. 'Catch the monster that has done this deed. One of you, ride for the physician and for the Holy One!'

The guards carried Simeon out of the room, and laid him on a couch in the neighbouring chamber. He had lost consciousness and was bleeding profusely. One of them, well used to wounds, bent over Simeon, trying to staunch the bleeding, and assess the situation.

'The blow missed the lung, had it penetrated there would have been bloody foam upon the lips and much coughing. The knife must have struck a rib, been deflected. He will live, not like that poor woman next door!'

'I have sent all the women of her household to her chamber,' muttered one of his fellows. 'The Centurion will have us all flogged for this! Who saw the intruder first? Why was not the alarm given?' He was sweating with fright, as he considered the retribution that would be wreaked on them. Perhaps if they could at least, catch the demon that had done this! 'You stay with the lad, Junias—I'm going into the grounds with the others!' He rushed out.

Inside Miriam's chamber, Sarah bent her head over the young woman's chest, listening for any sign of a heart-beat and there was a faint one. The wound under the breast, was gaping, white edged, blood welling out.

'Bring me clean linen strips. Hurry—hurry, or we'll lose her!' She packed the cloth against the wound, tying it firmly in position. Then she took a basin from Esther's hands and carefully washed the blood from between Miriam's thighs then she gasped. A contraction had stiffened the woman's abdomen and Sarah sobbed, as she realized that Miriam was losing her child.

It was two hours before a figure strode authoritatively between the wailing women who filled the bedchamber.

'Out, out all of you—except you, young woman and you girl!' The physician who had been in the villa a few weeks back, to attend young Simeon's fever, now turned his eyes on the young woman on the bed.

'Uncover her,' he said to Esther. 'Hold the lamp close, so! Now you, what is your name?'

'Sarah!'

'Tell me all you can? Ah, but first, is there fresh water for me to wash my hands!' Sarah explained the situation as she had found it.

'Is there any hope, doctor?'

He exposed the wound in the chest, and worked furiously.

'There, it will leave an ugly scar, but she may live! She has been incredibly lucky that the knife missed the heart, but the lung has been punctured, see you the blood on her lips? But it is very little and the damage may mercifully be slight. But for one in this condition, to go through labour, well it is asking a lot. If you believe in God Sarah, then I ask you to pray, for we will need prayers before this night's work is through.'

'I will pray,' said Sarah with a sob. 'Do you know Sir Physician, if any have seen the Holy One, Jesus of Nazareth?' Sarah's face was bright with hope, for the guards had been sent to find Jesus.

'I fear he is not in Capernaum,' said the doctor gently. 'We can only do our best for her and leave the outcome in the hands of Almighty God.'

It was late the following afternoon that Centurion Claudius returned to his villa, carrying the formal deed of divorcement for Joanna. There was a pronounced stillness about the house. No one rushed to greet him, no slave smiled a welcome. He scowled and glanced around him, puzzled. Then he spied Mencius, hiding behind a pillar.

'Mencius boy, come hither! Why, what ails you? Wherefore this long face?' Tears were welling from Mencius eyes, as he fell on his knees.

'Master—oh, master!'

'Tell me! Tell me, what's wrong? Simeon! Sarah! Where is everyone? Wife, Miriam? Come hither!' There was no reply at first, only the sound of the slave boy's sobbing. Then a figure slowly descended the stairs, white faced, strained with tiredness.

'Physician, what do you here? What has happened? It—it's not Miriam?' He did not wait for an answer, but bounded up the stairs, crying her name. He flung the door of the bedchamber open then groaned in horror. Miriam lay dead on the pillows, face waxen white, dark bruises against her fair young throat, her mouth swollen.

'Dead----dead! Oh, dear God—not Miriam, not my wife!'

'She is not dead, my Lord, she lives—just.' The physician rested a hand on Claudius arm. 'Here, be seated, and I will tell you all.' Claudius sat down, in a daze, hardly knowing what he did. 'She has lost the child, we have fought for her own life these many hours, the girl Sarah, and I.'

'But what evil mischance caused this to happen? Had she a fall and what are those bruises on her throat?'

Claudius sprang to his feet, and ran to the bedside, flinging himself on his knees beside it. 'Miriam, Miriam, dear wife,' he murmured. He made as though to lift her to him, but Sarah, who had been standing against the side of the room, ran forward.

'Do not touch her sir! She is wounded, a knife wound, almost to the heart!'

'What!' Claudius rose, and looked wildly at the physician. 'Tell me, doctor, and tell me everything! What happened here, whilst I was away?'

'Rape and attempted murder! There is no gentle way to say these things. Would that I could say something to comfort you, Centurion! Yet, she lives, may recover, but in what frame of mind, after such happening, I cannot tell. She will need all of your love, your understanding. She will feel herself defiled, which together with the loss of her child may be difficult to bear, for you see a decision had to be taken to save her life. There will be no more children. I am so sorry.' The physician bowed his grey head, dropping his eyes, before the agony in the soldier's blue gaze.

'What fiend did this deed and how did it happen, when the house was surrounded by armed guards? Where was my son? Where was Simeon?'

'Simeon lies next door. He attacked the wretch with his bare hands and was stabbed in the back. No, fear not! He is not dead. I've dressed the wound, which had already received rough attention from one of your men, and now he sleeps.'

Claudius stared down at his wife's still form. Another had placed his hands upon her, had pressed between her thighs. Even if she lived, would he ever be able to take her in his arms, without that memory driving like a wedge between them. Poor, beautiful Miriam—Miriam of the laughing green eyes and shining black tresses, what was it that the physician had said, she will feel herself defiled! Would they either of them be able to forget this?

'Claudius raised his hands above his head, the chords of his neck standing out, as he screamed, 'I will never forgive!'

Chapter Thirteen

The guards had been interrogated, to little purpose. One of those posted at the back of the villa, beneath the Centurion's chamber, which faced the sea, faltered that he had seen a black shadow slide from the bushes, but it had been a brief glimpse, seen in a flash of lightning. The wind had been so strong, that it had extinguished their lanterns and torches.

He had called to his fellow. The rain had been lashing down, blinding their eyes, the darkness almost stygian. Then another zigzagging flash had shown the shape of a man, clinging to the stem of the thick creeper that hugged the walls of the villa.

'We went inside, sir. Young Simeon asked what was wrong. We told him an intruder was mounting the wall and we rushed outside again, with Simeon carrying fresh lights, which we held up high, trying to see the man, to judge if he had gained admittance to the house.'

'Did you see him again?'

'Not so, sir, there was no sign! But the creeper extends to the southern walls of the villa, so we ran round to that side, in case he should be seeking a way in there.'

'Well, speak on, you fool! What next?'

'We saw no one, but called to the other guards, to help us in our search. Master Simeon decided to run within, to check that all was well inside. Sarah says that he flung open door by door. He came upon your lady's plight too late to save her, but tried to avenge her, and almost lost his own life in the process.'

'I suppose it never entered your thick skulls to check the house first, before seeking the assassin outside. Did it not seem remotely possible to you, that a man climbing a wall in a night such as that, in a violent storm, was there for one thing only! The balcony could be reached by a determined man, with one swift leap from the creeper and so in!' Claudius face was a mask of despair and impotent rage.

'Centurion, we are all so terribly sorry! All of your men, everyone holds the Lady Miriam in the highest esteem. We would give our lives for her, sir!' The soldier hung his head in shame. He knew that he faced a terrible flogging for his failure to protect his lady, maybe death even. As it was, he knew himself and his fellows, to be dishonoured.

'And afterwards?' Claudius forced his voice to be calm. 'Did you not pursue the criminal, who almost killed my wife, and robbed me of my son? You are seasoned soldiers! Yet the only person to come to grips with that—jackal was a beardless boy, Simeon!' The anger he was holding in, was the more terrible, for being so contained.

'I may have wounded him, am almost sure of it,' said a more confidant voice. 'I was stationed to the west of the villa, at the main gates, some two hundred yards away. I thought I heard voices, raised in the storm, but the wind was howling so loudly, I couldn't be sure and in any case it was my duty to guard the gates. Then there was no mistaking the shouts.

Someone was yelling, 'After him—after the assassin!' Then there came a terrific flash of lightning, lit the sky up, like day and in that flash I saw a man in a dark tunic, masked, with a turban on his head, running like a deer. I threw my spear. The darkness crowded in again, so I ran in what seemed to be the direction, I had seen him take.'

'And....?'

'He got away, in the dark. But by this morning's light, I recovered my spear, and on it, the bloodstained fragment of cloth I now show you! Also, there was this!' The sergeant of the guard held out a curved dagger. 'He must have been carrying it to protect himself and dropped it, when my spear caught him.'

Claudius could hardly make himself reach out and take that dagger, which had almost borne Miriam into the next world, but he did, looking at it curiously, almost analytically.

'It is of the type used by the Jewish party of assassins, the Sicarii,' said the sergeant. 'I looked for a trail of blood, but of course, there was none. The rain was very heavy last night, but by the position of the cloth on the spear head, I would hazard a guess, that the fellow was badly wounded.'

'Well done, sergeant! You at least are to be commended! As for these others, have them taken to the garrison, whilst I consider their fate!'

He stood at Simeon's bed-side. As though sensing his presence, the lad stirred. He was lying on his stomach, the bloodstained bandage on his back, bearing witness to his frenzied attack on the intruder. He attempted to raise his head, a slight groan issuing between his lips.

'Father?' Realization flooded back. Despite the Centurion's protests, he managed to swing his legs over the bed, to turn and sit up. The eyes he turned on Claudius were questioning, full of pain. 'Lady Miriam, is she...?'

'She lives, but her life hangs by a thread! She has lost the baby, a boy. She bears a stab wound in her breast, which almost killed her. She is deeply unconscious.'

Claudius had jerked the words out, the anguish almost too much to cope with. 'You—you know what he did, that fiend out of hell?'

'I know,' he whispered. He reached out, and took Claudius hand. 'Will you ever be able to forgive me, Father? If only I had been a few minutes earlier!'

'Simeon, had it not been for you, the assassin's knife would have struck true. If you think you can manage to, I want you to tell me everything you can remember. I will have every inch of flesh flayed from his bones, when I catch him, I....!' Claudius shrugged off the lad's hand, pacing the bedchamber like a caged tiger. Never before, had Simeon seen such cruel light in the Roman's blue eyes, and he shivered.

'There was no light in the Lady Miriam's room when I burst in, but there was light streaming in from the hall behind me. He was standing over her, knife upraised. He saw me, but the knife was already descending. I grappled with him. I remember banging his head on the floor several times. I had no weapon, fool that I was. We struggled, rolled over and over—then there was a sharp pain in my back!' He gingerly shifted his position on the bed. 'I suppose he must have stabbed me.'

'Can you recall his appearance, anything that would identify him?'

'Not really, he was black bearded, turbaned, kept laughing! Even when I smashed his head, he kept on laughing.'

'How was he dressed?'

'A short tunic of some dark material—there was a mask over his face, covering the eyes, but the mouth and beard are in front of my eyes still and I will never forget the sound of that laugh!' He looked into Claudius face, for the Centurion was standing over him, eyes boring down, as though he would transfer the remembered image, from the boy's mind, to his own.

'To think those imbeciles of mine could have prevented it all, had they only acted faster! You, Simeon, have my thanks and my respect, for the way in which you attacked an armed man, with bare hands. But as for those guards of mine, I will have them lashed until they cannot stand!' Fury was building up in the Centurion's brain, anger so great, that it clouded judgement, and all normal thought.

'But sir, you cannot do that! They did their best! The wonder is that they saw anything in that storm. One of them saved my life, for the physician told me I would have bled to death without immediate help. I beg of you sir, do not have them beaten.' Simeon looked steadily into the furious face of the Roman officer. 'Please, Father,' he said. Before Claudius could answer, the door burst open and Sarah rushed in.

'Lady Miriam, she has opened her eyes. Please come, sir, for she will have need of you!' Claudius followed her mutely. The physician raised a restraining hand, as Claudius approached the bed.

'She is very weak, but remembers what happened. I have had to tell her, that she has lost her child.' His grave eyes scanned the Centurion's face, gauging his mood. 'She needs your reassurance,' he said gently.

'Miriam, my poor wife—how is it with you? Are you in much pain?' He bent over her, but made no attempt to kiss her, or even touch her. He could not bear to and Miriam realized this and understood why. It was the final blow. Something died in her. She had joyed in her wife-hood, blossomed in the love that Claudius showered on her. Now he had a loathing for the soiled female flesh that once he had held so dear. He saw the flinching in her eyes, as she looked at him then buried her face in the pillows.

'Oh—why did he not kill me,' she whispered. 'Then at least you could have mourned me. Were it not against the law of Almighty God, I would take my own life. As it is, my sweet lord, I will remove myself, from beneath your roof as soon as I am strong enough to do so." He saw her shoulders shaking with suppressed sobs, reached out as though he would touch her then dropped his hands to his sides.

'You will be avenged, Miriam, that I promise you! But never let me hear such foolishness from your lips again. Your home is here, in this villa, at your husband's side. Rest now! I will send Sarah to sit with you!' There were tears in his eyes as he left the room, and they were of shame. What was wrong with him that he could have rejected in this way, the human being he so deeply loved? It was not her fault, poor child! How could he ever touch her again, without the image of the rapist rising up between them? He let out a string of oaths, as he stood in the garden, looking across at the sea lying so calm now, shining silver pink, reflecting the deeper rose of the spreading sunset. He would have to get away from Capernaum, ask Marcus for another posting. He would leave Miriam well protected this time. Perhaps, after the space of a few months, or a year, they could put this horror behind them.

Lady Joanna arrived the next day, accompanied by David and Mary of Magdala. There was another young woman with them, who was introduced as Susannah.

'Centurion Claudius, we heard. How is she? Please, may we see her,' requested Joanna. Her violet eyes were tender with compassion, as she gazed at Claudius.

'Lady Joanna, Mary, Susannah, you are very welcome. Sarah will bring you to my wife, but I must warn you, she is very sick, is not talking.' Joanna looked into his eyes, saw the suffering and the hardness, and knew the reason. She touched his arm, without saying a word. Then the three women climbed the stairs, leaving Claudius with David.

'Centurion, I heard the terrible news with deepest shock! Has the attacker been caught?' David looked at Claudius with genuine pity, no longer seeing him merely as a Roman, but as a man who had suffered deep hurt. Looking at the Centurion, he remembered his own feelings, when his parents had been murdered, the futile rage the sorrow that burst the breast, also what these feelings can do to a person.

'Thank you David. Perhaps you would like to go to Simeon. He also is sick of a knife wound. His intervention probably saved Miriam's life!'

'I had not heard this! Is he badly wounded?' Anxiety for his brother made him curt.

'No, not badly. The knife slid along a rib, without penetrating the lung. He has a painful wound, but it is clean and should heal well. Miriam was not so lucky.'

'How is she? I heard she had miscarried, sir. I am so sorry.'

'She was raped, boy, then knifed under the left breast, a most hideous blow, that almost killed her. The lung was affected and yes, she miscarried of our son, will never bear another.' The words were spoken almost objectively now, as though he were describing hurt to someone outside his family circle. 'Go to your brother boy,' he said.

'No need, for I am here,' said a quiet voice. Simeon had made his way downstairs, his forehead wet with sweat, from the pain the exertion had cost him. 'All day I waited for you to come to me, father, so I decided to come to you.' There was no condemnation in his voice, just understanding.

'You young fool, you should be abed. Get back there now!' Claudius spoke harshly.

'Wait, I will set my arm about you,' cried David, shocked to see Simeon's pallor. He rushed to his brother's side, as the younger lad swayed towards him. 'Centurion, help me get him upstairs!'

'No. Not yet! Father, the guards! I asked you yesterday to pardon them. Have you?'

Claudius face expressed disapproval of the boy's question.

'Simeon, the discipline of my men, is matter solely within my jurisdiction. They have already been dealt with, and mercifully.'

'You forgave them?'

'They received twenty lashes, Simeon, but a whip was used, not the flagellum. I could have had them scourged unto death. Instead, they got off with a whipping! I assure you, they were much relieved at the lightness of their sentence.'

He looked steadily into Simeon's eyes. 'Had I not punished them, it would have been taken as a show of weakness. There would have been a lack of respect, the respect and fear, upon which command rests.'

'Come brother, let me get you back to your bed,' insisted David. Then they all turned, as Mencius came in.

'A disciple of the Holy One wishes to see you, sir! His name is Simon. Shall I admit him?' Before Claudius could answer, Simon appeared on the threshold. He bowed before Claudius, eyes serene.

'David left message for me of what has occurred here. The Master is away, at Gennasaret, where he healed so many previously. I have come in his stead.' He looked at Claudius compassionately. 'How goes it with your lady,' he asked gently?

'She is very ill. The physician says she seems to have lost the will to live.' Suddenly his eyes hardened, as he stared at the disciple of Jesus. 'Tell me are you that same Simon, named the Zealot? You cannot be Simon Peter, for you have not the usual heavy Galilean accent!' Claudius eyed Simon suspiciously. There had been many unexplained matters troubling his mind, when he had heard that a prominent Zealot was a follower of Jesus, for it seemed incongruous that a member of the violent nationalist party should be associated with the Holy One, whose message was of love and peace. Claudius had deeply protective feeling towards Jesus, and knew that any association with those who promoted uprising would be seized upon as reason for arresting and possibly executing the Messiah. Simon read his thoughts.

'At one time, my whole energy, all my thoughts were of revenge towards those who killed my father and subjected my people. But that is behind me. Believe me, Claudius, you cannot follow Jesus of Nazareth, and breathe hatred. He changes the hearts of men, reshapes their lives! Now as a humble servant of the Holy One, I have only desire in life, to bring his message of the Kingdom of Heaven to all men.'

Claudius looked deep into the eyes of the dark skinned man, who stood quietly before him and read the truth there.

'I will take you to Miriam,' he said tonelessly. 'As you may know, it was premeditated rape, for she told the physician, that her attacker demanded to know whether she was 'Miriam—the Roman whore!' Simon, she was singled out because of her marriage to me, by a man who laughed, yes laughed as he violated her—and then knifed my son, young Simeon!'

'Of what description was the man,' inquired David breathlessly?

'Why do you ask? Masked, so not much could be seen of his face, but what was it that you said, Simeon, a rough, black beard, sneering mouth and laughed at what he did!' He watched David's face, as he spoke.

'Barabbas!' the name leapt instinctively, from David's lips.

'How say you, boy, Barabbas?' The Centurion seized David by the shoulders, causing him to unloose his brother. Simeon swayed and almost fell, but Mencius, ever watchful, steadied him.

'Barabbas? I know that name!' cried Claudius. 'He is one of the Zealot leaders. How is he connected with this? Is he the man?'

David shook his head, as he floundered miserably. 'I am sure he is not! It is merely that I met him recently, when he told me of how his own wife had been raped by six Romans and took her own life, in his arms! But although memory of what he said came into my mind, I know he would not have done this thing. He is a fighter of men, not a murderer of women.' But in spite of his words, David was remembering Barabbas threats against the Centurion and his household and his mocking laugh, as he had disappeared. Simon thought of that laugh also, but he had a keen insight into the heart of Barabbas and his motives. This was not his work.

'Barabbas is certainly not your man,' said Simon. 'In my opinion, you should look amongst the ranks of the Sicarii, for this is typical of their methods. Even in the sacred precincts of the Temple, none whom they suspect of disloyalty to Israel are safe. The dagger, from which they take their name, is ever beneath their robes, seeking home in an enemy's breast! Nor would the Lady Miriam be the first woman, to be attacked by them, for forgive my saying it, giving herself to an enemy.'

'We are married!'

'Centurion, they would not honour the difference anymore than they would accept Simeon as your adopted son! True it was at Miriam, that they struck, but it could equally well have been Simeon.' Simon shook his head sadly. 'One day, perhaps, Jew and Roman will be able to accept each other, as children of one Almighty Father. Those of us who follow the teachings of Jesus of Nazareth, already do this or try to, but extremists have their vision blocked by hatred.'

'Whoever did this deed was snivelling coward! No man of honour would raise his hand against a sleeping woman!' Claudius face was contorted with anger.

'Yet it happens. How many times, Claudius, have you sacked a city, destroyed a village, slain its men and let your soldiers have their way with the women?'

'How dare you draw such comparison? That is war and the things that happen in war are sometimes regrettable, but to be expected. You cannot equate war with murder!'

'But the sacred oil of forgiveness, has to be poured to bring healing in both cases,' said Simon quietly. His eyes met those of the furious Roman evenly.

'Forgiveness?' he choked. 'Go you look upon the shattered loveliness of the girl who was once beloved wife and mother of my unborn child!'

'Was once? Is she no longer your wife, Claudius?'

'By what right do you question me, Zealot? How do I know that you yourself were not involved with this crime? Barabbas is known to you, this matter of the Sicarii, may only be a blind for ought I know!'

Simon looked as though he would flare back at the Roman, but he swallowed, and replied, 'You speak not from wisdom, but from the spirit of revenge, that has entered your heart, and so I forgive your words. Do you wish that I should leave, or shall I go to the Lady Miriam?' Claudius glowered at him, then, jerked his head towards Mencius.

'The slave will conduct you. I have affairs to attend to at the garrison!' He stormed out of the door, his stentorian voice, bellowing for his horse.

'Will you follow me, my master,' said Mencius respectfully. Simon glanced at the two brothers and David nodded that he could manage Simeon.

When he knocked at the door of the bedchamber, the physician opened it. He knew Simon by sight, and admitted him. The disciple glanced towards the bed. Sarah and the three visitors sat around it on stools, their soft voices murmuring encouragement to the still figure, face buried in the pillows. Joanna saw him first, and rose to her feet.

'Simon,' she whispered softly, as she walked over to him. 'She is conscious, but has withdrawn into her own world of pain and misery. I know she recognizes our presence, but the words she breathed to me, when I first came in, explain her behaviour. Claudius is rejecting her!'

'I have already spoken with him. He is obsessed with revenge. Lady, will you and the others withdraw from the bedside.' She turned her eyes questioningly upon him, and nodded. Simon approached the sick woman.

'Miriam, you have suffered greatly, but healing will be yours, if you will accept it and forgive.' She heard the male voice, and slowly raised her head. He was shocked at the difference in her appearance, the extreme pallor, the dark obscenity of bruises to the lovely throat. The hurt in her eyes, like the dumb suffering in the eyes of a wounded animal, touched him to the depths of his soul. He placed a gentle hand on her head.

'Can you forgive,' he said, asking the impossible.

The faint whisper stole between swollen lips. 'Yes, Simon. I forgive, for that poor creature must have been out of his mind.'

'Then Miriam, in the name of Jesus of Nazareth, Son of the Most High, I bid you arise, you are healed.' He turned to Sarah, summoning her to Miriam's side. 'Assist the Lady Miriam to dress!'

'Wait—wait,' cried the physician in agitation. 'This could kill her, the punctured lung!' He ran forward, but stood in disbelief, as Miriam sat up in bed. Her hands went to the bandages that swathed her chest.

'I will not need these now, good physician,' she said softly, 'Loose these bandages, I beg you!' None now had eyes for Simon, who turned unnoticed towards the door and closed it quietly, behind him.

The doctor looked at her in bewilderment, for the bruises had disappeared from her throat, and a faint tinge of rose warmed her cheeks. His fingers shook, as he fumbled to cut the bandages then cried in amazement. The bloodstained linen came away in his hands, but beneath it, was whole, unsullied flesh. There was no slightest trace, of the hideous wound, that had almost killed her. Sarah burst into a flood of weeping, as she wrapped a cloak about Miriam's shoulders. The other women fell to their knees, crying out to God in gratitude, and deepest awe.

'All glory be to Almighty God,' breathed Miriam, through shaking lips, 'and to Jesus, His beloved Son—the Messiah!'

Then the women crowded about her, laughing and embracing her, in a joy that went beyond words.

'I have a great longing for a bath,' said Miriam suddenly. 'Sarah, will you have Esther attend me.' She walked towards the door then paused. 'Thank you—thank you, Physician, for your care, which saved my life!'

Sitting in the hot, almost scaldingly hot water, scented with essence of jasmine, Miriam examined her body, and found no traces whatsoever, of the cruel attack, except that the little mound beneath her breast, which had been Claudius baby, had gone. Tears ran down her cheeks, as she placed her hands over her flattened belly. Then she dashed the tears away, for she knew there were decisions to be taken.

Esther helped her mistress to dress, feeling totally confused at events that were beyond understanding. The young maid had thought her new mistress was to die, but now she was miraculously cured and giving order for the packing of her clothes in trunks.

While Esther with Sarah's help chose the plainest of Miriam's tunics, the women sat quietly around Miriam, as she explained what she wanted to do.

'I have to get away from the villa. I knew, from the look in Claudius eyes, that he would never be able to regard me as his wife again. Yes, there would be an outward formality, masking an inner coldness. I am not brave enough to face that sort of existence.' She spoke sadly, but with no self pity. 'Mary, have you room for one extra woman in that house of yours?'

Mary of Magdala slipped an arm about her, in rough sympathy. 'Men, sometimes I hate them all,' she said scathingly. 'Miriam, you will be very welcome and I mean that. I would say so, otherwise!'

'May I come too,' asked Sarah? 'Life will be difficult in this house, when the Centurion finds you gone. I would rather not be here—also, what about Esther?'

Mary began to laugh. She glanced about her. 'Well, let's see! That makes how many of us? Joanna, Susannah. Miriam, Sarah and Esther and of course, myself! Six of us and I have a feeling, that our number will grow. Jesus and his disciples will need the supportive caring of women, to supply their wants, and to guide those other women, who leave their past behind—and are born again.'

Miriam was dismayed to hear that Simon the Zealot had already left the villa, for she had not yet thanked him. But he had taken opportunity before he left, to minister to Simeon, who stood in the atrium, talking quietly to David.

'Lady Miriam! May God be praised,' cried Simeon. Then he glanced at the trunk, being carried downstairs by Mencius and Esther. Joanna was holding her jewel casket, which Miriam had kept safe for her. 'Why, what is happening,' he said, but he knew and understood. They told him that Miriam was to live in Capernaum at the house of Mary of Magdala and that his betrothed was to move there too

'Simon, we will be married at the end of a year, as we have pledged ourselves to,' said the Samaritan girl softly. 'Perhaps Claudius will place you in a school of medicine, so that you can train to become a physician.' She threw her arms about his neck and embraced him. 'Goodbye, dear Simeon. I will not be far away and one day, there will be no more partings.'

Simeon had Mencius strap the trunks containing the women's possessions, onto the back of one of the pack donkeys. He wanted to accompany them along the beach, to protect them, but was refused.

'You must remain, Simeon, to speak with the Centurion when he returns,' said Miriam. 'I have written this letter, it is to be given into--- my husband's hands.' Her voice almost broke, but she handed the little scroll to Simeon then moved out of the villa which had been her loved home, and where she had been so wonderfully happy. The women walked down the steps and along the pathway, banked high with summer's flowers, then down more steps, to the shore. Simeon watched the little party, proceeding along the narrow beach, where waves splashed gently on the pebbles, Mary leading a reluctant donkey.

Simeon reassured the anxious house-guards who had protested to him, when their mistress, miraculously restored to health, had made unceremonious departure with the other women. David was following closely behind, as he pointed out, and he would personally take responsibility for Lady Miriam's safety. Nevertheless, a spirit of unease enveloped the whole household.

It was night before Centurion Claudius returned to the villa. His men were smartly on duty, and Mencius ran to take his cloak, while another slave brought wine. Claudius gulped it down and held the goblet for more.

'How fares Simeon.'

'I am here, my Father.' Simeon stepped easily forward, from his corner seat. Claudius watched him, bemused. This was not the pale, fainting lad, who had clutched onto his brother, to keep his feet. This was Simeon, as he had been before the attack.

'How, did this happen? Your back, Simeon, show me your back, boy!' He almost wrenched the tunic from the dark shoulders, exclaiming in utter amazement, to find not even a scar. 'Has the Holy One been here? But he could not have been, for they told me in Capernaum, that he was on the other side of the lake!'

'It was Simon. Do you not remember, how David told us, that Jesus had sent his disciples out, to heal the sick, in his name! He prayed over me, in the holy name of Jesus, and all pain left me.'

Claudius smiled faintly. 'I must speak my thanks to Simon then. I fear I was less than polite to him. Well Simeon, you will be able to ride with me tomorrow, when we investigate the caves, any place at all where that unspeakable fiend may be hiding. Today, my men and I took Capernaum apart. We demanded admittance into every house in the town, broke down doors where they were not immediately opened, the only houses we did not touch, were those belonging to the disciples of Jesus and the house of Mary.'

Simeon winced, imagining the scene, and the loss of that very slight acceptance, shown to the Centurion, following his building of the new synagogue, this fragile bridge of understanding, would have irrevocably crumbled. He sighed, and Claudius frowned at the unspoken criticism.

'The man was wounded. Yesterday we scoured the countryside, behind the villa, found nothing. The probability was then, that the criminal was being sheltered by friends in the town. Unless he has got clean away, then the only other conclusion must be that he is in the caves. If he is there we will find him, smoke him out, as Herod did with terrorists in his day! Have you ever seen this done boy? Men are lowered over the rock face by cradle, baskets of reeds dipped in pitch are set fire to, and hurled into the cave, your man runs out, choking, and you drag him up with grappling hooks!

You shall ride with me tomorrow. You will enjoy it!' Only then did his thought lift from revenge, to remembrance of the wife, on whose behalf he was engaged in frenzied activity.

'Simeon, did Simon also—speak with Miriam?' He could not bring himself to ask the obvious. His blue eyes began to soften, as a wondrous possibility, dawned in his heart.

'Father, he did. Your Lady is healed. The physician tells me, it is as though the wound had never been, also that her other hurts have mended.'

'Why, what wonderful tidings! Why did you not tell me of this instantly boy?' He turned and started to mount the stairs, calling his wife's name, 'Miriam—Miriam!'

'Wait, she is not there! She has gone.'

'What's that you say?' Claudius halted, then continued up, throwing open the bedroom door. Crumpled sheets marked the spot where his wife had lain; a bloodstained bandage lay on the floor; a cupboard door hung open, Miriam's chests had gone; her combs and toiletries were no longer strewn on the dressing chest. 'No! No, it cannot be!'

He rushed back downstairs, seizing Simeon by the arm, his grip cruel. 'Where is she? Tell me at once, or I'll have you whipped!' Simeon blenched at the malevolence in the blazing blue eyes.

'She left this for you,' he said quietly, using his free hand to remove the letter from his tunic. Claudius snatched the letter, and broke the seal with impatient fingers. As he read, tears started to his eyes, and he sank down onto a chair.

"Dear Husband,

I call you this for the last time, Claudius, for I know how you feel towards me now, and that what has happened has drawn invisible veil between us. It is not your fault that you feel so. Any man would recoil from a woman who had suffered dishonour and perhaps it would have been better if I had died. It would have been cleaner. But I live and in fact, have been restored to health by the power of the Lord Jesus, vested in Simon, for which I give thanks to Almighty God, as I hope you will also.

Claudius, I am going to live with Mary Magdalene and Joanna and with some others. Sarah and my maid Esther are accompanying me. We intend to follow the Holy One, to help in whatever way we may, and to learn of his teaching so that we can guide others. Claudius, you will forever reign in my heart as dear husband but I release you from your vows to me. I suppose you will seek divorce. If you remarry, then I pray blessing on your new wife, and that she may be fruitful, and give you the son which I was unable to.

My last wish is that you release me, and that in time your memories of me, may be the happy ones of our first love. May Almighty God, have you in His keeping, now and for always,

Miriam."

Long Claudius sat into the night, reading that letter, over and over again, through eyes blurred with tears. He was tempted to bring her back, forcefully if necessary. But he knew that her words were true. Much as he still loved Miriam, and even though she now bore no physical scars of her ordeal, in his mind, there would always be the wraith of the dagger-man, crouching over her—and! Perhaps, yes perhaps, if he could find the man, take vengeance, have the sure knowledge that he no longer infested the earth, then this memory would no longer haunt him, and he could really take her home to his heart.

'Father!' Simeon shook Claudius shoulder gently. The Centurion had fallen asleep, face bowed over the letter. It was almost dawn. His face as he wakened looked tired and drawn. Memory flooded back and with it, the pain.

'Ah, Simeon, I must have fallen asleep. Why are you not abed yourself?'

'Can you not forget what has happened, Father, forgive?'

'Forgive? Are you deranged, to ask such a question?'

Simeon looked at him gravely. 'Because it is only in this way, that you will free yourself from hate and remove the barrier between Miriam and yourself.' He stepped back, for Claudius had risen, fist raised. 'Simon tells me that once the Lord's principal disciple, Peter, asked this question-----'Lord, how many times shall I forgive my brother when he sins against me? Up to seven times?' but Jesus answered to Peter, 'I tell you, not seven times, but seventy times seven!'

Simeon watched Claudius face.

The Centurion seemed to struggle with conflicting emotions then said icily, 'You must forgive me, Simeon, if I cannot regard the rapist of my wife, as a brother! I will never forgive! Never forget and will look for revenge upon him, until my dying day. Only when I hear his screams of agony, will I then perhaps, be able to put this behind me. Speak no further to me on this matter.' He walked heavily upstairs, to the empty bedchamber.

Chapter Fourteen

All day the soldiers surged amongst the hills. Claudius had sent a messenger to the garrison at Tiberias, in response to which summons, Julius Quintus arrived with a large force, to help in the search for the Jewish scum who had dared to dishonour a Centurion's lady.

Their voices rang out, as they worked with grim delight. There had been a relative peace recently and the men were spoiling for a fight, for excitement. Many a poor shepherd was seized and interrogated as troops marched through farmsteads, roughly raising to the ground any structure that might harbour terrorists. High amongst the hills they spread, in organized penetration of cliff and gully but their search yielded nothing, and their frustration grew.

A sudden shout rang out.

'Sergeant—here! Armed terrorists—Zealots, we think! There are about a dozen of them, cornered at the end of the ravine!'

Claudius heard the shout, and spurred his horse forward, shouting to his man to follow him. The descent was perilous, the sides of the ravine sheer.

'Don't let them get away!' He saw them then, boxed against the cliff face. Light was fading, he must act quickly. The Zealots were shouting their leaders name, waving their spears fearlessly against the far greater force, their only advantage, that the narrowness of the gully prevented more than a very few men facing them at any one time. Claudius heard the name they were calling. It was one familiar to him, both as that of one of the most infamous Zealot leaders and on another count, for it was that name which David had uttered, as possible suspect!

And he was here, within the Centurion's grasp. The blood throbbed at his temples, as he called to his men.

'Capture their leader alive. I want Barabbas delivered into my hands!' He led them forward, a solid wedge of soldiers, shields forming protective phalanx, inexorably advancing on their puny foe. Then, there was creaking noise above their heads. Claudius glanced upwards, and saw too late the shadowy figures above, who were levering great boulders with poles, loosening them to come crashing down upon the Roman soldiery. A shout of laughter—of triumph, echoed from the end of the ravine, as many of the hated Romans fell crushed and bleeding, felled by the huge stones and the lesser ones which rained down upon their heads. Then as Claudius tried to reorganize the confused remnant of his men, he saw the Zealots disappearing unbelievably into the rock face itself. He pushed forward, but his horse sank to its knees, hit by a spear, which had been meant for him, but had caught the stallion in the neck. He dismounted, rushing towards the end of the ravine, intent on capturing Barabbas at any cost. He heard the shouts of those of his men who were regrouping behind him.

Another volley of boulders, bounced down the steep slopes, causing further decimation of the force. Only one figure was now visible at the end of the gully. The man shook his spear, screaming a challenge, then fell, not through any act of the advancing Romans, but as victim of one of the heavy stones, which still cascaded from the sides of the hill. It ricocheted, striking him on the shoulder, catching him off balance. His men shouted to him and Claudius realized that an almost imperceptible crack in the rock face, was the entrance to a cave. Barabbas managed to raise himself to his knees, fighting against waves of nausea, wrought of the sickening pain.

'Matthias, help me!' But Matthias was already making his own way to safety. In a case like this, it was each man for himself and it would not take the Romans long to enter the cave and discover that it had another outlet, through a passage that led out onto the other side of the hill.

'Bind him!' Claudius held Barabbas in iron grasp, gesturing to his other men, to advance into the cave, whilst two of their fellows did his bidding. Once the Zealot was safely secured, Claudius turned to see how the wounded had fared. It had cost them dear, this sally into the ravine and the Centurion realized now that Barabbas had deliberately led them into a trap and cursed himself for all kinds of a fool for not having foreseen something of the sort. Mocking laughter rose above his head, those who had mounted the attack upon them, disappearing into the gathering darkness of a Galilean night. Within the cave, the Romans looked about bewildered. It was empty, the unseen passage blocked by a huge stone.

They were back at the garrison at Capernaum. Julius Quintus stood at Claudius side as they had the Zealot chieftain brought in before them. He had recovered from the first shock of blinding pain from his damaged shoulder, the bone was badly bruised, but not broken, and Barabbas cursed softly, at the evil quirk of fate that had made him victim of the very act he planned. But this was war, you took your chance!

'So, you are Barabbas, leader of that rabble,' said Claudius contemptuously. 'Men fight with the sword and spear, not stones!'

'Indeed,' said Barabbas harshly. 'Then tell me, Centurion, what do you Romans use in your siege machines, but stones! Or is it merely the fact, that we use our hands, instead of your infernal catapults that you object to!'

One of the guards struck him a blow across the mouth.

'Do not dare to address the Centurion Claudius so, you dog!' Barabbas spat, then stared appraisingly at Claudius. He had heard of the attack on the soldier's wife with grim amusement. His first thoughts had been, that here was poetic justice that the Centurion's woman had suffered such fate, he had thought of the terrible ordeal, which his own sweet wife had endured and of her resulting suicide!

'Centurion Claudius, I seem to have heard your name mentioned just recently, but I do not recall why!' He smiled crookedly, from his bleeding mouth. He knew they would kill him and without mercy. Perhaps if he could annoy them sufficiently, he might get a quick death, instead of the crucifixion, which was usually meted out to insurrectionists.

The blaze of anger in the blue eyes opposite him only served to amuse him. Claudius examined the face of the Zealot, feature by feature. Was this the man? He looked at the cruel mouth. Was it this mouth that had bitten down on Miriam's lips, the black, curled, bushy beard that which Simeon had described?

Those hands, had they encircled his wife's throat, was it he who...? It was all he could do, to remain calm, for he knew there was one way to be sure. His guard had wounded the rapist.

'Strip him,' he said, and watched as willing hands tore the tunic from the man's back. Claudius walked around him, his eyes raking every inch of the Barabbas hide. There was no trace of any recent wound, only the ugly contusion on his shoulder.

'Have him scourged,' he said thickly. 'Then, Julius Quintus, have a detachment bear him to Jerusalem for execution, so that Tribune Marcus may make an example of him.' He turned on his heel and left the room, the sounds of the descending whip, filling his ears, together with the Zealot's groans. Disappointment almost sickened him. This was not the man. His quest must continue.

For a week, Claudius men scoured the countryside. It was as though the earth had swallowed the man they sought. Of course, he might already be dead of his wound; this was possibility. But still Claudius insisted that they continue the search. It had become an obsession.

At last, almost when it seemed impossible to hope further, one of his men came to a room in the fortress which had become his centre of operations. He saluted, unable to contain the excitement that shone from his eyes.

'Centurion—sir!'

'Well, speak man, speak!'

'In a miserable hut sir, we had passed it a dozen times, we've discovered a man! He is badly wounded, in fever. We found this.' He handed a dagger sheath to Claudius. The Centurion exclaimed softly and walked over to the small cupboard. He unlocked it, and withdrew from the top shelf, a curved dagger. It slid into the sheath, like a hand into a glove. Nor was that all! The hilt of the dagger bore a letter 'S' carved into the bone, the sheath was embossed with the same letter.

'We have not moved him, Sir, because we fear he might not last the journey. We thought that you might care to come and examine him!' The man drew himself to attention, waiting an answer.

The hut was in fact, only two miles out of Capernaum, the wounded man lying where they had discovered him, in a scooped out area of the mud floor. The soldiers explained that, when the legionaries had burst into the hut on a previous occasion, they now guessed that the suspect had been lying there, covered by a sleeping mat. His elderly father, had stretched himself on top of his son, disguising his presence with his own body, whilst his crippled wife, had pleaded her husband's infirmity, as reason that he did not rise before the Romans. Today, however, one young soldier had approached the hut alone, making no noise, had entered and found the couple on their knees, tending the dangerously ill man. He had quickly realized the situation and called his comrades.

Claudius exclaimed in disgust at the foul smell pervading the hut. He looked down at this figure, wearing a torn, dark brown tunic, forehead beaded with sweat, face emaciated, skin a shade of grey against the black beard. The man's eyes were wild with fever. He kept muttering to himself and every so often, a high-pitched laugh burst between his lips.

'You—get up!' Claudius spoke sibilantly. His words had no effect upon the Sicarii. He continued to babble incoherencies, interspersed with the inane laugh.

One of the soldiers bent and jerked the wounded man unceremoniously, into a sitting position. The man screamed in agony and the ring of soldiers exclaimed, as the suppurating wound in his back, was exposed. There was much pus, the surrounding area black and evil smelling.

For a moment, he focused on the tall officer, standing over him. He saw the red cloak, the scarlet plumes of the helmet, and he knew who this was and again he laughed. He raised a shaking hand towards Claudius.

'How is it—with your wife—Centurion?' Then he appeared to have some sort of seizure, for his face contorted, the mouth opening wide, in soundless scream and he fell back, dead!

The sergeant in charge shook his head regretfully. 'I'm sorry, sir, he's cheated us, gone to Hades!'

'Then take the carrion outside, and burn it, 'choked Claudius, face working with frustration. 'Raise this hut to the ground!'

'What about them, sir,' said the sergeant anxious to please? 'Shall we put them to the sword?' Claudius glanced at the elderly couple, prostrate with grief, as they stared at the dead body of their son. A thought came to him, what purpose would it serve? They looked half dead already.

'No, let them go free, that they may tell their friends, that it is impossible for enemies of Rome to escape our vengeance.' Then he hesitated, grabbed the old man by the front of his tunic. There were things he had to know.

'Your son, how was he called?'

'Zeke, honoured sir, we called him Zeke.' The old man answered wearily. He had known that this son would end up dead one day, had warned him so many times.

'He was a member of the Sicarii?'

'Yes! My wife and I pleaded with him many times not to mix himself up in these matters. Why could he not work in the fields like I do, as my father did, and his father before him? Poor people like us we cannot afford to involve ourselves with politics. I beg that you will spare our lives, sir, at least, that you spare Elizabeth. She has ever been a good wife, a good mother!' Tears were streaming down his cheeks.

'Can you give me the names of other members of the Sicarii? Your life depends on it! Names man—names!'

'I cannot! As the Almighty is my witness, I cannot, for my son never mentioned anyone. He rarely came near us, honoured sir. He spent most of his time in Jerusalem. If we tried to aid him, to hide him, well what parent would not seek to succour a child even such a one as Zeke!' Claudius read the truth in the man's eyes and trembling lips. With an exclamation of disgust, he gestured that they should get out of the hut.

'You may as well set torch to the hut and burn the filth where it lies. It will save touching it—that wound was gangrenous, and if a man has even a small scratch on his hand, the evil humours from such as this, can cause death!' He turned on his heel, leaving his men to do his bidding. As he rode his new horse back to the fort, he realized a terrible emptiness inside his breast. His vengeance, what had it achieved? He reined his horse, and looked back, as the flames from the Sicarii's funeral pyre, shot up into the sky. Soon, there would be nothing left but ashes. That was what his life was now, ashes, ashes of despair! Slowly realization of how much he had actually lost was borne in on him.

'Oh, Miriam—Miriam,' he cried brokenly. 'How could I have been so foolish—so unfeeling? If only I could reverse time. If only I had taken you into my arms!'

But perhaps it was still not too late. He would ride to Capernaum, go to the house of Mary of Magdala, and ask Miriam to come home. Then his head drooped. But of course, he could hardly do that now. He had swept through the town with his men, in that first wild burst of fury, breaking into the towns people's houses, flattening the market stalls, in abortive search. Too much had happened. But then, if she truly believed in the teachings of the Holy One, well, didn't he encourage people to forgive!

He entered the villa again, for the first time in a week. During all this while, he had not stopped to consider how Simeon was faring, for the lad had declined to accompany the search parties. Much as he wanted to see the criminal brought to justice, he feared that Claudius would act purely in vengeance and sensed that this might take terrible form.

He stood at the front door waiting, for he had seen the Centurion approaching from the roof top, where he had spent so much time straining his eyes, over the last few days. His gaze swept over the tall, weary figure who marched in listlessly.

'You did not find him, Father?'

'I did,'

'Well tell me, who was it? Where is he now?

'A member of the Sicarii party and he is dead.' He smiled, a cold grimace, as he added, 'He died of his wound from that spear thrust, not at my hand, Simeon. He baited me with his words, before he died. And he laughed, lad, he laughed.'

'I'm glad you got him, Father, and that he no longer lives, to practice his foul trade. I must admit to some admiration of the Zealots, but none for the dagger-men!'

'I suppose you must have heard, that the Zealots cost me dear, killed and wounded many of my men.'

'I did and that you captured their leader, Barabbas!'

'I wondered at first, whether your brother David, was right in his suspicion of the man, for he is an evil looking creature. I had him scourged and by now, he should be in Jerusalem, awaiting execution, as Tribune Marcus thinks fit, probably crucifixion.'

He thought he saw an expression of wry amusement on Simeon's face, but the lad looked suitably grave, as he said carefully, 'I take it then, that you have not yet received the news of Barabbas escape!'

'How say you, he has escaped? Why, this is thing impossible! He was sent off in chains, with a guard of fifty. Where did you hear such nonsense, boy?' Claudius snorted disbelief.

'A messenger came here a few hours ago and we dispatched him to the garrison. Did you not meet him there?'

'No. I left the garrison hours back, to go to the miserable hovel, where the Sicarii had taken shelter. I rode back here directly, from his fiery exodus, we burned the hut down, so that no trace should remain to pollute memory.' He made for the door. He knew he must return to the garrison, to get news of this fresh disaster, but paused, for he heard the guards shouting challenge at the gates as the two soldiers marched briskly to the villa.

'Centurion, the sergeant gave me this letter for you.' The man tendered the badly written parchment. Claudius unrolled it, exclaiming in anger at its contents.

'Back to the garrison you two! Tell Sergeant Lucius, that I ride to Tiberias tomorrow morning. Have an escort of twenty mounted men, outside the villa at sunrise.' They saluted and hastily retreated. They thought they had never seen such fury in their Centurion's eyes. Many would be flogged over this affair, but luckily the troop guarding Barabbas, had been drawn from the garrison at Tiberias, where far greater numbers of men were available. They were safe this time!

'Unbuckle this breast plate for me lad.' Claudius placed the heavy helmet on a shelf then waited, as Simeon's fingers busied themselves. At last, his trappings laid by, he sank down on a couch. Simeon tactfully asked no questions, but waited for Claudius to enlighten him, as to what had actually transpired.

'It seems it happened on the road just past Nazareth,' he said at last. 'A large party of Zealots descended from the slopes above, seemingly they held mirrors, flashing the sun's rays across the soldiers faces, blinding them for brief moment, but long enough, for them to seize Barabbas and away, with the loss of only one of their men, who was killed!'

A feeling very like exultation, shot through Simeon's breast. It was not that he enjoyed Claudius humiliation, but that he delighted that his small nation still found the courage to stand against mighty Rome, to dare to pit inadequately armed, untrained men, against the seasoned troops of the most ferocious fighting force the world had ever known. At that moment, Simeon realized, that whatever bonds of affection he might have for his adoptive father, he was a Jew, would always be one and could no longer live in a false position. He had to separate himself from Claudius; but how to do this, without hurt to one who had shown such kindness towards him? Silently he prayed for help, for this difficulty to be resolved, and it was.

'Come here, Simeon. Sit—sit beside me. We must talk.'

'Yes, Father?'

'I intend to leave Capernaum for a considerable time. Maybe I will return one day, to what had become to feel like home. Tribune Marcus has given me the option of becoming second in command of the Antonia, directly under him, and now, I feel is the time to avail myself of this position. How would you feel about accompanying me there?' He watched Simeon's face and saw the expression of dismay, which he interpreted as dismay at being parted from Sarah. 'It would serve to fill the time of your year's betrothal,' he said gently. 'Indeed, it would be test of how deep your love for Sarah is. Marriage is a very serious affair, as once I told you.'

'Father, for some time now I have wanted to speak to you regarding my future, but so much has been happening. Is there not a chance, that you will be reunited with Lady Miriam? I am young, with no experience in such matter, but I know her love for you fills her whole life, and that you...!'

'Enough boy! None of us knows what lies ahead in life, and perhaps it is well that it is so. I know you speak from concern, but ask you to say no more on this subject. Now you began to speak of your own future. What were you going to ask me?'

'I want to study to be a physician,' blurted Simeon. 'I intended to ask you whether I could study at the university at Tarsus, even had ideas of Rome, the Greek school there, but then I confided my ambitions to Stephanus, and he suggested that I might instead, become apprentice to him. He has studied under Celsus, and....'

'Not so fast, Simeon! You want to study medicine? Well, it is no bad profession. I have given up thought of trying to make a soldier out of you. But who is this Stephanus and the other you mentioned—Celsus?' Claudius smiled guardedly at the boy's enthusiasm.

'Stephanus is the physician who treated the Lady Miriam and me!' Simeon looked amazed, that the Roman had not learned the name of the man who had served him so well.

'Ah! Well to me, a physician is only addressed as such, however, continue!'

'Master Stephanus is gifted as a surgeon. Celsus whom I named, has written a treatise on surgery. He is held in highest esteem, and Stephanus has studied with him.' Simeon looked at the Centurion pleadingly. 'May I become apprenticed to Stephanus? It will cost you nothing, for I will live in his house, and work as his assistant!'

'Very well, I agree if this is what you want. However, I am perfectly willing, should you prefer to send you to whichever school you select. In any case, I shall see that you are provided for. Don't forget, Simeon that you will have a wife to support in a year's time.' Claudius rose and wandered over to the window.

'What I suggest is this, that I place you officially in charge of this villa, I will leave a few men to guard the premises. Melchus is capable of running things smoothly and he is completely trustworthy. He has been with me for considerable time. As an auxiliary he will be more easily spared from the garrison, and he has often been to the villa. You personally will only need to come here from time to time.' He paused, and continued softly. 'Of course, this villa is home to my wife, whenever she wishes it to be, and I hope that before long, she will be sensible and return, the more especially as I will not be here.'

'May I dare to hope, that both of you will one day be reunited,' said Simeon feelingly. 'If you think I am not too young, to hold responsibility for the villa, then I willingly accept this charge.'

During the night Claudius sat before his writing table, composing a letter to Miriam and enclosing Joanna's divorce papers. Tomorrow morning, he would delay his start, long enough to meet with Physician Stephanus and arrange Simeon's future; also see that funds were placed with a lawyer he knew he could trust, to provide for the needs of his wife and young Sarah.

The sun was high in the heavens before Centurion Claudius spurred his horse forward, leaving Capernaum behind. He turned on the brow of the hill, staring down at the huge crowd, who were congregating along the shore. He did not need to be told the cause. The Holy One had returned. He saw a boat put out a little from the shore, and watched briefly, as the white robed figure stood up in the bows, hands outstretched in blessing. He turned away, calling on his men to follow and knew that the pain in his heart was not only for his loved ones he was abandoning there, but because of what amounted to rejection of the Messiah's message of forgiveness and love. He was glad when the contour of the hill cut off sight of the bay. Now for Tiberias, to wreak reprisal on those idiots, who had allowed Barabbas to escape—and then on to Jerusalem!

Mary's face was flushed from bending over the oven, as she lifted hot bread from the glowing embers. The kitchen filled with its fragrance. She set it to cool, exclaiming at the burn on her finger.

'My sister Martha is the one designed by nature for cooking, not I,' she declared crossly then chided herself for the outburst of temper. Her lifestyle had changed in an extraordinary manner over recent weeks. Gone were her jewels and fine clothes; no paint now emphasized the dramatic beauty of her face, and instead of smooth hands, with painted nails, were blistered fingers. Yet never had Mary of Magdala looked more beautiful. Now as she called to those she had come to name sisters, she had a glow about her as though a lamp shone within. Sometimes a wind would disturb the flame of that lamp, as when Mary would explode with all of her old fire. But always serenity returned, as she would repent her tempestuous behaviour.

'Why don't you let me do the cooking,' cried Sarah. 'I am well used to it and it will be good practice against the time when I will have to cook for Simeon.' She looked around. 'Where is Miriam?'

'In her chamber, weeping. No. Don't go in yet. While you were out at the market, Simeon called with a letter from Claudius. He has left Capernaum for good, gone to Jerusalem! Although Miriam had accepted their separation at surface level, it is still a blow to see matters made final.' Mary's face was sad, for she had genuine affection for Miriam and felt deeply for her friend in loss of both baby and husband.

'Where is Simeon now?' Sarah made to run into the street, but Mary restrained her.

'He will see you later. He said he had matters to arrange first. However, Sarah, he did say that you would be very pleased at his news.' Sarah's face was bright with curiosity, but Mary would say no more on the subject.

'Where is Joanna then?'

'She is comforting Miriam. Simeon also brought her document of divorcement, which Claudius had meant to deliver on return from his earlier visit to Chamberlain Chuza. She is well rid of the man. I often saw him, an obnoxious creature, who fawned on Herod, whilst greedily amassing a fortune of his own.'

'Judge not, that you be not judged, as the Lord said,' said a laughing voice. Susannah came in, bearing two heavy baskets of vegetables. 'However, I must agree with you about Chuza. Nor was he faithful to Joanna. Because I made my living, by singing and playing the lute, he thought he was entitled to make free with me as he did with many others!' She started to unpack her baskets. 'See, we have plenty of beans and onions for the soup and peppers and fresh herbs. Then I bought melon and figs, yes—and more honey.'

'Did he have his way with you,' asked Mary bluntly?

'No! One worse than he tried though, Herod! I refused him, bit him! That is why I will bear these scars until death!' The young woman bared her shoulders, showing a criss-crossing of raised white scars, against the dark skin. 'I screamed so much, that my voice became hoarse and I could never sing again! I used to hate all men, would attack them as I told you. My whole world was full of hate, until I heard about the Holy One. I walked for miles to find where he was teaching and screamed my hatred of men to him.'

Mary had heard the story before, but still enjoyed hearing it again, for it ran so nearly parallel to her own. 'Tell me,' she said softly.

'The Lord Jesus looked at me and the compassion and love in his eyes, washed through my soul like a shower of cool rain on parched earth. Then he raised his hand and I felt a touch on my head, so gentle. Then my whole being seemed to fill with light as I heard him rebuking the spirit of hatred, bidding it to come out of me! It did! I fell to the ground. When I rose, I found myself singing in full voice, my throat restored, singing as I did before but with greater range, and I believe with that love I now feel for all mankind pouring out in the melody.' Her black face glowed with emotion and her large expressive eyes were bright with tears. Mary took her in her arms, and hugged her.

'You have a voice like the angels,' she said. 'I myself have been a singer, love singing, but I have not that deep vibrancy of tone which sets your voice apart. You have been blessed with a wonderful gift, Susannah!' And so the day continued, the women, comforting and supporting each other, as they prepared food for the master and his hungry disciples, who would be coming there later, weary from a day of teaching and healing, tired also, from dealing with the increasingly sarcastic attacks made upon them by the Pharisees, who now for the most part, resented Jesus popularity with the people as they tried time and time again, to catch him out with trick questions before departing, discomforted.

Jesus had been teaching from the boat for two hours, using parables, stories that illustrated deeper truths. Always he used examples taken from events in their daily lives, things familiar, as with the story he was now telling of the sower scattering seed. The crowd hung on his words.

'Some of the seed fell along the path, and the birds came and ate it up, some fell on rocky places, where it did not have much soil. It sprang up quickly, because the soil was shallow, but when the sun came up, the plants were scorched, and they withered, because they had no root.'

The farmers amongst the crowd, nodded understandingly, and strained their ears to hear the rest of the parable. Jesus continued-'Other seed fell amongst thorns, which grew up and choked the plants.' He searched their faces, and went on,

'Still other seed fell on good soil, where it produced a crop, a hundred, or sixty, or thirty times what was sown.' He saw that some of the listening upturned faces, registered comprehension of the stories real message.

'He who has ears, let him hear,' said Jesus. The boat put in to shore, and he stepped out, wading up onto the wet shingle. Immediately the crowd surged about him. A cry was raised among the people. 'What like is the Kingdom of Heaven, Lord?'

Jesus answered, 'The Kingdom of Heaven is like a mustard seed, which a man took and planted in his field.' He smiled at them-'Though it is the smallest of all your seeds, yet when it grows, it is the largest of garden plants, and becomes a tree, so that the birds of the air come and perch in its branches.' Again, some few nodded, as the meaning took shape in their minds.

A group of women stood looking puzzled, so Jesus looked at them and smiled. 'The kingdom of Heaven is like yeast that a woman took and mixed into a large amount of flour, until it worked all through the dough.' They exclaimed in delight at his words. This they could understand.

Jesus saw a rich merchant, listening intently, brows furrowed.

'The Kingdom of Heaven is like a treasure, hidden in a field. When a man found it, he hid it again, and then in his joy went and sold all that he had, and bought that field!' The man's face struggled with the meaning, and finding it, shook his head—was this teaching such, that he had to give up all else, in order to have the joy and peace he glimpsed? As he shuffled off, he heard other words following him, 'Again, the Kingdom of Heaven is like a merchant, looking for fine pearls. When he found one of great value, he went away, sold everything that he had and bought it!' He turned back, looking at Jesus, torn with indecision. But he thought of his thriving business, his carefully hoarded wealth. Then he shook his head, and clasping his hands to his temples in hopeless regret, was swallowed up in the crowd.

Jesus sighed slightly as he walked amongst the people. He knew only too well, that few had the perception, to interpret the true meaning of his parables. Even those who did, had all too often, just a surface interest in a teaching, which although it offered a truer, deeper happiness, than any fleeting experience offered them now, made demands too high to be met. Who could really repent of all the vicarious pleasures that distracted them, from the stresses and pressures of life? Who really wanted to forgive those who had offended them, when hugging resentment against the offender, gave release of the smouldering anger for all other of life's ills and who indeed, would wish to take their hard won possessions and share them with those in need! The teaching was of a noble order, it touched the heart, but to make decision to follow it and be born into a new life, an altered mental state, was asking too much for most.

And so they crowded close about him, watching for those miracles of healing, which always occurred when the sick and lame knelt before him, crying on his name, or merely touching the fringe of his robe as he passed in faith that they would be healed, their faith always realized. They wanted to believe, but the price exacted was too high. Yet still they came, watching, waiting, as did the Zealots. They hovered like hawks, always hoping that Jesus might declare himself as Messiah. The nationalistic fervour had its nucleus here in Galilee, and even those who were not party members, were often sympathizers. Why did he not seize the initiative, taking advantage of his enormous popularity to raise a banner as King of the Jews? Thousands they knew would flock behind his leadership, drawn by the charisma, which he alone in the land displayed.

Word had flown, from village to village, of Barabbas dramatic escape from almost certain death at Roman hands, and this, taken together with the successful engagement in the hills behind Capernaum, fired enthusiasm. Now surely, would be the perfect time, yet always and always, Jesus spoke of love and forgiveness. Perhaps eventually, it might be possible to force the Holy One into a situation, where they could acclaim him despite himself, by force if necessary.

Jesus was looking very tired now, and his disciples muttered between themselves, that they should get him home to rest. Peter raised his deep voice, remonstrating with a group of women, who were pushing their way towards the Holy One, holding babies in their arms and dragging toddlers for Jesus to bless.

'Make space there,' cried Peter. 'Can't you see that the Master is weary? Take the children away!' Many of the little ones were wailing, frightened at the pushing, noisy throng, who surrounded them. Jesus saw what was happening and turned on Peter reprovingly, but Peter did not see, and continued to scold the mothers. Then Jesus drew his brows together in indignation, and his disciples suddenly aware of his displeasure, drew back before the lightning flash in those shimmering gold flecked eyes.

'Let the little children come to me and do not hinder them, for the Kingdom of God, belongs to such as these.' He indicated that they should make a space about him, and as the people fell back instinctively, Jesus seated himself on the grassy bank, and held his arms out to the children. The little ones hesitated, relieved that the pressure around them had abated. They stared at Jesus then one after another, left the shelter of their mother's garments to which they had been clinging—and ran forward, to climb on his knees and rest their little heads against him. The minds of these innocents were receptive to the living force of love which radiated from the gentle Son of God, who held them tenderly to him, blessing them, as he laid soothing hand on their heads.

Then those who carried tiny babies came forward now, holding their precious burdens out to Jesus, that he might bless them also. Only when he had so blessed every single child, did Jesus arise and beckoned his disciples once more about him.

'I tell you the truth—anyone who will not receive the Kingdom of God, like a little child, will never enter it.' They bowed their heads in contrition, minds grappling with the meaning of his words. Now at last, he consented to make his way back into the town.

Jesus and his disciples had eaten, and now the women cleared the table, bearing the dirty bowls out to the kitchen. They did not stop to wash them now, but returned to seat themselves unobtrusively, as Jesus explained some of the parables he had used during the day, the meaning of which had eluded some of them. As he explained, he wondered ruefully, how the busy crowds would ever comprehend, when even his chosen twelve sometimes had difficulty. But they must be made to understand, for one day, all too soon, theirs would be the task of spreading his message to all mankind. He looked at them, these large children of his, quarrelsome, perhaps too full of their own importance following their mission to the villages, where they had taught and healed in his name. They now enjoyed the adventure of all that was happening, even discussing their relative positions of seniority when they thought he was not listening. How was he to prepare their minds for what lay ahead—how to explain to them.

So it was, that Mary of Magdala was one of the first, to hear Jesus announce the unbelievable, the terrible tidings, that the 'Son of Man was going to be betrayed into the hands of evil men, to be tortured—and crucified!' There were cries of denial of his quietly made statement. He held up his hand for silence, as he looked around the room, his eyes resting on first one and then another of the twelve, and on to the women, who were sitting shocked in the shadows.

'On the third day, I will rise again,' he said.

He had left, the disciples following him out, as they dispersed to their homes, Jesus going to the house of Simon Peter. The women busied themselves in the kitchen, clearing up and trying to understand, what their beloved lord had said. Miriam had been shaken out of her mood of lethargy, into which she had fallen after reading Claudius letter. What were her small problems now, compared with the fateful news she had just heard. Joanna clasped her hands together in despair.

'It cannot be allowed to happen,' she said, tears spilling unchecked down her cheeks. 'Mary, if any other than the Lord had said it, I would not have believed it!'

'Yes, I know,' said Mary, her face torn with anguish. 'All any of us can do, is to watch over him carefully, tell his disciples to be vigilant and try to keep him away from Jerusalem, for I have heard the Pharisees muttering, that it is the High Priest Caiaphas and the Sadducees, who seek his death.'

'Then we must help to spread his teaching, until he has so many followers, that neither the Sadducees, nor the Pharisees, will attempt to harm him, for fear of the populace.' So spoke the Lady Joanna, her violet eyes glowing with ardour. But fear stole upon her heart, as she remembered the death of the saintly man who had gone before the Holy One, to announce his coming. John the Baptist had been slain without mercy by Herod Antipas, merely to satisfy the whim of his most cruel wife's, spoiled daughter. She knew that Herod would not hesitate to bring a similar fate to Jesus of Nazareth, if he came to suspect that the Holy One, descended both on the side of Mary his mother and Joseph, his late guardian, from the royal house of David, from which it had been prophesied that Israel was to expect the long awaited Messiah, King of the Jews! If then, Herod thought Jesus to be a threat to his own position as Tetrarch, he as well as the Sadducees, would seek his death!

'We must keep him away from Herod also,' said Joanna, uttering her fear. Then she looked behind her, sensing another presence in the room. The other women followed her eyes, staring at the veiled figure that had just entered quietly. The woman was simply dressed, her dark blue robe heavy with dust, as were the worn sandals on her dainty feet. She dropped her veil, and they stared curiously at her face, wondering why the lovely countenance seemed vaguely familiar. They looked at the dark masses of her hair, silver winged at the temples, the classical lines of beautifully planed cheekbones, curved mouth and firm chin and at the gentle eyes, which stared back at them, with so tender a light.

'My name is Mary,' she said softly. 'I am Jesus mother.'

They surrounded her almost with awe. This then was the favoured of God, mother of His most precious Son. 'I am a woman such, as you,' she said gently. 'I know that you are caring for my dear son. I have come to help you.'

Chapter Fifteen

Well, Claudius, I'm delighted you've decided to forgo rural domesticity to join me here in Jerusalem—but I don't have to tell you, how much I regret the evil happening that brought about your decision.' Tribune Marcus held his friend close against his chest, in brotherly clasp of affection. He released him. 'You will wish to bathe and rest, after your journey. Tonight we will talk—you can give me your duty report then.' His dark eyes swept over the Centurion's face, seeing the strain beneath the surface appearance of brittle gaiety. For Claudius had presented himself with a smile about his lips and a flash of fire in his blue eyes.

Claudius smile faded, as soon as he was private in the bathroom. He dismissed the slave Marcus had sent to attend him, stepped down into the steaming water and scrubbed himself vigorously, then let himself relax. As he did so, pictures of Miriam formed behind his eyes, and his spirit groaned. It was almost two months now since he had last seen his wife and he had begun to banish memory of her during his working day. But now here in the Antonia Fortress, where they had made that visit last spring—at the Jewish Feast of Passover thoughts of her came flooding back.

How he missed her, Miriam of the merry laugh and jade green eyes. He remembered the radiant picture she had presented, in her white silk tunic, worked in gold, the glittering veil over her midnight hair—that same wonderful hair, cloaking her bare loveliness in his bed. But he must forget her. She had been defiled. Even though her body would bear no outward trace of the Sicarii's vile embrace, he would never again be able to take her in his arms, without that evil face interposing itself between them—or the sound of that insane laugh, drowning out her own sweet voice!

He scowled ferociously, angry that he could still feel so affected. He ran the few steps down to the cold bath in the small recess below. That was better! Nothing like ice cold water to drive away mental distemper! At last, refreshed in body if not spirit, he climbed the steps that led to the top most chambers of this the tallest of Antonia's four towers. He peered out of the open shutters of the room allocated to him. This tower was over a hundred feet high. It gave complete view of the Temple buildings below him and of the vast city of Jerusalem, held this afternoon in a dusty haze, as a fierce desert storm carried stinging sand in its breath, to release it high up in this mountain citadel. The October wind moaned eerily across the city's housetops, rattling through the palm trees, tossing slender cypresses in its swift embrace. Dark mountains fell away from this rock cradle of Zion, in a strange landscape of bleached gold and beige, stroked with grey.

'What would I not give, for the verdant green of Galilee once again,' he murmured, 'The blue rippling waters of the lake!' He turned away from the window, the shouted orders of the guard infringing on his consciousness. Of course, it was a feast again. The Feast of Tabernacles! The huge porticoes fringing the Temple precincts bristled with armed legionaries, waiting for any sign of trouble among the enormous crowds surging through the courts. But this was a joyful feast, commemorating the end of the Israelites wanderings in the desert centuries before, as well as a thanksgiving for the riches of the harvest. Thousands had converged outside the city walls from all the surrounding area, carrying baskets of lustrous purple grapes, golden sheaves and luscious fruit. They had built shelters of Palm and Willow branches, and dwelt in these during the hours of darkness, every smallest space on the slopes was covered by these booths. He reflected that they would give little protection from the stinging sand that sometimes swept in on the desert wind

The smell of incense from the Temple drifted through the open window, mixed with the rich odours of charred meat causing dryness to the back of the throat from the ongoing daily sacrifices of sheep, oxen and doves. The sonorous chanting of the priests, hauntingly beautiful, in praise of the One God, penetrated the room. With an exclamation of near anger Claudius clapped the shutter down. He had thought that here in Jerusalem, he would be able to forget the magnetic pull of Jesus of Nazareth—Son of God, in a dusty robe! But no! Even here, Jesus words flowed through his mind seeking out the barbed defences of his damaged spirit with healing grace. What was the phrase Simeon had repeated? 'Come to me, all you who are heavy laden, and I will give you rest!' And again--'Forgive your enemies!'

'Peace—love and forgiveness! Huh! I will never forgive,' vowed Claudius savagely.

His face was flushed from the heady wine Marcus continued to press on him, dark red, full bodied wine, putting new vigour into a man's soul. It had loosened his tongue over the excellent dinner they had just enjoyed, helping him release his heavy load of grief and frustration to the only man he could fully trust. Marcus let him talk, knowing that like a boil after lancing, poison needed to drain if it were not to gather again. He made no judgements, gave no advice, just listened sympathetically but with a deep sadness for Miriam, whose bright spirit had stirred him with her fearless honesty.

Long after Claudius had retired, Marcus stood staring out into the night. A myriad twinkling, pinpoints of light, shimmered from the Israelites torches and their campfires, which now surrounded the walled city, whilst within its ancient walls, brighter illumination poured from the houses of the rich, and the brilliant bulk of Herod's palace. Then his eyes strayed below him, to the soaring beauty of the mysterious Temple of the Jews, its pure white and gold, rippling with flame in the dark night, where the vigilant guard's fiery torches caressed it, and as he stared, he wondered about the Rabbi Jesus. Would he risk coming to this Feast of Tabernacles, knowing that the Saducees and the more vehement amongst the Pharisees, sought his life?

He thought of all he had gleaned from his long conversation with Claudius. Time and again it would seem, Jesus had rejected those who tried to thrust the Messiah-ship upon him, in its earthly conception of power, speaking only of a heavenly kingdom of peace. Certainly, such idea was impossible of human implementation in the real world of greed and crude desires. Strength! That was what the world was all about—being stronger than your neighbour, taking what you wanted from life, enforcing your wishes by might—military prowess. If you didn't, you went under, were subject to the authority of others less scrupulous.

He shrugged philosophically. Tomorrow, he would have Claudius speak with Pontius Pilate. The Governor was himself, much taken up with the exploits of the Galilean teacher, towards whom he had a softness, following the incident last Passover when Jesus had disrupted the sale of cattle for slaughter, from which the detested Caiaphas extracted such rich pickings. Although Caiaphas, crafty High Priest, together with the Saducees, the Rabbinical hierarchy ruling Israel were toadies to Rome, outwardly fawning on their masters in order to retain their own authority—Pilate had very little respect for them, and no trust. The idea of a simple Galilean rabbi taking them to task for their avarice, in their own stronghold, the Temple, had caused him much amusement.

Not that the incident at Passover, had been Jesus only brush with the priests. He had also made a visit during another feast, Pentecost it was called, when he had healed a man paralyzed from birth at the Pool of Bethesda, which lay just immediately behind the Temple, not a stone's throw from the Antonia, near the Sheep Gate. He has made the mistake of healing the man on the Jewish Sabbath, telling the totally helpless fellow who had never walked of his own volition to-- 'Get up! Take up your mat, and walk!'

It had stirred up a real hornet's nest about Jesus head, for when the man was seen carrying his mat, classed as performing work, which was totally prohibited on the Sabbath, the priests had immediately seized on this as excuse to persecute Jesus. Marcus chuckled, as he remembered the Holy Man's reported reply.

'My Father is always at His work to this very day, and I too am working!'

They had accused him of putting himself as an equal with God, and had plotted in their fury, how they could trap him, but the people held him in highest esteem, and if they laid hands on Jesus, there might well have been uprising. Well, it would be interesting to see whether Jesus would reappear at the Temple, during Tabernacles!

The brothers of Jesus were also wondering whether he would decide to join the crowds converging on Jerusalem. Over recent months they had been amazed, at his mounting popularity in Galilee, grudgingly acknowledging that he possessed extraordinary powers of healing. But still they were resentful of claims made of him by others, either that he was a prophet much favoured of God, or might indeed be the Messiah— and they, the sons of Joseph, refused to believe that he was the Son of God.

Nevertheless, they began to realize, that it might be opportune for them to ride on the wave of mounting respect and enthusiasm that greeted Jesus wherever he went. Why did he not take advantage of the popularity he was enjoying and why restrict his teachings to the confines of Galilee. After all, just supposing that he should indeed be named as Messiah, then surely Jerusalem, the Holy City, centre of their faith was the place where Jesus should be acclaimed. Yes—and it was almost Tabernacles!

They were not troubled by the fact that his disciples had told them that the authorities in Jerusalem, the Sadducees, through their council the Sanhedrin and the ruling scribes and Pharisees, sought to take Jesus life. They came to him, faces taut with expectancy.

'You ought to leave here and go to Judea, so that your followers there may see the miracles that you do. No one who wants to be a public figure acts in secret. Since you are doing these things, show yourself to the world!'

Jesus looked at them—Joses, Jude and Simon, with a world of sadness in his eyes, for he knew their hearts, their unbelief. Alone of the brothers, James, who had been a follower of John the Baptist, acknowledged Jesus as the Christ. He stood apart, ashamed of his brothers, hoping that Jesus would not be swayed to go on the perilous journey.

Jesus continued to stare at the three, who now dropped their eyes before that searching gaze.

'The right time for me has not yet come; for you, any time is right. The world cannot hate you, but it hates me because I testify what it does is evil. You go to the feast. I am not yet going to this feast, because for me the right time has not yet come.'

They went away murmuring angrily, disappointed that they had been unable to persuade him to accompany them. They had dreamed of entering Jerusalem at Jesus side, with a great multitude in tow, listening to the plaudits of all Judea. The brothers had heard talk amongst the Zealots, of proclaiming Jesus King of the Jews, leading a victorious army against the Romans. Improbable perhaps, certainly impossible if he took this self-effacing attitude! Reluctantly they made their way, together with the other crowds leaving Galilee for Judea.

When he was sure that all who sought to accompany him had already left, Jesus went apart to a lonely place high on a hill to pray, watching the crowds disappearing from sight along the rough track that wound amongst the grassy buttresses girding the lake. Twilight descended, the sky pulsing with the wine deep effulgence of a crushed grape, until the stars swung scintillating out of a hushed haze as night fell. The Holy Son of God prayed to his Father, communing, seeking guidance. Then filled with the Spirit he rose from knees bruised by night's vigil into a golden dawn, and made secret way towards Jerusalem.

Centurion Claudius was roughly awakened by the blaring of a hundred silver trumpets. First just one short blast, but it brought him instantly to his feet to thrust the shutters open. It was dawn, and the Temple blazed with golden light, as the early rays of the sun lapped its gold crested, white marbled structure, caressing the colonnades, stroking the priests white robes to bright peach. Claudius watched bemused, as a long column of priests entered the Temple courts, in attendance on one of their rank carrying an apparently heavy golden pitcher.

'Good morning, Claudius! You slept well I trust?'

He swung around, guiltily aware that for the first time in many months, he had overslept. Tribune Marcus eyed his confusion in amusement.

'Those confounded trumpets wakened me—and just as well! I would normally have been abroad an hour ago. It must have been your most excellent wine that caused me to sleep late!'

'The sleep will have done you good, my friend. As for the trumpets, you will have to accustom yourself to their early morning assault on the eardrums, the more especially this week.' Marcus joined him at the window. 'See the priest bearing that golden pitcher. He has been to the south of the city to the Pool of Siloam to draw the water. Each morning for a week he will repeat the trip and!-' His voice was drowned by the shrilling of trumpets, as the priest carried his golden burden up the steps leading to the temple. Blast after blast splintered the early morning air, as unseen by all he entered the sacred precincts. The water he had brought was ceremoniously poured into the golden bowl at the foot of the High Altar by Caiaphas, resplendent in his blue, High Priestly regalia. The multitude flooded into the Temple courts, closely watched by the hundreds of armed Roman legionaries manning the tops of the colonnades. Thousands poured into the city from the hillsides, leaving their night time booths to join their fellows already assembling, whilst on everyone's lips was the question—Will he come? Is he here? Has anyone seen the Holy Man from Galilee?

The next few days were busy ones for Claudius, as Tribune Marcus prepared his friend for his new responsibilities. Thoughts of Miriam receded in his brain as he stored the information that Marcus threw at him; ambition which had lain dormant in his breast now burgeoned forth, as he had glimmerings of what life could hold for him should he ever attain equal rank with Marcus. The tender shoots of peace and kindness towards his fellow man, born of seeds implanted by the Holy One, were strangled by new desire for power and advancement.

He dined with Marcus and Pontius Pilate. The Prefect spoke graciously with him, confiding his future plans for building a new aqueduct. Pilate smiled, as he explained that he intended to finance the much needed water supply to the city, by helping himself from the Temple treasury.

'Friend Caiaphas grows fat on the Temple funds—as does that crafty father-in-law of his, Annas. It will be most amusing, to watch his reaction, when he learns of the excellent means I will put at his disposal, for dispensing some of the wealth he had garnered, for the common good of the inhabitants of Jerusalem!' Pontius Pilate laughed and belched good- humouredly. He then proceeded to question Claudius very closely on everything that had happened in Galilee since their last meeting—and all his questions centered round Jesus of Nazareth. Were the stories of the many miracles all true, or of course an exaggeration? What of the Zealots? He had heard that trouble might be fermenting again in that region—had Jesus shown any signs of seeking to gather into his hands, the reins of political leadership, or was he still preaching his message of love and forgiveness and repentance for sins?

Claudius answered him that Jesus spoke only of peace and healed all those who came to him. Pilate nodded, satisfied, and stared broodingly into his wine goblet, letting his fingers caress its jewel encrusted stem.

'Strange that he has not come to this Feast of Tabernacles, I had thought that he would. Well—the feast still has three days to run.'

They spoke of other things, amongst them of Barabbas and his infuriating escape.

'He may well be dead now,' Tribune Marcus mused. 'If your man who wielded the flagellum knew his job, then Barabbas would have been near death, even without the rigors of the journey that was interrupted by his followers. I have seen many a man, with the flesh hanging in strips from his body, torn by the metal tippings attached to the leather thongs. Countless men have died under a scourging, as you well know, Claudius!'

'Well, I must go! My lady wife awaits me, anxious to hear whether Jesus has arrived yet or not.' Pilate arose and looked at Claudius with commiseration. 'I am more sorry than I can say to hear of the dastardly attack on your wife, Centurion. My wife holds Miriam in much affection. They say that time heals all things.' He paused, trying to consider how he would act, should such evil as rape ever touch Claudia? He had to admit to himself, that he did not know how he would behave. 'If ever Miriam should come to Jerusalem again, then Claudia will wish to receive her—as indeed will I,' he said bluntly, and was gone.

The following morning, the trumpets rang out as usual, heralding the carrying of the golden pitcher and the sound of chanting rose from the

Temple area, as the thousands of worshippers joined in the sacred songs of praise to the One God. The soldiers ever alert, gazed down at the mighty sea of people below them, as the chanting gradually ceased and a sudden a murmur passed through the crowd.

'He is here—the Holy One from Galilee has arrived! He is teaching under Solomon's Porch.' Word passed from one to the other, until it reached the High Altar, where Caiaphas was stepping back to join his colleagues.

'Jesus of Nazareth is in the court of the Gentiles—and the people are listening to his words, some falling on their knees around him, deep in prayer. Others are calling on him to perform a miracle, for there are many sick present.' The young priest, who had brought the news, scanned Caiaphas face, to gage his reaction. Caiaphas reacted savagely.

'Order my temple guards to seek opportunity to arrest this trouble maker!' His face glowed with anger under the tall blue head-dress, as he toyed nervously with the twelve glowing jewels attached to his short ceremonial cloak surmounting his flowing blue robe, fringed with its gold bells and pomegranates. Fury lit a fire in his brain, as he considered the audacity of Jesus, to dare to present himself again at the Temple for a third time—after his presumption in overturning the money changers tables and disrupting the sale of beasts for sacrifice, at the last Passover. This time he would pay for his temerity with his life! Then caution took over, as reason dawned. The Rabbi Jesus was well liked by many of those misguided individuals, who now thronged the Temple precincts. The arrest must be accomplished diplomatically, when most of the people had dispersed, perhaps towards nightfall. He gave the necessary orders, to the approval of his bevy of attendant Sadducees and those high ranking Pharisees who were there.

A mother wept with happiness as she held her small daughter to her breast, seeing once emaciated tiny limbs, plump out with firm flesh as this little one so close to death, now glowed with health. As she cried out her thanks to Almighty God, a moan of awe swept through the crowd, whilst others behind, tried to see what was happening. But it was that firm, majestic voice, sweeping amazingly to the furthest corner of the Temple that held the people entranced. Never had they heard such words—such a profound teaching and those who lived in Jerusalem had taken opportunity to listen to the most learned rabbis of the day; men who had studied for years at the rabbinical schools. Yet here was this apparently untutored Galilean, teaching with an authority as though he wore Elijah's mantle, the beauty of his words exceeding those of the Prophet Isaiah. It was thing incredible, and they listened with amazement, tinged with fear.

He heard their whispered words.

'How did this man get such learning, without having studied?' Jesus answered. 'My teaching is not my own. It comes from Him who sent me. If any chooses to do God's will, he will find out whether my teaching comes from God—or whether I speak on my own.' He gazed at their expectant faces, reading doubt on some, belief and joy on others—and easing their way gently between the mass of people he saw the Temple guards, and he knew their purpose.

'He who speaks on his own, does so to gain honour for himself, but he who works for the honour of the One who sent him, is a man of truth; there is nothing false about him. Has not Moses given you the law? Yet not one of you tries to keep the law!' The guards were closer now. He threw back his head and demanded—'Why are you trying to kill me?'

'You are demon possessed,' cried some of those nearest, taking affront. 'Who is trying to kill you?' They had not noticed the guards.

But a confused version of his words sped from lip to lip, as people began to question each other.

'Isn't this the man they are trying to kill? Yet here he is speaking publicly, and they are not saying a word to him! Have the authorities concluded that he really is the Christ?'

'But we know where he is from,' cried others. 'When the Christ comes, no one will know where he is from!' Their faces were puzzled, uneasy, as their minds grappled with the confusing facts, that this man possessed all the attributes of the expected Messiah, his miracles, his wondrous teaching touching their hearts—but he was an ordinary carpenter from Nazareth, not a mysterious being descended in majesty from another world. It was not even as though he were from Jerusalem, city of culture, but from a miserable village in Galilee, where the people were poor, unsophisticated and spoke with uncultured accent.

The soldiers on the colonnades peered down curiously, hearing the raised voices in the crowd, waves of sound, vibrating dully, the ever present tensions in Jerusalem could flare at the smallest spark. One of the sergeants recognized the name that was being shouted—Rabbi Jesus! The man from Nazareth! He dispatched a man for the Centurion.

Claudius walked swiftly to the point from which he could oversee the focus of the pushing, striving throng and there below him, arms outstretched, stood Jesus, throwing back his head in impassioned speech.

'Yes—you know me, and you know where I am from. I am not here on my own but He who sent me is true! You do not know Him—but I know Him—because I am from Him—and He sent me!' At this identification with the Almighty, some of the Pharisees within the crowd leapt forward, shouting to the temple guards to move in, to arrest Jesus. The guards moved in towards Jesus, then hesitated before the light blazing in his eyes and knowledge was born in their hardened hearts, of the stature of the one they were called upon to deal with and their spirits quailed in fear. Their feet, when they attempted to march forward, were rooted to the ground. High from his vantage point on the colonnade, Centurion Claudius stared down. He had seen the high ranking Pharisees giving orders to the Temple guards, and their apparent unwillingness to act. His instinct was to send some of his men amongst the crowd, to collect Jesus and remove him from danger, but he knew such partisan action, might cause sudden flare up, in the seething mass below him.

Jesus was speaking again.

'I am with you for only a short time, and then I go to the One who sent me. You will look for me, but you will not find me—and where I am, you cannot come!' Then as the Jews debated as to the meaning of these words, wondering perhaps if he intended to go to preach to those Jews scattered amongst the Greeks, he was gone.

It was the last day of the feast. As before, the golden pitcher was borne into the Temple courts, to the resonance of the silver trumpets, and the priestly procession proceeded to climb the Temple steps, bearing the water to be poured before the High Altar. Then suddenly, a loud voice arose, reverberating around the whole temple precincts, rising even above the sonorous chanting of the priests.

It was Jesus. The crowd fell back from him, their mouths opening in awe, for the Spirit of the Living God was upon him, and each man and woman present, found themselves trembling and sorely amazed. He gestured to the priest carrying the pitcher, who had just ascended the topmost step leading to the Temple door. The man turned, spilling some of the pitcher's contents, to run dripping down the marble steps.

'If anyone is thirsty, let him come to me and drink. Whoever believes in me, as the scripture has said—"Streams of living water will flow from him!" The newly risen sun poured a cloak of flame over his white robe. But it was at his face that they stared, for light seemed to blaze all about him, surely a trick of the sunrise, for his eyes shone with the heart of flame, glowing with unearthly brightness. They raised shaking fingers towards him, as they murmured to each other—'Surely, this man in the Prophet!'

'He is the Christ!'

And Caiaphas heard their words, as he stared from an open window in the Temple building; words that were now being tossed from lip to lip, all around that huge open area, that bordered the Temple and he cursed in fury and frustration, calling to his underlings to act, to send the guards to arrest Jesus—and not to fail this time, if they valued their skins!

Now others amongst the people started to question their fellows. It was the place of his birth that seemed to be their stumbling block.

'How can the Christ, come from Galilee? Does not the scripture say that the Christ will come from David's family and from Bethlehem, the town where David lived?' Everywhere small groups started arguing, for none knew Bethlehem to have been Jesus birthplace, and again Centurion Claudius was sent for, as the Roman soldiers sensed a possible riot. This time, Tribune Marcus walked at his side, as together they stared down at Jesus, where he stood teaching the crowd, while the Temple guards once more attempted to close in around him. But as the guards looked on him and heard his words, they were again transfixed with fear.

'Look at those guards! It's obvious that Caiaphas has sent them to arrest the teacher,' said Marcus, resting his hand on Claudius shoulder. 'I watched them march down the Temple steps and work their way between the crowds! They are within six yards of him now, yet they are making no slightest move to carry out their orders! Why? I have seen more arrests down there on feast days, than I can remember. No nonsense with those fellows—as well trained as some of our own men! Yet they look as though they have been turned to stone!'

'It is the power of God,' murmured Claudius tightly. As he spoke, Jesus suddenly raised his head, seeming to gaze straight at him, stripping through the ambition and lack of forgiveness rankling Claudius soul. A sudden shudder shook Claudius frame, as he came face to face with his inner self, and was appalled at what he saw. He stumbled slightly, and

Marcus tightened his grip in surprise, in case the Centurion should fall, for it would be certain death to fall from that height.

'Are you unwell?'

'No—it was merely the reflection of the sun on one of the guards shields that dazzled me,' managed Claudius, trying to keep his tones level. Marcus nodded, satisfied.

'Where is the Holy Man now,' he suddenly exclaimed for during the slight period of time during which he had taken his eyes off the court of the Gentiles, Jesus had disappeared. No, the guards had not taken him, for they were still standing spellbound. But of Jesus, there was no sign. Slowly the noisy throng became less agitated, as the sound of harps and viols stole upon the air, and the hauntingly beautiful psalm being intoned by the priests, was taken up by thousands of throats. Yet as they sang, most of those present, still disputed in their hearts, as to whether the man from Galilee, was indeed the Messiah—the Christ?

Caiaphas was almost livid with rage as the guards stood trembling before him, hard set not to cringe before the malevolence in his burning eyes.

'No man ever spoke the way this man does,' they mumbled shamefacedly, afraid to admit that they themselves believed the Nazarene to be the Christ. Caiaphas and the Sadducees lashed the guards with their tongues, as did the leading Pharisees. They had had him within their grasp and let him go! What if those fools in the Temple courts believed his rash words? They were unlearned men, easily swayed, looking for excitement! Could not the guards realize, that there was not even one of the ruling priestly hierarchy who supported Jesus claims!

Yet, one man raised solitary voice in Jesus defence. It was Nicodemus. He had been a changed man since his encounter with Jesus on the Mount of Olives at the time of the last Passover. His fellow Pharisees noted a difference in him, his needle sharp gift of repartee less obvious, his exaggerated insistence of pursuing each slightest point of the law, dissecting minutiae, seemingly dispensed with. His eyes sometimes held a slightly haunted look, as though he was at war with himself.

'Does our law condemn a man without first hearing him, to find out what he is doing?'

His question rang out its challenge across the meeting hall, which formed the southern boundary of the Temple platform.

The other men looked at him in amazement then erupted into angry retort.

'Are you from Galilee too? Look into it, and you will find that the Prophet does not come out of Galilee!' Having silenced him with this incontrovertible fact, they set their minds as to how best to accomplish the Nazarene's death. Perhaps it would be better to destroy his credibility with the people first—trap him into openly disobeying the law! But of course, Tabernacles was now finished, the multitude would be dismantling their booths and returning to their own districts. So, would Jesus remain longer in Jerusalem, or return to safety in Galilee?

Claudius was relieved to hear merely the blast on a single trumpet, to herald the dawn. It was the customary signal from a priest set on the Pinnacle of Trumpeting, but it was taken up by other silver trumpets as the cry arose that the sun had risen over Hebron, signalling the knife to fall on the first sacrifice of the day. Far fewer people were milling below in the Temple courts than during the week of the feast, as thousands had taken their departure, and could be seen streaming away from the city walls. Smoke soon drifted upwards from the great horned altar within the Temple, as the burnt offering to the Unseen God, was attended by the chanting of the priests.

Claudius had been advised by Tribune Marcus that a smaller force need man the walls today, as life returned to normal, until the next feast that of Dedication, the Feast of Lights—but that was not until December a winter festival. As he stared from his window in the great tower of the Antonia, he hoped that Jesus had made safe retreat from this dangerous city, which always reminded him of a crouching lion! For Jerusalem resembled the king of beasts in its leonine colouring, the golden browns of the buildings caught in the fierce light of the risen sun—an alien beast, ready to spring, to rend and tear those who ventured within its tension filled walls.

'Centurion, Sir! There's a disturbance in the court of the Gentiles—at the southern end, where the remaining phase of work on the Stoa is taking place!' The man looked apologetically at Claudius, for the Centurion was staring gloomily at several parchments, showing the accounts for provisions, others for accoutrements for the soldiers. A military scribe had submitted the figures for his approval. He sprang to his feet, glad of excuse to leave the figures, for which he had no liking.

'I will come!'

'Oh, no sir, I merely wanted permission to bring a few of the men down into the Gentile Court, in case things get difficult. It doesn't take much to provoke a riot situation. If I may suggest that about twenty men should suffice—there is a woman struggling to escape from the priests. I heard shouts of stone her!'

'I said I would come,' replied Claudius. 'Lead the way, Captain, and twenty men would sound about right. Alert the colonnades and bring extra men out!'

Below in the huge court open to Jew and Gentile alike, a respectful circle of people surrounded the seated figure of the Holy One. Jesus had spent the night on the Mount of Olives, and returned to the Temple this morning, to teach those who had ears open to his message, despite the ever present danger of arrest. He paused then glanced about him as a woman's screams pierced the air.

'Mercy! Mercy sirs, I don't want to die—I'll do anything you say! I repent!' Suddenly the circle of reverent listeners standing around the Holy One, parted, to allow passage of a purposeful band of priests, dragging the dishevelled figure of a woman. They pushed her to stand in panting confusion, before Jesus. They closed ranks behind her, to prevent possibility of escape. Their faces were cruel as they sneered at Jesus, who did not rise, but sat composed, silent, reading the evil on their faces.

One of the Pharisees addressed Jesus.

'Rabbi, this woman was taken in the very act of adultery. In the law, Moses instructed us to stone such women! Now—what do you say?'

The group of Pharisees watched him like vultures about to rend their prey, for he would lose face with the crowd whatever he should say. They knew all too well, that Jesus spent much time preaching repentance and forgiveness to those whom they considered to be the dregs of society—to tax collectors, drunkards and sinners and also to women such as this one, who took the dark path of prostitution, whose premises had been watched for the specific cause of catching her in the act of pursuing her trade. If he took her part, pleading mercy for her, then he would be guilty of openly flouting the Law of Moses. But should he condone the cruel death sentence of stoning, to be carried out immediately then he would be discredited amongst the great multitude of the poor and afflicted, to whom he personified peace and forgiveness.

Jesus looked impassively from the weeping, terrified woman, in her torn, tawdry spangled garment, to the leaders of the Jewish faith, some of whom had seized stones from the demolished columns that were being replaced, the final phase of the forty-six year long rebuilding of the Temple. Their intention was plain—they had only to drag the woman outside the Temple gates, to accomplish their grizzly purpose; hurl her down the steep slope and throw the heavy stones, until she was merely bleeding, lifeless lump of clay.

Pain, grief—the almost impossibility of his task amongst them, made him lower his head and there was anger at their inhumanity, their disruption of his ministry with such base motives. He did not raise his head, even when the sound of marching feet were heard, and halted just behind the group.

'What's the teacher doing?' Those whose view was obscured by the encroaching Pharisees tried to push forward.

'The Holy One is writing in the dust with his finger!'

'What is he writing?'

'He writes words, just words! Avarice, pride, untruthfulness, anger and fornication....!'

All eyes were trained upon the gracious figure, in the white gown, who continued to write further words on the marble tiled courtyard, which bore fine film of dust, from the efforts of the busy workmen priests on their high ladders. The Pharisees faces darkened with anger and they started to call out to him in their impatience, demanding an answer. Then their eyes descended curiously, to see what he wrote—read those accusing words.

Slowly he lifted his head, and his dark eyes shimmered with golden light, as the sun blazed down on the scene. He gazed at the woman, kohl smudged eyes wild with fear; on the rigid priests; the curious men and women and saw behind them the double line of Roman legionaries, armour glinting, their Centurion with his scarlet cloak and plumed helmet. The Pharisees moved uneasily beneath that stare, as the Messiah read their souls, looked into the aridity of their hearts.

He spoke. 'If any of you is without sin, let him be the first to throw a stone at her!' He bent his head again and their eyes were drawn down to what he wrote and each one of them saw his own particular sin written in the dust—and it was as though the words leapt at them with all the flames of hell. They started to tremble—to drop the stones—then one by one they turned blindly away, slinking under the colonnades, heads bent in discomfiture.

The crowd murmured to each other that it was noticeable, that it was the elder and most respected of the Pharisees who walked away first. Then—at last, Jesus raised his head again, and looked full at the shaking figure of the woman. She returned his gaze with awe and deepest gratitude in her eyes, as she shifted uneasily.

'Woman, where are they? Has no one condemned you?' She shook her head as she heard the gentle words.

'No-one, sir!' There were new tears in her eyes now, as the ice in her heart cracked, and a seed of hope was born, hope for new life, for cleanliness—for healing.

'Then neither do I condemn you! Go and leave your life of sin!'

She dropped to her knees before him, weeping openly now, then rose, new purpose on her face, as she hurried off, in the opposite direction to her erstwhile tormentors. She turned once, casting a look of adoration on the Son of God, who had given her new life.

Claudius had observed the whole incident in wonder and delight in the humiliation of the Pharisees. He spoke a quick word to his men, and they marched back to the Antonia. As he dismissed the men, the young captain said to him soberly-

'He made it impossible for them to stone her, didn't he?

After all, there cannot be a man alive, who has not committed sin!'

'There is one who has not,' murmured Claudius to himself. 'But then, he is not just man—but God!' Frustration filled him, as he realized the impossibility of his situation. How could he continue to serve Rome and the god emperor, Tiberius, when he knew that the Jewish Unseen God was the only true God and Jesus of Nazareth his Son!

Chapter Sixteen

The disciples and the women had arrived on the outskirts of Jerusalem. For Miriam, it had been a vastly different journey from her previous visit, when she had travelled with Claudius, enjoying the comfort of her litter. Now she walked, under the blazing Judean sun, which scorched the strange, baked hills to bleached bronze. Her feet were sore from the rough stones and burning sand, which seared even through the stout sandals.

Mary Magdalene rubbed her arm across her forehead, wiping away sweat beading her brow and smiled at Joanna, who walked determinedly at her side. The last few days had been her first experience of the rigors of travelling on foot, but she had proved herself to have an endurance not expected in one gently nurtured and pampered in palaces. Susannah walked behind, chattering with Sarah. Esther had been left in Bethsaida, with Phillip's family.

The disciples halted and John looked respectfully at the serene figure, seated on the shaggy donkey. Mary of Nazareth looked apprehensively at the huge, walled city which lay before them. She had visited it on other occasions in the past, for Passover, but had ever felt uneasy within Jerusalem's narrow, tension filled streets. There was always an atmosphere similar to that experienced before one of those violent storms, which swept across Galilee's waters—a brooding intensity, expressed in the watchful, slightly aggressive manner of the city's inhabitants. It was as though some malevolent force was concentrated there, waiting to be unleashed!

The last stage of their journey had been difficult, for thousands had been leaving Jerusalem, at the conclusion of the Feast of Tabernacles, and many shouted at the little party, asking good-humouredly whether they had mistaken the date of the feast!

It lacked a couple of hours to sunset. They must get the women safely to the house of Lady Joanna, before seeking Jesus, if he were still there. He had not told them of his intention to attend the feast and they had assumed that he had retreated into the hills for a few days; but a shepherd had reported seeing Jesus on the road to Jerusalem. Immediately they thought of his words regarding his eventual fate at the hands of the authorities there, so now they were come to find him in the hope that he was still safe.

As they passed beneath the huge gates, Mary shuddered, her fingers tightening on the reins. Everywhere in those winding streets was noise. Shopkeepers shouted their wares to those who hesitated in their progress, disdainful camels loped between donkeys heavily laden, and slaves shouted passage for some rich merchant in his litter. Roman soldiers smiled boldly at lightly veiled women who walked slowly past, calling out to them suggestively, while Pharisees held their robes close about them, that they should not be contaminated by contact with unbelievers, frowning as urchins darted between the crowds, begging for some small coin. The cobbled streets were dusty and the air thick with smells of over ripe fruit, garlic flavoured meats and smoked fish, and the droppings of the pack animals. Smells also arose from the sores of beggars, who waved pleading hands to all who passed. All this was mixed with the stench from the sewers and the pungent odour drifting across from the street of cheese-makers. Only when they passed a garden, hidden by high walls, belonging to one of the rich Israelites who collaborated with the Romans, did the sweet fragrance of roses and jasmine charm their suffering nostrils, wafted towards them by swaying tops of tall palms.

They had left the smaller houses behind, until here, close by Herod's palace, now used by Pontius Pilate, was a modest villa, glimpsed behind iron gates.

An attendant opened the gate, and looked suspiciously at the party of women and plainly dressed Galileans, covered with the dust of their journey.

'Who are you? What do you want here?' demanded the door attendant, opening to their knock. 'This is the house of Chuza!'

'Do you not recognize me, Titus? I am the lady Joanna!' The divorced wife of Chamberlain Chuza, smiled at the young slave in his orange striped tunic, who stared back bewildered. Another older man appeared behind him. He also stared bemused at the strangely assorted party seeking admittance. Then he saw a woman who looked familiar and as he glimpsed the slightly haughty glance in Joanna's violet eyes and he knew her.

'My lady, we had orders from Lord Chuza, to keep the house in readiness for you at all times. These, are your guests?'

'Yes, Samuel. Please have rooms prepared.'

'Not for us,' said John quietly. 'We are going to seek the Master. We know where he usually stays. But certainly it would be good to wash away the dust of the journey.' He helped Mary to dismount. Then they filed into the cool confines of the villa. After the relief of a refreshing wash and hastily eaten meal, the men followed Peter to the door and said farewell. They were going outside the city walls, to the Mount of Olives, where they hoped to find Jesus. Judas Iscariot cast one final approving glance at the marble hall, examining the rich carpets and exquisite vases. He smiled unctuously at Joanna, before he left.

Lady Joanna gave a slight shudder, as Judas Iscariot departed in the wake of the other disciples.

'That man fills me with a spirit of unease,' she said. 'I have never felt him to be a real disciple of the Lord. There is something cruel in his make-up. Why do you suppose that Jesus chose such a one to follow him?'

Mary of Nazareth turned, a serious expression crossing her usually serene features, as she said, 'I can only tell you, that all that is happening now is in fulfilment of prophecies made by God through his holy men over past centuries. Perhaps it is ordained, that this Judas has a part to play in whatever lies ahead.' She was silent for a few minutes then said quietly-'When Jesus was tiny babe, Joseph and I brought him to the temple, to consecrate to the Lord. It was at this time, that an elderly man, filled with the Spirit, took my son in his arms. He said—"This child is destined to cause the rising and falling of many in Israel, and will be a sign that will be spoken against, so that the thoughts of many hearts will be revealed—and a sword will pierce your own soul too!"

Mary of Magdala watched her Lord's mother with unaccustomed tenderness, realizing perhaps for the first time, how most wonderfully favoured Mary was of all women on earth, that she had been chosen to be the mother of the Son of God. She had held him in her arms as a babe, comforted his childish woes, taught him at her knee, shaped his early years, and now stepped back gently worshipping and adoring the wondrous being who was the awaited Messiah.

'Lady,' she said, and slipped to her knees before Mary, resting her head against the older woman's lap, 'I feel so unworthy to be in your presence, when I think of the life I once led! You are his gracious mother—and I---!' Her voice broke on a sob. A hand reached out, stroking her hair.

'Be comforted child,' said Mary. 'I feel that you also have been chosen for special purpose and that men will always hold your memory dear.' Her dark eyes seemed to pierce the mists of the future and a tremor passed across her face. Then she smiled at Miriam, Joanna, Susannah and young Sarah, whose faces were solemn and full of apprehension, as they worried about the safety of Jesus. Where was he now?

'We will retire,' she said. 'We all need sleep to calm our spirits. Let us pray Almighty God, to have his hand upon His Son Jesus—and to guide us, in our ministering to his needs.' The soft beds were an unaccustomed luxury and they lay mingling their prayers to the glorious voice of Susannah, as the night wind poured over Jerusalem.

While the women slept, the disciples searched the Mount of Olives, then finding him not, built a small fire, and sat disconsolate. Where was he? Had the authorities taken him? The night was full of strange rustlings and a bird of prey shrieked eerily into the starlit vault above. Then as their hearts were consumed with heaviness and they muttered their nagging thoughts to each other, a figure stole towards them, and stood smiling down on the small group. The leaping firelight illuminated his face, its reflection glittering in his eyes, outlining hair and beard with shimmering intensity—it also showed his torn robe and a smear of blood at his forehead.

'Master! We have been so worried about you!' They sprang up, their relief patently obvious. Nothing mattered now though, except that they had him safe among them again. Later that night, as their Master slept exhausted, they talked in whispers about what he had told them. He had almost been stoned this afternoon in the Temple, had been seized but had managed to escape the emissaries of the Sadducees, who had disguised themselves amongst the crowds and attempted to discredit him with the people. They had suggested that Jesus was a Samaritan and demon possessed. But Jesus had confounded them with his words.

'I tell you the truth, if anyone keeps my word, he will never see death!' They had cried out at him again screaming that he was possessed of demons. They were closing in around him, these paid flunkies of Caiaphas, dressed in the robes of the common people.

'Are you greater than our father Abraham? He died! And so did the prophets! Who do you think you are?' Their faces strained to contain their rage.

'I tell you the truth—before Abraham was born—I am!' They caught at his robe and raised the stones they had held in their hands, hidden behind their backs until now.

'Kill him-----stone him!' they cried.

But Jesus had torn away from them, slipping behind a crowd of those sympathetic to him, who closed ranks against the furious secret agents of the Temple. He had remained quietly in the Temple grounds, only managing to escape as night fell, and the crowds streamed out of the gates.

David held whispered conversation with Simon, being careful not to disturb the Master's slumbers. His heart was filled with anger towards those who dared to raise hands against Jesus. Simon's face was grave, as they all realized for the first time, how very real the danger was, that threatened the Messiah in Jerusalem. His words spoken in Capernaum, that he would be captured, tortured and crucified, came flooding back to them and the stark reality, that this could indeed happen filled them with fear, and a firm resolve to protect their Master with their lives.

When dawn broke, Jesus was already afoot, calling on his disciples to follow him. He was going into Jerusalem. They tried to dissuade him, but to no avail. As they washed themselves in the Kidron brook, they were shivering slightly for although the days were still hot, nights out in the open when the temperature dropped dramatically caused stiffness. Now Jerusalem's tawny shape spread menacingly before them.

They tried to remonstrate with him one last time, before entering.

Miriam was the first person to rise. She stared out of the bedroom window at the unfamiliar surroundings. This side of the villa, looked upon the soaring towers of Herod's palace, where she had dined with her husband last springtime. Tears filled her eyes, as she realized that Claudius was less than half a mile away at the Antonia fortress, but now it might have been a thousand miles. She sighed then hurried to the bathroom, to wash away those tears of weakness. What did her own small problems matter when there was the greater worry over the safety of the Holy One?

The women had almost finished breakfasting when Titus announced an early visitor.

'A lady wishes admittance. She will not give her name, Lady Joanna, but says you know her.' The young slave's eyes were bright with curiosity, for the veiled woman, although plainly garbed in a dark green cloak, wore a fortune of jewels on her slim, patrician hands.

'Why—bring her in,' said Joanna.

'Dismiss your slave, Lady Joanna,' said a cool authoritative voice. Joanna hesitated then she knew who this was! They all rose to their feet.

'You may go, Titus,' she said. She waited until the slave had closed the door then looked expectantly at the lady Claudia, wife to Pontius Pilate. Claudia removed her veil and slipped the concealing cloak from her slim shoulders. Her beautiful face looked tense, but she smiled as he eyes fell upon the two women she had come to see.

'You are welcome, Lady Claudia,' said Joanna warmly. Claudia took her hands, then embraced her, and turned to Miriam, looking compassionately at the young Jewish woman, seeing the slight traces of redness about the lovely green eyes and knowing the reason.

Miriam—dear Miriam, I am so sorry,' she said softly, taking her in her arms in swift embrace. Then she stepped back, looking interrogatively at the other women, inclining her head slightly, as Joanna introduced them. Her eyes lingered on Mary of Nazareth, with an unfathomable expression.

'How did you know we were here,' asked Joanna? 'None knew we were coming!'

'Your slave mentioned this to a girl of my household whom he loves. She spoke of it to one of my maids, who repeated to me that Chuza's wife had arrived at her villa next to the palace with a group of women, amongst them the wife of Centurion Claudius and the mother of Jesus of Nazareth!' She looked at Mary with strange wistfulness. She who was descended from Rome's Imperial house, brought up amongst wealth, intrigue and great power, had knowledge of the emptiness of soul that such things bring. Things rarely acknowledged, such as the despair, the inner loneliness wrought as days rush by to what else but eventual annihilation. She then, stared with a world of longing in her eyes at the quiet figure, humbly dressed, silver winged hair drawn back from her gracious brow, dark eyes gentle. This was Mary, mother of—the Son of God? A thousand questions pricked her mind. Claudia, embittered by a loveless marriage of convenience, now knew her spirit struggling to free itself of the pain such bitterness breeds.

'You lady, are his mother,' she said? Then Claudia, married to the most powerful man in Judea, knelt before Mary, and stayed thus, wordless for a minute. Mary's hand rested gently on her head, as she said softly-

'You believe in him then—you know?' She took Claudia's hand, raising her. Claudia's eyes misted with tears.

'When we were together, at your Jewish Feast of Passover, Miriam spoke of your son, said he was the Messiah, the great leader long awaited by your people, but more that he was the very Son of God. She told me of her visit with her Centurion husband, to your carpenter's shop at Nazareth, of all you had told her of the wonderful events surrounding your son's birth and of the miracles. When Miriam returned to Capernaum, I was filled with desire to learn more of Jesus and his teaching, but as you may know I spend most of my days at the coast, at Caesarea. I only accompany my husband to Jerusalem, during the Jewish festivals, when he takes command here in case of—well trouble.' She paused for a moment and sipped the fruit juice Joanna had offered her.

'Have you seen my son—heard him preach,' asked Mary?

'Yesterday I visited the Antonia. My husband and Tribune Marcus were at the chariot races at the Circus and I persuaded Centurion Claudius to escort me along the top of the colonnades, on the chance that Jesus might be preaching below in the Court of the Gentiles.

'Was he there,' asked Mary?

'Yes, but for much of the time, although I could hear his voice, I could not see him, for he was immediately below me, on the steps of the colonnade, by Solomon's Porch. I heard his words, wonderful words of peace and love. Crowds of people were surging towards him, first one group after another, pushing forward to question him. There were some agitators amongst the crowd, trying to discredit him, but mostly they were shouted down.'

'Did he seem to be in any sort of danger?' asked Mary Magdalene, face deeply troubled.

'I would say that he is permanently in danger,' replied Claudia, glancing at her. 'The lives of men are ruled by greed, covetousness, anger and pride—they are not going to swing away from these forces which dominate their lives easily, nor smile upon one who makes them aware of the evil which holds them in bondage.'

'He knows of the danger,' said Mary of Nazareth. 'But his mission is more important.' Her mothers' heart beat like a fluttering dove, as she fought down fear.

'His words will one day encompass the whole world—change it,' said Claudia. 'I knew this as I listened to him. He moved out amongst his people and I saw his face for the first time. I sense that your husband believes in him, Miriam! Do you know what Jesus said? "I am the light of the world! Whoever follows me, will never walk in darkness, but will have the light of life!" That is what he is, the Light of the World!'

'Would you like to learn more of my son,' asked Mary? 'Let us sit and I will tell you everything you wish to know.'

Before she left that quiet villa, Lady Claudia had made lifelong commitment to the one she now acknowledged as Son of the One God and as she slipped unobtrusively back into the palace, her eyes were shining.

Peter and John walked on either side of Jesus, as the party passed through the city gates and paused by the Pool of Siloam. A blind man sat near the pool, his begging bowl held laxly in his left hand, whilst his right hand was outstretched to passersby, imploring charity. The man had been blind since birth. It was widely believed that disability and sickness were inflicted on an individual as a result of sin. David heard some believers of Jesus, who had attached themselves to the disciples, murmuring amongst themselves about the beggar, who was well known to them. At last they questioned Jesus.

'Rabbi? Who sinned, this man—or his parents?'

'Neither this man, nor his parents—this happened so that the work of God might be displayed in his life!'

The disciples knew instinctively that Jesus was about to heal the man, but they also knew that it was the Sabbath, not that this had ever prevented the Lord from a work of healing, despite the protests of the Pharisees that he defiled the Sabbath. But surely he should be extra careful in Jerusalem at this time, when there were spies everywhere, those seeking any excuse to arrest him. Peter whispered quietly to Jesus. But it was to no avail.

'As long as it is day, we must do the work of Him who sent me! Night is coming, when no man can work. While I am in the world, I am the light of the world.' Then as all watched, he touched the man on the shoulder. The blind man, whose other senses were acute, as is often the case with those denied sight, had heard every slightest whisper of those around him. The firmly positive tones of Jesus, registered their significance in his brain. He did not know who placed a hand on his shoulder—only felt warmth radiating through him, as his limbs started to tremble.

Then Jesus bent, spat on the ground, mixing the dust with his saliva, put the mud on the man's eyes. The man gave a grunt of surprise, as he felt the physical presence of the substance.

'Go, wash in the Pool of Siloam,' said the unknown one, guiding him in the direction of the pool. The blind man, heard those around him, calling out in excitement and naming the stranger as—Jesus? He knelt at the edge of the pool, gripping its sides with his hands, then assured of his balance, leaned forward and cupped the water in his hands, splashing his face, washing the mud away.

His cries of amazement and joy shattered the peace of the early morning. For the first time, he saw the radiance of the sun, and glancing down into the pool, saw his own reflection and knew for the first time, how he appeared to others. His incoherent utterances caused a crowd to gather around him. Jesus and his disciples had already moved on.

The man went to his home rejoicing, with gratitude in his heard, too great for words to the unseen Rabbi, who had touched his eyes and given him this wondrous gift of sight. If only he had used his eyes, to try to identify the Holy One, to give him thanks! He would find him though, glory to his name—the name of Jesus!

Neighbours regarded him in disbelief. How was this possible, perhaps it was not the same man? But it was. His parents identified him. He was carried off to appear before the Pharisees to give an account of himself! He looked into the angry faces of Jerusalem's spiritual leaders and wondered at the difference between these cruel looking men, their arrogance and disbelief in what he told them and the Holy One, who had done the impossible, given sight to one born blind.

'I tell you, he put mud on my eyes and I washed—and now I see!' His parents were summoned to give evidence, and confirmed that he had been born sightless. They were furious, these Pharisees, who refused to see the light, to accept truth. They reviled the man, who answered them with spirit, defending the wonderful man who had healed him.

'One thing I know, I was blind, but now I see!' They had him thrown out of their presence, so great their fury that they could not destroy his credibility. He picked himself up and stared back scornfully. How dared they to suggest that Jesus was a sinner. 'If this man were not from God, he could do nothing!' Having yelled his parting shot at the top of his voice, he set off to examine this disturbing world, where good was descried.

Jesus was told of what had happened to the man. His face clouded with sadness, then he turned on his heel and accompanied by his disciples, went to seek him. He was followed by some members of the Pharisees, who were carefully watching his progress, eager to further discredit him.

They found the man in one of the city squares, where stone seats were placed around a gushing fountain, and glossy leafed shrubs were starred with brilliant pink flowers. He was throwing his arms up high in an excess of exuberance, as he cried wonder of his new gift of sight. He became still, as Jesus stood before him.

'Do you believe in the Son of Man,' asked Jesus? The man recognized his voice.

'Who is he, sir,' the man asked respectfully? 'Tell me, so that I may believe in him!'

'You have seen him in fact he is the one speaking with you!' The man's face became bright with joy, his eyes sparkled with tears. His lips trembled as he said in a shaking voice, 'Lord—I believe!'

He sank down on his knees, raising a face radiant with praise to Jesus, and worshipped him. His disciples smiled at each other, at this public acclamation of faith, then formed protective shield about Jesus as the Pharisees began to throw jeering comments. David murmured to Simon, that he would like the chance to wipe the sneers from their faces, and felt Simon's restraining pressure on his shoulder as he started towards them. Jesus was speaking again, his very calm in contrast to their ireful presence.

'For judgement I have come into this world, so that the blind will see—and,' he looked directly at them, 'those who see, will become blind!'

One Pharisee cackled in high-pitched laughter. 'What! Are we blind too?' Jesus looked at them his face stern.

'If you were blind then you would not be guilty of sin—but now that you claim you can see, your guilt remains!'

A crowd now gathered in the square, pressing to get close to the Holy One. Among them were his mother and the women, who followed him. Mary's face was bright with relief and so grateful was she that he was safe, that she did not concentrate at first on what he was saying, only that he was likening himself to a shepherd with his sheep, then as she became calmer, she heard him say-

'I am the good shepherd. I know my sheep and my sheep know me, just as the Father knows me and I know the Father and I lay down my life for the sheep.' He glanced around the crowd, amongst whom he saw some Greeks and Samaritans—Phoenicians and even a couple of curious Roman soldiers. 'I have other sheep that are not of this sheep pen. I must bring them also. They too will listen to my voice, and there shall be one flock and one shepherd.'

The Jews started to murmur amongst themselves at this, whilst the Pharisees exclaimed once again that he was demon possessed. How dare he put Gentiles on a footing with those of Israel!

'The reason my Father loves me is that I lay down my own life, only to take it up again! No one takes it from me, but I lay it down of my own accord. I have authority to lay it down, and authority to take it up again. This command, I received from my Father.'

As he finished speaking pandemonium broke out, as the Pharisees screamed out that he was blaspheming, was crazy. Nevertheless, the majority of those present, who had spoken with the man healed of blindness, believed him to be the Messiah.

'Master, come quickly, for I fear they will send for the guard,' said John urgently.

'Lord, if you would like to refresh yourself at my house,' murmured Joanna? 'It is not far.' She was rewarded by a warm smile as she led the way. Behind them, a large, noisy crowd were shouting vociferously at the Pharisees, whilst the Roman soldiers shrugged their shoulders at this incomprehensible people who allowed themselves, to become so involved over matters of their religion.

'Why do the priests dislike this Jesus so much?' asked one soldier of the other. 'He is always calm, preaches forgiveness, and heals the sick.

You would think they would applaud him for his teaching.'

'Not so, they are jealous of him, my friend.' He spat reflectively. 'They will kill him one day, if we Romans do not arrest him first for causing disturbance. It's a pity, for there is something about him that draws you to him. Bah! Let's get out of here!' They pushed their way good-humouredly between the crowds, returning to their garrison.

They were to return to Galilee, preaching through Judea as they went. But first, there was to be a brief stop at Bethany, the little town where Mary Magdalene had been born, and where once she had lived with her brother Lazarus and her sister Martha, before leaving with a rich merchant, who had promised marriage. The journey north, in a swaying litter, clad in silk and dreaming romantic dreams, had led eventually to the lowest forms of degradation in Magdala and Tiberias, with a pain that burned her soul for her lost innocence, until Jesus had cast out the demons that afflicted her.

She walked ahead of the little party, and knocked hesitantly at the door of the family house, unsure of her reception. This was the first time she had returned home since leaving two years ago. Many there were, who would have delighted in telling Martha and Lazarus, what had happened to their beautiful young sister, whom all the men in the town had hungered for, yet who had rejected all who came to Lazarus, asking her hand in marriage, a girl who had fled in disgrace, with the Greek merchant of the oiled black beard and flashing eyes. Yes, and tales would have arrived back here, of Mary the prostitute, who had danced and flaunted herself in Herod's palace, shouting bawdy songs, as she tripped and swayed her way home to her house in Magdala. Who had at other times journeyed to that other small home in Capernaum, to which she escaped when the agony in her heart was too great to bear.

Martha came to the door and looked in amazement at the veiled figure in the plain dusty robe. Surely it could not be? But it was—Mary! The sisters stared into each other's eyes. Martha's arms opened, and she folded Mary to her.

'Praise be to God, you are home,' she said simply. No recriminations, no hesitation, and Mary burst into tears, as this older sister, who had mothered her since their parent's death, gathered her to her ample bosom.

'Mary, can it really be you?' a young man had followed Martha to the door. His hair was blond, his beard slightly darker and his eyes the blue of a summer sky. Mary lifted damp eyes and smiled a little apprehensively. They exchanged a long, poignant stare. She lowered her head.

'Lazarus! Can you forgive me, the shame I brought on our name?' For answer, he embraced her then looked beyond her to the group of people who had approached them. Their leader, tall, white robed, was watching the emotional family reunion, a most tender expression softening his lips. Suddenly Lazarus knew who this was, for he had been amongst those, who had crowded into the Temple courts at Jerusalem to hear Jesus preach. But what did he here, the Holy One of Israel?

'Lord,' he said simply, bowing deeply before Jesus. 'Welcome to my humble house, you and your disciples.' He turned to his elder sister. 'Martha, prepare food.' He ushered them inside, still holding Mary by the hand.

They stayed for a few days in that welcoming house at Bethany, the warmth they experienced here in direct contrast to the suspicion and gathering resentment shown by some in Jerusalem. By day, Jesus taught and ministered to all in the small town, people also from outlying villages flocking in with their sick, once they heard of his presence. But during the evening, Jesus would teach his disciples, as they reclined at their ease, enjoying the comfort of the sister's care. Jesus always included Lazarus in those special moments, when he would speak of his Father and the Kingdom Heaven and the fair haired young man listened with an earnestness and depth of understanding to match that of the disciples.

When at last, Jesus announced that the time had come for him to return to Galilee, Lazarus face fell. He would dearly have liked to follow the Holy One, but knew his duty was to remain. He was a mason, a hard worker and employed several craftsmen. He was in much demand, both in Bethany and Jerusalem. One thing lessened his sorrow that Jesus was leaving, the teacher had told a crestfallen Mary, that it would be good for her to stay in Bethany for a while, that the relationship between herself and her family could completely heal. Although Martha was delighted to have her young sister back, it nevertheless rankled that Mary spent most of her time listening to Jesus, instead of helping her about the house.

It was their final evening. Martha was preparing a feast, had gone to extraordinary care to prepare the meal, and now stood in the entrance to the large room where Jesus sat, explaining one of his parables. She was hot from the stove, flustered and feeling somewhat aggrieved to see Mary sitting on a mat at the Lord's feet, completely enwrapped in his words, as were the rest of the company.

'Lord—don't you care that my sister has left me to do the work all by myself!' Jesus turned a gentle but reproving glance on Martha, cutting through herself pity.

'Martha—Martha, you are worried and upset about many things. But only one thing is needed. Mary has chosen what is better, and it will not be taken from her!' But Mary had leapt guiltily to her feet, and followed by Miriam and Joanna, hurried through to the kitchen, to help bear in the dishes. Mary's lovely face held chastened expression, as she felt herself to blame for her sister's discomfiture, yet she knew herself to be in the right. She realized that these few precious occasions, on which she was privileged to learn the Messiah's teaching from his own lips, were to be utilized and treasured, for one day it would fall to her, as it would to his disciples to spread his message. Every word he uttered had to be committed to memory—and guarded within that memory for generations of men as yet unborn.

Centurion Claudius had been summoned, together with Tribune Marcus, to a meal at the palace. Pontius Pilate welcomed them, full of his plans for the new aqueduct. Work was to start almost immediately. Lady Claudia listened to her husband's enthusiastic plans impatiently, for she sought a quiet moment to speak with the Centurion. Pilate's dark eyes flashed irefully, as he confided that he had sent a written request to Caiaphas to release a large proportion of the Temple funds, for the implementation of the work and had received rejection! Not that this would stop him. If Caiaphas refused to co-operate, well, Pilate would appropriate the money anyway, and replace the High Priest if he had any further problems with him.

'Centurion, do you know that your wife was recently in Jerusalem,' inquired Claudia softly, managing to claim his attention.

'Miriam! She is here, in Jerusalem,' cried Claudius in amazement. 'Where—where is she?'

'She was staying in the house of Lady Joanna, next to the palace, just minutes from here. But alas, she has gone now. I had hoped to see you before she departed, in case you should have wished to meet her. As you probably know, she is accompanying the other women following Jesus of Nazareth.'

'What is that you are saying,' put in Pilate, turning curious eyes on his wife. 'That Miriam is with the miracle man and his disciples? How did you come to hear this, my dear?'

'You should know, Pontius, that it is impossible to keep a secret from women, even in this most secretive city of Jerusalem,' she replied lightly. Her eyes rested speculatively on Claudius face. Surely one day he would relent and take his wife back, for he loved her still, of that she was sure. Poor Miriam, to be raped, half killed, to lose her child and then be rejected by her husband. Any other woman would have been eaten up with bitterness, yet strangely, Miriam faced the world with serenity and calm, all her thoughts for the safety of Jesus, whom she was honoured to serve. She had a glow about her now, a spirituality born of her faith in the Son of God, and Claudia envied her! She glanced down now at her jewels, her silken garments, at the table heavily laden with exotic food, at the respectful slaves serving her from golden vessels and she knew herself to be poor in comparison with Miriam.

Claudius paced up and down his bed-chamber that night, like a caged leopard. Below him, the lights of Jerusalem glittered dimly through a curtain of sluicing rain. Dense clouds masked the stars and the crescent moon peeped fitfully through the enveloping dark. But the moisture that dampened his cheeks was not born of the weather, but of grief and frustration and anger against fate, against himself. Miriam—Miriam! Why, oh why had it happened? He poured some of the amber coloured spirit Marcus had given him, gulped it down, and felt the fire spreading through his limbs. He would forget her. Drown memory of those trusting green eyes in this heady ambrosia, fit for the gods—only there were no gods, just statues of stone and bronze symbolizing man's quest; the only real god, the Unseen God of Israel, and Jesus Christ, His Son.

David sat with his brother Simeon, on one of the black basalt rocks bordering the Sea of Galilee. Although late in the year, the weather was still hot and sunny. The boys watched in amusement as a small lizard flicked a fly onto its tongue then darted across the rock, back into the golden grasses. It was so peaceful here. Bright red lilies starred the valley floor, and water gurgled in a thin stream, to lose itself in the unruffled inland sea. The surface was so clear, that they could observe the tiny fish, which darted close to the shore.

'I wish I had been with you,' sighed Simeon, regretfully. 'Yet I have been busy and already I have learned much of Master Stephanus. I have with my own hands, delivered a woman of a breech birth, which the midwife had despaired of. I have assisted Stephanus when he operates and know how to mix the opiates that make such surgery bearable. Have watched Stephanus detach a small piece of the intestine, ripe with infection, which would have killed the man, should it have ruptured—then there was a man who had suffered a crushing blow to his head, the skull pressing upon the brain beneath. Stephanus bored two holes with a special drill and lifted the depressed section of the skull! Marvellous, David, it was marvellous! But still, this is doctoring the body, whilst you are privileged to be with the Holy One who heals souls who makes men whole, completely whole in both mind and body. Besides this, what I am learning is of complete insignificance!'

'Our Father, Ezra, would have been very proud of you Simeon,' said David. 'Who would have dreamed that my young brother would one day be a respected physician? Yes, your training will take many years, but of all professions, surely that of doctor is the most noble.'

'What you say is true, I know it. But I have my whole life in front of me to study medicine and who knows how long the Holy One will be among us? Oh, David, David, sometimes I have terrible dreams concerning the safety of the Messiah, of men using him with a cruelty beyond words. I just know this that I wish to be with him, while I yet may! I have mentioned my feelings to Master Stephanus. He says he will allow me to take a year away from my studies with him, to follow Jesus. He also believes him to be the Son of God!' Simeon's face displayed a rigid determination, and David did not attempt to dissuade him from his purpose.

'It will be good to have you with us,' he said, throwing an arm about his brother's shoulders. 'What about the villa though? Are you not supposed to oversee its security?

'The soldier Claudius left in control is completely dependable, but I will try to visit it every two months and will get word to Claudius, that such is my intent.' He trailed a dark skinned foot in the water, a foot that once had been clubbed, but was now as straight as its fellow. 'How do you find Miriam,' he asked?

'She seems to have come to terms with her grief. Certainly she shows no sign of the pain she endured. She and Joanna are like sisters, as are Susannah and your Sarah. We all miss Mary of Magdala. She has remained with her brother and sister at Bethany, her place of birth, but the Lord will be passing through Bethany again towards the Feast of Lights, Hannukah. Mary will rejoin us then.'

'What of your dreams of driving the Romans out of the country? Are you ultimately going to throw your lot in with the Zealots,' probed Simeon?

'I no longer support the Zealots and nor does Simon, though like him I suppose I will always hold them in respect for their ideals. You see, I now realize, that however hard life is, however unequally men are treated, violence is no answer. You have to reshape men's thinking, change conditions for the better by peaceful means where possible, keep yourself complete, inviolate within life's hurricane. Providing you have absolute faith in God our Father and His Son, the Lord Jesus, then whatever mental and physical hurts you have to endure, you cannot be damaged spiritually.' Both young men were silent, looking pensively across the silver water, perhaps each reflecting how much the other had changed. A shadow fell across the rock and they turned, startled.

'Your pardon, young sirs! My name is Nathan. Peter the fisherman directed me hither. He said that one of you might be able to give me news of my daughter? Her name is Miriam!' The man, who spoke, was dressed in a brown tunic. He seemed to be about forty, sprouted a new beard, and wore his black hair, short cropped. His eyes, as he stared down at them, were kind.

They exchanged glances. Simon had mentioned a leper, who had received healing from the disciples' mission, when sent out by the Master in two's; a leper who had claimed to be Miriam's father. Could this be the man? They rose and questioned him. Miriam had decided to visit the villa, the first time she had done so, since she had left Claudius. She had insisted on going alone and so the brothers awaited her here, some five hundred yards from the gardens.

'The Miriam I know is married to a Roman centurion. But her father is a leper. She has not seen him for years.'

'I was indeed a leper, my young friends, until healed by the power of the rabbi Jesus, vested in his disciple Simon, once called Zealot.' As they looked into his eyes, they were struck by the glowing ardour of his glance, as he mentioned Jesus name, and they knew he spoke truth.

'Come,' said Simeon. 'I'll bring you to your daughter!'

Miriam sat in the atrium, staring into the steady gaze of Melchus, the auxiliary whom her husband had left to guard the villa.

'The Centurion sent this, to be placed into your own hands, lady,' he said respectfully, then tactfully withdrew, as Miriam broke the seal on the parchment scroll. Tears sprang to the young woman's eyes, as she saw her husband's firm handwriting. She perused the missive swiftly. He spoke of his love for her and that she should refrain from following the Holy One, to be sensible and take up residence again in the villa which was her rightful home. But there was no indication in the letter that Claudius was prepared to take her back to his heart, as his wife. She blinked away the tears, unwilling that the auxiliary should see her distress. After all, he had written that he loved her—was obviously concerned for her safety. A smile softened her lips, as she stroked the parchment Perhaps, one day, the Master would heal the bruised spirit of her soldier husband. Until then, she could only wait, continue to love him with all her heart and place her faith in Almighty God and his Son Jesus.

She raised her head as she heard voices. Melchus strode to the doorway, to return with Simeon and David, both smiling broadly. With them was another. Her eyes widened in disbelief—then with a broken cry, Miriam stumbled forward, into the arms of her father.

Chapter Seventeen

Caiaphas stood before Pontius Pilate. Although his face was calm, his eyes were burning pools of hatred. A detachment of soldiers had marched from the Antonia to the Temple, headed by Centurion Claudius and halted outside the low wall which divided the inner courts of the Temple from the Court of the Gentiles, the area open to non Jews. Claudius had smiled wryly, as he read the warning inscribed in Greek that was displayed there. "No foreigner is to enter within the balustrade and enclosure around the Temple area. Whoever is caught, will have himself to blame for his death which will follow."

He translated it to his men, who already knew that the inner Temple to be sacred to the Jews and forbidden territory to them, then as he walked on he saw the notice again this time written in Latin. He gestured to one of the temple guards, standing watch over one of the four entrances on this the northern side of the Temple.

'Here—you fellow! Come here!'

'Sir?'

'Go immediately to the High Priest, Caiaphas, and bring him hither. He is commanded to the presence of Pontius Pilate—and the Prefect will brook no delay.' Claudius noted the gleam of anger in the guard's eyes, as he turned to do the bidding of the detested Romans. Caiaphas soon appeared, flanked by a contingent of priests.

'You will not require them,' said Claudius shortly, with a dismissive gesture to the priests. 'Allow me, to escort you to the Prefect, Lord High Priest.'

And now Caiaphas stood before Pilate, trying to contain his rage, as the all powerful Governor demanded a huge sum of gold to be paid from the temple treasury, to finance the new aqueduct that he was planning to build. Pilate expected him to acquiesce with that same enthusiasm with which he requested the money, saying that the people of Jerusalem would jointly praise Roman initiative and priestly generosity, in providing the much needed extra water supply.

'The temple funds are purely to finance the needs—the work of the Temple,' seethed Caiaphas. 'The gold is sacred to the house of the Lord our God!'

Pontius Pilate gave a contemptuous laugh.

'Say sacred to your own needs, High Priest! I have heard that the God of the Jews is a just God. Surely he will be better pleased to see funds raised in his name being used for the common good of the people of Jerusalem, rather than supporting the thousands of priests and attendant temple staff. However—I do not have either the time or inclination to argue the point with you. Your father-in-law, Annas awaits without. I have already spoken with him. He is to bear your order to the Sanhedrin, to release the gold forthwith and have it brought hither.' Pilate's dark eyes measured the furious spiritual leader impassively, as he leant back indolently, in his throne chair. 'Summon Annas,' he commanded.

'Ah—Lord Annas, your son-in-law requests that you call a sitting of the Sanhedrin and vote the agreed sum of gold to be released to my officers. Centurion Claudius will provide you with suitable escort and in the meanwhile, Caiaphas shall remain as our—guest!'

'But it will take time to convene the Sanhedrin,' writhed elderly Annas, former High Priest. Some of our members live without the city.'

'Then we will take their wishes as being favourable to financing the aqueduct, and just rely on those members of your ruling council who are available. Should I not receive the co-operation I require, that Rome demands, then I may be forced to replace those officials who are insensible to my wishes. I do not think, Lord Caiaphas that you would wish to see another wearing that splendid blue robe, with its golden bells and pomegranates!'

Grudgingly, their hearts black with fury, the priests allowed Pilate to sequestrate the Temple funds. It was not only the deprivation of the enormous sum that rankled, but the indignity of being subject to this the most unfeeling of all governors who had reigned over them in recent years. Word of what had happened, sped swiftly through Judea, eventually reaching Galilee, where members of the Zealot party decided to strike back at this latest insult to their religion.

News was received that Pilate was to make a special visit to Jerusalem, to see for himself how the work on the aqueduct was progressing. From the hills behind Capernaum, men gathered in a certain cave, Hundreds of fists cracked into cupped hand in sign of greeting and accord, as a great shout arose, for Barabbas it was who held up a hand for silence and addressed them.

'Fellow Zealots—I greet you and commend your swift attendance on this meeting. We are here, as all know, to plan how best we can avenge the latest outrage perpetrated against our nation by Pilate and his minions. He is on his way back to Jerusalem within the week. I suggest a direct confrontation with the Romans, take them by surprise. Rouse the citizens of Jerusalem to uprising. Kill as many Romans as we may—and then slip away again to the Judean hills! How say you?'

'But I thought that we were to wait for the Holy One, Jesus of Nazareth, to proclaim himself king,' said Samuel, a fisherman from Bethsaida.

'I have it on good authority, that Jesus has no intention, of ever voluntarily seeking Kingship. You all know Simon, son of the founder of our movement and esteemed member of the Zealots, well we must now accept he has become a disciple of Jesus of Nazareth and no longer an active participant in our affairs. I spoke with him yesterday. Jesus will never lead us against Rome! That is final.' Barabbas sighed in frustration and continued, 'Perhaps, it might be possible in the future, to put him in a position where he might be proclaimed king, in spite of himself. But we have to plan the uprising in our own strength!'

They spoke long into the night. A plan was made. Vows were taken and three hundred men made their way separately to Jerusalem.

But even within the Zealot movement, there were those few, willing to turn traitor for Roman gold. Pilate had halted at a small village on the road from Caesarea to Jerusalem. He listened to the good-humoured shouts of the force that protected him, as they enjoyed this break in their march. He glanced at them in pride, these handpicked men of the Legion.

'My Lord Governor, there is a man here who asks to speak with you,' said Rufus, a young centurion. 'He has information about a planned uprising in Jerusalem—the Zealots!'

'Indeed? Bring him here,' said Pilate.

Pilate gave his instructions to his centurions. Carefully selected soldiers were to be disguised as Jews, clothed as countrymen in the rough homespun robes favoured by the Galileans. They were not to be armed, except by heavy clubs and would infiltrate the crowds to deal with any trouble-makers. In this way, Pilate would be free of responsibility for any undue bloodshed and no uncomplimentary reports reach the Emperor. He had no doubt, that any move by the Zealots, would be on a very limited scale, and satisfied, he waited in his village encampment, until suitable clothing had been procured for his men.

Pontius Pilate was certainly not prepared for the howling, shrieking mob, which came at his men from all directions, as they entered Jerusalem's narrow streets. Heavy fighting broke out around the Tower of Siloam part of which collapsed causing much carnage. The whole of Jerusalem was in uproar. Pilate was at last safe within the Antonia fortress, but below him in the Court of the Gentiles, his soldiers in their disguise of homespun robes, produced their murderous clubs and completely losing all control, lashed out in a frenzy of killing. At the end of the day, some Roman soldiers had lost their lives, as had very many of the Galilean Zealots and the blood ran red in the gullies of the Temple courts.

Caiaphas stared impassively into the eyes of the dying Zealot, who had been carried before him.

'Let my blood be mingled with that of the sacrifices on the altar,' breathed the lad, for he was no more than fourteen. 'This day, Priest, Pilate has mixed the blood of patriots, with that of sheep and oxen—but we will prevail! Others will rise and---aghhh!' His dying scream was cut off, as a gurgle of blood issued between his pale lips.

Word of the uprising passed on men's lips. A caravan stopped in Nazareth, wounded Zealots made their back to their native villages. Jesus heard of it and grieved the futility of wasted lives.

'Do you think these Galileans were worse than all the other Galileans, because they suffered this way? I tell you, no! But unless you repent, you too will all perish. Of the eighteen who died when the Tower of Siloam fell in on them, do you think that they were more guilty than all others living in Jerusalem? I tell you, no!' He sighed and started to explain the futility of violence. It was not the way to change men's hearts and gradually wounded spirits subsided, as they heard his words.

After a brief rest at Capernaum, the Holy One took his disciples into the many scattered villages, both around the shores of Galilee and those set back in the hills, spreading his message of repentance and love, healing the sick as he went. Nor did there seem to be any end, to the procession of crippled and diseased folk who came to him with faith shining in their eyes, for they had seen countless others who had been restored to physical and spiritual health.

Many members of the Pharisees were now favourably inclined towards him. Here in the county areas, they were of a gentler disposition than their cynical counterparts in Jerusalem. Simeon and David watched now as a party of Pharisees, faces troubled bowed before Jesus. They had come from Tiberias, bearing word that Herod was seeking to arrest Jesus.

'Leave this place—and go somewhere else! Herod wants to kill you!' Their voices were urgent.

He drew his brows together and his eyes smouldered angrily.

'Go tell that fox, I will drive out demons and heal people, today, tomorrow and on the third day I will reach my goal. In any case, I must keep going today, tomorrow and the next day—for surely no prophet can die outside Jerusalem!'

His description of Herod as fox, reached the ears of that irate ruler, who paced his bed chamber, kicking the shins of the nearest slave, boxing the ears of another and vented his fury into the ears of his wife Herodias.

'Kill John, you said---and I did! But what good did it do? Here is another risen up in his place that is far more dangerous! Thousands flock to him. It is surely a matter of time before the Zealots mass behind him to march on Jerusalem. The country is like a vast, tinder dry forest, it needs only a spark to ignite it, and the fires once lit will burn us all!' Saliva flecked the corners of his mouth as he continued,

'Caesar will not stop to consider the slight threads of friendship which bind us together. You and I will be expendable as having been unable to contain the situation here. The Legions will march in, the population will be decimated, and at the best, dear wife, you and I and your clever little Salome, will be banished in disgrace!' He snarled the words out, and for once, Herodias did not attempt to talk back. She had never seen her husband in such an ugly mood. Many in the palace dungeons would suffer tonight, to assuage his anger. Shrieks and groans would arise from those foul, foetid places, where Herod whiled away many a weary hour experimenting with some novel form of torture, before seeking his wife's bed, to slake the lust which his fiendish activities always produced.

'Bring Chuza here,' he screamed! When his chamberlain bowed low before him, Herod broke into an almost hysterical tirade, seeking to reduce the man to the gibbering condition of fear his outbursts usually produced on his victims. But Chuza merely nodded gravely, agreeing with everything that Herod said.

'Your wife is a disgrace to our household,' raged Herod! 'What kind of man are you, Chuza, that you allow Joanna to roam the countryside with the other half demented followers of this wandering trouble maker, who names me fox!'

Chuza sighed with measured regret.

'But my Lord—Lady Joanna is no longer my wife. We are divorced, as you know! I no longer have jurisdiction over one free to follow her own devices! Nor would I presume to interfere with one who is remotely related to your own family!'

'I disavow that relationship,' cried Herod angrily.

'My Lord, in my humble opinion, the Lady Joanna is more sinned against, than sinning.' He paused and watched Herod carefully.

'How mean you, chamberlain?'

'I feel that Joanna was bewitched by John the Baptist! Until she heard him, she was dutiful wife and loyal subject of yours, sir.' He spoke slowly, carefully.

'But John is dead his powers would surely have died with him?' Antipas regarded his chamberlain uneasily.

'You say truly, Sire, but who knows what new spells the Nazorene Jesus may have cast on her!' He sensed he had diffused Antipas anger, and had no compunction for the smear he had cast on Jesus. There was a hint of fear in the eyes of the despotic ruler now, as he considered whether the Nazorene might direct his magic on him.

'It is said—that he has never harmed any man—preaches love and forgiveness,' said Herod, drawing comfort from the fact.

'Yet—he almost provoked riot in the Temple during Passover, when he overturned the money lender's tables and disrupted the sale of beasts for sacrifice. Do you wish to give orders for his arrest, my Lord?'

Herod Antipas chewed his lower lips, as his cunning eyes darted back and forth over his chamberlain's face. Much as he wanted to arrest and kill Jesus, he feared the possible consequences to himself. Yet the miracle man had to be stopped, before whole scale uprising occurred.

'Send word to the High Priest, Lord Caiaphas that I wish to meet with him when I next visit Jerusalem for the Feast of Lights, in a few weeks time.' That was the answer. He knew Caiaphas detested Jesus of Nazareth for his interference in the lucrative business of selling the sacrificial beasts. All knew that Caiaphas reaped rich pickings from the money so raised—and that he wholeheartedly abhorred the Holy One for his teachings, the liberality of which ran contra to the rigidity of the temple teaching. Also, it was reported, that Jesus had referred to the Sadducees and leading Pharisees as whited sepulchres—freshly painted tombs acrawl inside with festering dead men's bones. Ah yes, friend Caiaphas had many a bone of his own to pick with Jesus. Let him be the one to arrest him then—and kill him!

David and Simeon were conversing in low voices. They were sitting slightly apart from Jesus and his apostles and had built a small fire of their own. Simeon tossed some more drift-wood on it and pulled his cloak about him, for a chill breeze had sprung up, across the lake. The stars glittered and the half- etched face of the moon was huge.

'I know I should not really have listened to words the brothers James and John thought private—but once I had heard a little of what they spoke, I just could not make myself move away.' He paused, as though uncertain of how much to tell Simeon.

'Well David, go on. You say they were talking of a recent occasion when they had accompanied the Lord Jesus onto a mountain to pray. Surely there was nothing unusual in this, for we all know that the Holy One loves to retreat to the high places, to commune with God his Father.'

'Brother, it was what happened there on the mountain! John said that as Jesus was praying, the appearance of his face changed—his clothes became as bright as a flash of lightning!'

'What, happened next,' asked Simeon in awe?

'Two men appeared. Moses and Elijah, in most glorious splendour! I heard James say, that they were speaking to Jesus about his departure, which he is about to bring to fulfilment in Jerusalem. It seems that Peter, who was with them, had been as sleepy as they were, until this happened. As they became fully awake, they saw his glory and the two men standing with him.'

'They must have been so amazed. What did they say to Jesus?' Simeon hung upon his brother's words.

'Peter said, "Lord, it is good for us to be here. Let us put up three shelters—one for you, one for Moses and one for Elijah." Even while he was saying this, a cloud appeared and enveloped them and they were very afraid as they entered the cloud.'

'Go on—go on!'

'A voice came from the cloud, saying, "This is my Son, whom I have chosen. Listen to him!" Then, after the voice had spoken, they found that Jesus was alone!'

Simeon reached out and took David's hand and held it wordlessly. They both turned, and glanced with reverence at the still figure of Jesus, who knelt in prayer some yards from his sleeping disciples. He seemed to sense their glance, for he turned towards them and beckoned.

'We go to Jerusalem, for the Festival of Lights—Hanukkah.'

The little party started upon the road to Jerusalem, the early sunlight giving way to a heavy cloudburst, penetrating their clothing, causing their homespun garments to cling wetly about them. Many there were who saluted them, as they splashed through the mud. One man darted out from the side of the track to intercept Jesus.

'Lord, I will follow you, wherever you go!' he said this in dramatic tones. Jesus looked him full in the face. How little the man understood what he was offering?

'Foxes have holes—birds of the air have nests, but the son of man has nowhere to lay his head!'

Joanna and Miriam were supported on the strong arms of John, as they clung to him. Lightning slitted the sky and thunder boomed threateningly among the hills. Then as suddenly as it had started, the storm stopped, and steam rose from the undergrowth, as the sun poured down. But it no longer held the heat of summer and they were wet as well as hungry, as they approached the next village. Here Jesus was received with respect, yet many of the men seemed to hang back from the group. The Zealots had become disillusioned with the Holy One. Still holding him in esteem for his teaching and his miracles, but they no longer endued him with the charisma of kingship.

They knew that he possessed miraculous powers, had showed tremendous courage, for had he not enforced the ruling priesthood in the Temple, had risked stoning, so why, oh why would he not consent to lead them against the Romans? He alone of Israel had the stature to draw the whole nation about him. It made no sense. They were still smarting from their abortive attempt to cause full scale uprising in Jerusalem over the aqueduct affair. Well, perhaps they had managed to give the invaders a bloody nose, but their latest sally had produced nothing but a fleabite on Jerusalem's leonine loins. The power of Rome nowise diminished

But the poor came, the elderly, mothers with under nourished children clinging to their ragged garments, those with no hope, a beaten look in their eyes, as their pitiful savings were surrendered to the voracious tax collectors in Roman employ. These then came out of their villages and gathered in forlorn groups along the road to Jerusalem, as word of his approach reached them. Joanna, Miriam and the handful of other devoted women who followed Jesus and his disciples, paid for their sustenance out of their own means, so that the party was never a drain upon the poor people they ministered to. Yet many of these would have given their last small coins to assist the Messiah. He stopped many times, to reach out a hand in blessing, in healing. The words of gratitude and joy, uttered from the trembling lips of a once blind beggar, Bartimaeus, rang after them. 'Glory be to God—and blessings upon thee, Jesus, Son of David!' Instinctively, Bartimaeus placed his benefactor in Israel's royal house.

As they reached Jericho, the disciples were muttering angrily about the poverty of those they had left behind on the road, the iniquitous taxes that reduced hard working people, to such extreme poverty. Matthew bowed his head, as he heard them, and remembered with shame that he had been a collector of those same taxes. Simon the Zealot glanced at him and guessed his thoughts. He reached out a hand and clamped it down on Matthew's shoulder.

'We all have to let go of our past, Matthew,' he said gently and Matthew raised his brooding gaze upon him. In spite of having received forgiveness at the Holy One's hands, he still felt remaining twinges of guilt for a past that had cost so many in Galilee dear. He forced a smile now.

'Mine was such a hateful profession,' he murmured. The small exchange had not gone unnoticed by Jesus. Crowds came surging out of the city gates to greet them, and in the press, many were hurt by that jostling throng. Nor did the wave of enthusiastic curiosity cease, as they made their way through narrow streets, shaded by palm trees, to one of the many squares where abounded houses of those affluent Jews, who wintered in Jericho, because of its favourably mild winter climate and accessibility from Jerusalem. Set in a luxuriantly green oasis, an emerald glowing in the scorched semi desert and arid hills, this was the oldest town known in the world. The people were shouting to Jesus, to show them one of his miracles—to teach them—and to answer one question. Was he the one who was to come?

His gaze swept over them, then rose above their heads, to the branches of a sycamore fig tree, where a black bearded figure, in a red tunic worked in gold, sat perched, swinging red sandaled feet, as he waited for Jesus to approach closer. This was Zacchaeus, the chief tax collector of Jericho and accordingly, one of its richest citizens. He had heard much of Jesus of Nazareth and when the people shouted that the Holy Man was coming, he had tried to push his way amongst the crowd, to get a sight of the controversial rabbi, whose name was on all lips. But Zacchaeus was short of stature and had no chance of seeing, or being seen. So he had used his wits, climbed the sycamore tree, deciding that the vantage point, was worth the slight loss of dignity involved in reaching his objective, to get the closest possible view of Jesus.

Jesus stopped. He raised a hand in greeting to Zacchaeus, beckoning him to descend.

'Zacchaeus—come down immediately!' His firm gaze held that of the startled collaborator, who started to tremble under that shimmering gold glance. How had Jesus known he was up there? How had he known his name?

'I must stay at your house today,' continued Jesus with a smile and watched quietly, as Zacchaeus slithered unceremoniously down the tree, leaping the last few feet. He stared up at Jesus now, where moments ago he had looked down.

'Lord,' he whispered breathlessly. 'Lord, your servant humbly bids you welcome, and your disciples!' He led them off towards his imposing white villa, with its many verandas, set in exotic gardens, where even in winter, flowers cascaded in brilliant abandon. He ignored the angry murmuring of the crowd, as did Jesus.

'Did you see that? The Holy One has gone to be the guest of a sinner!'

'What is that?'

'He's gone to eat in the house of a sinner, the notorious Zacchaeus, that son of a camel!' The mutterings grew to an angry roar, but the crowd did not quite dare, to physically obstruct their progress.

Zacchaeus offered of his best to Jesus and the disciples, setting servants to wash their dusty feet, offering scented water to rinse off the dust of their journey. Jesus looked about him as he entered the marble tiled dining hall, where couches were piled with embroidered cushions, richly woven carpets in jewel shades scattered on the floor, tapestries clad the walls and everywhere was the gleam of gold, from lamp-stands, candlesticks, vases and ornate goblets. Zacchaeus was a squirrel and this was his nest, furnished in flamboyant taste, letting this show of affluence counter his lack of inches—and all had been paid for, by his unjust dealings as chief tax collector, exacting far and above the sum laid down by Rome.

Zacchaeus knew of course, that the Romans were aware of what went on, and turned a blind eye on the devious dealings of those they employed to collect the all important tribute to Rome. It was expected, that a tax collector would feather his own nest as compensation for the aversion, with which he would almost inevitably be regarded by his fellow countrymen.

They sat down to a wonderful meal, served by quiet servants. Zacchaeus attacked his seasoned lamb with enthusiasm. Eating was one of his chief delights then as he glanced to see that his honoured guest was enjoying his meal, he found once again, that strange look of the Holy One, directed on him. He suddenly lost his appetite. He tried to look away, but could not. He wiped his greasy fingers on a napkin, trying to unlock his gaze then he placed his hands upon the table edge, to disguise the trembling which had set in. Still Jesus looked quietly into his eyes. Then Zacchaeus rose to his feet, glancing wildly about him. Each costly item in the room shrieked the toll of misery that had purchased it and the deeper wound the purchase had made to his soul! And a cry burst forth from the very depths of his being!

'Look Lord—here and now, I give half my possessions to the poor, and if I have cheated anyone of anything, I will pay back four times the amount!' Then Jesus smiled approvingly at him, nodding his head. Zacchaeus walked unsteadily towards Jesus, and knelt at his feet. A hand was placed on his head and a feeling as of fresh spring water, coursed through his veins and the look in his eyes was now one of pure joy.

Jesus spoke to Zacchaeus and those around him.

'Today, salvation has come to this house, because this man too, is a son of Abraham—for the Son of Man came to seek and to save what was lost!'

Zacchaeus bowed his head, so that none should see the hot tears that pricked behind his eyes, but there was one who did see them. Matthew rose, and went over to Zacchaeus and bent over the man, who would never be little again.

'I was once a tax collector too,' said Matthew quietly. Wordlessly, the other took his hand.

Even before Jesus and his disciples had left Jericho, a queue of bewildered citizens, summoned by Zacchaeus, left his presence with small bags of gold in their hands. They hurried amazed into the streets to tell their neighbours of this most wondrous miracle that Jesus had wrought in their midst, turning their hated and feared tax collector into benefactor.

Two days later, Jesus and his companions arrived at Bethany, where they decided to stay overnight before proceeding on to nearby Jerusalem for the Festival of Lights, sometimes known as the Feast of Dedication. It commemorated the purification and rededication of the Temple, almost two hundred years before, by Judas Macabeaus, following its defilement by Antiochus Epiphanes. Of all the Jewish feasts, this was perhaps the most beloved of children, who delighted to sit in their brilliantly lit homes and listen to the stories of the Macabees, told to them by their elders. It was always a time of great celebration too in the Temple at Jerusalem, and hundreds would leave the surrounding villages to celebrate the festival in the holy city.

Mary Magdalene saw them coming and ran from the door to greet them, bowing before Jesus, tears of joy in her eyes at seeing him again. Martha and Lazarus followed closely upon Mary's heels. Mary had a special smile for David and Simeon and plied them with questions, then gave a cry of delight as Joanna and Miriam came down the slope towards the house, together with Jesus mother, followed by Sarah and Susannah.

It was a very happy party who sat down to eat that night, but the happiness dimmed as Jesus warned them of what must ultimately happen to him, that he would be arrested, crucified—and rise again on the third day! A knot of grief formed in each heart at the thought that the Holy One, their dearest Lord and master, must suffer these things. But perhaps after all it could be avoided and Hannukah was coming, the bright lights of the festival, would serve to disperse the gloom that had fallen over their spirits.

The wind moaned fitfully in the streets of Bethany that night, its chilling breath seeking out any badly fitting door or shutter, with spiteful persistence. The disciples thought back to the mild weather they had left behind in Jericho. But at least here there were solid walls about them, sleeping mats to lie on, rugs to cover them! Miriam's eyes were heavy with sleep, as she heard the Holy One instructing Lazarus and the disciples that everything that was yet to pass, was to take place to fulfil all that was written in the Law of Moses, the prophets and the psalms.

Then Miriam's mind wandered. She fell asleep dreaming of Claudius, reached out for him in the night and woke to find her hand touched the shoulder of Joanna.

'Hush, dear,' sighed Joanna. 'You will wake the others, you were crying for your husband—for Claudius.'

'I'm sorry,' murmured Miriam, stricken faced.

'Don't be. My heart tells me, that one day you will be reunited with your soldier husband.' She patted Miriam's hand as the two young women once more composed themselves to sleep.

Morning dawned brightly. Jesus glanced back almost regretfully at the happy little house in Bethany, which had begun to feel like home. Lazarus had suggested that the Holy One might care to use it as a base whilst visiting Jerusalem, for it was a scant two miles outside the walled city.

Soon David and Simeon stiffened in excitement, as they entered the city gate under the watchful gaze of the Roman soldiers who surmounted the walls. It was the first time David had re-entered the city of their birth since they had left it with such light hearts, so long ago it seemed, to seek out John the Baptist, together with their parents and a multitude of others. Now John was slain at the hands of Herod, as were their dear parents at the brutality of Roman soldiers and David sensed the poignancy of this return together to Jerusalem.

'Did you ever go near our father's shop, when you came here with the Centurion,' asked David?

'It wasn't possible then. Perhaps now though, we will be able to slip away and look at our old home.'

'No, Simeon! I don't even want to see it again. It's the past and the present is so much more important.' David swallowed and clapped a hand manfully on his younger brother's shoulder, propelling him forward. They sauntered nonchalantly as they could past a group of laughing soldiers, who were tormenting an elderly man, who cowered against a wall, hands in front of his face. They longed to go to the man's assistance, but dared not draw attention to themselves. Jesus had preceded them by another route, the party splitting up, so as to mingle more easily with the busy crowds. Simeon spun about as a hand touched him on the shoulder.

'Greetings, young sir—it is Simeon, son of Centurion Claudius?' It was the Pharisee Nicodemus who spoke, he who had been the first man to whom the Lord Jesus had explained the necessity—of being born again. Simeon now also knew that this same Nicodemus was a member of the Sanhedrin, the powerful ruling body of the Jews.

'Lord Nicodemus! I am honoured that you remember me. May I introduce my brother, David?' He hastily murmured Nicodemus status in his brother's ear as David stepped forward to bow before the keen eyed, bearded Pharisee, in his heavily fringed robe. Nicodemus questioned them as to their presence in Jerusalem. It seemed that he was aware of Claudius estrangement from Miriam and that Simeon had not accompanied his adoptive father when Claudius had taken up his new duties at the Antonia. Indeed, the two lads began to realize that there was little that this powerful and wealthy member of the Sanhedrin did not know of current events.

'You are a follower of Jesus of Nazareth, David? I know that he is even now within Jerusalem, would wish to warn him that he should proceed with extreme caution. There are those who wish his death!' He had lowered his voice as he said this. Nicodemus knew well that Jerusalem was full of spies, both in the pay of Caiaphas and of Rome. After brief exchange, Nicodemus moved on.

The young men hurried towards the Temple, faces tense with worry. Nicodemus would not have given his warning lightly. The street along which they proceeded was packed with those intent on enjoying this joyful festival and people jostled each other good-humouredly as they crowded about the stalls of sellers of sweetmeats. Yet even this surface jollity was merest veneer, masking the suspicions and fears of the inhabitants who had suffered the most appalling cruelties over recent years, as one emergent ruler after another besieged Jerusalem and put its citizens to the sword. Now under Roman occupation there was brooding resentment, which could flare up in an instant with unimaginable intensity. Jerusalem was like a caged leopard, pacing proudly, quietly within its cage, yet let its keeper once make careless move, and this leopard would spring—rend and tear, sinking swift teeth into cracking bone.

Jesus was walking in his favourite place, under the shadow of Solomon's colonnade. Those in the Court of the Gentiles, rushed forward, as word passed from lip to lip, 'He has come! The prophet from Galilee is here! Come and listen to Jesus—Jesus of Nazareth!' They crowded about him, shouting for a miracle, a new demonstration of his healing power. Word was sent to Caiaphas, that the Galilean was here again, and Caiaphas peered from a narrow window, set high in the Temple, as he fixed baleful stare on this man he hated, detested, yet almost feared. Suppose—just suppose that Jesus strange powers should so move the people that they would announce him publicly as the Messiah, the Christ. There would be open rebellion and he and his fawning colleagues would lose their lives in the Roman repression which would follow.

Jesus must die! He called to the Captain of the temple guards.

'Be prepared to arrest the Nazorene! Send agents into the crowd, men skilful in debate to trap him into blasphemy----then Captain, you and your men move in. There will be no mistakes this time, nor any excuses accepted for failure!'

Roman soldiers, stationed high above Jesus head, on the colonnades, leaned forward as they heard the excited shouting of the crowd. Was this to be yet another uprising? Centurion Claudius positioned his helmet and adjusted his cloak as he responded to the news that Jesus was teaching in the Temple courts. With feelings still running high after the aqueduct affair, he knew it would take very little to bring the hostile inhabitants of Jerusalem to uprising. He was also aware, that Caiaphas had made no secret of the fact, that he sought Jesus life!

One of Caiaphas agents was shouting, 'How long will you keep us in suspense? If you are the Christ, tell us so plainly!'

Claudius listened intently as Jesus reply rose to his ears, his answer clear.

'I did tell you, but you did not believe!' He raised a hand for silence, as he continued firmly, 'The miracles I do in my Father's name speak for me, but you do not believe because you are not my sheep!' The agents coloured angrily as he continued, 'My sheep listen to my voice, I know them and they follow me. I give them Eternal life, and they shall never perish—no-one can snatch them out of my hand!' His eyes flashed as he glared at the agents and at the slowly advancing contingent of Temple guards.

Peter drew closer to Jesus, beckoning the disciples to gather about the Master.

'My Father, who has given them to me, is greater than all! No-one can snatch them out of my father's hand—the Father and I are one!'

He had said it! He had identified himself with Almighty God and it was what they had been waiting for, and the people began to cry his name in praise. It was also what the Sadducees and Pharisees had been waiting for—and stones began to appear in the hands of the temple agents. It would be better this way, no arrest, just on the face of it, a stoning resulting from an outraged populace affronted by blasphemy. Claudius shouted orders to his men. They started streaming from the fortress into the Temple area, advancing on the disturbance from the opposite end of the Court of the Gentiles.

Jesus looked at those who held the heavy stones up threateningly now.

'I have shown you many great miracles from the Father. For which of these do you stone me?' His courage was unbelievable, as he confronted them. Those Jews who trusted his words and now regarded him as Messiah moved forward against the phalanx of belligerents brandishing stones. They called to Jesus, to save himself, to retreat.

Again Jesus voice rang out, as his assailants attempted to shout him down.

'We are not stoning you for your miracles. We are not stoning you for any of these, but for blasphemy, because you a mere man—claim to be God,' they howled!'

'Blasphemer! Blasphemer,' others joined in!

Claudius could barely make out Jesus words, so great was the hubbub. His own men now forced their way past the Temple guards, blocking their access to Jesus, as they themselves now advanced on him. Jesus was still remonstrating, as hundreds of supporters backed him.

'Why then do you accuse me of blasphemy, because I said I am God's Son? Do not believe me, unless I do what my Father does. But if I do it, even though you do not believe me—believe the miracles, that you may know and understand that the Father is in me—and I in the Father!'

One of the agents ran at Jesus, seizing his robe, as he yelled to his colleagues to capture Jesus, drag him outside the Temple away from the crowd—and stone him. Throw him down the precipitous side of the building and finish him off! A Roman officer rapped out an order, directing his men at the seething, struggling mob surrounding Jesus, who now, with a quick twist of his body, broke away from those who laid hands on him.

'Where is he?' This question was asked, by friend and foe alike, for Jesus had disappeared. The Romans returned to the fortress, grumbling at yet another daily disturbance by this unruly people, who gave more trouble than any other subject nation in the Empire. Claudius relaxed, but sent his own agents out into the streets to discover the present whereabouts of Jesus, and Caiaphas raised one of the curved sacrificial knives aloft, as with a howl of rage he acknowledged that Jesus of Nazareth had eluded him once again!

The wife of Pontius Pilate knew where Jesus was, for a breathless group of men had pushed past her as she left Lady Joanna's villa, imploring the tall figure in the torn robe to hurry. He turned and looked at her and Lady Claudia bowed low, before returning to Herod's palace. She was draped in one of her maid's cloaks, with the hood pulled low over her face, masking eyes that brimmed with repentant tears.

Those tears continued to spill down her cheeks later, as she sat at her window, staring unseeingly below at wondrously wrought palace gardens, where fountains splashed and the statues forbidden by Jewish law but set there by Herod the Great, peeped coldly white beneath tall swaying palms and bushes. A sharp breeze had arisen, stripping cupped flowers of pink and cream from the bushes. Its sound blended with the turmoil in her heart. In that glance Jesus had laid on her, had been an uncovering of her past, forgiveness and a call to the future.

They left the city at dusk, before night suddenly fell and the lights which gave Hanukah its name, blazed within the hearts of the homes and within the mighty Temple. But the flaring Temple lights were as nothing to the ferocity that shone from the narrow eyes of Caiaphas, High Priest.

They left a protesting Mary and Sarah at Bethany. Martha had slipped a protective arm about the pretty Samaritan girl's shoulders, as Simeon confided that he would feel happier knowing that his betrothed was safe within this family home, until such time as he was able to take her to wife. Indeed, it had been great strain upon his young manhood, to be in such close proximity to Sarah, yet unable to enjoy the fruits of their love. Nor was it only his promise to Centurion Claudius, to wait a full year that restrained him from seeking early fulfilment of the marriage bed, but the honour and respect in which he held his betrothed.

Mary sighed rebelliously as she swept the floor. Obviously the Lord must have had reason for wishing her to remain with her brother and sister. Instinctively, she realized that she did indeed need this quiet time, to let the last of the tensions which had been coiled like a tight spring inside her, to completely relax. So, as she bowed her head over her broom, she heard in her mind the gentle words of the Holy One. 'Ask— and it will be given to you! Seek—and ye shall find! Knock—and the door shall be opened to you. For everyone who asks, receives. He who seeks—finds and to him who knocks, the door will be opened!'

Yes, the door in her heart had opened to the words of the Holy One, but perhaps not enough. It had to be thrown wide open, to completely allow the teaching of Jesus to enter in, and to live forever in that rebellious heart and as she swept the tensions drained away, and she started to joy in this simple task of service to others. Mary of Magdala, who had flaunted herself in the palaces of the rich, offering her body in exchange for gold and jewels, now at last understood life's real treasure, as cleansing tears splashed down into the dust. She was again, Mary of Bethany.

'Do not be sad, Mary,' cried Sarah, as she picked over a bowl of fruit. 'Jesus and the others will be back soon, they promised!'

'I am not sad, dear Sarah, nor will I ever cry again,' she added stoutly. She could not guess, how in a few short weeks, she was to break that promise.

Chapter Eighteen

In a small grotto on Jordan's banks, under the shade of willow and tamarisk, Miriam sat at ease with Joanna. The women were resting after washing garments in the river. Miriam's fingers caressed the scarlet petals of one of the small wild lilies that quivered to the warm breeze sighing along the valley. Even in winter, it was lushly green here, in this deep rift in the earth, where the meandering river, linked the sweet, clear waters of Galilee, with the chemically salted, lifeless depths of the Dead Sea. Barren hills rose around them, flanking the adjacent semi desert.

'I wish I could have been here, when John the Baptist baptised the Holy One,' Miriam sighed wistfully. 'Simeon has told me of it many times and I never tire to hear how, John proclaimed Jesus as the Son of God!'

Joanna's eyes were tender, as she replied, 'To think we are sitting quite near the spot where it all began. But that is wrong, isn't it. It really commenced when a tiny boy child began to grow beneath Mary's heart—seed planted by God.' She bowed her head as she indicated the mighty Jehovah, the God of Abraham, Isaac and Jacob, of Moses and the prophets, the Holy God of Israel, whom Jesus had told them was Father of the whole world, of all peoples. Their task it was to tell the world of Almighty God and of the message of Jesus, his only begotten Son.

'Even before that Joanna dear, John says that the Holy One explained that he was with the Father when the world was made, in the beginning—that he is the Word of God made flesh.' The whispered words blended with the soft splashing of the water against the tall reeds, as it swept lazily on. Above their heads they could see Susannah bending over the flat rocks over which they had draped the clothes to dry, and heard her give a shout of greeting.

'Simeon! He's back! It's Simeon!' She raised a dark skinned arm in gesture of welcome to the young man, who was clambering down towards them. They had all been missing Simeon, whose heart had led him to leave the disciples for brief visit to Bethany, to see his betrothed, his beloved Sarah. Although he knew she was perfectly safe with Mary Magdalene and her family, he had still fretted for a sight of her and a week ago had left Peraea, fording the Jordan, in order to feast his eyes on his lovely Samaritan sweetheart.

'Simeon dear, oh but it's good to see you again,' exclaimed Miriam gaily. Then she noticed his sombre gaze, the look of deep anxiety etched around his eyes. 'What's wrong,' she asked? 'Is it Sarah? Has something happened?'

'No, Miriam—Sarah is well and sends you her warmest greetings. But Lazarus alas is ill, sick I fear unto death!' he swallowed and continued. 'He has a fever against which my meagre knowledge is helpless. It burns him up. His face is yellow, skin stretched tight over bone, eyes sunk back into dark pits, he has an evil smelling sweat, is unable to eat, and keeps lapsing into unconsciousness. Martha sent for a physician from Jerusalem, who purged him, shook his head and departed. I fear, oh I very much fear, that he is lapsing into the coma of death.' His voice broke on a sob.

'We must get word to the Holy One,' cried Joanna in deep distress. 'Jesus loves Lazarus dearly. We cannot let his friend die without telling the Holy One. He will be able to heal him, however ill he is! I know this!'

'Well, that's why I have hurried here so fast,' replied Simeon. 'So, where is he? Where is Jesus?'

'He could be in any of several villages,' said Miriam, face puckering with worry. 'We expect him either tonight or tomorrow morning. You had better remain here with us, Simeon. If you go looking for him, you might go in quite the wrong direction. Come, let's return to our camp. We are still in the two large caves, as we were when you left. You shall rest there and eat and we will pray that our Lord returns soon!'

Stars sequinned the stygian night, as the tired dusty band of men led by Jesus, returned to their camp in the caves above Jordan. Warmth, welcome and hot food awaited them. They waited until Jesus had blessed the food and the men assuaged their appetite, before breaking the terrible news that Lazarus was at the point of death. They had reasoned that if they had told him beforehand, he might have made immediate journey to Bethany to aid his friend, brother to Mary Magdalene, who was also Mary of Bethany. No, let the Holy One eat and rest first.

'Lord,' murmured Simeon at last, coming from the shadows at the back of the cave. 'Lord—the one you love, is sick.' He gulped, and added, 'Lazarus is sick unto death!'

All the disciples rose to their feet in shock, fixing eyes on Jesus, waiting his command to action. A pang crossed his face, the muscles at the corner of his mouth tensed. He lowered his lashes in concentration. For a few minutes he sat in utter stillness then raised his eyes, staring beyond the entrance of the cave into the chill night. At last he spoke.

'This sickness will not end in death. No. It is for God's glory, so that God's Son may be glorified through it!' The disciples stared at him bewildered. What could he mean? Simeon licked his lips nervously, wanting to speak again, to ensure that Jesus realized the seriousness of Lazarus condition. But as Jesus gaze rested on his face, Simeon knew that the Holy One did know, even as he knew all things.

Jesus remained there for two more days, nor seemed to hear the agitated whispering of the women and the surprised comments of the disciples, who decided that Lazarus could not really be in truly desperate plight or Jesus would have made immediate journey.

On the third morning, Jesus spoke.

'Let us go to Judea!'

His disciples reacted in agitation. Much as they wanted to see Lazarus recover, they knew the extreme danger Jesus would place himself in by returning to Bethany, just two miles outside Jerusalem and within easy access of Caiaphas secret police.

'But Rabbi,' they said, faces tense with worry, 'A short while ago the Jews there tried to stone you, and yet you are going back there?'

Jesus beckoned them outside the cave, where the rising sun shot up through the dawn sky, above the hill that sheltered them, flooding the valley with an intensity of light, lining Jordan's course with liquid flame. Below them, the wild olives and willows shivered in the early breeze.

'Are there not twelve hours of daylight? A man who walks by day will not stumble, for he sees by this world's light. It is when he walks by night that he stumbles, for he has no light.'

They stared at each other in perplexity. He spoke again. This time he smiled, his lips parting with a most tender expression, telling them to be of good cheer, they were going to set out immediately. Simeon took a deep breath of relief, as he helped the women gather their cooking pots together, it was to be hoped, that they would not reach Bethany too late.

'Our friend Lazarus has fallen asleep,' said Jesus quietly, as he led them to the fording place. 'But I am going to wake him up.' The disciples followed him into the shallows, helping the women, their faces relaxed.

'Lord, if he sleeps, he will get better,' they exclaimed, not realizing that he meant Lazarus had died. They stood briefly on the opposite bank of Jordan, before clambering up the steep sides of the hill. Jesus faced them, his face stern.

'Lazarus is dead!'

They cried out at this, bewailing the fact that he had not been there, to have prevented this disaster.

'For your sake I am glad that I was not there, so that you may believe! But let us go to him.' They stared at him in mixture of sorrow and bewilderment then followed mutely behind him.

In Bethany, Martha held Mary to her bosom, comforting her sister, trying to remain calm when her own heart was almost breaking. Lazarus had been laid to rest in his tomb four days ago now. Both women had prayed that their message would reach Jesus in time, that Simeon would be able to find him, and bring him back before the inevitable death that attended such terrible fever. Now mourning friends not only from within the little village community, but also from Jerusalem had come to comfort the two sisters. Each day, more people arrived and Martha knew she must prepare refreshments for those who would arrive today and the everyday tasks helped her to contain her despair. Mary showed her grief more intensely. She had been so sure, that Jesus would come. Even to that moment when Lazarus had fetched a last sigh, as soft as a butterfly's wing, she had thought that her beloved Master would appear to heal the brother who was so dear to her. Martha left Mary's side, to sweep the dust out of the door. She raised a hand to her eyes, for people were running towards the house. She dropped the broom and hastened to meet them. Instinctively, she knew that there must be news of Jesus—and even if he came too late, at least he would be able to bring comfort.

'The Holy One approaches,' cried several of the village lads, who had seen his party coming as they tended their goats outside the village. Mary followed Martha to the door, white to the lips. She stood rooted to the spot—but Martha ran along the village street and beyond to greet Jesus and his disciples, her face hot from exertion and swollen with tears. She came to a halt, stood awkwardly before him, her weary face working with sorrow.

'Lord—if you had been here, my brother would not have died!' She stood looking at him, her chest heaving, then her eyes met his, and the angry note left her voice as she said quietly. 'But even now—I know that God will give you, whatever you ask!'

The disciples glanced from one of them to the other. No one moved or spoke.

'Your brother will rise again,' said Jesus, looking full at Martha. She swallowed, not daring to believe what he said.

'I know he will rise again at the resurrection, at the last day!' This must be what he meant—mustn't it? It couldn't mean that—no, that was impossible!' Her eyes were fixed on the Holy One's face, her body quivering. Jesus opened his arms, wide.

'I am the resurrection, and the life! He who believes in me will live, even though he dies—and whoever lives and believes in me will never die! Do you believe this?'

'Yes, Lord,' breathed Martha. 'I believe that you are the Christ, the Son of God, who was to come into the world!' Then she turned, and walked quietly back to her house.

'Mary---Mary! The Teacher is here and he is asking for you.'

Mary was still standing on the spot where Martha had left her, in trance-like appearance of sorrow. Now she started to move, to hurry along the street out beyond the confines of the village, where Jesus still remained with his disciples, where Martha had met him. The mourners who had congregated near the house had watched Mary's abrupt departure with surprise. No doubt, she was going to the tomb to mourn.

Jesus advanced to meet her. Mary was weeping bitterly, as she fell at his feet. The veil had fallen back from her long dark hair as she knelt in the dust, her tears splashing onto his sandalled feet. Great, choking sobs shook her frame, as she blurted out, 'Lord—if you had been here, my brother would not have died!' Pain at her brother's death, pain that Jesus had not arrived in time to prevent that death, when she had been so sure, so absolutely sure that he would, now left her devastated by a grief that jarred the innermost recess of her soul, tearing at her faith.

A hand descended on her head and gradually her sobs subsided. She raised her tear filled eyes to his saw there a compassion that spilled itself in precious drops from his own eyes. A soft groan broke from the gentle heart of the Son of God. Then Martha was at Mary's side and helped Jesus to assist the distraught girl to her feet. Sarah stood further back, weeping unashamedly.

A procession of people had followed Martha out of the village. They stood before Jesus, heads bowed in sorrow, weeping and wailing for their dead friend, as was the custom. Now Jesus own face was working with grief, his spirit deeply troubled.

'Where have you laid him,' he asked?

'Come and see, Lord,' they said, and whispered amongst themselves, to see the Holy One so distressed. It was obvious that he had cared deeply for Lazarus, so why then, had he not healed his friend, when he had healed so many others! Jesus knew what was in their hearts, but he made no reply to their criticism. Instead, he walked with head bowed, overcome with emotion. He wept. He followed the villagers, who led him up a barren hillside now, their feet slipping on the scree, loose stones falling behind him, the sharp thuds the only sounds punctuating the silence in that desolate place. At last they pointed to the mouth of a cave, sealed by a huge stone.

'He is there, Lord!' They stood well back from the entrance, not wishing to be defiled by approaching too close to this place of death. Jesus pointed to the stone.

'Take away the stone!'

Reluctantly, three of the mourners moved forward to do his bidding. The disciples stood behind him, bewildered that their master should want to expose the horrors of corruption. Miriam and Joanna were standing next to the bereaved sisters, their faces troubled. Martha raised a hand in remonstration to Jesus, as she saw the men place hands upon the boulder. In shrinking gesture of dismay, she blurted out a warning.

'But Lord—by this time there is a bad odour—for he's been there four days!'

Jesus turned calmly and looked at her. Although his face bore signs of tears, his gaze was steady. Martha stared back at him nonplussed. She made to speak again, but he shook his head. There was a glow about him now, a feeling of energy emanating from his form. Martha began to tremble and clutched onto the arm of Mary, who was staring fixedly at

Jesus, an incredulous hope beginning to form in her mind.

'Did I not tell you, that if you believed, you would see the glory of God?'

For answer, the sisters clasped each other more tightly, hardly daring to breathe. They watched from grief stricken eyes as Jesus gestured to the men to proceed, then as the heavy stone was moved, and the men sprang hastily back from the tomb, Jesus stepped forward. He clasped his hands and turned his face upwards, as he breathed a prayer.

'Father, I thank you that you heard me. I knew that you always hear me, but I said this for the benefit of the people standing here, that they may believe that you sent me!'

He turned back a brief minute, his eyes sweeping the faces of the women, his disciples and the troubled, wondering villagers, with sprinkling of their more sophisticated neighbours from Jerusalem, amongst them a spy from the temple. Then his face took on a stern expression, his gold flecked eyes flashed with strange, unearthly light as he approached the mouth of the tomb. His voice rose like thunder—and all trembled at his words.

'Lazarus—Come out!'

Then—as all watched the mouth of the cave in stupefaction, a figure shuffled clumsily forth, shrouded in grave clothes, his hands were wrapped in linen, as were his feet. He stumbled, unable to see for a cloth masked his face, and the voice of Jesus rang out again-

'Take off the grave clothes—and let him go!'

There was joy in the little house in Bethany, like to that in the courts of heaven, the only tears now those of happiness and gratitude. Lazarus sat on a couch, a sister on either side, embracing him. He had bathed and now wore his favourite tunic. His blue eyes held a strange, faraway look, as he stared at those dear to him and whom he had never expected to see again in this life. People had started to stream into the house, pushing forward, to look with blatant curiosity at this man, whom all knew to have been dead. For had not his cold and stiffened corpse been laid to rest, and now, four days later, unbelievably, he had been raised from the arms of death, by the command of the Holy One.

'He is indeed the Messiah! Jesus is the Holy Son of God,' they cried, 'for none but God, can give life back to those held in the corruption of the tomb!' They offered congratulations to Lazarus, wanting to shake his hand, but fearful to touch him.

Then they streamed out of the house, dispersing to every corner of the village, whilst those from Jerusalem started upon the two mile walk back to the city, each wanting to be the first with the news, that Jesus of Nazareth was indeed the Christ! But the temple spy ran before them on trembling legs. Panting with exertion, he stood before the High Priest, Caiaphas, jerking out his story, his face white with the shock of what had happened.

Caiaphas drew in a sibilant breath, as his face darkened with suppressed anger. He forced himself to remain calm, to question the spy carefully, noting that although the man was in the grip of strong emotion, he nevertheless had the look of truth about him, was after all one of his most reliable agents. Yet the story was incredible! How was such a thing possible! His mind raced. Even supposing that the impossible had happened, and that was not to say that he believed such fantasy, well there were other powers than those of Almighty God. Suppose that Jesus had called upon the power of demons! He refused, absolutely refused to recognize the truth, for to do so would be to abdicate his power, his all important authority. Yet at the back of his mind, knowledge was forming, that this Jesus was indeed the Messiah. But he must not be acknowledged as such, for if this thing should happen, the people who already loved and respected the wandering Nazorene, would without doubt rise behind him and crown him king. Yes—and what would be the result of that? Thousands would die! The country would be put to the sword, by the ruthless fighting force that was Rome. Now at least, there was a tenuous peace, perforated it was true by the continual pinpricks of the Zealots, but at least the people had some stability, even though bowed down by taxes and most importantly, the temple was flourishing! This domain of gold and marble, sacred to mighty God, where he, Caiaphas held sway, this temple must be preserved for all posterity. Nothing must interfere with this.

Jesus must die! Better that one man should be sacrificed for the sake of all. He clapped his hands. He ordered a meeting of the Sanhedrin, the ruling council. All must be done according to the law, so that none could raise a finger afterwards! In the meanwhile, Jesus must be arrested, before the news of the raising of Lazarus spread too far and before the Zealots could muster in Galilee. But Jesus could not be found. He had left Bethany, with his disciples for a region near the desert.

Tribune Marcus burst into a peal of hearty laughter, which did not abate, despite the look of discomfiture on the face of his Jewish informer. The soldiers standing near him, who had also heard the man's words had ill disguised grins on their faces. The only man not to laugh was Centurion Claudius, who walked over to the window to stare thoughtfully from this high turret of the Antonia fortress, in the direction where Bethany lay.

'I promise you, Lord Tribune,' the informer gave Marcus the title obsequiously, 'that my words are true! I was there. I saw Lazarus come forth from the tomb, wearing his grave clothes!' A look of near terror crossed the man's face, as he relived the awesome experience.

Tribune Marcus composed his features, as he watched the informer curiously. He knew enough about men, to realize that the man was not lying, that he truly believed what he was saying.

'My dear fellow,' said Marcus in kindly tones. 'I am indeed willing to believe that a living man was released from the tomb. The problem lies with the custom you Jews have of insisting on the burial of a corpse before sundown, on the day the unfortunate departs this life. There are some states of coma which closely resemble death, mistakes can be made as obviously happened in this case. The man was lucky that Jesus arrived in time to have him released from the tomb, an appalling situation to find himself in surely—entombed alive!'

He shook his head, and made to dismiss the man.

'Lord Tribune—the man had lain at the point of death for several days before expiring. A young lad, with some knowledge of healing by the name of Simeon attended him, as later a respected physician from Jerusalem did also. Lazarus had been suffering from that foul fever which yellows the skin and in which the patient is afflicted with a distemper of the bowels, and is unable to eat. He was in a state of extreme emaciation when he died. The man who issued forth from the tomb was fresh faced and in the full vigour of manhood. It was a miracle, Lord! Word of it is spreading all over Judea and Jesus is now openly being declared the Christ!'

He bowed, as the Tribune threw some silver coins to him, and made to depart, slipping the money into a purse concealed within his tunic. But he could not retreat, before trying one more time to get this stubborn Roman to believe him.

'Lazarus was four days in the tomb, Lord. Four days, his body embalmed, his limbs wrapped in grave clothes, a cloth over his head—and he walked out—came forth at the command of the Holy One!'

'He was a fortunate man,' said Marcus smoothly.' Let me know if you hear any further developments in this matter, any sign of the people acclaiming Jesus as military leader. Ah, and yes, I want to know the moment Barabbas shows his head in Jerusalem!'

The man nodded and was led down a staircase by a soldier, to pick up the empty provision baskets, which gave him excuse to enter the fortress without attracting suspicion. Any person found acting as an informer to the Romans would be mercilessly dealt with by either the Sicarii or the Zealots.

Claudius turned away from the window to find his commander's eyes upon him.

'Would you have any objections, to my taking a few men and visiting Bethany? The sister of the man Lazarus is known to me. Mary is a friend of my wife.'

Marcus smiled slightly. 'Of course you may go. After all, this young man named Simeon, with knowledge of healing, could be your adopted son, eh! Just remember one thing though.' His words were low, as he accompanied Claudius to the door and spoke out of earshot of the men. 'Your life is linked to an unfortunate degree with the Jewish people, both through your wife and your adopted son. It is not by chance that soldiers are not allowed to marry, Claudius! This rule prevents unions being formed, which can give rise to divided loyalties. Obviously, in your case, nothing was said. After all, your twenty years official service are over, and whenever you wish it, you can retire from the service with a very handsome sum of money, honoured position and land—or, you can take the decision to stand as tribune. You have your five campaigns almost twice over, to commend you and with Pilate's backing, you would be sure to be elected.' His dark eyes bored into Claudius blue gaze. 'Claudius, old friend—I know how you feel over Jesus of Nazareth. That you admire the rabbi and hold him in respect.'

'I would never allow my respect for him, to stand in the way of duty,' jerked out Claudius, stiff lipped.

'Maybe not, but at the moment I feel that you are walking a tightrope. Don't fall!' He flung an arm about Claudius shoulders in a rough embrace. 'You still love Miriam, don't you, despite what happened?' Claudius brow furrowed. He sighed.

'Yes, I do. But too much has passed. She will never be able to forgive me, for the way I rejected her after that fiend raped her.' At length he was now able to talk about it. 'Yes, Marcus, I know I have been all kinds of a fool, for I do love Miriam—would do anything to have her back as my wife. But she is completely absorbed in following Jesus. It is too late!' He spoke wearily, face dejected.

'Claudius—take the advice of a friend find her and tell her how you feel! I warrant you, she will return to your arms. Well—off with you!' He grinned as Claudius clamped his helmet down, and set off down the steep stone stairs, with almost unseemly haste. Marcus returned to his desk, to write a letter to Pilate. He mentioned the story of Lazarus without comment, except to state that with Passover now approaching, the most sensitive time of the year as far as the Jews were concerned, perhaps extra care should be observed in case of insurrection. It seemed that many were now openly declaring Jesus of Nazareth, as the Christ.

One of the young goatherds spotted the small contingent of Romans approaching the village and ran to alert the people of Bethany. The women disappeared into their houses and the village looked almost deserted, as Claudius and his men entered. Only a few stray dogs snarled warningly and just one small boy stood in the square, looking up wonderingly at the helmeted soldiers, with their burnished breastplates and rust coloured tunics and the huge four-foot long shields. Too young to be afraid, he smiled a greeting.

'Shalom,' said this little one. Claudius slipped from his horse and bent down to the child.

'Where is the house of Lazarus,' he asked in halting Aramaic? For answer, the child pointed, then suddenly shy, ran away. Claudius glanced about him, at the poor houses, few shops and to the left in the square, a tavern with benches set outside under the shade of two straggling palm trees. The village had no containing wall, was of insufficient importance for that, nor was there an imposing synagogue, although a long, low building on a small rise might have served that purpose.

Claudius walked towards the house the boy had indicated. It was bigger than the others, with the usual flat roof. Someone had attempted to make a small garden, for flowering shrubs struggled for existence against the fierce breath of the desert which parched all vegetation, the wonder being that the few miserable goats he had seen as they approached the village, could find sustenance amongst the yellowed spiky grass.

He knocked. The door was opened by Martha. She looked nervously at the tall imposing Roman officer who stood there. She rubbed hands damp from washing vegetables, on her tunic, as she forced herself to look him in the eyes.

'This is the house of Lazarus?' inquired Claudius gently.

'Yes, why do you ask, sir?' Martha seemed to draw courage, and placed hands on her hips, a somewhat truculent expression on her face. Then another voice called out, and suddenly, Sarah was there. She had recognized his tones and pushed past Martha. Claudius smiled in amazement, to see the young girl, who had been his wife's slave, but was now freedwoman and betrothed to young Simeon. Whatever was she doing here, could it mean that Miriam was here also? Sarah pushed her tangle of black curls back from her forehead, wishing she looked tidier to greet him, for she had been working.

'Centurion Claudius!'

She bowed and was caught up in his arms. He hardly dared to phrase the words. 'Sarah child, how do you come to be here—is Miriam....?'

'No,' she said sadly. 'She was here, just a few days ago. But she has gone with the other women who minister to Jesus and his disciples. I used to be with them too, but Simeon thought it better if I remain here with Mary's family, as we are not yet married!' She stopped and looked guiltily at Martha, realizing her discourtesy, in not introducing Claudius. 'Martha, this is Centurion Claudius, Miriam's husband!'

'Greetings to you, Centurion,' Martha's face relaxed slightly, but she glanced uneasily towards the troop of soldiers lining the street. He saw her glance and gave a short order to his men to go to the tavern, wait for him there.

He followed Martha into the house and looked around the white washed room into which she led him. His inquiring glance took in the two couches, one spread with a beautifully woven rug in muted jewel shades, the other with goatskins. Between them stood a long, low, tiled table, its base of skilfully carved stone, in the corner a chair covered with a faded rug and blue cushion, while in the corners of the room, there were smaller tables holding lamps of burnished copper. He was struck by the feeling of peace he sensed in this place.

Mary, he learned, as he gratefully accepted a cup of wine, had also gone with Jesus. The news surprised Claudius. After all, if all he had heard about Lazarus illness was true, then surely she should have been here to have nursed her brother back to health?

'I heard stories, that your brother was very ill, Martha?' He knew he must proceed tactfully.

'My brother died—was dead and in his tomb for four days! But the Holy One came, and commanded my dead brother to come out of his tomb. And he did! Glory be to God, and to his Son Jesus!' There was no mistaking the note of truth in the woman's voice, or the intense joy with which she spoke these words.

'Would it be possible to see your brother? I take it that he is in bed?' Martha glanced at Sarah, and both burst into gales of happy laughter.

'Come with me, Centurion,' said Martha, and led him back along the deserted street. They turned into a narrow alley, which led to another street. The sound of metal on stone rang out loudly on the quiet air. Martha stopped outside a partly erected new dwelling, calling on her brother's name. Lazarus came striding round from the back of the house. He dropped his hammer with an exclamation of surprise, to see Martha in company with a high ranking Roman officer. Claudius stared back in stupefaction. Surely this bronzed, well muscled young man, blond hair damp from exertion, blue eyes shining with health could not be the man he had heard spoken of by the informer? Yellowed skin, emaciated? It was impossible, only he knew it was not!

'You are Lazarus?

'Yes, Centurion, but what do you want with me?'

'Just, to speak with you. I am a friend of your sister Mary. I met her in Capernaum, where I used to live.'

'Ah, now I understand. You are Miriam's husband?'

'I am. Lazarus, I'll be honest. I heard the story of your miraculous return to life, the news is circulating Jerusalem and although I had personally seen proof of Jesus wondrous powers in Simeon's healing, I must admit that I doubted. When I heard that you had been dead, in your tomb for four days—this was thing incredible!'

'Say rather, possible only through the power of the Living God, vested in His Son, Jesus. He is the Messiah, Claudius! But I think you already know this?' Lazarus placed a steadying hand on Claudius arm, for the soldier had gone very pale. 'Come back to my home,' he said gently. 'We have many things to discuss.' He called an instruction to one of his workmen, and led Claudius back to the little home that Jesus loved. Martha brought a simple meal of bread and cheese and olives, a bowl of grapes and a jug of fresh goat's milk. Claudius relaxed in the chair spread with a faded rug.

'That is where he likes to sit,' said Lazarus quietly. 'Now tell me, Claudius, why are you really here? Is it to gather information for Pilate? Do the Romans seek to arrest Jesus?' the blue eyes met his steadily, demanding truth.

'Pilate has no quarrel with the Holy One,' said Claudius slowly, 'At least, not unless he leads an uprising against Rome! Now I know enough about Jesus, to realize that he does not seek power, does not wish to set himself up as a military leader. But Lazarus, as we both know, the Zealots are determined to find a figurehead, one they can acclaim as King, to enable them to mobilize the whole country against us, which would be entirely futile. We have the greatest army in the world! None can stand against us. Even if the Zealots were to score victory in a few minor skirmishes, our forces would wipe them out completely, and with them, a great many innocent people. So it must not be allowed to happen. Jesus must beware the Zealots!'

'You need have no fear of his involvement with them,' replied Lazarus. 'Jesus is a spiritual leader, to bring our people to repentance and to loving knowledge of our God—to spread the word of Almighty God, to Jew and Gentile alike. For this purpose he was born, he who is both man and the Son of God. Do you understand what I am saying to you, Claudius?'

'I am not sure. The concept is almost beyond my power of comprehension! Because once you accept this, that there is one mighty and invisible God, who according to you, cares for all humanity, for Jew and Gentile alike, who is a God of love—how then if men believe this, can one nation fight and dominate another?'

'My brother, let me explain it to you, the way in which Jesus taught me and his disciples.' Lazarus reached out and took Claudius hands in his, and for two hours, the men sat together, Claudius listening with an intensity of spirit, knowing as he listened, that eventually he must come to the decision that Marcus had spoken of. He must retire from the army and become a private citizen. Then he would be free to follow his conscience, to start living out his life as laid down by Jesus—who was the Christ.

'I must return to the fortress,' said Claudius at last. 'If you see Jesus, tell him to keep away from Jerusalem, for Caiaphas has agents out seeking for him to destroy him. Obviously, I will do all in my power to protect him, but political decisions will be taken over my head. Tell the Holy One to stay away. Barabbas is only waiting for another opportunity to attack, and may try to use Jesus as a rallying spark, to set his people on fire.' He rose to his feet, 'Remember, tell him to stay away from Jerusalem!'

'I will tell him if he ever comes here. But he will do, what he must do,' replied Lazarus sombrely. 'Go now, Claudius. But I know that one day, you will be one of us!'

He remounted his horse and collected his men, who had enjoyed an unusual rest and break from routine. The sound of marching feet, receded along the street, as the Romans returned to Jerusalem. Lazarus climbed to the roof of his house and knelt there in prayer. A Jew was praying for a Roman enemy—who was now a friend.

Chamberlain Chuza looked down from the balcony of his bedchamber, onto the main palace courtyard, surrounded by the amazingly beautiful gardens which were famed in all Galilee, only none but the guests of Herod Antipas ever saw them. Tiberias, this beautiful city created as his new capital by Antipas and completed just ten years ago, was shunned by all devout Jews, as it had been built on ancient tombs and was accordingly, a place unclean.

A caravan had halted just outside the main gates, the noisy bellowing of the truculent, thirsty camels, jarring the silence of the afternoon, when most people reclined. Hawk nosed Arabs supervised the unloading of the camels, as bales of silk, loads of ivory and chests heavy with treasure for the eyes of Herodias, were carried through the courtyard, to the palace gates. Herod's slaves swept silently out to meet the newcomers; then a murmur was heard, which grew to an excited shouting. What was this disorderly conduct about? Chuza snatched a small whip from the wall and hurried downstairs.

'You there—Eliab! What is the cause of this commotion?'

Chuza stood legs apart, glaring at a youth, who had been one of the more vociferous. The slave bowed low to Chuza, his eyes frightened. 'Well, have you no tongue? If you have one, use it, or I will have it plucked from your mouth!'

At this threat, the lad pointed towards a wiry looking member of the caravan, a Phoenician.

'My Lord, this man says that the rabbi Jesus has raised a man dead four days, from the tomb, that there are many witnesses! People are acclaiming Jesus as Messiah!'

Chuza let forth an oath of exasperation. Not another of the incredible stories of the Nazorene, which managed to circulate even here, in the palace! The man was becoming a danger to peace in the area, disturbing even the normally placid slaves by the extraordinary happenings that surrounded his ministry. He had better bring this matter before Antipas, because his master would in any case, hear of it. He beckoned to the Phoenician, asking whether he had personally witnessed the event he was disturbing all by relating.

'No, my Lord—this wonder happened just outside Jerusalem, in the village of Bethany. But I heard it as we passed through Jerusalem, from a man who was present, cousin of a Pharisee.'

'Come with me. You will be rewarded for giving an accurate account, to Herod!'

Herodias thrust her splendid bosom before her husband's eyes, flaunting the barbaric necklace of huge turquoises and lapis lazuli, set in gold. A diadem of matching stones adorned her brow.

'Think you this jewellery looks well on me, my Lord? The merchant assures me, it once graced the neck of the Egyptian queen, Cleopatra— she who loved Anthony and took her own life!' The heavy musk of the perfume she wore, rose to his nostrils, but Antipas was unmoved, indeed was tiring of his wife's charms, which no longer attracted his jaded senses now that Herodias daughter, his niece Salome, was blossoming into even more flamboyant beauty than her mother. Why could he no longer find joy in the sexual pleasures, which once meant so much to him? Why in frustration, was he drawn to the torture chambers deep in the basement of the palace for stimulation, usually culminating in the deflowering of one of the virgin slave girls, constantly bought for his delectation? Yet in a strange way he still loved Herodias, loved her for her ruthless ambition and cruelty, which matched his own, making them one.

'You do not care for the necklace,' pouted Herodias, stripping it from her throat and throwing the priceless creation onto her bed.

'It is becoming, wife—but do not trouble me with women's trifles. I am concerned with matters of greater import!' Herod's brows were drawn heavily together and he ground his teeth into his lower lip in a way that presaged a coming storm. He seized a wine goblet, tossed off its contents then hurled the empty goblet at a waiting slave. The man managed to dodge and picked it up.

'I suppose you are worried about this latest story, of the carpenter's doings, supposedly summoning a dead man from his tomb? Complete nonsense! Who would believe such incredible tale?' Herodias sneered and cast an angry glance at Salome, who had sauntered in, and was reaching for the fabulous turquoises.

'Leave that, and have yourself announced before entering,' she snapped. Salome cast a languorous glance at Antipas, who for once ignored her. She flounced out. 'Why are you so concerned about this Jesus,' Herodias continued. 'Why do you not just have him arrested, and deal with him as you did with John the Baptist?'

'Because, dear wife, this Jesus is loved and revered by thousands of our people. They hated my father, in spite of all he did to better their lot. They will never forget that we are of mixed race. But we have discussed this matter before. I do not want open rebellion on my hands as being responsible for disposing of the pestilential rabbi. But Caiaphas must act soon. Passover is in two weeks time. We will travel to Jerusalem ahead of the festival, so that I may speak urgently with the High Priest on this matter. Even the people will not dare to gainsay the High Priest. However, if there are problems, then let Caiaphas bear responsibility before Pontius Pilate. But certainly, Jesus of Nazareth must die!' Having hissed out the last words, he stalked out of the bedchamber. That night, Herod Antipas slept alone, his sleep disturbed by recurring fear. What if Jesus had really raised the dead? If such indeed was the power at his command, could he not likewise strike the living dead, in similar manner? Herod sat up in bed sweating.

'If only I could see him for myself, satisfy myself as to the truth about him. Demand that he demonstrate his power, by producing one of his miracles,' he muttered. Then he sighed uneasily, 'Safer not to come in contact with him though!' He threw himself back against the silken pillows. A thought came into his mind, suppose—just suppose that all they said of Jesus were true, that he was the long awaited Messiah! Bah, his brain was becoming as addled as that of his superstitious slaves! Just let Passover come and friend Caiaphas would put an end to all these suppositions. Jesus must not survive the Feast of Passover.

Chapter Nineteen

A priest stood on the Temple pinnacle as dawn flushed the sky over the Mount of Olives and the sun splattered blood onto the froth of clouds. He cried his message of the new risen sun then raised the trumpet to his lips, the shrill, silver blast shattering the air, causing a flock of birds to rise, speeding like a shower of black arrows across the Kidron valley. Vultures circling high over Hinnom, swerved in flight, as they crested the air currents. Donkeys and camels submitting their backs to early loads raised their voices in protest and devout men knelt in prayer.

It was the sign for the first sacrifice to be offered to God, and smoke and incense rose on the air from the great horned altar. The little trembling lamb had yielded up life beneath the sacrificial knife, as man attempted to atone for the stain of sin by offering up this innocent unblemished life, the day's round had started in the magnificently gilded Temple, the thousands of priests busy at their appointed tasks. Caiaphas looked broodingly from his window, set high in the small room near to the Holy Place, across to the Antonia fortress. His spies had informed him that Pontius Pilate was expected today, although it was a full week before Passover. Moreover, it would appear that Pilate and the Lady Claudia would be residing in their apartments in the Antonia on this occasion, instead of at the Citadel, in the splendour of Herod's palace.

Pilate must have some good reason, for this change in routine and Caiaphas could only conjecture that the Prefect must be expecting trouble. He stroked his beard thoughtfully, his dark eyes narrowing. What was it that Pilate feared? There had been word that Barabbas had entered the city, but none knew where he was hiding. Of course, it might be mere rumour! But more likely, it was the strong impression among the entire population that Jesus would be publicly proclaimed Messiah, following the miraculous raising of Lazarus from the tomb. Hundreds had started to stream to Bethany, to see the man Lazarus for themselves. Bethany? Should he order Jesus arrested when he came there, as surely he would? He shook his head, his eyes darting with indecision. Perhaps it was not the best place. Simon the Pharisee, who had been driven out of Jerusalem with that most dreaded scourge of leprosy, and who had been healed so it was said by the Nazarene was now living in Bethany. He had many friends amongst the Pharisees in the temple, including Nicodemus, respected member of the Sanhedrin.

Caiaphas snapped his fingers for his attendants. He would visit his father-in-law Annas, who had previously held the High Priesthood. Annas was very old and very wise. Annas received Caiaphas warmly, as they walked in the large, flower bordered courtyard of his splendid villa in the upper city.

'My dear son-in-law, over the last few months I have made it my business to find out what I can of the lives and backgrounds of those who so closely follow the Rabbi Jesus. I will not bore you with unnecessary detail, merely to mention, that in my opinion, there is one man amongst his intimates, who could be a weak link.'

'Oh?' Caiaphas looked up, intrigued.

'His name is Judas Iscariot. It is rumoured that he may have had connection with the Sicarii at one time. Certainly, he is a highly nervous individual, who makes no secret of his wish to see Jesus as king, heading rebellion. He is also avaricious, but above all a fanatic! Such men are unstable. They will give their lives for an ideal, but if disappointed, betray the one who has negated their hopes.

'Well, I thank you for this information, but...!' He broke off, as a priest approached them, bowing low before Caiaphas. 'What is it then?'

'My Lord High Priest, I have hurried here from the Temple, to tell you that Herod has arrived at his palace and has sent a message, that he wishes to speak with you most urgently!'

'Send back my greetings to Herod and say that I accept his invitation to see him. I will visit the palace within the hour!' Annas and Caiaphas exchanged meaningful glances, before Caiaphas made swift return, by the underground passage that connected the house of Annas with the Temple.

Caiaphas litter was borne on the shoulders of twelve priests, a company of the Temple guards clearing passage for him, and flanking his progress, in their shining armour. It was but a short march, from the temple to the Citadel, the three huge towers adjacent to the imposing palace dominating the skyline. Herod the Great had named them, Hippicus for a friend, Phasael after his older brother—and Mariamne for the best beloved of his nine wives and whom he had murdered. But it was the son of that long dead Herod, who had rebuilt the magnificent temple and this most glorious palace with its two great wings who now enjoyed the splendours wrought by his notorious father, whose fame as a builder had been acclaimed as far as Rome and whose cruelties would groan down the centuries. Usually, Antipas felt himself there under sufferance when Pontius Pilate was in residence, even though both had their own equally splendid suites of rooms in the enormous building, but this time, to his delight, he had been informed that Pilate preferred the Antonia, where special preparations were being made to receive the Lady Claudia.

Antipas, was sitting on the throne in the great hall surrounded by his nobles, with Herodias and Salome seated on either side of him. He rose to his feet, and gestured for Caiaphas to approach, and the two men who in all Palestine, had the most to lose in the case of uprising, bowed courteously to each other.

'Greetings, Lord Caiaphas. I thank you for your kindness in coming so promptly to my invitation. There are matters of import which I wish to discuss with you.'

The priest bowed again, watching Antipas impassively. He knew he was the centre of attention, as the throng of richly clothed nobles and diplomats stared curiously at the mysterious figure of the Temple's spiritual leader, standing quietly before them in his flowing robes, robes to be exchanged in a week's time for the splendid regalia, withheld by the Romans in between festivals in order to curtail his power. Traditionally, the High Priest needed this outward sign of authority to fulfil leading role in any political sense, with the people. But even without his jewelled breastplate and blue embroidered gown, the hem bordered with gold bells and pomegranates, he was an imposing figure and many viewed him uneasily. Very few of those assembled there retained the faith of their fathers, merely paying lip service, to the mighty God of Abraham, Isaac and Jacob and visiting the Temple only for the great feasts. Some indeed, worshipped in the temples of the Roman gods, built by Herod, in deference to his contemporary, Augustus Caesar, great Emperor of Rome, himself worshipped as god by his people, as now was his successor Tiberius Caesar. Temples to both Roman and Greek deities abounded in most of the major cities in Palestine, some towns being peopled almost exclusively by Gentiles. Here in Jerusalem, were to be found theatres, public baths, and the great arena where men pitted themselves against beasts and the circus where chariot races were held. Yet dominating the great tawny city, was the splendid temple, built by Herod to replace the previous, less imposing building which had survived over five hundred years, itself replacing the original wonder of antiquity, Solomon's Temple. A thousand priests had been trained as masons, to undertake the mammoth task of rebuilding the temple, no man not of the priesthood was allowed to profane the building work by his touch; carpentry, decoration, gilding, all being effected by the priesthood.

Now Caiaphas ruled this most imposing edifice in Jerusalem, soaring high on the hill of Zion, slightly larger even than this magnificent palace, built also by Antipas father, in the shadow of the Citadel, with its three massive towers. And Caiaphas enjoyed his power as master of the Temple and great army of priests and scribes, his supreme authority in the High court, the Sanhedrin, just as Antipas delighted in his position as Tetrarch of Galilee and Peraea. So they stared at each other, Caiaphas, with the cruel eyes of a wolf and Herod, whom Jesus had named fox, with the crafty face and manner of that predator.

'Matters of State should perhaps be discussed in more private setting,' suggested Caiaphas.

'You are right!' Herod signalled dismissal, with peremptory wave of his hand and the High Chamberlain ushered the company into a neighbouring reception hall. Caiaphas eyes now slid over Herodias and Salome.' You have leave to retire,' said Herod. Looking slightly affronted, nevertheless they rose reluctantly and strolled away.

'Now Lord Caiaphas, may I offer you refreshments.'

'Thank you—perhaps later.' They seated themselves. 'You wished to speak with me about?'

'Jesus of Nazareth!'

'Ah!'

'What do you think of him, Lord Priest?'

'What thinks your Highness,' replied Caiaphas, tossing the question back.

'That he is a danger to peace in Palestine—a menace that must be removed!'

'Removed—my Lord?'

'He must die. Thousands are acclaiming him Messiah, since the story of Lazarus. It is only a matter of time, before the people fuelled by nationalistic fervour of the Zealots rise against Rome, with what disastrous results we can both envisage!' Herod's face had mottled with anger, as he made this statement. Since arriving in Jerusalem, he had heard nothing but talk of the Holy man from Galilee on all lips. So now he threw discretion to the winds, knowing that Caiaphas would be in similar danger, should the anticipated rebellion take place.

'What action do you intend to take,' asked Caiaphas, watching Herod's face.

'I cannot afford to move against him myself. His greatest support is in my territory in Galilee. Should I seek to arrest him, I may well precipitate the very thing I seek to prevent—the Zealots will retaliate. As you know, my brother Archelaus was removed from his position in Judea by the Emperor, as result of the complaints against him by the common people, which is why we now have to endure the presence of this succession of Prefects! I do not wish to end up in exile, in like fashion!'

'So, you wish me to intervene in this matter,' purred Caiaphas. 'As it happens, I feel as you do. But all must be accomplished according to law. Yes, Jesus must die, even though I have respect for him as a just man, healer and teacher. Sometimes—one man has to die, for the sake of a nation!' They drew their chairs closer. The net that was to close about Jesus was already being cast on the waters of time.

On that same day when Caiaphas and Herod secretly conferred, Jesus and his disciples returned to Bethany, together with Mary Magdalene and the other women, including Mary, his gentle mother. They had spent the last few weeks in the comparative safety of the village of Ephraim, near the desert. Now Jesus knew the time was drawing near for him to return to Jerusalem, to fulfil prophecy and to accomplish the task for which he had been born into the world.

He had calmly explained to his disciples, that the time had come for him to die, to suffer many things—but that on the third day he would rise up again! But still they could not accept what he said, although a terrible apprehension placed strangle net around their hearts.

Judas Iscariot walked out into the desert the night before they left Ephraim, his soul torn in torment. He knew that Jesus was the Messiah, the Holy Son of God. So why then, all this talk of suffering and death, when all he had to do was to proclaim himself King, to have the whole countryside rise up behind him. Judas stared up wildly into the glittering stars, which seemed to swim above his head in a black ocean. Jesus had the power, the wonderful, supernatural power that emanated from

Almighty God. Nothing could harm him, if he did not wish it. Surely then, if he were to be put in such a situation, when his life was in actual danger, then he would be forced to act and to unleash the awesome forces at his command. Perhaps he mused, even to call upon a legion of angels, wings brushed with sparks of eternal flame, to come to his rescue, and bring him to his rightful position as King!

Judas snatched his dagger from beneath his robe, and lifted it in flashing movement high to the sky, as he breathed an oath, a plan, that was to change the course of the world. A plan that though he knew it not was in fulfilment of a divine plan, that would offer up sacrifice of the spotless Lamb of God, for the redemption of all those throughout the ages who would then believe. A plan that would make his own name accursed for all time, by those who did not know his motives! He returned quietly to their camp, and slipped down silently beside the other disciples, wrapping himself in his cloak against the desert chill, where all snored in slumber, except one. Jesus raised himself on one arm, and stared at the man who would betray.

Lazarus was at the doorway, to welcome the Holy One. Simeon had brought advance notice that Jesus was coming and Martha had been up before dawn, preparing the house. She bowed deeply before Jesus, before turning to Mary to hug her sister in greeting as she ushered the party inside.

David and Simeon together with his betrothed, Sarah, slipped away from the house, which was full to bursting point.

'Sarah, I declare you grow more beautiful, every time I see you,' said David admiringly. 'It is only the knowledge that I will have such a delightful sister-in-law, which compensates for the fact that I did not meet you first!' She was indeed looking extremely lovely, her waist length tangle of black curls shining in the sunlight and her dusky cheeks warm with praise that made her lower long lashes over her dark eyes.

Word had already passed from house to house, that Jesus had arrived, and curious villagers were pouring into the dusty street, starting towards the house of Lazarus in order to get a glimpse of the Holy man and his disciples, would he perform another great miracle in their midst? Amongst the people who crowded past Sarah and the brothers was an autocratic figure wearing the deep-fringed robe of a Pharisee. It was Simon, once named Leper, he who had once been driven out of Jerusalem when his dreaded skin disease had been diagnosed as leprosy! He had been healed a year ago, when as a lonely broken man he had knelt humbly at the feet of the Rabbi from Galilee, to have the weight of sin lifted from his soul, and the equally terrible disfigurement that afflicted his body, removed at a word from the gracious Son of God. Simon had appeared before the priests and submitted to amazed examination, before officially being declared cleansed and able to once again take up his position amongst men. But Simon no longer had desire for the great ceremonies in the Temple, even his wealth which was considerable, meant little to him.

He had moved to Bethany, preferring to live in comparative obscurity, in this small village, a mere two miles from the walls of Jerusalem, in a villa that was modest by his previous standards, and set slightly beyond the little community on the side of the hill. He was a friend of Nicodemus, respected judge and member of the Sanhedrin, and his fellow Pharisee would occasionally visit the villa on the hillside. Word had come from Nicodemus, that Jesus would be in danger of his life, were he again to enter Jerusalem. He must warn him!

The Pharisee's eyes swept over David and Simeon. He recognized their Galilean homespun garments and immediately guessed that they were followers of Jesus.

'Your pardon young sirs, are you of the party of Jesus of Nazareth?'

'We are, sir,' replied David, watching Simon uneasily. He realized from the man's cultured accents, that he was no simple villager. Besides which, he wore the robes of a Pharisee.

'Your master once healed me,' said Simon quietly. 'Will you please take me to him?'

They retraced their steps. Lazarus welcomed Simon into his house. Jesus was seated in his favourite chair, the disciples standing about him with troubled looks on their faces. They looked up, as Simon advanced into the room. Peter gave a slight start, as he saw the robes of the Pharisee. Then John, who had the best memory of any of them, recognized Simon as the man who had knelt before the Lord, in a lonely place, weeping bitterly—holding leprous hands over a face from which the nostrils had been eaten away by the disease. Jesus had spoken quietly, laid hands upon him and he had walked away healed.

'Your name is Simon,' said John with a smile. 'You wish to see Jesus?'

'Lord,' said Simon, walking straight up to Jesus, and bowing low. 'I have a favour to ask, that you will honour my poor house, by dining with me tonight, you and your people and you too of course, Lazarus!' So it was, that Martha accompanied Simon the Pharisee to his home to help prepare the dinner, knowing that there was no woman in this bachelor household, to attend to important culinary matters. The other women were to follow later.

When the others had departed, Mary Magdalene prayed alone, in the tiny room which was hers as it had been when she was a child. Tears were welling up in her eyes as she prayed, for Mary knew deep in her heart, that when the Holy One said that he was going to face the terrible death of crucifixion, this most horrific of all deaths, that he meant it. The others all tried to blot out the reality that he was deliberately drawing near to Jerusalem, knowing that his enemies lay in wait there for him, with inevitable consequences.

Long she knelt there, deep in prayer. Then she rose to her feet and opened a wooden chest, which held her few possessions, most of which remained in the house at Capernaum. She lifted out an alabaster jar, containing a priceless perfumed ointment, which some instinct had caused her to retain when she had left jewels and embroidered silk tunics behind with her past. She started out of the house, along the street, and climbed the narrow track leading to the house of Simon the Pharisee.

The dinner was already in process when she entered. The men were all seated in traditional fashion, reclining on couches, leaning on one elbow, leaving the right hand free to eat, feet extended behind them. Jesus reclined in place of honour, with Simon on one side and Lazarus on the other. The women served, Martha in particular overseeing the carrying in of the courses.

'Lord, I have asked you here tonight, for a special reason,' said Simon softly, leaning closer to Jesus. 'One of my colleagues of the Great Sanhedrin has sent word that you face certain arrest and I fear death, should you enter Jerusalem. Even here in Bethany it is not safe.' His earnest words commanded Jesus attention and the disciples sitting closest, who had heard Simon's warning began to whisper together in agitated tones.

'We go to Jerusalem for Passover,' was all that Jesus said in response to the warning, but there was a world of sadness in his eyes and he bowed his head. It was at this moment, when the disciples were silent, watching his face that the sound of weeping stole upon the air, and Mary Magdalene came quietly in, tears pouring down her cheeks. She was carrying an alabaster jar which caught the eye of Judas Iscariot. He watched as she broke the seal on the jar, and the heavy fragrance of the costly spikenard ointment filled the room.

Her sobbing continued, as she moved in almost trance like motion to stand immediately behind Jesus then knelt behind the couch, her tears splashing onto his bare feet, for he had removed his sandals on entering. He did not turn his head, but continued to sit, face drooped upon his breast. Faster and faster the tears flowed, as great choking sobs now shook Mary's slender frame. Then she opened her eyes and saw her master's feet wet with her many tears and setting down the perfume, she tossed her long tresses forward over her face, until they covered his feet. Slowly, in almost ritualistic manner, she seized handfuls of her hair and began gently drying skin hardened by hundreds of patient miles of walking, as he had ministered to those sick in mind and body. She dried it as one would dry the skin of one prepared for the tomb, then her fingers scooped the perfumed ointment from the jar and smoothed it on his feet, crying as though her heart would break.

Not a sound broke the stillness, except the poignancy of the woman's sobbing. Simon had taken uneasy glance behind him to see who so disturbed the propriety of the occasion and saw it was Mary, whom all knew to have left Bethany in disgrace! Even though it would seem that she now accompanied Jesus and his disciples, nevertheless her present behaviour was completely lacking in decorum. No wonder Jesus sat so still, yet at the same time, surely he should realize that it was not fitting, that such a one as Mary, should behave with such indelicacy.

But if Simon the Pharisee was perturbed, Judas Iscariot was absolutely outraged. He sprang to his feet face working with fury, and pointed with trembling finger to the alabaster jar, which she still held. Mary rose to her feet, as an impassioned shout broke from Judas lips, as he pointed an accusing finger.

'Stop wasting that ointment!'

'Be silent, Judas,' said John sternly, eyes smouldering. But the other disciples now began to pick up on Judas remarks, for the purse bearer who kept their common funds, was working himself into a fiery rage wrought of his inner turmoil at his guilt, as he contemplated his secret plan to betray Jesus.

'Why wasn't this ointment sold, and the money given to the poor,' raged Judas. 'It was worth a full year's wages!' Still Jesus did not move. But Mary did. She stood to full height, and then with a very perfect dignity, she poured the remainder of the perfumed cream, over Jesus head and hair. One hand stole gently forward, gently massaging the cream into his forehead. Then with a withering glance at Judas, she dropped the alabaster jar onto the tiled floor, where it splintered into a dozen fragments.

Now at last Jesus spoke and the look he cast on Judas, was one of brooding sorrow.

'Leave her alone,' said Jesus. 'Why are you bothering her? She has done a beautiful thing to me. The poor you will always have with you, and you can help them any time you want. But you will not always have me!' At this a hum of protest arose from the disciples, who could never bear it, when he made them face what lay ahead.

'She did what she could,' continued Jesus. 'She poured perfume on my body beforehand, to prepare it for burial. I tell you the truth, wherever the gospel is preached throughout the world, what she has done will also be told, in memory of her!'

Judas stood shamefaced at the Holy One's rebuke. Then he rushed out of the room, his mind made up, but he could not remain in the presence of the one he was determined to betray. He rushed between the crowds waiting outside Simon's house, some having come from as far as Jerusalem, now that word had circulated that Jesus was again in Bethany. A chill wind moaned from the heights of the Mount of Olives, on the lower eastern slopes of which Bethany was situated. He raised his head into the wind, staring at the dark bulk of the hill before him. On the other side of it separated by the Kidron valley lay Jerusalem.

He hesitated. The city gates would be locked at night, the Roman soldiers mounting heavy guard—but perhaps he could gain entrance by the Golden Gate of the Temple. None saw him, as he slipped into the shadows and started up one of the worn pathways, panting as he forced himself to hurry ever faster up the sharp incline. The moon pooled its light stingily on the shaly steep sides of the hill. Every so often, Judas glanced guiltily below him, where the lights of Bethany cradled all that he held most dear, the wonderful rabbi, Son of the Living God, but who refused to accept the worldly mantle of his kingship. There was still time for Judas to change his mind. He stood poised on the crest of the hill.

Should he return to Bethany before he was missed? The dim lights of Bethany lay behind him the blaze of Jerusalem beckoned before him. A cry burst from his lips, wrenched from the agony of his soul. He ran wildly down the slope, in between the olive trees, across the Kidron brook—and on.

'Halt! What seek you here, fellow? Know you not that the Temple is locked until morning.' The Roman soldiers guarding the gate brought their lances up in threatening movement. They were on perpetual alert, in case Barabbas and his Zealots should try to take advantage of the crowds converging on the city, to enter and attack. Some indeed said that Barabbas was already in the Lower city, that warren of souks and narrow alley ways, where the sunlight never penetrated.

'I have important information to deliver to the High Priest,' said Judas, trying to control the trembling of his limbs wrought of guilt and fatigue.

'Well, can it not wait until sunrise?' asked an officer, staring at the man curiously. But he beckoned one of his men. 'Go fetch one of the Temple guards,' he said. Judas stood quietly, head bent. It seemed an eternity, before a figure in the distinctive uniform of the temple guards, stood before him, glancing at him by the light of the flaring torch he held.

'Who are you fellow,' he asked haughtily?

'One, with information for the High Priest—regarding the Nazarene, Jesus,' Judas faltered.

'So? Well you had better come with me.' The Romans stepped aside, allowing Judas to enter. Sweat was pouring down his forehead. There was no turning back now!

Strangely, now he was talking to Caiaphas, in this long, narrow hall lit by the many olive oil lamps and spluttering candles set above their heads in wall branches, he had become almost icily composed. The man he was proposing to betray was no longer his dearest master, but an anonymous figure, that he could discuss dispassionately.

'What are you willing to give me, if I hand him over to you,' asked Judas, arms folded. One of the priests glanced towards Caiaphas. The High Priest's lips moved, naming the price for the greatest infamy ever to be perpetrated on the earth.

'Thirty pieces of silver!'

Judas watched impassively. Not as much as he had hoped, about as much as a labourer could earn in three months. But at least, it should serve to get him clear of Jerusalem, should his plan go awry. Suppose Jesus refused to act when arrested, if he refused in this extreme to take the reins of authority into his hands, and call upon the people to rise, and the heavenly hosts to support him the Son of the Most High, against those cruel eyed priests? Well, then surely Jesus would have only himself to blame! The man who could heal the sick, feed the crowd of five thousand with a small boy's meal, drive out demons and even call the dead back to life, could if he wished, slay these Sadducees, Pharisees and Levites with a glance. He had the power—yes, Jesus had the power, to become King of the Jews! This action of Judas would only precipitate that which Jesus had so far been refusing to do, would force him to take dramatic charge of the situation!

'Here you are—Judas Iscariot. Thirty pieces of silver!'

The priest gestured to the Levite to count the money into Judas cupped hands, as he closed the treasure chest. 'Now, when may we hope to get return for our money?'

'At Passover!'

'Too late, Jesus must not be allowed to disrupt Passover.'

'I will do my best to arrange matters before then. You have my word!'

Caiaphas almost sneered as he heard the disciple's reply. The word of a traitor! Yet he knew, as he looked into the fanatical gaze of Iscariot that this man would keep faith with him, but for whatever twisted reasons Caiaphas did not know, nor wished to. Already it had been discussed within the Sanhedrin that Jesus must die. Caiaphas had made his own views plain. Better that but this one man should die to save his people from reprisal from the Roman forces. What more apt time for the sacrifice of the Galilean rabbi, than the time of Passover! A mental image of an unblemished sacrificial lamb, pure, blameless, to take away man's sin through the shedding of its innocent blood became strangely fused in his mind, with the form and face of the Nazarene. He gave an involuntary shudder, and gestured that Judas should be dismissed.

During the early hours, Judas dragged himself, dusty and exhausted to the door of the house at Bethany, where his comrades lay beside their leader in sleep. The door creaked as he entered, but none stirred. Only Simon the Zealot watched uncomprehendingly, as he saw Judas sink gently down on his mat, and a very faint sigh issued between the lips of Jesus.

Centurion Claudius glanced through the reports on the table, made by officers of the night watch. He paused as he read of an incident at the Golden Gate. He gave an order.

'You wished to see me, sir?'

'Ah, yes. I understand that you admitted a man through the Golden Gate, shortly after midnight. 'Tell me, what was his name—and what his mission?' he asked. The Centurion's blue eyes bored into the man's face, noting the alertness of the officer's expression, despite the fact that he had been on duty all night. He smiled encouragingly at the man.

'He was a Jewish informer. He asked to see Caiaphas, with news of Jesus of Nazareth. I had one of the temple guards escort him to the High Priest. He was less than an hour in the Temple, before being brought back to the gate by one of their officers.'

Claudius gave an exclamation of dismay. He already knew that Caiaphas was poised to arrest Jesus, should opportunity arise. Who could the informer be, surely not one of the Galileans?

'Had the informer the heavy accent of those from Galilee?'

'No sir! In my opinion, he spoke like the Jews from Judea. I wasn't able to get his name, didn't realize it was of any importance. But he was obviously under the influence of some heavy emotion, fear I suppose, for he was sweating profusely.'

'Thank you, Lucius. You did well to mention this matter, now off to your bed, but be ready to resume emergency duties should it be necessary!' The Centurion sat scowling at his desk for a few minutes then shrugged. There was nothing he could do at present—only hope that Jesus would have enough sense not to enter Jerusalem. Spies had already brought word that the Holy One was just outside the city, at Bethany. Well, providing he kept a low profile, Rome had no quarrel with him, Pilate was indeed, prepared to tolerate the rabbi from Galilee, if for no better reason than that Caiaphas detested Jesus—but perhaps more importantly because the Lady Claudia was much taken with the Galilean's teachings. Claudius wondered musingly, whether perhaps the wife of Pontius Pilate possessed any inkling that Jesus was the Messiah, the long awaited son of the Jewish God, who would save his people.

How much longer could Claudius himself lead a double life, believing Jesus to be the Christ, while continuing to serve Rome? He had almost decided to speak with the Tribune, for Marcus would surely understand his wishing to retire. Just let this Feast of Passover go by, for he could not leave Marcus with tension running so high in the city, and then he would return to Galilee and if fate were kind be reunited with Miriam. But first, there were reports that Barabbas had been seen in the Lower City and Claudius had taken a vow to see the Zealot leader safely lodged in the Antonia's dungeons, before meeting his just end!

Pontius Pilate lay on the marble slab. He had just emerged from the bath and was now being massaged with perfumed oil, by two deft fingered slave girls. He was for once feeling completely relaxed within his luxurious suite of private bathrooms, where he could momentarily shuffle off the cares of his office with his clothes. His skin was glowing from the earlier application of the curved strigils which scraped away dirt and dead cells. The bath from which he had recently stepped was of black marble, set in an alcove, above which two warriors sculpted in white marble, were locked in mortal combat. The floor in black, red and white mosaic echoed the colours of the panelling, whilst all fittings and basins were of solid gold.

His eyes closed, as muscles relaxed under the skilled massage, then, he sat up in startled outrage as a slave rushed in. He recognized her as Maria, one of his wife's body slaves.

'Maria! Why this intrusion?' he scowled.

'Your pardon my Lord, but my Lady Claudia requests your presence!' So unusual was this urgent summons from his wife, that Pilate quietly snatched a towel, as he snapped his fingers for his robe.

Claudia awaited him in their bedchamber, where their huge couch, was resplendent with spread of dressed leopard skins. She was standing by the long, narrow, south facing window, gazing over the top of the Temple to where the city fell away below them and further still, without the city walls, to the smooth soaring Mount of Olives. She pointed a slender finger, to a huge crowd surging along the rough track from the summit, and even from here, they could hear the shouts of the people.

'It is the Holy One!'

'How do you know?' He scowled in irritation. More trouble on the way! His spies had reported that Caiaphas was seeking the death of Jesus of Nazareth, whilst other sources suggested that Barabbas and his Zealots were waiting to foment more unrest, that there could be more bloodshed now than at their abortive uprising during the aqueduct affair. If Jesus and Barabbas should both descend on Jerusalem at the same time, then the situation in this turbulent city could erupt like a ripe volcano.

'One of the slaves mentioned, that when she went to market to buy the fresh figs that you like, for the traders from Jericho are always waiting outside the city walls for the gates to be opened at sunrise with their fresh fruit, it was whispered that Jesus was coming. Crowds immediately started streaming out through the gates to welcome him!' She laid eager hand on his arm. 'Promise me, my Lord, that no harm will come to the Holy One?'

'I can make no such promise! My duty here is to keep peace. If the Galilean rabbi places himself in such a situation, that he becomes the focal point for insurrection even innocently, then we may have to arrest him, if Caiaphas guards don't get him first!'

'But Pontius—Jesus isn't as other men, he is---,' her voice trailed off, as Pilate placed a hand over her mouth, with a regretful smile.

'Hush, lady. You above all people, with your ancestry, should know that duty ever comes before personal desires.' He almost believed his own words as he hurried off to find Tribune Marcus. Yes, Pilate did believe in justice, providing it did not impinge on his own desires or comfort. He wished that Claudia would cease to show this peculiar interest in the man from Galilee.

'Ah, Marcus, it would seem that we face trouble even before Passover! I understand that Jesus of Nazareth approaches the city?' Pilate's face bore slight traces of amusement, as he thought of the annoyance of the detested High Priest, that the Galilean was again daring to enter Jerusalem. In spite of his own irritation that disturbances might once again mar one of the major Jewish feasts, he could not but admire the courage shown by Jesus, in thus running the gauntlet of Caiaphas enmity.

'I have men dressed in the garb of the Jews, mixing in with the crowds, as well as a cohort lining the route the Holy One is taking. Claudius is in charge!'

'Claudius—ah, well!' Pontius Pilate sighed in relief and returned to complete his ablutions.

Claudia remained at the window. She could see the serene figure, seated on a donkey, followed closely by his chosen twelve, but before and about these a huge crowd surged, shouting ecstatically. She strained her eyes. They seemed to be throwing something in front of the Holy One. She sighed in exasperation, wishing desperately that she might be amongst the noisy throng. The sound of singing rose on the air. Men, women and children were intoning one of the sacred Jewish chants, not a mournful song this though, but textured with pure joy, beautiful, wildly haunting and above all, the shouts of Halleluia—Halleluia!

Claudius spurred to meet the head of the procession, his men flanking the approach to the Golden Gate. As his practiced eye took in the sheer size of the crowd, which he had underestimated, he quickly realized that the five hundred men he had with him would be ousted by the sheer weight of numbers should the multitude become aggressive. At the moment they were tearing off their outer garments, all were wearing their best holiday clothes, and strewing them in the path of the quiet man on the donkey. Others waved branches torn from the palm trees and tamarisks, throwing them also before Jesus. Children were darting about the lower slopes of the hill, swiftly gathering armfuls of the bright Spring flowers, then racing back to the procession, pushing as close as possible to the wonderful rabbi, whom their parents told them was the long awaited Messiah. There was adoration in their dark, shining eyes, as they tossed their floral tributes before him.

'They are naming him as King, sir,' said Lucius, who despite a few hours sleep, had accompanied Claudius. 'What are your orders?'

'He is a spiritual leader, no threat to Rome,' replied Claudius. 'But we must watch that factions within the city do not use his advent as pretext for riot.'

'Look, sir—that man! One of the Rabbi's followers, I'll swear he was the man who arrived during the night watch two days since, seeking Caiaphas with information about Jesus!'

Claudius eyes followed the direction in which Lucius was pointing. All the disciples were glowing with excitement, but one, the man whom Lucius indicated wore an expression of pride and satisfaction. Claudius stared at Judas, was this one who would betray the Son of God? Claudius felt a cold rage well up inside, would have gladly plunged his sword into that infamous breast. But he must not let his respect for Jesus become apparent. If he were to be of any help to him, he must appear completely impartial.

Two Pharisees plunged forward, into the path of the oncoming donkey. They had become enraged at the cry of the disciples, which was being echoed by the crowd.

'Blessed is the King, who comes in the name of the Lord! Peace in Heaven and glory in the Highest!'

The Pharisees glared indignantly at Jesus, raising their hands in affronted disdain

'Teacher—Rebuke your disciples!'

Jesus raised his eyes, and they shrank back before the shimmering fire of his gaze. His eyes swept the Temple walls, built of the massive stone blocks, each weighing several tons.

'I tell you,' he said, 'If they keep quiet, the stones will cry out!'

The crowds were increasing all the time, as people started running down into the Kidron valley to meet the procession, for thousands were already encamped outside the city in readiness for Passover. Some had come from the coast, from Tetrarch Phillip's lands, others from Galilee or from the cities of the Decapolis where many Jews lived interspersed with their Grecian neighbours, some even some from lands afar, coming to the holy city for the sacred feast. They had heard the shouting, the cry of Messiah, seen the ecstatic crowds and now watched with incredulous joy on their faces that the wonder foretold through the ages by all the prophets had come to pass, that the Messiah was amongst them.

But could this really be the Messiah? This quiet man, dressed in simple white robe, riding a donkey? One ancient scribe raised his voice, quoting scripture to them, using the words of the Prophet Zechariah.

'Rejoice greatly, oh daughter of Zion! Shout, daughter of Jerusalem! See, your King comes to you, righteous and riding on a donkey—on a colt, the foal of a donkey!'

Claudius caught his breath as he heard the words, then with a nod to Lucius, was about to reign his horse about. His heart was too full to remain there. He glanced once more towards Jesus, and started to tremble as their gazes locked. He was sure that Lucius must sense the great, throbbing wave of spiritual emotion washing through him. What was it? What was happening to him? For a minute he sat immobile, then kicked his horse's sides. As the horse jerked into obedient motion, he saw her—his wife Miriam!

She was walking with Mary Magdalene and Joanna and some other women. She saw him, and reached out a hand towards him, her eyes brimming with tears, caught in the triumphant ecstasy of the exultant crowd. He saw her for but a few minutes before she was swept from view amongst the people.

Claudius stared after her in utter frustration. But this was not the time for his personal affairs. Claudius had a growing certainty, that he would meet with Miriam again soon and in the meanwhile, he must do all in his power, to prevent the present situation become dangerously out of hand. He turned to Julius, a seasoned centurion, well used to crowd control

'Julius, remain in command here. Lucius, come with me. I'm returning to the fortress to bring a second cohort out into Jerusalem's streets, in case of insurrection. This crowd is too volatile. Should the Zealots seek to infiltrate it, I fear there could be a bloodbath! I must warn Marcus!'

Lucius nodded and spurred his horse, following close behind Claudius, as together they retraced the short distance back to the walled city.

Herod watched the immense crowd converging down from the slope of the Mount of Olives towards the city. He was standing on the battlements of the palace, which gave panoramic view of all that was happening. His face went grey, as he heard the tremendous shout, 'Hosanna! Hosanna to the King!' His eyes narrowed in concentration and he bared his teeth, in very truth resembling the fox, for which Jesus had named him. This man on the little donkey—he was the king? Surely not! Herod burst into a gale of relieved laughter, which quickly subsided as he realized how great was the crowd, now surging out of his view, upwards towards the Golden Gate of the Temple. Good! Just let Jesus enter the Temple, and friend Caiaphas would have this Galilean trouble-maker safe in his web, and all their problems would be no more! But as Herod turned away from the tower, he felt a sudden unease. The crowd had been amongst the greatest that Herod had ever seen assembled—suppose fighting was to break out? Pontius Pilate could be ruthless, as witness the innumerable executions—people disappeared, never to be seen again, once within the Antonia!

A man pushed between the throAttachmentDownload crowds who struggled before his ruthless buffeting. Matthias the Zealot was determined to reach Simon, who had once been one of them, and hopefully would soon be so again. He reached out an urgent hand, dragging on Simon's robe.

'Here, Simon—stop! I must speak with you, urgently!

'Matthias—what do you want?'

'A word in private, follow me!' And Simon did so fear clutching his entrails, for he knew that only evil could follow any plan of the Zealots. Yet his instinct told him to investigate what lay ahead. That way he might be able to prevent Jesus becoming entrapped in any action planned by the Nationalists, whose aims for the freedom of their country, had once dominated his every waking thought and his dreams. Now, he saw his erstwhile comrades as friends still, but from whom he was now removed as absolutely spiritually, as though they lived in different worlds.

They sank panting on the shaly bank that ascended towards the Temple. The crowds passed barely yards from where they crouched, sweeping inexorably upwards, bearing the Messiah to the steps of the Golden Gate.

'What is it, Matthias? I must return to the Holy One at once!' Simon's dark face stared interrogatively into the cruel visage of Barabbas lieutenant. The Zealot placed a pincer tight grasp on his wrist, preventing his rising.

'Gently, Simon—let me congratulate you, on the Holy One's success! It is more than any of us could have hoped for. Listen to the shouts! Hosanna—to the King! The King, my young friend! And what a King he will make, one that both you and I and Barabbas and our people, will be proud to unite behind and serve. How wonderful for you Simon, that you are one of his chosen disciples. I hope you will not forget old friends, eh!' and Matthias spat in satisfaction.

'It cannot be! Matthias, the Holy One does not seek temporal power, and I have told you that many times.' Simon's voice was low, urgent.

'Well, whatever he wants, he will now have to take up the burden of kingship, for the people will never understand it, if he rejects them after they have acclaimed him in this fashion. If he disappoints them, Simon, they will turn on him. Believe me, my young friend there is nothing more fickle than a mob, nothing more dangerous, than a mob thwarted in its just desires. They look for freedom! Isn't this what the Messiah is supposed to bring them, freedom from oppression—freedom from Rome?' He pushed his face within inches of Simon's, still bruising his wrist in that implacable grasp. 'Now listen to me, Simon! Barabbas is in the city. He saw Jesus coming, and some of our own people are amongst that crowd. Tell Jesus, to accept what all want. We already have a rich gown and diadem ready for his use. But first he must outface Caiaphas in the Temple before the people, as we the Zealots, will pour in our hundreds into the courts, will rush the gate of the Antonia!'

'This is madness! You must forget such impossible idea. Apart from the fact that Jesus would never agree, never, never, never—just think of the bloodshed! The Romans are mounting the colonnades in even greater numbers than usual, one of Joanna's friends got news of it to us. You would bring death and terrible suffering to thousands of innocent people. Go Matthias—tell Barabbas to forget this madness!'

'We will act, with or without your co-operation, Simon.' Matthias swore savagely and flung away from the disciple.

'Do you believe Jesus to be the Son of God, Matthias?' the question, quietly asked, startled the Zealot. He shook his head nervously, exploring the actuality of what Messiah meant for the first time and perhaps at last, the awesomeness of who Jesus really was, was born in upon him. He swallowed, stood poised in thought.

'I must go, Simon.' He reached out briefly clasping the younger man's hand in rough friendship then was gone. The disciple hurried after Jesus party, desperately worried now. Somehow he managed to position himself next to Peter and John.

'The Zealots are about to rise,' he whispered. They looked at him appalled. They had been riding a great surf wave of jubilation! They had heard their master proclaimed as King with delighted amaze. They had always known that one day this would happen. Yet now that it had, for all of their ever present squabbles about which of them were the most important, the realization that Jesus must be involved in savage fighting in furtherance of kingship, was something they had not seriously contemplated. They were none of them cowards, told themselves that they would defend their master to the death, but not now with no time to think!

Jesus had dismounted and strode serenely into the Court of the Gentiles, where he had stood so many times before. The tumult about him was ear splitting. The Romans on the colonnades leaned forward, staring down into the mass of people, watching, vigilant.

'Hosanna! Hosanna to the son of David,' some children were singing, their sweet voices causing Jesus to smile tenderly at them. People were singing the psalms now, their massed voices raised in great chorus of praise. Then others amongst the crowd, who had been there before they entered the Temple, started to question what was transpiring? Who was this, why was this mob of pilgrims behaving with such undue solemnity, there was a time for psalms and what was this talk of the Messiah? One could hardly get past the sellers of doves and incense, nor reach the tables of the money- changers.

The situation was getting chaotic, the people a solid wedge of struggling humanity. Jesus raised his hands and the silence that followed was electric. High above, from his window in the Temple, Caiaphas watched in futile anger. He knew the impossibility of trying to arrest the Galilean amongst his thousands of supporters.

Jesus began to preach. They listened eagerly, those who had come to greet him, waiting for him to announce himself as Messiah. The words he spoke were wonderful ones, of seeking through repentance, the Kingdom of God. But they were more interested in the kingdoms of this world. Surely he would say it now, that he was their long expected King—the Christ?

They waited, hands itching to applaud, voices to rise in tumultuous acclaim. Then, before they could fathom what was happening, Jesus raised his hands in final blessing, and as the people fell back instinctively before him, he quietly walked out of the Temple gate. He left a flurry of questions in his wake. Why had he not acted? He had raised Lazarus, they had all heard of his miracles, some indeed had witnessed them, he could teach, as no man ever had before, no not even Hillel! So why had he vanished, without explanation other than it was getting late!

'He has left the Temple! He was not proclaimed king after all!'

The young Zealot, who had brought this impossible story, stood with chest heaving, face streaked with sweat from the effort involved in freeing himself from the multitude in the Temple courts. He had moved as swiftly as possible, through the Lower city, to where Barabbas, with several hundred men, was hiding in an area with so evil a reputation, that even Roman soldiers did not venture in amongst these dank, dark alley ways. The people who lived here were incredibly poor, and would kill for a few pence and willingly sheltered the Zealots who always made it worth their while.

Barabbas stood baffled, his bearded face working with frustration and anger. He had waited, had hoped for so long. He had been so sure that today they would have used Jesus as figurehead for just uprising! Was it all to be for nothing? Their plans brought to naught? Something in Barabbas brain cracked! He threw caution to the winds, forgot all he had taught others.

'Follow me! I want a hundred men only. More than that would attract too much attention. We are going to the Temple, we are going to find Caiaphas, and kill him and his priestly friends. The people will then be even more eager to acclaim Jesus—who is with me?'

They poured along the narrow streets, weapons concealed beneath their cloaks, until now they were on the main street that led upwards to the Temple and then it happened. Centurion Claudius mounted, before a long, disciplined troupe of seasoned legionaries, who were marching with chilling precision, came down the temple ramp from the south-eastern gate. The gap between the two groups was rapidly closed by the Romans, who would have marched by this motley group of apparently ordinary pilgrims, except that Claudius happened to glance directly into the eyes of Barabbas. Even with that prayer shawl over his forehead, Claudius recognized the Zealot chieftain who had killed many of his men, and escaped from his captors when being dispatched to Pilate.

'Barabbas!' he shouted the word at the top of his voice, indicating the bandit with his whip. Then he dismounted and rushed towards his enemy, his men behind him. Suddenly the Zealots produced their swords and daggers, desperately trying to surround their leader. The fighting that ensued was short and savage. The Zealots were accustomed to using surprise as their weapon, making swift attack and away. Here, trapped by a vastly greater force and unable to manoeuvre in the confine of the street, they fought valiantly, then fled leaving a pile of dead behind and their leader in the hands of the Romans. But Claudius did not witness his triumph. He lay stunned on the cobbled street, dealt a vicious blow from a heavy stone, dropped from above, by a Zealot who had climbed onto a neighbouring rooftop.

Barabbas struggled ineffectually between his captors, a string of curses pouring from his lips, as he was borne in triumph into the Antonia by the delighted Romans. As for Claudius, his men placed him gently on two of their shields as stretcher, and carried him carefully to Pilate's own physician.

Barabbas was placed in the dungeons, to await his fate, which he already knew would be death by crucifixion—the most cruel death devised by man!

Chapter Twenty

Barabbas groaned. The blow the jailer had just struck him, adding to the throbbing discomfort of his other injuries. He was lucky to be alive, for the sword thrust dealt him by the young Centurion at Claudius side would have brought certain death had it not been for the breast plate of chain link, sewn on strong leather that he ever wore under his loose tunic.

Claudius had wanted Barabbas captured alive, and had shouted a warning to Lucius not to administer a mortal blow; but the young soldier, keen to shine in his commander's eyes had already thrust, whilst at that same moment Claudius whip had whistled about Barabbas legs, jerking the Zealot off his feet. He had been immediately seized upon by four legionaries, and pushed, stunned and sick with pain, through the Roman ranks to the rear of the fighting. Minutes later, the pile of corpses in the streets bore witness to Roman efficiency. Fifty of his best men, lay dead or dying, the others had fled ignominiously saving their own skins. Yet, was it not what he had always told them to do? To save their own lives in such a situation in order that they might fight another day to free their beloved country!

His only consolation was that Claudius, felled by a heavy stone dropped from above by a Zealot, was like to die from his injury. He had heard the jailers discussing this just now, and had thrown taunting comment to them. He spat out blood which was trickling from his mouth, the jailer's fist having just driven his teeth through his tongue, as he had gloated to the man over Claudius near demise.

'Watch your filthy tongue, Zealot,' said the jailer calmly. 'The man you speak of is one of our most honoured soldiers.' He pointed to the hunk of bread, the dried fish and cup of water. 'Refresh yourself, Barabbas. You must keep up your strength for a few days. After all, we want you in good shape for your crucifixion! We have been reserving one of our highest crosses for you—Chieftain!'

'But you cannot crucify me yet. I have not been tried! It is the law, that a man must have fair trial before sentence.' Barabbas spat out the words, together with more blood, from his painful tongue.

'Have no fear, Zealot. You will receive proper trial and sentence under Roman law, probably be judged by Pilate himself, but there will be no escape for such as you. You are for the cross, Barabbas!' The jailer signed to his fellow, to secure the lock, as they went on their rounds.

Barabbas waited until they were out of sight then sank down onto the soiled straw covering the stone floor. Tears filled his dark eyes, tears of humiliation and frustration. He had let his men down when they so desperately needed his leadership, all because patience had snapped. But why, oh why had Jesus not acted? If Jesus were indeed the son of their mighty Jewish God Jehovah, as so many believed then surely Jehovah would want the Holy One to bring freedom to his people?

'I had thought that Jesus had come to set men free,' raged Barabbas, his voice breaking on a sob, nor realized that he spoke greatest truth.

Matthias nursed a broken arm, splinted by one of his men. They were devastated by this sudden catastrophe, the loss of their comrades and worse, of their leader. They held brief conference and elected Matthias to lead them.

'There is no reason for remaining in Jerusalem now,' he told them. 'The Romans will be on full alert. No second attack would stand a chance. So we will do what we always do in such case, make escape from the city by two's and three's, mingling with the crowds who leave Jerusalem at night to camp on the hills. My heart is heavy for Barabbas. If he were anywhere but the Antonia there might be some hope of rescue, but not from that thrice damned fortress!'

So they stole away at sunset, bitter with despair, until they regrouped on the Jericho road and there between the frowning mountain buttresses, swore once more the Zealot oath of freedom. One day, all Jews should be free! Free to rule their own land—free to worship the One God—free to work out their own destiny! Nor did any think of the quiet words of love, spoken by the gracious figure who had that day ridden into Jerusalem, humbly upon a donkey, teaching that the Kingdom of God can be found in the hearts of all men and where, if they will let him in he will so gloriously reign.

Jesus and his disciples were once again in the house at Bethany. Of all the thousands who had followed him to the city that day chanting Hosanna, none now came close to the house of Lazarus. But thousands speculated on the hillsides and within the city, hearts tingling with bitterness and disappointment that the man they had acclaimed as the

Christ, had made no move to take upon himself the majesty of that office. Had it all been a mistake? But then—what of the miracles and all the prophecies that were fulfilled in him? Perhaps—tomorrow! They went to sleep, hearts sorrowful, but still not relinquishing hope that maybe Jesus could indeed be the Messiah.

Eleven of Jesus disciples sat with him, heads bowed, as he instructed them, emphasizing once more, that this visit to Jerusalem would culminate in his death. All that was happening was within the plan of Almighty God, laid down from the beginning of time, that they should not despair as the day of his death drew nearer, but have faith in him and his words, and that if he left them, he would return. John, Peter and Matthew mouthed his words, committing them to memory, as they did with all he said, but having no real understanding of them. That would come later.

David and Simeon were exhausted from the day's excitement. They stood now on the flat roof, talking in whispers before lying down to rest under the awning, wrapped in thick cloaks against the cold. The house was full to overflowing, some even lying in the small courtyard in the centre of the house. Clouds brushed the face of the half full moon and the wind moaned in from the desert. It was a restless night, as the prince of this world tensed for action against the Son of God—a fight he was to lose, even as he had done in that earlier encounter in the wilderness. But now he dripped his poison, into the heart of Judas Iscariot. The twelfth apostle walked outside the house, his thoughts burning darts of pain. Why had Jesus not taken the opportunity given to him by thousands, to be King? Well, Judas would give him one more chance, but that chance would be before the might of Caiaphas, whom the Holy One would have to smite with the power from on high, if he were to survive. If Jesus would not accept power at the hands of the multitude, then surely he would have to exert his own mighty power as the Son of God, to free himself of the authority of the High Priest. Surely, in this way, he would be forced to prove himself to all Jerusalem in most spectacular fashion, and would perhaps forgive Judas for pushing him into decision of kingship. And thus Judas tried to justify himself in the role he was determined to play, that of traitor.

'Look at Judas.' Simeon spoke softly. 'I don't trust that man, David.'

'Nor does Simon! He asked me to watch him. All he seems to think about is money. He was standing down there just now, muttering to himself, shoulders hunched, pouring silver coins from one hand to the other—and then he uttered a strange cry!'

'Look at him now. Pacing up and down—up and down! He seems to suffer from some distemper of the mind.' Simeon gave a quick shudder.

'Call that distemper greed for power,' murmured a low voice, and startled they turned to see Simon's dark face smiling down on them. But the smile vanished, as he related news just brought in, that Barabbas had been captured.

'I cannot pretend any great sorrow for that,' declared David. 'Yet for all his evil ways, there was that about Barabbas I admired. If he was ruthless and cruel, it was for one reason, his commitment to free our country.'

Simon sighed. 'He was once good friend of mine and although I no longer support the Zealots, yet my heart is heavy for him. They will kill him of course. There is only one death meted out to those who offend Rome. Crucifixion, the cruel, the most painful death ever man devised!'

'And this is the end our dear Lord says awaits him,' cried David. 'But why—oh why does he rush on such a fate, as to be lifted up! Can't you persuade him to leave now, while he yet can?' The youth's face was full of anguish.

'Think you we have not all tried? He merely says that it was for this reason that he came into the world that through this men may have eternal life! And because he is who he is, the Son of God—even though we do not understand all these things, yet our duty is just to obey.' Simon put an arm about both their shoulders, before leaving them to sink down on their sleeping mats, to toss restlessly until dawn.

Mary Magdalene put a gentle hand on Miriam's shoulder. The Centurion's wife was breathing heavily in sleep.

'Miriam—Miriam!'

'What is it?' Miriam struggled into a sitting position.

'Simon brought news just now that Barabbas is captured by the Romans.'

'Barabbas? You mean the Zealot Chieftain, whom my husband once captured, had flogged and who escaped when being sent to Jerusalem?' Miriam rubbed her eyes, as she became fully awake.

'It was your husband who captured him this time. There was a fight close to the Temple precinct. Miriam, I am so terribly sorry to tell you this, but Claudius lies gravely wounded!'

'Oh, do not say so,' cried Miriam. She turned very pale. 'Did Simon say how he was wounded—by sword or by spear?'

'They say a huge stone was dropped on his head from a house top—so the force must have been considerable.' Mary looked at her in commiseration. 'Maybe I should not have told you. But I thought you would want to know.'

'Thank you,' whispered Miriam tears welling up into her eyes. Another hand stole out to comfort her. It was that other Mary, mother of her Lord. Then the other women woke as though by instinct.

'Let us pray for Claudius,' said Mary of Nazareth and drawn by common purpose, the women clasped each other's hands, as they prayed for enemy Centurion, whose heart had been touched by knowledge of Almighty God and his Son Jesus. As they prayed, a feeling of great peace descended on each heart. Rising, Mary slipped quietly to the inner room, to speak with her son.

The following morning, Jesus set his face once more for Jerusalem and this time he wanted only his chosen twelve with him. Joanna was to take the other women to her villa near Herod's palace. They would be safe there. Simeon and David would act as escorts and remain with the women and although they desperately wished to be with the Messiah and his disciples, they did not question his wishes. Simon told them they were to remain at the villa for at least the next few days, as the house at Bethany was too well known now. Even Lazarus was to move into Jerusalem, into the house of a widow who was a secret supporter of Jesus. She had a son, John Mark, who had once had long conversation with Peter in the Temple, and this young man, having heard Jesus preach, had accepted in his heart that he was indeed the Messiah. Jesus and his friends, would always be welcome in this house, but would have to approach it carefully at all times, for it was close to the house of High Priest, Caiaphas. Now Lazarus was going there, for he knew his own life was in danger from Caiaphas, for Lazarus was walking proof of Jesus power over death and Caiaphas wanted that proof destroyed.

Joanna cried out in relief as the heavy gates of the villa closed safely behind them. The streets had been seething with people of all nations, jostling, pushing impatiently towards the Temple. The Roman legionaries were much in evidence, trying to ignore the taunts of the people, many of whom were outraged at the arrest of the Zealot leader. Barabbas was almost a legend, and even those who did not actively support the Zealots, admired the handsome, black bearded chieftain, who was said to fear no man. But the soldiers had been instructed to show restraint with the populace. The days leading up to Passover, could be explosive ones and Pilate demanded that this feast should pass off without incident.

Mary of Nazareth looked from the window of her room, towards the shining crest of the Temple, which gleamed in the fierce light of the noon sun like molten gold. Its marble flanks, split into the hundreds of columns of the colonnades, appeared to her at that moment, like gigantic teeth set to crush her son. A soft moan escaped her lips, as the words of that elderly devout man who had blessed her infant, her first born, in the temple, prophesying of Jesus future, returned to her mind. Old Simeon had been under the power of the Holy Spirit of God, as he blessed Mary and said—

'This child is destined to cause the falling and rising of many in Israel and to be a sign that will be spoken against, so that the thoughts of many hearts will be revealed and a sword will pierce your own soul too!'

A spasm crossed her face. 'That sword is poised now, Simeon,' she murmured, 'and how will I sustain its fall!' She fell to her knees, praying passionately for her son—her Master.

Joanna instructed the servants to keep her informed of anything that transpired out of the ordinary and released them from their duties, so that they could visit the Temple. Titus and Oram highly delighted put on their best tunics and set forth. They were in time to witness a sight that filled Caiaphas and the Sadducees with blind fury, and Pilate to stare from the Antonia in wry amusement, mixed with irritation.

For Jesus had appeared in Solomon's Porch with his disciples. His progress was impeded with those using the porch as a thoroughfare to carry in the goods they were selling to the thousands visiting the Temple and there in their accustomed places, were those selling lambs and doves, as well as the tables of the money changers. He placed his hands on the nearest of the tables, and with a hard shove sent it onto its side. The cages of doves shattered, freeing some of the birds. His disciples moved forward, opening the cages of those still imprisoned. Crash! Another table fell, and yet more birds soared skywards, circling the colonnades— crash and another of the moneychanger's tables fell, despite the anguished attempts of its owner to steady it. There were cries of delight, as children scrambled forward to snatch up the scattered coins.

It was chaos. Jesus seized with inner fury at the base use the Holy Temple was now serving, stormed the full length of the colonnade, calling on his disciples to release the penned lambs. None had realized the power of his limbs, as he tossed the heavy solid wood tables, as though they were parchment. At last it was finished! He called upon his disciples to bar the way of any others attempting to move merchandise into the area.

Pandemonium broke out, as strangers to the Temple demanded to know who was this impassioned figure in white and by what right did he do these things? Pharisees clasped their hands to their temples in despair, almost dislodging their phylacteries in their agitation. Was it not enough, that Jesus had disrupted the traders last Passover? Must he repeat the offence!

But now the anger had disappeared from Jesus face, as he stared at the great crowd pressing to get closer to him, seeing the obvious concern on their faces for an incident they did not understand. His eyes still blazed, but his words were calm.

'Is it not written—'My house shall be called a house of prayer for all nations?' He paused and pointed to the trail of overturned benches with one hand, whilst with the other, he gestured upwards to the towering beauty of the Temple.

'My house will be called a house of prayer, but you are making it a den of robbers!'

Then understanding dawned. Everywhere, men were nodding their heads in agreement. It was wrong to use the precincts of a place sacred to the Lord God, as a market! Many openly acclaimed his action, as hundreds more who were present yesterday at his triumphant entry, explained that this was the wonderful rabbi from Galilee, he who performed miracles! Yes, it was Jesus of Nazareth, the Messiah! They surged about him. Surely his demonstration against the corruption of those running the Temple could mean only one thing. He was about to announce himself publicly as king! Many of the children started to chant at the top of their voices, 'Hosanna! Hosanna to the son of David!'

Jesus raised his hands and commenced to teach, his voice vibrating on the air, as all fell silent, straining to catch every word. Titus and Oram managed to squeeze their way to within a few feet of the Holy One. Soldiers on top the colonnades, peered down on the listening multitude curiously, for all faces were turned towards Jesus, those who had some knowledge of Aramaic, pondering the passionate call to repentance, in his teaching of the forgiving love of the Most High. With a piteous cry, a mother raised a child up in her arms—the boy was blind.

A moan of awe went up, from those who witnessed the wonder on the little boy's face, as he saw his mother for the first time and instinctively bowed his little head beneath the healing touch of Jesus. As though a signal had been given, the blind and lame were helped forward by their friends, for great numbers of the afflicted had come today in the hope that Jesus would be present, that through him they would receive healing and Jesus rewarded that faith. Their cries of gratitude and praise blended with the ecstatic shouts of the children, as their enthusiasm for their hero filled the whole temple area.

'Hosanna! Hosanna, to the Son of David!'

Caiaphas was consumed with rage. Jesus was now dominating the temple. He, Caiaphas, the chief priests and teachers of the law, were being set at naught. As far as the huge crowd was concerned, the official upholders of the rigid religious structure they so jealously upheld were no longer of any account. Even numbers of the Pharisees were listening intently, with parted lips. Caiaphas gave an order, and a band of the most important temple officials, the chief priests and the most learned amongst the teachers, issued forth from the sacred building, calling upon the people to allow them passage. They bore down upon Jesus, in solemn procession, their leader holding up his hands for silence, as he positioned himself in front of Jesus.

'Do you hear what these children are saying?'

'Yes,' replied Jesus calmly. 'Have you never read--"From the lips of children and infants, you have ordained praise!"'

They stared at each other, baffled, humiliated. And they, his enemies, were silenced.

It was evening, as they left the temple, and returned to Bethany. Martha awaited them with supper. She had refused opportunity, to go to Joanna's villa in the city. She would remain she said to serve in any way she could be of most help. The gentle smile on the tired face of her master was treasured reward for long hours in the kitchen. Jesus gave a blessing, before they sat and ate, discussing the events of the day. But there was unaccustomed tension on the disciples' faces now, as a heavy spirit of foreboding seeped into their minds, only Judas sat in outward calm, to await the trap that would snap shut before the end of that week.

Joanna questioned the two servants eagerly, and only when satisfied that Titus and Oram had repeated everything they had heard and seen, did she dismiss them and turn towards the other women.

'Praise be to Almighty God that Jesus is still safe. But how much longer can he survive? The risks he is taking entering the Temple and preaching openly are enormous! Even though the ordinary people love him and believe him to be the Messiah, Caiaphas and the Sadducees will act against him soon, I know it!' Her face was deeply troubled.

'He is going to die,' said Mary Magdalene softly. 'We all know this, Joanna. But there is nothing that we can do, for he himself has said it is inevitable.'

'But remember, he said also—that he would rise again!' It was Mary of Nazareth who had spoken and though there was deepest anguish in her eyes, there was also hope.

Early the next day, Jesus announced his intention to visit the Temple once more. His disciples no longer attempted to protest, for it would have done no good. They panted their way up to the crest of the Mount of Olives. Once Jesus looked back, staring at the tawny beauty of the hills and desert, where glittering far beyond lay the brilliant blue waters of the Dead Sea, framed by the smudged violet of the Mountains of Moab. Then he turned his head northward, seeing in his mind's eye, the lush green banks, of that other stretch of water he loved so well in his beloved Galilee. He breathed a faint sigh and stepped resolutely forward, towards this city which had murdered the prophets—Jerusalem!

The Sadducees were waiting for him today. They sent representatives to confront him as soon as he appeared. Their leader threw back his head challengingly.

'By what authority are you doing these things?'

'I will ask you one question,' replied Jesus.' Answer me, and I will tell you by what authority I am doing these things!'

'Well—?'

'John's baptism, was it from heaven, or from men?' Jesus stared at them serenely. 'Tell me,' he said?

The assorted band of temple representatives murmured together in perplexity, for he had put them in a dilemma.

'If we say from heaven, he will ask, why didn't you believe him then? But if we say from men—well?' They knew that all Jews held John the Baptist to have been a prophet, so could not risk offending the people. They turned furious eyes on Jesus, confusion in their eyes.

'We don't know!'

'Neither will I tell you, by what authority I do these things,' replied Jesus and watched in slight amusement, as the affronted priests departed back to Caiaphas, twitching their robes in annoyance, as they went.

All throughout that day different officials pushed their way towards Jesus, only to retire discomforted. His disciples listened in fascination, as Jesus dealt with each group in turn, deftly avoiding traps set for him, by giving answers that dumfounded these experts in the law, for his words excised the cunning of their ploys with the knife of truth.

At length, some Pharisees and two members of Herod's court approached, for they believed that they had found a way, to either make Jesus openly flout the law or destroy his credibility with the people, as being unsympathetic to their miserable lot under the detested tax system of Rome. Jesus stopped preaching, as the Pharisees in their deeply fringed shawls, made haughty advance to him, accompanied by the brilliantly clad courtiers. The mid-day sun burned down with fierce heat and Peter murmured to John that the master should rest—then he with the other disciples became quiet as they noticed this new band of inquisitors. One of the Pharisees bowed gravely before Jesus, his outward show of courtesy, belying the venom in his heart.

'Teacher,' he purred. 'We know you are a man of integrity. You're not swayed by men, because you pay no attention to who they are, but you teach the way of God in accordance with truth.' He smiled unctuously at Jesus, and glanced around to ensure that the crowd was listening.

'Is it right to pay taxes to Caesar—or not? Should we pay, or shouldn't we?'

Every head in the crowd pressed forward, as a great hiss arose at this question. All eyes were fixed on Jesus. But Jesus knew the hypocrisy of his questioners.

'Why are you seeking to trap me?' The men shuffled uneasily under his shimmering gaze that stripped their souls bare. Then he held out a hand. 'Bring me a denarius, and let me look at it!' One of the courtiers produced a coin and held it out to Jesus. He looked down at the coin.

'Whose portrait is this and whose inscription,' he asked the questions in crisp tones.

'Why—Caesars,' they declared!

'Give to Caesar, what is Caesars—and to God, what is God's!' The dexterity of his answer left them standing in amazement as the crowd relaxed. Thomas gave a sigh of relief, for he had doubted the Master's ability to fend off this dangerous question, whilst Simon still maintained his protective stance at Jesus side. And so the day went by, the Holy One teaching the crowd by a series of parables. But still the temple authorities attempted to trap him, either into blasphemy or into misinterpretation of the law, but each time they had to return to Caiaphas in humiliation. At last, the western sky blazed with scarlet, rivulets of flame spreading into bruised contusion of crimson, purple and indigo clouds. The disciples followed Jesus out of the Temple, exhausted and amazed at his endurance, but as they went, exclaiming to each other, about the beauty of the building, the glory of its decoration, and turning back, they drew his eyes to the enormous size of the huge stones, in the outer wall. Jesus turned with them, a strange look on his face.

'As for what you see here, the time will come when not one stone will be left on another! Every one of them will be thrown down!' His eyes looked into the future, seeing the siege and sacking of Jerusalem that would follow, with the destruction of the magnificent Temple, the desolation that was to come.

They looked at Jesus in amazed unease, glancing around in case any should have overheard this devastating statement. Surely, it was thing impossible, that the mighty temple, already in the forty-sixth year of rebuilding, massively crowning the Mount of Zion, should ever be destroyed!

Peter whispered with his brother Andrew, as his band of disciples were hard put to keep pace with the master as he forded the Brook Kidron and started up the steep flanks of the Mount of Olives. At last Jesus halted, and signed that they should seat themselves under the sheltered seclusion provided by a grove of ancient olive trees. It was a favourite resting place of his where they had spent many a night in the past. Here, in this quiet spot, with the night wind soughing through the trees and stars casting a glittering net over the velvet black immensity of the sky, the disciples questioned Jesus about his prophecy of the destruction of the Temple.

'Tell us—when will this happen? And what will be the sign, that all this is to be fulfilled?' Peter asked the question they were all worrying over.

Jesus looked at them urgently. 'Watch out that no-one deceives you. Many will come in my name claiming—I am he—and will deceive many,' Jesus leaned forward, staring into their faces. 'When you hear of wars and rumours of wars, do not be alarmed. Such things must happen, but the end is yet to come!' Then his voice was charged with emotion, as he cried, 'Nation will rise against nation, and kingdom against kingdom. There will be earthquakes in various places and famines! These are the beginnings of birth pains!'

A moan of distress burst from their lips, as they moved restlessly. He continued.

'You must be on your guard! You will be handed over to the local councils and flogged in the synagogues. On account of me, you will stand before governors and kings as witness to them. And the gospel must first be preached to all nations!'

They looked at each other. How could they, simple fishermen for the most part, stand and witness before the great of this world?

'Whenever you are arrested,' Jesus continued, 'and brought to trial, do not worry beforehand about what to say. Just say whatever is given to you at the time, for it is not you speaking, but the Holy Spirit!'

Before that night was over, Jesus had prophesied to them not merely of events to come within their own generation, but of the End Times in distant centuries ahead, and they trembled as he said—

'The sun will be darkened and the moon will not give its light. The stars will fall from the sky and the heavenly bodies will be shaken!' Then he smiled at them comfortingly, as he said, 'At that time, men will see the Son of Man coming in the clouds, with great power and glory. He will send his angels and gather his elect from the four winds, from the ends of the earth, to the ends of the heavens!'

They sat in stupefaction, as he threw his arms high, wide and ended with a loud cry, 'Heaven and earth will pass away, but my words will never pass away!'

Stunned by all they had heard, in an apocalyptic address that dealt not only with events forecast for their own lifetime with attendant warning signs, which they found almost too terrifying to contemplate, the onrushing disaster that was to overtake their land and people, but even more difficult for them to absorb, those cataclysmic happenings that would herald the end of man's existence in the world! When in the millenniums to come, a risen Christ, in light more brilliant, than the lightning flash that cleaves the sky, would come in Majesty to collect his own, those who followed the Way!

At last, they all arose, leaving the shelter of the olive grove, intending to take the path over the hill to Bethany, when Simon put a restraining hand on Peter's shoulder, and John stifled an exclamation of dismay, for a file of guards, dimly outlined by the rising moon, were making their way up to the brow of the hill, their destination, Bethany! They could not return there, the only alternative to camp over night under the stars, as they had done so often before.

Three men stood around the couch on which Centurion Claudius lay outstretched, still and pale as though already dead, as helpless beneath the physicians touch as a new born babe, and for once unable to come to attention before the gaze of Tribune Marcus and Prefect Pontius Pilate.

The Prefect gestured towards the inert form of this soldier, whom he had come to respect, not only for his courage, but because of his connection to one of Rome's wealthiest families. Marcus had related to him the fact that the Senator, his friend's father, had quarrelled with Claudius many years before. Claudius had left Rome and enlisted in the legion. Had he so wished, the soldier could have graced a far higher rank than that of centurion. As far as Pilate was capable of showing emotion he did so now, knotting his eyebrows in grief.

'Is there no hope, physician?'

The doctor shook his head sadly. The force of the stone that had wrought this evil, lessened slightly by the strong metal helmet, which had dented beneath the blow had been immense. No doubt the humours within the brain were affected. He pointed to the huge bruise at the back of the head, inviting Pilate to feel it for himself. As the Prefect did so, he glanced curiously at the scarred body of the Centurion, each one of those long healed wounds, in the service of Rome. Well, they would give him an honourable burial if he expired. But by the gods, it was a shame that one such as Claudius, should die.

'There is an operation, Lord, one that I have performed several times. It involves boring holes through the skull, and lifting a piece of it up to relieve pressure on the vital tissues beneath. But such surgery is fraught with danger for the patient, and most die. Yet if you wish, I will attempt it?'

Pilate looked at Marcus then spread his hands in gesture of indecision.

'He deserves any chance we can give him,' said Marcus firmly then raised his head in annoyance, as one of his men knocked and entered.

'Did I not say that I wished no interruption?'

'Tribune, sir—there is a young woman below, who says she is the centurion's wife. She wishes to see him. She is humbly dressed, after the fashion of the Jews.' He turned, as he heard a commotion behind him.

'Let me pass! Where is my husband?' Miriam's green eyes flashed determination. She saw the supine figure and held out her arms, 'Claudius! Oh—Claudius!'

She pushed past the legionary, completely ignoring Pilate and the Tribune as she fell on her knees beside the couch, tears splashing onto the still, upturned face of her husband.

'Claudius!' She lifted one of his hands in hers, remembering the way in which this same hand had grasped hers lovingly at their wedding. She pressed a kiss on it.

'Miriam, it is good to see you, despite this sad occasion,' said Marcus, helping her to her feet. She looked at him, a dazed expression on her face, her wet eyes polished jade.

'He has lain thus for four days. I fear he is mortally hurt,' he continued. 'But at least, lady, he sustained his injury in arresting a man who would have brought turmoil and bloodshed to the feast. I speak of course, of Barabbas!'

'You should be proud of him, Lady Miriam,' said a courtly voice, and she turned to see Pilate's inscrutable gaze upon her.

'I am proud of him, my Lord. But I am more concerned for his health at this moment, than his deeds.' Her chin jutted out with all her old determination. She looked at the Arab physician, in his flowing robes, who was surveying her sympathetically. 'Has his condition altered in any way, since he first received his injury?'

'Why—yes, lady,' he replied slowly. 'When I was first called to attend him, which was shortly after he was brought into the fortress, he was breathing very heavily, almost snoring, and this continued until midnight. I feared a fatal seizure at any time, then strangely his breathing became normal, his face peaceful. He has lain thus ever since. But soon, a decision must be taken, as to whether to operate on his skull.'

'You say, Sir Physician, that his breathing became quiet—at midnight of that first day?' Her eyes shone with a kind of joy. 'Glory be to God,' she murmured, for it had been at this time, that she had linked hands with the other women in prayer, in that little house in Bethany. She held out a hand decisively. 'Claudius is my husband, decision regarding his health mine, until he is recovered. There will be no operation. It is not that I doubt your skill, honoured Physician, but it will not be needed here. Claudius will recover!' Her voice was calm, her bearing commanding. The doctor bowed courteously, but looked towards Pilate for advice.

'Lord Pilate, Tribune Marcus, I would be alone with my husband!' she spoke with authority. The men looked at each other, then shrugged and started towards the door. Marcus hesitated, hand on the door frame.

'Perhaps, Miriam, your Holy Man from Nazareth, might have helped here,' he said evenly. 'He was not at the temple, either yesterday or today though. Would you have any idea where he might be?' She shook her head, a wealth of sadness in her eyes.

'No, Tribune.'

'Then I will leave you. The doctor will be in the neighbouring room. I will have refreshments sent up for you. If there is anything you want, anything at all, then ask the man I will post at the door.' The moment the door had closed, Miriam loosed her cloak and tossed off her veil then she sank down beside her husband. She knew he was gravely ill, but at the same time, she experienced no fear of the situation.

Instinctively she raised her hands in prayer, calling upon Almighty God, not just for help, but praising Him for His goodness in all things and as her praise rose between trembling lips, she experienced a strange feeling, as though enveloped by an unseen power, which spread through her whole being, a sensation as of deliciously cool spring water, flowing through her veins.

'Father, in the name of the Lord Jesus,' she pleaded—'I humbly pray that you heal my husband!' Saying this, she reached out and placed a gentle hand onto the Centurion's bruised head. He stirred. His head moved slightly from side to side, as he seemed to hear the words— 'Praise to you Almighty Father, from everlasting to everlasting! Amen and Amen!'

'Miriam? Miriam—wife!' and Claudius opened his blue eyes, focussing on the sweet face above him, hearing her impassioned praise to God. 'Oh, wife, dearest wife,' he whispered, kissing her lips and tear wet eyes, 'What miracle is this? How came you here?'

But questions could wait. Again and again he kissed her, until at last, she pulled back from him. Then he tried to recall how he came to be in bed, for his last recollection was of the confrontation with Barabbas. He frowned, desperately trying to remember the sequence of events following, and could not.

'Miriam, I remember coming upon the Zealot leader, Barabbas, we captured him! But I do not remember returning to my room—or?'

'You were wounded, Claudius! They say that a huge stone was dislodged from a rooftop, by one of the Zealots. It caught you on the back of your head, causing loss of consciousness.' The Roman glanced towards the partly open window, where the night stars shimmered dimly through an enveloping mist.

'Why, but that must have been hours ago,' he said.

'Not just hours but four days ago! You were slipping away into death, when I came here tonight.'

He shook his head, bewildered then his fingers ran over his skull exploringly. Nothing!

'But—I do not understand! There is no cut, nor bruise, nor have I the slightest pain!'

'I prayed to Almighty God, for your healing, asked it in the name of Jesus! Even as I prayed in his name, God answered, for in that very minute you opened your eyes!' He looked deeply into his wife's eyes and read the truth there. With a choking cry, he slipped out of bed and fell to his knees, his own lips murmuring in prayer. And the stubborn heart of the Roman Centurion cracked, as he accepted God, and the majesty of His Son.

There was a quiet tap at the door, and the Arab physician presented himself. He had heard cries coming from the sickroom. He stood transfixed on the threshold, as he beheld his erstwhile dying patient, kneeling beside Miriam, both of them praying and praising the great God of Israel. They rose to their feet, as they noticed him, the centurion seeking his robe.

'Centurion, I pray that you return to your couch,' cried the physician in distress. He knew that even though the miraculous had happened, and that his patient had returned from the anti-chamber of the world of shades, any precipitous movement might still cause death. Claudius smiled, and obligingly sat on the end of the couch, as the physician explored his head with careful fingers, then raised his head in amazement.

'But this is thing impossible,' he cried! 'The huge bruise has disappeared! What happened here,' he said, turning to Miriam?

'My husband has been healed by the greatest physician, sir, Almighty God!'

The doctor swallowed in awe. Then, not knowing what else to do congratulated Claudius and withdrew to seek out Pilate with the amazing tidings. For Miriam had explained, that she had asked for healing, through the name of Jesus of Nazareth—the Messiah!

Pilate sat shaking his head, in the privacy of his chamber. Claudia was still enjoying the ministrations of her women, in their private suite of bathrooms. Could it be that the Nazarene was indeed more than mere man? If this were so, then what did this bode for Palestine and for Rome! Bah! This land was full of problems. He would go below and join his officers at table, and check that no fresh incidents had been reported—for this was the Eve of Passover! At least this year he was free of the necessity of making polite conversation with the Herodian royal family. He felt a twinge of guilt that he had made no gesture of diplomatic friendship towards Antipas on this present visit, although he was aware that Herod had been in residence in the Citadel for a whole week. Yet much as he disliked Antipas, he knew that as Rome's representative, it was beholden on him to cement the continuing good relationship between

Herod and Emperor Tiberius.

'Well', he mused, 'perhaps tomorrow inspiration would dawn of some small way of placating Antipas. In the meanwhile, he would return to Centurion Claudius bed chamber, to see the soldier's remarkable recovery for himself!

In a long, low ceilinged chamber, in a spacious house in the Lower city, John, James and Andrew checked the last details of the Passover meal, soon to be eaten by the Holy One and the rest of the disciples. Even John Mark, whose mother owned this pleasant villa, was not to be included for Seder, this special feast which yearly marked the Jews escape from bondage to the Egyptian Pharaoh centuries before and also commemorated the giving of the sacred law to Moses, on Mount Sinai by Almighty God. Although they did not yet know it, this meal was one of farewell to them, by their beloved master, a meal that would be shared throughout all time to come by the faithful in Christ, as sacrament of love.

John checked that the four large goblets were in place on the table, for the four traditional toasts that would be drunk, the platters of unleavened bread, the dishes of bitter herbs and bowl of relish sauce. Thirteen places had been set, John making it clear to his brother James that he would sit in place of honour, next to Jesus, yes, and James could sit on his other side, if Peter did not object that was! As John stated this, Simon Peter entered the room, closely followed by Simon the Zealot and the others, with Phillip bringing up the rear, bearing the succulent roast lamb on a large platter. Peter immediately began to argue with John as to the seating arrangements, claiming the place of honour for himself, which John stoutly denied him. The other disciples looked on, tired and irritable, nerves still jangling from the problem of entering the city without being detected, for they knew that the Temple guards were seeking Jesus to arrest him, and feared that Herod's troops might assist them in this.

Jerusalem was full of spies, neighbour betraying neighbour, either to Caiaphas agents, or to the Romans. Yet there were hundreds within the city who loved Jesus and believed him to be the Messiah. Even though so many had been bitterly disappointed that Jesus had not attempted to oust the Romans through armed uprising, yet they revered him for his teaching and his miracles. So it was that although several had recognized the gracious figure making his way through narrow alleyways and market courtyards, none betrayed him, but murmured swift prayer for his safety.

He was the last to enter. As he stood there silently looking on these quarrelling children of his, he breathed a sigh! Always they squabbled about seniority, had done so many times in the past when trudging along the dusty roads in Jesus wake, the sons of Zebedee even persuading their mother to ask that they should have the highest places in his kingdom, once Jesus entered it!

Jesus raised his hands in blessing and intoned the opening prayer of Passover and then reclined on the couch. As he broke the unleavened bread, he was aware of the tension coiling about the room, heard muffled whispers of annoyance, as a dispute arose as to which of them was considered to be the greatest. His sad eyes examined them questioningly, then his gaze fell on Judas and his lips tightened. So little time—there was now so little time! They must be made to grasp the essence of his teaching. He rose silently from the table, and made his way downstairs. When he returned, they looked at him in amazement, for he had divested himself of his outer garments and had tied a towel around his waist. There was bewildered silence. Then Jesus knelt before a startled Thomas, positioned the bowl of water and commenced to wash the disciple's feet. Thomas almost spluttered in outrage. It was thing incredible, that his Lord should so demean himself, taking upon him the duties of a servant! Jesus moved to Phillip, eventually reaching Peter.

'Lord—are you going to wash my feet,' asked Peter incredulously?

'You do not understand now what I am doing, but later you will understand.' A hot flush of shame rose to Peter's face, for he dimly realized the point that his master was making.

'No Lord, you shall never wash my feet!' His eyes were bright with embarrassment.

'Unless I wash you, you shall have no part with me,' replied Jesus calmly.

'Then Lord, not just my feet, but my head and my hands as well,' for even in this, Peter was attempting to benefit more fully than his fellows in Jesus love, but Jesus understood his heart, a heart that was soon to break beneath the dagger blow of his cruelly exposed weakness. Yet that heart would mend, lapped by God's forgiveness in the crucible of eternal love, forging this most wilful of his disciples into the rock on which his future church would stand.

'A person who has had a bath needs only to wash his feet—his whole body is clean!' Peter lowered his eyes, and Jesus moved on to Judas Iscariot. He glanced back at Peter, before saying, 'And you are clean, though not every one of you.'

The Holy One knelt before Judas, washing the feet of the one who would betray, seeing the fine beading of sweat, which broke out on the Sicarii's brow. At last the task was finished the Lord resumed his garments and took his place back at table. All tensions of jealousy had gone, washed away with the dirt of the road by the Son of God. They sat abashed.

'One of us should have done the washing, since there was no servant present' muttered Andrew.

'Do you understand what I have done for you? You call me teacher and Lord, and rightly so, for that is what I am! But now I, your Lord and teacher have washed your feet, you also should wash one another's feet!'

It was a lesson none of them would ever forget. They started to smile slightly at one another, suddenly alert to the normal niceties of care, helping each other to bread, a succulent sliver of lamb, pushing the sauce dish, the bitter herbs. Into this relaxed atmosphere, Jesus next statement jagged like cold lightning.

'I tell you the truth—one of you is going to betray me!'

Simon leapt to his feet, all his dormant Zealot instincts surfacing, as his eyes slid fiercely from face to face. Let him but know the man, and he would be dead before he reached the door! Peter's thick black brows bristled with rage, whilst John stared in shocked amaze. The only face not to show concern was that of Judas, who was making great show of masticating a slice of meat. Mathew glanced at the purse bearer thoughtfully. Peter leaned across, calling to John who was reclining next to Jesus.

'Hsst! Ask him which one he means,' hissed Peter? Obediently John leaned back closer to Jesus.

'Lord, who is it,' he whispered through trembling lips, wanting to know, yet shrinking from knowledge that would brand one of the chosen twelve as, impossible even to frame the thought, traitor! Jesus heard the question from this the most beloved of all his disciples and he answered John, Son of Zebedee, in voice as soft as a sigh.

'It is the one to whom I will give this piece of bread, when I have dipped it in the dish.' So saying, he broke off a piece of unleavened bread and dipped it in the sauce, and offered the sop to Judas Iscariot. Judas met his eyes defiantly for brief minute then dropped his gaze in confusion, as he took the sop. Jesus looked at the lowered face of this man who had shared so closely in his ministry, realizing even as Judas received the sop that Satan entered into him. Keeping his voice low and even, Jesus said, 'What you are about to do—do quickly.' John sat wondering if he had misheard Jesus words, and stared after Iscariot.

All had noted the Holy One's brief murmur to the purse bearer, but none heard the exact words, so when Judas rose quietly to his feet and walked swiftly to the door, they merely supposed him to have been sent out on some errand by the master.

One other man saw the Sicarii leave. John Mark stood stroking his young beard, enjoying the peace of the evening, on the flat topped roof, from which vantage point he noted Judas leave the villa, glancing uneasily around, before scurrying with some furtiveness towards the Upper city. Mark drew his dark winged eyebrows together in a frown. When the Zebedee brothers had told him that the Holy One wished to eat Passover in their large upper room, together with the twelve disciples he had felt honoured as had his mother, Mary. Although they knew the danger to themselves in giving sanctuary to Jesus, when it was openly rumoured in the city that the Temple authorities were seeking to arrest him, they would nevertheless have risked their lives for the wonderful man they acknowledged as the Messiah.

John Mark had been wrestling with a problem. The Holy One had descended from the supper, asking for a basin of water. Rhoda, one of the young servants, had whispered to John in stupefaction that the Rabbi Jesus, had tied a towel about him, and was going to wash the feet of his disciples. She had hastily offered to go upstairs to perform this basic function of necessity and courtesy, but had been quietly denied.

John Mark shook his head. Here in Jerusalem, as well as in his native Cyprus, only slaves performed this office. His thoughts were distracted from this enigma, by the sight of the fast disappearing Judas Iscariot. On instinct, he called one of his slaves, instructing the man to follow Judas and let him know where he went. Then he went below, to where his family was waiting for him to take his place as head of the family for their own Passover feast.

In the upper room, much of the tension had disappeared, with the absence of Iscariot, only Simon the Zealot frowning uncertainly, as he worried about Judas and exactly where he had gone, for Simon completely distrusted the Sicarii! But Jesus seemed to be gathering himself to impart further instructions to the eleven. But first he rose to his feet, seeking their attention. He broke bread before them, and gave it to them.

'Take and eat—this is my body!'

Then as they were eating the bread, a strange look on their faces, as though they dimly realized that Jesus was revealing new mystery, he took the last of the four goblets which was drunk at the conclusion of the meal. He blessed the cup, raised it symbolically to his own lips, before offering it to them.

'Drink from it, all of you!' His voice was throbbed with amazing power. 'This is my blood of the covenant, poured out for many for the forgiveness of sins!' He looked on them, his gold eyes luminous. 'I tell you—I will not drink of this fruit of the vine, from now until the day I drink it anew with you, in my Father's Kingdom!' Tears of emotion filled their eyes, as they listened to his next words.

'My children, I will be with you only a little longer. You will look for me and just as I told the Jews, so I tell you now. Where I am going, you cannot come!'

They looked at him uncertainly. What did he mean? He raised his arms wide, throwing back his head.

'A new command I give you. Love one another! As I have loved you, so must you love one another! By this, all men will know you are my disciples—if you love one another!' They looked at each other, and almost awkwardly, each man reached out and took the hand of his neighbour, as the flow of love and energy radiating from Jesus, swept through them, as new and tender emotion gentled their spirits. Peter was the first one to bring the conversation back to what was troubling them all.

'Lord—where are you going,' he asked, as he tried to imagine life without the master and could not do so.

'Where I am going, you cannot follow now, but you will follow later.'

'Lord, why can't I follow you now? I will lay my life down for you!' He turned his flashing black eyes pleadingly on Jesus. And Jesus looked at Peter, at his earnest face, framed by shock of thick, coarse black curls and springy beard, and shook his head sadly.

'Will you really lay down your life for me?'

'Yes, Lord!'

'I tell you the truth, before the cock crows, you will disown me three times!'

Peter sat shaking in appalled silence as Jesus continued to teach them for a brief spell, before concluding,

'But the Councillor, the Holy Spirit, whom the Father will send in my name, will teach you all things and will remind you of everything I have said to you. Peace I leave with you, my peace I give you. I do not give to you as the world gives. Do not let your hearts be troubled and do not be afraid!'

He looked at their strained faces, wishing he could spare them the anguish of the days ahead, praying that they would have the strength to hold faith. He led them in the traditional closing hymn, which carried poignantly into the night, his voice soaring above theirs.

'Come now—let us leave!' He knew there was no turning back now. There would just be a few precious hours left to pray with them. They were going to that secluded wild garden on the side of the Mount of Olives which Jesus loved, and where they had so often spent nights before. Its grove of olive trees surrounded an old oil press, around its protective low wall an ancient vine swarmed. Wild flowers closed their heads in sleep, beneath the misty stars—Gethsemane.

Chapter Twenty-One

When the door had closed upon an intrigued Pontius Pilate and equally amazed Tribune Marcus, Claudius led his wife over to the window gazing with her into the night. A heavy mist drifted upwards from the floor of the Kidron Valley and even the stars seemed hazy. There was a brooding quality to the scene, illuminated by a moon almost full, but of subdued light, vaguely defining the bulk of the Mount of Olives, down whose slopes Jesus had ridden in quiet majesty upon a young donkey acclaimed by thousands mere few days ago.

'I wonder where he is now,' muttered Claudius. 'I feel very uneasy about him Miriam.'

'We all do, husband, we who follow him,' Miriam said quietly, 'You see—we know he is to die. It is inevitable. He has told us to accept this, but not to fear. Death will not hold him. On the third day, he will rise again!' She gave a muffled sob and held on to Claudius hand as she whispered, 'But oh, why should such cruel fate await one who is all gentleness and goodness.'

'But surely Miriam, he can still escape, make his way back to Galilee? We Romans wish him no ill will, for he has taken part in no act against Rome. Pilate even has grudging respect for him on account of his stand against Caiaphas!' He raised her hand to his lips in gentle salute, then realized what she had just said. 'Miriam, what mean you, by saying that he will rise again? Those who die as a result of crucifixion—well let it be that none survive.' He said the words grimly.

'Claudius, we none of us know what he means, only that for months now he has been preparing us for the fact that he is to be lifted up—but will rise again on the third day.' Miriam's eyes were swimming with tears, but her voice was steady.

'But it must not be permitted to happen,' cried Claudius harshly, voice urgent with concern. 'He is needed far too much in this cruel world of ours and how can even he be sure, he will rise again?'

'Hush, dear love. You must not agitate yourself, come back to your couch!'

He stared one moment more, eyes sweeping the gleaming white and gold Temple, outlined as usual by the flaring torches of the temple guards, its shape soaring majestically into the night and he shuddered.

'Miriam, I have a weird sense of impending doom tonight, similar, yet different to the feeling that soldiers experience on the eve of battle. It is as though nature itself is holding its breath, waiting for some awesome, cataclysmic happening.'

'I feel it too and am fearful!'

'Well, let us try to talk of happier things.' He led her to the couch and as they seated themselves, thought back to all the weary nights he had sat here longing for the sweet wife he had so cruelly rejected, before retiring to his lonely bed. He took her in his arms now and kissed her gently.

'Miriam, can you ever really forgive me, my thoughtless, despicable treatment of you?' For answer, her hands swept up, pulling his head down, as she kissed away the tears that were seeping into his blue eyes. She stroked the silver hair at his temples and traced with gentle finger, the lines of bitterness, that had formed about his mouth.

'There is nothing to forgive, sweet Lord! Are you sure though, that you really wish me to return to you as your wife, for there may be times, when you will remember—the Sicarii?'

'Miriam, all I can say, is that you will be even dearer to me, for how could I have continued living, if you had died!' His voice was husky with emotion.

'But what of the fact, that I can no longer give you the son you have always longed for?' She asked the question probingly, for she knew how much he wanted a son.

'Why Miriam, we already have a son, young Simeon and soon a daughter-in-law, the lovely Sarah. Yes, and one day, who knows, a quiver full of grandchildren!' He smiled as he thought of the Jewish lad who had become so dear to him and whom he had not seen for some months now.

'Where is Simeon?'

'He is at the house of Joanna, together with David, as are all of the women who follow Jesus! Simeon escorted me to the Antonia so that I might come to you, but returned to the villa in case he was needed. He had complete faith that you would receive healing, looks forward to greeting you soon!'

Satisfied, Claudius took her in his arms again. To his surprise, she pushed him back gently.

'What's wrong, wife?'

'Claudius, I want to wait until we are back in our beloved Galilee, before we lie together again. At the moment my heart is full of worry for the Holy One. It would just not seem right to—do you understand what I am trying to say?'

Claudius nodded soberly.

'So then, we will wait until we return home. I know that Marcus will arrange for my official retirement at any time I choose and now that day cannot come quickly enough. No more soldiering, wife. But how I will fill my days, I cannot yet imagine.'

A strange, faraway look spread across Miriam's face, as she said in a voice of altered timbre. 'A new work awaits you Claudius, a work where you will follow a different banner, a work that will bring you to another land!' He looked at her curiously, about to ask her what she meant, when there was a knock at their door. He rose to his feet. The wife of Pontius Pilate stood on the threshold.

'Centurion, my husband told me of your miraculous recovery which I had to see for myself! Also, that Miriam is here, that you are re-united?' Her eyes fell upon Miriam's radiant face. 'I am so happy for you both! Claudius, may I borrow Miriam for an hour or two? I wish to speak with her over a private matter.' She came forward and embraced Miriam, looking at her almost pleadingly. Miriam saw the need in that glance and nodded.

'Of course I'll come! Claudius, you should rest now.' She pressed his hand, before following the Prefect's wife out of the room.

The room into Lady Claudia escorted her guest was richly appointed. Soft footed slaves, bowed as their mistress entered, and Miriam glanced around amazed at the luxury of her surroundings. Exquisite paintings adorned the walls, the beautifully wrought gold based lamps pouring soft light upon couches draped with white skins, and everywhere the sparkle of crystal, gemstones and gold. Huge vases were filled with sweet smelling flowers, and a small fountain bubbled musically into a pool set in the centre of the room. Miriam exclaimed in delight and stood looking down at the orange and silver fish, which darted below the surface.

'I never thought to see such a sight in a fortress,' she confided in surprise.

'Don't forget that the Antonia was originally built by Herod the Great, to serve as both palace and fortress and that he himself lived here for many years before rebuilding the Citadel. True, I have tried to place my own touch on the rooms that Pilate and I occupy, and later dear Miriam, I will show all to you. But now please sit, for I wish to speak with you of Jesus of Nazareth. But first I must offer you refreshments.' She clapped her hands and obediently a young slave girl bowed before her. 'What would you like to eat, Miriam?'

'Nothing, well, perhaps some fruit, a cool drink.'

'Is that all?' Lady Claudia gestured to the slave, to bring what her guest required. Then she dismissed the other slaves and stared earnestly at Miriam.

'I have been afflicted of terrible dreams recently, Miriam! Every night I toss upon my bed, scared to close my eyes, because of these dreams.'

'What form do the dreams take, Lady Claudia?' Miriam's green eyes were full of concern.

'The Holy One features in all. First I see him ministering to the sick, walking fearlessly amongst those with all sorts of loathsome disease, healing, blessing all those who come to him in supplication. I seem to hear the sound of the most exquisite singing, as though a choir of angels is chanting in heavenly praise. Then suddenly, everything changes! The Holy One is now surrounded by men with cruel faces, eyes burning with hatred. I hear the sound of a malevolent chuckling—and then I wake up sweating with fear! Miriam, am I going mad? What does it all mean?' Lady Claudia's eyes were wild with trouble. 'I know he is in some kind of danger,' she whispered. 'I think this is a warning sent to me, a warning of some terrible fate about to overtake the Lord Jesus.'

'I believe you have been given insight in the form of dreams, of the cruelty soon to surround the Lord. Claudia, we know, we all know that he is to die soon. He has been preparing our minds for what is to happen and we have the choke of fear at the back of our minds, for his dear sake. But

Claudia, he has also said that after he is lifted up, he will rise again, on the third day!'

'To be lifted up—crucifixion? Oh, never that, Miriam. Never that! It is the most cruel of deaths—torture beyond comprehension. First there is the scourging. Have you seen the flagellum, the many thonged whip they use, tipped with metal and with pieces of bone, set along its many thongs, used first to cut the flesh from the victim's back, then the huge iron nails used to attach the sufferer to the cross piece, the nails hammered through the wrists. Then the man lifted up as the cross piece is slotted into the upright and another huge nail hammered into the bones of the ankles, which are drawn one over the other. Hours, sometimes days of long torture, thirst, flies, hallucinations. Finally the legs are smashed, so that the victim can no longer support his body on the small peg between his thighs. He then dies of asphyxiation, as the weight of his unsupported body, prevents his drawing air into the lungs!' She looked at Miriam despairingly. 'As a soldier's wife, I have often had to witness the most terrible sights, Miriam, but that of crucifixion is the most horrible end that one man can sentence another to endure.'

Miriam's arms went about her, as the two women started to sob together. Then Miriam took one of the long patrician hands into her own, stroking it, as she murmured words of strength and comfort.

'Do you believe Jesus of Nazareth, to be the Son of God,' she asked?

'Yes, I do!'

'Then believe this also, dear Claudia. His Father, Almighty God, sent this dear only Son to this earth, to teach repentance and forgiveness of sins. In a way, which we do not yet fully understand, Jesus is to die, to take upon his innocent shoulders, the sins of all of us—of you and me— of the whole world. All that we have to do is to love him and to believe.' Miriam sank to her knees, and indicated that Claudia should do likewise. 'Let us pray together, as he has taught us to do.' The two heads, one fair, one dark, were bowed together in prayer.

'Will you stay close to me tonight, Miriam? I will have a chamber prepared for you, next to the one I share with Pontius. Send word to your husband.' She gave a sigh of relief as Miriam agreed, and retired in lighter mood than she had done for many weeks. Pontius Pilate also breathed a sigh of relief that the strained look seemed to have disappeared from his wife's face. He belched noisily, before lurching into bed beside her, his stomach churning with the excess of wine he had taken at table with his officers. Their one topic of conversation had been the Galilean. Pilate was beginning to wish Jesus had stayed in distant Galilee, however he seemed harmless enough. Pilate caressed his wife absently and fell asleep.

They had left the upper room. Jesus walked swiftly through the maze of interlocking courtyards of the Lower city, along the narrow alleyways and by deserted souk, and ever as he walked, he talked calmly with his disciples.

'When I sent you without purse, bag or sandals, did you lack anything?' They thought back to those early days in Galilee, when the master had sent them out, giving them authority to heal and cast out demons in his name, such exciting, happy days! Months later, seventy other disciples had been sent out on similar mission, this at the climax of his popularity. But many had fallen away from his side, the crowds also diminishing in size once they realized he was unlikely to seize political power.

'Nothing! We lacked for nothing!'

Jesus nodded, remembering and also knowing what lay ahead, the possible danger to them his little flock.

'But now if you have a purse, take it! Also a bag! And if you don't have a sword, sell your cloak and buy one!' They gasped, as he continued, 'It is written—"And he was numbered with the transgressors." I tell you, that this must be fulfilled in me. Yes, what is written about me, is reaching fulfilment!'

The men whispered together in agitated question.

'See Lord, we have two swords!' Simon the Zealot produced one, Simon Peter the other.

'That is enough,' Jesus nodded, satisfied. At last they reached the lower slopes of the Mount of Olives, tendrils of mist floating about the gnarled olive trees, the faint perfume of the dew damp wild flowers and crushed grasses, rising sweet to their nostrils, as they paused by the broken stone wall enclosing the olive press. Fitful gleams of pale, silver moonlight, stroked the leaves of the strong vine that swarmed over the old stones. Jesus laid a hand, on the sturdy stem of the vine.

'I am the true vine, and my Father is the gardener! He cuts off every branch that bears no fruit, whilst every branch that does bear fruit, he prunes, so that it will be even more fruitful.' He glanced at them, to see if they had understood. 'You are already clean, because of the word I have spoken to you. Remain in me, and I will remain in you. No branch can bear fruit by itself—it must remain in the vine. Neither can you bear fruit, unless you remain in me!'

They nodded their heads, the meaning clear. He continued,

'I am the vine, you are the branches. If a man remain in me, and I in him he will bear much fruit, apart from me, you can do nothing!' He bent and picked up a dead branch that had fallen from the vine. 'If anyone does not remain in me, he is like a branch that is thrown away and withers, such branches are picked up, thrown in the fire, and burned.' He cast the dead branch from him.

'If you remain in me and my words remain in you—ask anything you wish—and it will be given to you. This is to my Father's glory, that you may bear much fruit, showing yourselves to be my disciples!'

As he leaned against the old wall, he continued to teach them this last time, his eyes glowing with golden lustre in the moonlight. His voice rose, each word imprinted upon the still, damp air, 'As the Father has loved me—so have I loved you! Now remain in my love, just as I have obeyed my Father's commands and remain in His love. I have told you this, so that my joy may be in you and that your joy may be complete!'

A faint sob was heard, as Peter's heart, close to breaking, brought choking cry to his lips. Jesus raised his arms in blessing, as his voice, rich and low carried to each mans soul.

'My command is this. Love each other—as I have loved you! Greater love, has no-one than this, that he lays down his life for his friends,'

They turned grief stricken faces upon him, hanging on his words, sensing that this was his final message to them, but they were tired, emotionally, mentally tired. They heard him say gently,

'When the Councillor comes, whom I will send you from the Father, the Spirit of Truth who goes out from the Father—He will testify about me. And you also must testify, for you have been with me from the beginning. All this I have told you, so that you will not go astray.' His voice rose prophetically.

'They will put you out of the synagogue and in fact a time is coming, when anyone who kills you will feel he is offering a service to God!'

They looked at each other, as he continued to warn them of the trials ahead, but telling them over and over again, of the Holy Spirit, the Councillor, whom he would send to them, to help them in all that was to happen.

'I have told you these things so that in me, you may have peace. In this world you will have trouble, but take heart! I have overcome the world!' He rose to his feet and seemed to become deeply distressed. He raised restraining hand to his disciples.

'Sit here, while I pray.' He beckoned to Peter, James and John to accompany him, and they followed him to a point a little apart from the others.

'My heart is overwhelmed with sorrow, to the point of death. Stay here—and keep watch with me.' He watched, as the three sank to the ground, then he walked a few steps further on and fell with his face to the earth. A muffled sob broke from him.

'Father, if you are willing, take this cup from me! Yet not my will, but yours be done.' As he prayed thus, a bloody sweat poured from him, as the anguish of the heavy load of pain and sin he was to bear, the sin of all mankind, started to fall on his shoulders. He cried aloud in his agony. Then suddenly, the scene was illumined by strange, brilliant light as an angel appeared, sent from heaven to minister to the Holy, Son of God. His wings were crested with eternal flame, his face gleamed like the risen sun and he raised shining hands over Jesus, whispering words to strengthen, to comfort. The light faded. The angel had gone. But now Jesus rose to his feet, looking questioningly at his three chosen disciples. They seemed to be sleeping, completely exhausted from sorrow, only John blinked uncomprehendingly, through half open eyes. He had thought the angel part of a dream.

'Simon Peter, are you asleep?' He touched Peter's shoulder. The disciple sat up guiltily, waking James, shaking John by the arm. 'Could you not keep watch for one hour? Watch and pray that you will not fall into temptation. The spirit is willing—but the body is weak.'

Again he went apart, falling to his face and praying in agony of spirit, with his Father, his frame shaking with emotion. An hour sped by. He rose to his feet again, and returned to Peter, James and John. Again, he found them sleeping, although this time they opened their eyes, sensing his presence. They looked at the anguished face of their Master, and could find no words to say. Even Peter, was for once silent. Jesus sighed. What lay ahead, he must face alone—completely alone. For now, he was to be the sin bearer of mankind. Again, for the third time, he went apart and fell to his knees, his face buried in the grasses, while his spirit groaned. At last, drawn by instinct, Jesus rose to his feet and stared across the valley, to the steep sides of the hill atop which the Temple gleamed in the light of fiery torches. A dimmer line of dancing lights, was proceeding down into the Kidron Valley, where a detachment of Caiaphas guards, together with supporting crowd of priests and Pharisees, were following a man whose infamy, springing from tonight's action, was to stain the history books of time. Long before the vicious faced men panted their way up the slope towards him, Jesus knew that he who led them was one of his chosen twelve—Judas Iscariot!

Jesus dashed the stain of tears from his eyes, his face calm and authoritative again. He called firmly to his disciples, but as he did so, a young man, wrapped about in a linen cloak, burst wildly into the olive glade. It was John Mark. His servant had returned when John Mark had already retired, with the news that Judas Iscariot had entered that part of the Temple private to Caiaphas. John Mark had jumped out of bed, not even waiting to dress, merely throwing a linen cloak over his shoulders. Hugging it to him, he had run like the wind, cresting rooftops, leaping, rushing up and down steps, taking every short cut he knew until he was outside the city and once across the Kidron Brook, made his way to the place he knew that Jesus frequently retired to. He sank panting and exhausted before Jesus.

The soldiers had seen him rushing ahead of them and had shouted to him to stop, but he had not heeded.

'The temple guards!' he gasped. 'Judas Iscariot leads them!' His young face was urgent with fear. 'You must flee—there is yet time,' he said.

Jesus made no answer, but looked at the fast approaching lanterns and torches. He called to his disciples in crisp tones.

'Are you still sleeping and resting? Enough! The hour has come! Look!' He pointed to the lights. 'The Son of Man is betrayed into the hands of sinners! Let us go, here comes my betrayer!'

The three leapt to their feet, suddenly wide awake. They called to the others, who had also been sleeping. Simon the Zealot rushed to Jesus side, as did Simon Peter. The large group of armed men, chief priests and

Pharisee, with Judas in their midst, halted in front of the disciples glancing uncertainly from face to face.

'Who is it that you want,' asked Jesus calmly?

'Jesus of Nazareth,' they cried! Then Judas walked forward, as though in a dream. He approached Jesus and stood looking at him, unable to move. Then he lurched into action, seeking to give Jesus a greeting kiss, the signal previously arranged with the soldiers to indicate the man they were seeking.

'Judas—are you betraying the Son of Man, with a kiss?' The gentle words broke into Judas consciousness. Suddenly, the full enormity of what he had done overcame him and with a choking cry he blundered away, knowing he was leaving behind all that had made his life worthwhile, his beloved master, his Redeemer. Blackness enveloped his soul and he ran shrieking hoarsely from the scene pursued by the hounds of hell!

'Where is Jesus of Nazareth?' asked the guards, wishing to be sure.

'I am he,' Jesus said. His eyes flashed in the light of the lanterns, gleaming with unearthly brilliance. In sudden terror, the men drew back from him, and fell to the ground, nor could they move. The Holy One looked down on them.

Again he asked them, 'Who is it that you want?'

They stumbled to their feet, trembling. 'Jesus of Nazareth—we seek Jesus of Nazareth!'

'I told you that I am he,' Jesus answered calmly. They seemed to gain sudden confidence and started to advance on Jesus, their Captain indicating they should also round up the disciples. Jesus held restraining hand in front of them, and again they froze.

'If you are looking for me, then let these men go!' Minutes before, he had lifted up the disciples to his Father in prayer, asking that he would protest them, by the power of his name, the name given to him by God, so that they should be one, even as he was one with the Father. 'While I was with them,' he had prayed then, 'I protected them and kept them safe, by the name which you gave me. None has been lost, except the one doomed to destruction, so that scripture would be fulfilled!'

And God honoured his Son's request. The soldiers ceased to make threatening move against the apostles, only one soldier recognized young John Mark as the youth who had run in front of them to warn the Nazarene.

'Hold that man,' he exclaimed, and ready hands stretched out to seize John Mark. But the youth twisted in their grasp. His cloak came away in their hands. He snatched it back from them and fled away naked, trailing the cloak behind him, but made his escape!

The Commander of the Temple guards came to decision. He ordered his men to lay hands on Jesus and to bind him. But Simon Peter leapt into action, producing his sword. Malchus, Servant to Caiaphas was vehemently urging the soldiers to hurry, to arrest the blasphemer. It was more than Peter could bear, to hear his beloved master spoken of thus. He raised his sword, a weapon with which he was not familiar and made sweeping blow towards Malchus, slicing off his ear. The priest screamed aloud in pain, blood pouring from his ear, which was still attached to his head by a sliver of skin.

Then Jesus voice rang out clearly, as he signed to Peter to put aside his sword, his gaze also taking in Simon the Zealot, who had produced his own weapon and was making ready to use it. Simon's eyes were flaring dangerously, expression of utmost outrage on his face. It was plain he intended to protect his master to the death.

'No more of this! Peter, put your sword away!' He glanced also at Simon. 'Shall I not drink the cup my Father has given me?' He waited as the two men slowly put away their weapons, seeing the look of hopelessness and fear that spread over their faces in the dancing shadows cast by the torches. 'All who draw the sword will die by the sword,' he continued. 'Do you think I cannot call on my Father, and He will at once put at my disposal, a legion of Angels? But how then, would the scriptures be fulfilled, that say it must happen this way!' He was saddened by the look of utter dejection he read on the rest of his apostles faces, longed to speak words of comfort to them, but his time had come. Now it but remained to do the will of his Father and to trust, that they would hold faith, until the Holy Spirit came to strengthen them. He cast one last yearning look of love on them then moved forward to the Commander.

'Am I leading a rebellion that you have come out with swords and clubs to capture me? Every day, I sat in the Temple courts teaching and you did not arrest me! But all this has taken place, so that the writings of the prophets might be fulfilled!' The commander signed to his men to seize Jesus, but he gestured that they should wait. He walked over to Malchus, who shrank back from him in fear, blood pouring in a dark stream from his injury. Jesus raised his hand to the wound and healed him!

For a moment, there was awed silence. Then, almost reluctantly, the guards placed frightened hands upon Jesus, producing cords and binding him. Suddenly, like a flock of nervous sheep, the disciples fled, leaping up the hillside, running as though their sides would burst. Matthew had tears running down his cheeks. John only hid behind the low wall, calling to Peter. But Peter was running faster than any.

John stood up at last, sobbing as though his heart would break. The Holy One had warned them so often, that this was to happen only it had sounded unreal. How could the Almighty let this horror come upon his Son? Then to his wounded spirit, the teachings of Jesus came back. He remembered how many times the Lord had explained that he must die, taking upon his shoulders the sin of all peoples, past and present and in time to come, so that through his most Holy, perfect sacrifice, man should receive forgiveness from a loving God. But oh—what a price for the sinless One to pay! John dashed the tears from his eyes. He did not know what he could do, they had been forbidden to attempt to protect Jesus, told by him to make their escape. To wait until he would rise again and come to them!

'I am going to follow, to see where they are taking him,' he cried.

'Wait for me,' said a gruff voice. It was Simon Peter. He had halted in his wild flight and returned to Gethsemane, where to his relief he saw John. The two disciples fell into each other's arms, then made their way down, to cross the brook Kidron and then upwards towards Jerusalem. They found that by hurrying, they were able to catch up with the guards and the excited priests and hangers on. Somehow they managed to enter the city in the wake of these, without attracting notice.

Pontius Plate shot up in bed with shock! His wife Claudia was screaming, in the throes of nightmare. He bent over her.

'Quiet, wife—hush! All is well. You did but dream!' He shook her shoulder gently and sighed in relief, as she opened her eyes.

'Husband, I had the most terrible dream, but now!'

'You cried out!'

'I'm sorry.' She sat up in bed, trembling, her eyes filled of tears. Pilate patted her hand.

'Shall I call Miriam to you?' He looked at her anxiously.

'Yes, please do so!'

Pilate clambered out of bed and rang a bell for a servant.

'Fetch the Lady Miriam.'

She came, eyes still heavy with sleep. Pilate explained the situation. He was going to a couch in a neighbouring chamber. He had heavy duties waiting in the morning, must get some sleep. Would Miriam stay with Claudia? He smiled his relief and closed the door behind the two women.

What affliction of the mind was this that had overcome Claudia of late? Descended from the Rome's royal line, she had an aura of dignity about her that he admired above all things and appealed to his rough soldier's nature. She possessed the strength and delicacy of an exquisite piece of porcelain and in an ever changing world he was through her not too far removed from the throne. He cherished her for this, as well as his deep affection for her.

'Miriam, will you share my bed with me? I fear that the dream will return!' asked a trembling Claudia.

'Of course, murmured Miriam, and as though she received comfort from her friend's proximity, Claudia dropped into fitful sleep. Miriam remained awake. She had dreadful feeling of apprehension, laid upon her heart. Something ill was happening to the Holy One and she prayed silently to Almighty God, to keep Jesus safe.

David and Simeon were wakened from their sleep by a heavy pounding on the door. They leapt out of bed and ran into the atrium. Mary of Nazareth, Mary Magdalene and Joanna joined them there, together with the other women. Titus asked his mistress whether he should attempt to open the door at that time of night when marauders might be about.

'Go and inquire who it is,' said Lady Joanna calmly. They looked at each other uneasily, as they heard a voice raised in agitation.

'It is the son of Mary of Cypress—John Mark,' said Titus, leading the young man in. They stared at the youth, who was holding his cloak tightly about him.

'Forgive this intrusion in the middle of the night. But I knew you would wish to know that the Holy One is arrested! He is in the hands of the Temple guards. They have taken him to the house of Caiaphas!' His face was white and streaked by sweat and tears. He sank down onto a stool, sobbing. For a moment, there was an appalled silence then Mary of Nazareth gave a scream and fell half fainting, into the arms of Joanna. Mary of Magdala poured a glass of water and lifted it to Mary's lips, with shaking hand.

'The sword has fallen,' whispered His mother, between trembling lips, 'Oh, my son, my son! May the Almighty have his hand upon you, and keep you safe under the shadow of His wings!' Then she rallied. They must keep calm. Above all things they must remember all that he had laid upon them. She looked at the young man pleadingly.

'John Mark, if it be possible will you try to find out what is happening now? I do not wish that you endanger your own life but...' Her voice trailed off, as she searched his face piteously.

'I will go at once, lady. But do you all remain here, at least until you hear from me!' he spoke sternly. In this moment, he had become a man. Accepting their whispered assurances, John Mark cautioned David and Simeon to watch over the women. Then he departed, hurrying on silent feet, keeping ever watchful eye open for patrolling legionaries.

The house of Caiaphas, was near to that of his father-in-law, Annas, himself once High Priest for many years and still the ultimate power behind Caiaphas, who relied on Annas wisdom and experience to guide him in his precarious position as Judea's spiritual leader, and guardian of the mighty Temple. Caiaphas never resented the diplomatic hand that rested on his own reins of government, rather he was grateful for the elderly priest's wisdom garnered over the years and freely shared.

Annas had been summoned to his son-in-law's house, in the middle of the night. Those who came respectfully seeking him, mentioned only one word—the Nazarene! It was enough! His lower lip trembled with anticipation as he hastily pulled on his high linen nether garment, and drew his priestly robes about him, fastening his girdle of intertwined gold, blue, purple and crimson, then adjusted his high linen turban, worked in gold and especially designed for him. He enveloped himself in heavy cloak to warm his old bones, for the night was chill, as a swirling mist had descended on the city, as though nature sought to hide the horrors about to befall.

He was escorted to the house of Caiaphas. His son-in-law came eagerly to greet him, dismissing his priestly attendants.

'We have him! We have captured Jesus of Nazareth!' Caiaphas eyes burned with ferocious joy. 'One of our spies ran ahead to tell me that the guards have him secure, are bringing him here now! See...' He pointed through an open door, to the courtyard that lay in the centre of this huge ornate house, with its gleaming mosaic floors, splendid rugs in glowing colours, its rooms filled with treasures of gold and ivory, hung with rich tapestries; a house which was almost a palace. Into that courtyard an excited crowd of priests erupted, on the heels of a large contingent of guards, who marched in with a prisoner in their midst. Caiaphas lips parted in satisfaction, as he recognized the features of the man in the white robe. It was indeed the Nazarene, the so called Messiah! Well, now to make him admit to his blasphemies, then—execution!

'Congratulations, Caiaphas,' purred Annas, placing an affectionate hand on his son-in-law's arm. 'What do you plan to do next, interrogate him I suppose? You will of course need to convene the Sanhedrin, always remembering that some few of its members have a slight sympathy for the Rabbi Jesus. A verdict must be unanimous! This means, I suggest, that as a matter of emergency, we call out only those members of the Council on whom we may absolutely rely! They will sit in early session say about dawn, so that the matter may be expedited with little fuss.'

Caiaphas nodded thoughtfully, before uttering a slight objection. 'But Lord Annas, all must be done according to law, that none may accuse us afterwards of acting illegally. He has many thousands of followers and we cannot afford uprising. Supposing those members of the Sanhedrin not summoned, Nicodemus for instance, should stir up trouble?' Caiaphas face was perturbed. He wanted no slightest hitch.

'Think the matter through further, son-in-law! After the special sitting of those members of the Sanhedrin, whom we shall carefully select, who will of course, ask for the death penalty, why—it will then be necessary to go to Pilate, to authorize the execution, since we Jews lack the authority to do this.' He smiled triumphantly. 'The people will then blame the Romans for the crucifixion, which will follow. The guilt will not be on us!' He paused, as a sudden tremor passed over his face. Why had he thought in those terms, of being held guilty for the just killing of a blasphemer? He stared out into the courtyard, his face grim, as he looked upon the noble face of the prisoner standing gravely relaxed between his guards. A feeling almost of fear, shivered through his frame, then he straightened.

Annas spoke. 'Would you like me to undertake the initial examination? It will give you time to make the necessary preparations to summon the Sanhedrin into session!' His fingers played absently with his decorated golden girdle, as he bent his crafty old eyes on Caiaphas. Caiaphas gave a wolfish smile. The idea pleased him. After all, Annas was a master of interrogation.

'I leave him in your capable hands,' he agreed. 'Yes, what is it?' A servant approached hesitantly and bowed low.

'My Lord Caiaphas, there is a man present who says his name is John, son of Zebedee and he is from Galilee. His Father has visited us here in the past, when orders have been placed with him for large amounts of the smoked fish from Capernaum.'

'Well—what does this individual want, at such a time,' inquired Caiaphas testily?

'Merely to watch the excitement in the courtyard, he is a simple countryman, my Lord.'

'Think you he is connected with the Nazarene? I seem to remember hearing of one John, a fisherman, amongst Jesus followers. Yet it cannot be the same fellow. The disciple would never be so foolhardy as to venture here. Yet supposing he is one of the Nazarene's followers, what better record of the legality of our intentions, than that this John should be allowed in the vicinity.' He came to a decision. 'Yes—admit him!'

So it was that John the beloved disciple followed his Lord into the house of Caiaphas. Peter waited without, nervously pulling at his beard. A maid servant admitted him, for John had demanded entrance for his friend too. Peter was shaking with cold, and with apprehension. His eyes darted nervously back and forth, as he looked around, pulling his hood down over his face. A large brazier had been lit in the courtyard, its coals glowing invitingly. He drew close to it, warming his hands, gradually daring to lift his head and look about him. His hood slipped back. In the far corner, beneath a huge soaring archway, which gave access to the spacious antechamber, Jesus stood quietly. His arms were pinioned behind his back with cords, as his guards, now full of confidence and embarrassed at their earlier show of fear, before this strange holy man, shouted sarcastic remarks at him. Their Commander rapped out an order for silence. He had been amazed at the healing of Malchus, and felt growing unease in the presence of one whom he realized was not as other men.

Peter longed to go over to his Lord's side, but crippling fear, seized his entrails. But still he stared towards Jesus. His face framed by his dark curly hair and beard was outlined in the firelight, as were his Galilean homespun robes. The young servant girl who had admitted him, walked over from her position at the entry gate. She surveyed Peter thoughtfully.

'You are not one of this man's disciples, are you,' she asked curiously?

'I am not!' Peter made the denial, through lips stiff with fear and turned his head away from the girl. She shrugged and walked away. It was bitterly cold in the courtyard and many of the soldiers and officials drew closer to the flaming brazier. One of the men glanced at the tall, thick set Galilean, his eyes narrowing speculatively.

'You are not one of his disciples, are you?' He jerked his head towards Jesus.

'I said I am not,' said Peter loudly, glaring angrily at the man, who stared back, not quite convinced. Then all became silent, as a haughty figure appeared framed in the archway. It was ex High Priest Annas, still one of the most powerful figures in Israel. He walked up to Jesus, staring at him sombrely.

'Are you, Jesus of Nazareth?'

'I am he,' replied the stately man in the torn robe.

'Bring him inside,' said Annas coldly, and preceded the guards, who handled Jesus roughly, jostling him and swearing, as they thrust him headlong into the marble anti-chamber. He retained his balance and stood, face serene, before the threatening scowl of Annas.

'Now, Jesus of Nazareth—I demand you tell me of this pernicious teaching of yours, that you have been infecting the countryside with, even subverting the Jews in Jerusalem! Well—speak!' He thrust his grey bearded chin aggressively forward, fixing his haughtiest glance on Jesus. To his annoyance, Jesus merely stood impassively before him, answering nothing.

'Answer me! Tell me of yourself and of your disciples?'

'I have spoken openly to the world,' Jesus replied calmly. 'I always taught in synagogues, or at the Temple, where all Jews come together. I said nothing in secret! Why question me? Ask those who heard me. Surely they know what I said!'

On hearing these words, Annas gasped. He was used to men cowering before his interrogation. Seeing the anger on the High Priest's face, one of the guards brought up his hand and struck Jesus a savage blow across the face. Blood trickled from a cut on Jesus mouth. Jesus looked the man full in the face, and as he met that kingly glance, the man looked awkwardly down at his hand.

'Is this the way you answer the High Priest,' he blustered?

'If I said something wrong,' Jesus replied reprovingly, 'Testify as to what is wrong. But if I spoke the truth, why did you strike me?'

Annas face went white with anger. Never had prisoner behaved like this one! He sensed the growing unease of the guards. Just then, a Pharisee twisting the fringe of his prayer shawl nervously edged his way towards Annas.

'My Lord, the Lord Caiaphas awaits at the council. He is ready for the prisoner!'

'Take him away then,' hissed Annas! The guards jerked Jesus about, back into the courtyard. John son of Zebedee managed to slip quietly among the crowd surrounding Jesus.

Peter was bending down by the brazier, head bowed. He heard the commotion about the archway, saw the guards coming out and he arose to his feet. His forehead was trickling with perspiration in the cold night, as a sweat of fear made his body clammy. Suddenly a man came up and put an arresting hand on his shoulder. He was a relative of the servant of the High Priest, whose ear had been cut off by Peter, and he now recognized the Galilean as the man who had dealt Malchus the blow.

'Didn't I see you with him, in the olive grove,' he cried in excitement?

'Man, I don't know what you are talking about,' exclaimed Peter belligerently. Then he burst into a stream of abuse, denying any connection with the prisoner. At that moment, Jesus turned his head towards Peter and the cock crowed twice, heralding the dawn. Peter raised his eyes, his glance locking with that of the Holy One. Then he pushed his way out of the courtyard, through the lobby and into the street beyond. His face was flushed with shame, his hands trembling. Half fainting with shock of conflicting emotions, he held onto the gatepost of a neighbouring house, and wept great choking sobs. He, whom the Lord had named the rock, had betrayed the Son of God, even as Jesus had predicted that he would. How could he ever face Jesus again or the other disciples! Blindly he pushed his way through the curious crowd, who were now surging out of the courtyard. He saw John amongst them. But he did not respond to his friend's gesture to accompany him. He turned on his heel and fled, and the sound of his sobs was heard in heaven.

The guards decided to have some sport with Jesus, before escorting him to the council. A cloth was tied over his head. Now they would not have to endure the majestic look in those strange gold eyes that seemed to examine their very souls. One of them gave him a push, as another and another repeated the assault, as they commenced to strike the helpless figure about the face and body. They used the flat of their swords.

'Prophesy! Prophesy who hit you?' they called. 'Show us your powers now, Nazarene!' At last, there came an order from their Captain, the Strategios. It was time to get the prisoner to Caiaphas. Reluctantly they regrouped, pushing Jesus forward. They had removed the blindfold, revealing the bruising to his face. One eye was swelling badly, and his lip was bleeding, his white robe stained with the blood that dripped unchecked.

John Mark was once again admitted to Joanna's villa. Mary of Nazareth hurried to him, her eyes frightened.

'He is taken before a special sitting of the Sanhedrin, before Caiaphas. 'I will not stop. I want to find Nicodemus, for he is well disposed towards Jesus, this I know. Then there is another, the Lord Joseph of Arimathea. I will get word to you again, as soon as I may.

'Please-----please do what you can, whispered Mary.

'I fear it may be little enough,' replied the young man sadly. 'Just remember, remain here for now.' He bowed to the other women, seeing the strain on their faces. Simeon and David accompanied him to the door.

'May we not come, for we love the Lord dearly?'

'Then stay here and protect his mother and the other women. They are in your charge!' He slipped away, just as dawn was flushing the sky. He saw a distraught figure walking aimlessly along. It was Simon Peter.

'I have to get away from Jerusalem,' Peter muttered, trying to push past the young Cypriot. Mark quickly saw that something traumatic had overcome this leader of Jesus disciples.

'Come with me!' He led him to his own house and pushed the door open, ignoring the young serving girl Rona, who hurried forward and looked at her master questioningly. 'Lazarus is within. Tell him, all he needs to know,' said John Mark, and wearily, Peter went inside. John Mark took a short cut, making back towards the Upper City.

Jesus stood, hands still bound, before the semi-circle of cruel faced men in that long, narrow chamber. Their faces were drawn with tiredness, for they had been up all night, waiting for this their moment of triumph. Their eyes, reflecting the light of the spluttering torches and seven branched candelabra, were relentless. Now at last, he was in their grasp— the man who was spoken of as the Son of God! Blasphemer! Soon he would disfigure this world no longer. They stared at him. At his swollen face and stained robe, but something in his eyes, those eyes with the golden flecks, seeming to shimmer in the torchlight, brought quiver of fear to their breasts.

Caiaphas had a procession of false witnesses waiting in the small anti-room. He had one last word with them, before coming in to take his place on the throne like chair reserved for the High Priest. Annas was already seated at his right hand side. He checked that all the men he had summoned were there and nodded satisfaction. Then his eyes darkened, for he saw one man who should not have been present. Nicodemus! Then the door opened, and another man entered, about whom Caiaphas had grave doubts. Joseph of Arimathea! What did he here? Caiaphas managed to keep his face impassive.

Caiaphas made a short opening address, first of all asking the prisoner to confirm his name.

'Are you the Rabbi Jesus, out of Nazareth?'

'I am he,' replied Jesus, staring straight back into Caiaphas eyes. The High Priest shifted uneasily under that stare.

'You are accused of preaching blasphemy. Witnesses will be brought to testify against you. You will receive fair and impartial trial before this the High Court of the Sanhedrin.' He paused. 'Have you anything to say about yourself before proceedings begin?' He scanned Jesus face, but his prisoner stood impassively before him.

'Very well,' he said. He then proceeded to lead the assembled Sadducees and Pharisees into a short traditional prayer. It was soon over, amidst coughing and clearing of throats. The Sanhedrin now settled itself for the coming climax. Caiaphas summoned his first witness, a shifty faced fellow who accused Jesus of performing work on the Sabbath. Another mean mouthed man stood waiting without, ready to give his corroborative evidence. It was essential that two witnesses should give evidence confirming the accuracy of an accusation.

'I accuse this man of instructing a cripple at the Pool of Bethesda, to take up his mat and walk on the Sabbath, all know that the carrying of such articles constitutes work,' said the man self righteously.

'Wait fellow, did you not mean that the Rabbi Jesus healed a man who was lame from birth?' It was Nicodemus who now stood up. 'Is it right to do good or ill on the Sabbath,' he demanded of the assembly? 'Surely it is according to God's will, to take pity on one's fellow man and to bring relief from suffering!' He smiled blandly at Caiaphas, who waved the witnesses away angrily. There were plenty more such. Better to have a clear cut case, than rely on evidence which might be even slightly discredited. He called for the next witness. Jesus stood, unmoved.

Witness after witness was called. But in each case, they either contradicted each other, under the skilful examination of both Nicodemus and Joseph of Arimathea, or were exposed as unreliable. Caiaphas face became blacker by the minute. He knew that he must complete the case soon, get the conviction that he sought before the people who would soon be streaming into the Temple would hear of what had befallen their so called Messiah. The situation was delicate in the extreme. He gestured angrily to the guards to bring the next two witnesses.

Two men stepped forward, bowing obsequiously before Caiaphas.

'This fellow said—I am able to destroy the Temple of God, and rebuild it in three days!' They blurted this out in chorus glancing at Jesus nervously, not daring to encounter his eyes. Caiaphas sprang to his feet.

'Are you not going to answer?' He shouted the words at the silent figure that merely looked at him with that disturbing, luminous gaze.

'What is this testimony that these men are bringing against you?' Still Jesus held his peace. At last, his face quivering with rage, the High Priest cast accusing finger at him, throwing back his head dramatically shouted-

'I charge you, by oath of the Living God! Tell us—tell us, if you are the Christ—the Son of God?' He hurled his challenge to the prisoner. At this moment, Jesus drew himself up to his full height, and seeing that he was about to speak, Caiaphas held up his hand for complete silence. He leaned forward, eyes boring into the prisoner's face.

'Well?'

'Yes—it is as you say!' Jesus eyes swept the whole assembly. 'But I say to all of you—in the future, you will see the Son of Man sitting at the right hand of the Mighty One—and coming on the clouds of heaven!'

A low moan of horror ran round the council. Even Nicodemus and Joseph looked stunned. What could they say to help, in face of this? They looked hopelessly at Caiaphas, whose face was almost radiant in relief. His hands rose up to the front of his robe, rending the material in traditional gesture. He faced the council, suitable expression of shocked amaze on his own features.

'He has spoken blasphemy! Why do we need any more witnesses? Look, now you have heard the blasphemy!' He raised his hands to them. 'What do you think?'

'He is worthy of death! He is worthy of death—death—death!' The howl that arose from their throats was like the baying of hounds. They were all standing now, shaking their fists. All control went; all slightest semblance of legality. They brushed Nicodemus and Joseph of Arimathea aside, in their mad rush to approach Jesus. They started to strike the bound man and to punch him. He was beset on all sides. But a restraining call from Caiaphas made them pause.

'All must be done according to the law! He must be brought before Pilate.' But they were in no mood to listen. Let Pilate condemn him, but first, they wanted him beaten. Again there were willing hands among the guards, to blindfold him. His hands were fasted to two metal rings set in the wall, his back exposed, and the cruel whip rose and fell relentlessly. He uttered no cry, merely slumped against the restraining metal rings. They released him, their bloodlust stirred to explosion point. The guards followed Caiaphas instructions, removing the blindfold and jerking the tunic back over his lacerated shoulders. He looked at Caiaphas and

Caiaphas gave sudden shudder, but pushed down into the furthermost recesses of his soul, the knowledge just born of what this man was. But he could not afford to stop now.

Pontius Pilate was rudely awakened, by one of his officers, who had sought admission to his bedchamber. Reluctantly Pilate opened a jaundiced eye. He had slept but little that night! First Claudia waking him with her screams, now this summons at dawn!

'What is it man?' The Prefect sat up in bed, staring at the soldier resignedly.

'My Lord Prefect, there is an unruly mob of Jews led by the High Priest Caiaphas, asking admittance! That is, they say they do not really want to enter the fortress, as that will mean defiling themselves at Passover.'

'Well, do they want to come in, or not?' Pilate's hackles had risen at the name of Caiaphas.

'Actually, sir—they ask that you be kind enough, to come down and see them!' The young soldier looked slightly shame faced at carrying such a message to the Emperor's representative.

'Tell them to wait—and bring Marcus to me! Incidentally, what do they want me for? Did they say?'

'They have a prisoner, sir, a man called Jesus of Nazareth!'

'Jesus!' Pilate gave an exclamation of surprise, and leapt out of bed. Just then, there was another knock at the door.

'Good morning, my Lord,' said a young officer. 'Tribune Marcus wished me to remind you early this morning, that you wished to deal with the matter of the insurrectionist, Barabbas!'

Pilate sighed ill-humouredly, another day of problems! With a command to wait for him he hurried to his suite of bathrooms, and plunged into an ice cold bath. Shivering, he towelled himself dry. It had helped, although last night's wine was still sour in his stomach. He was surrounded now by anxious slaves, worried at the sight of their master attending to himself.

'Ah, Marcus! What is all this nonsense about Caiaphas and the Holy Man? He turned relieved eyes on his senior Tribune, as he stood whilst his slaves arranged the folds of his toga. Marcus eyes were grave, his usual state of equanimity, disturbed.

'They have arrested Jesus of Nazareth. They are downstairs, outside the South Western tower of the Antonia demanding that you come out to them, and sentence Jesus to crucifixion!' Marcus looked at Pilate's enraged face. 'Caiaphas leads them!'

'They are demanding? They are daring to demand—that I follow their instructions! Now by Jupiter and all the gods, how dare they so insult my office?' He tossed off a goblet of wine, his cheeks flaming with temper. That Caiaphas! He would crucify him, if only it were possible!

'I will come down,' he said in quieter tones. 'Oh—and Marcus! Perhaps it would be better if certain persons did not learn of what is going on, at this stage.'

There was no need to specify that he meant his wife, who luckily was still sleeping, also Centurion Claudius and Lady Miriam. Tribune Marcus gave swift order to one of his men and followed Pilate below.

The huge gates between the two western facing towers were guarded by several hundred armed men, weapons at the ready. Pilate walked towards the gates, across the great tiled courtyard, called the pavement—or Gabbatha. His soldiers were brought smartly to attention, by Centurion Lucius. Pilate looked at their numbers

'How many are without?'

'I would say about two thousand, my Lord. Can you hear them?' The sound of a heavy chant was rising on the air. 'They are shouting—death to the Nazarene!'

'We'll see about that,' cried Pilate savagely. 'Summon another cohort and make sure the temple colonnades are well manned.' He waited as Tribune Marcus shouted an order, and in a short space of time, another five hundred men appeared. They surrounded the courtyard. Two of their number, carried an ornate throne seat, which they deposited in the centre of the huge, tiled area.

Then Pilate, flanked by Marcus and his other tribunes, brought from Caesarea for Passover, advanced to the gates, which were being subjected to a heavy pounding. At his order, the massive gates were slowly opened, to reveal a furious mob, headed by Caiaphas and his ancient father-in-law, Annas. Behind Caiaphas, firmly held by two temple guards, was

Jesus of Nazareth, hands bound before him, almost unrecognizable from the terrible assault he had endured. Only his golden eyes and the graciousness of his carriage confirmed his identity to those of the Romans who knew him.

'Lord Caiaphas, an unexpected pleasure,' breathed Pilate. 'Come in, you and the Lord Annas!' His face challenged them.

'We would prefer not to enter your palace, Lord Prefect. To do so would be to make ourselves ceremoniously unclean, at Passover, you understand,' purred Caiaphas.

'Bah! Nonsense,' said Pilate, eyes glinting. But he signed to his tribunes, to keep at his side, as he stepped out of the gates. His eyes took in the size of the crowd, which seemed to be growing every moment. The sun had not long risen, and Caiaphas squinted as the brilliant rays shot between the towers of the fortress, almost blinding him. Pilate noticed his discomfiture and smiled blandly. Then his smile froze, as he saw the figure of Jesus properly for the first time. It was obvious, that they had gone as far as they dared towards killing him themselves.

'What charges are you bringing against this man?' The crisp question made Caiaphas draw himself up trying to look as authoritative as he could, in his bedraggled robe. How he now despised his flamboyant but traditional gesture, in tearing his robe. Of all the times he wished to look imposing before Pilate, was now!

'If he were not a criminal, we would not be handing him over to you!'

Pilate shrugged his shoulders. He wanted no part in what he was sure, was a purely religious controversy, nor did he wish to give satisfaction to Caiaphas.

'Take him yourselves and judge him by your own law,' he prevaricated.

'But we have no right to execute anyone,' objected Annas.

Pilate swore softly then he gestured towards Jesus.

'What has he done?'

'We have found this man subverting our nation. He opposes the payment of taxes to Caesar and claims to be Christ—a King!' Caiaphas eyes were narrowed against the sun, as he burst out into this tirade. Pilate studied the battered figure, in the once white robe, noting the bruised face and from the stiff way the man held his shoulders, Pilate suspected he had been whipped.

'Are you the King of the Jews,' he asked curiously?

'Yes—it is as you say!' Jesus looked at Pilate calmly. The Prefect stared at him in surprise. He had not expected Jesus to admit it. He signed to his guards to bring the prisoner into the fortress then preceded them into the Lithostratos, the paved courtyard. He went to his chair of justice and seated himself, indicating that Jesus should be brought before him.

'Well now, Jesus of Nazareth, you are really the King of the Jews?' Pilate placed his hands on his outstretched knees, leaning forward intently.

'Is this your own idea, or did others talk to you about me,' asked Jesus? Astonished at the temerity of his bearing and slightly aggravated, Pilate considered his reply.

'Am I a Jew?' There was muffled laughter amongst his officers at this sally. But Pilate continued evenly. 'It is your people and your chief Priests, who have handed you over to me! So, what is it that you have done?' Pilate really wanted to know, to understand. Jesus raised his eyes above Pilate's head, as he said slowly,

'My Kingdom is not of this world. If it were, my servants would fight to prevent my arrest by the Jews. But now, my Kingdom is of another place!' His eyes returned to Pilate's face, seeking comprehension of his words.

'Ah—you are a King then,' exclaimed Pilate, glad to have clarified that point!

'You are right in saying I am a king. In fact, for this reason I was born, and for this, I came into the world! To testify to the truth! Everyone on the side of truth listens to me!' His golden eyes blazed the sincerity of what he said, between those broken lips. Pilate shook his head, bewildered.

'What is truth?' he wondered, nor were his words meant to be facetious. He rose to his feet, and walked towards the gates, where the vast mob was still howling. The guards brought Jesus in his wake.

'I find no basis for any charge against this man,' he said firmly. He stared balefully into Caiaphas eyes

'He stirs people up all over Judea by his teaching,' cried Caiaphas, with enthusiastic backing from the huge collection of priests and Temple staff. 'He started in Galilee and has come all the way here!'

Galilee! Herod Antipas territory! Suddenly Pilate realized he could release himself from his present dilemma and at the same time placate a possibly offended Herod, whom he had neglected to invite to dine with him. He would send the Rabbi Jesus to Herod. After all, he was under Herod's jurisdiction!

'Take him to Herod, let him be the judge of this matter,' said Pontius Pilate.

The soldiers handed their prisoner back to the Temple guards, but Pilate instructed a half maniple to accompany the mob, to ensure that Jesus was safely delivered to Herod. He wrote out a brief message to be handed to the Tetrarch. Then heaving a sigh of relief, he ordered that the gates be shut on the mob and started to relax, as the sound of their baying, disappeared on the air!

Chapter Twenty-Two

Herod Antipas was amazed at the news! Chuza had just come to him, saying that Pontius Pilate had sent a prisoner to him for trial and sentencing. The man was Jesus of Nazareth.

Antipas broke the seal on the short missive. Pilate had interrogated the prisoner and found no wrong in him. But as this Galilean was within the jurisdiction of Antipas, then perhaps Antipas would care to interrogate the man himself, advising on sentence, the more especially as the matter in point seemed to be peculiar to the Jewish faith.

Antipas stroked the letter thoughtfully. He had planned over a long period that eventually Jesus should be arrested and executed, but had not wanted direct involvement because of the Rabbi's popularity in his kingdom, hence his plea to Caiaphas to manage the matter for him. And now it would appear that Caiaphas had acted, was waiting outside with Jesus and expecting Herod to call for the Holy Man's death. But then what of this note from Pilate, who obviously was reluctant to implement the death sentence. Pilate was noted for his lack of respect for human life and if his cruelty was not on a par with Herod's, certainly he allowed no scruples of mercy to affect his judgements. So why now, when presented by this trouble-maker not react in his normal way and order summary execution. No—this needed thinking on.

He gave an order to Chuza then glanced lazily around at his courtiers. Herodias and her daughter Salome, their eyes bright with cupidity, were speaking with some rich merchants from the far Eastern lands who were displaying a casket of priceless gems. He called to the women to take their places at his side. Chuza called for silence, and the whole court looked expectantly to the door. What was happening? There were sounds of shouting and chanting without and Antipas drew his brows together menacingly. Who so dared to disturb the peace of his palace?

'Chuza, admit the High Priests Caiaphas and Annas, the chief priests and a few guards to control the prisoner and have all others removed from the palace grounds!'

Chuza acted swiftly. The captain of the Herodian guards produced a contingent of his men and the noisy throng of priests and Levites and the Temple hierarchy, who had followed Jesus, were dispersed into the streets beyond. Those in Joanna's villa heard the shouting and stole up onto the rooftop, to stare down at the vicious screaming throng, hearing the cruel chant, 'Death to the Nazarene! Jesus for the cross! Death to the blasphemer!' The women held onto each other in fear, Mary of Nazareth's face grey with terror for her son. Mary Magdalene supported her, whilst Joanna leaned over the balustrade, looking for any familiar face and saw John, son of Zebedee. She raised her voice, crying his name, never expecting him to hear amongst the confusion. But John raised his head, saw her, and started towards the entrance to the villa.

Herod Antipas leaned forward on his throne. He had instructed his wife and Salome not to interfere with his handling of the Nazarene in any way. Jesus was standing before him now, and Herod shook his head slightly. He had expected a replica of John the Baptist, a firebrand with matted hair and beard, dressed in goatskins like the prophets of old. But this man carried himself with a strange dignity. His face although badly contused was calm, his eyes those of—a king? As he looked into those eyes, something strange happened in Herod's mind, for he suddenly saw portrayed before him, every screaming, tortured soul whose sufferings he had ordered and gloated over. As one face disappeared another took its place, Herod placed a hand in front of his face, terror clouding his eyes. He made himself look away and the visions ceased.

His courtiers stared at him. Why did he not commence the interrogation? There was a rippling of subdued conversation, as the gorgeously apparelled men and women moved restlessly. Herod glanced at them, glad to fill his normal sight with these, the wealthy and powerful in his kingdom, and ambassadors from distant lands. He looked at the women, graceful, dressed in brilliantly coloured silks, necks glittering with jewellery, faces boldly painted, those who were veiled with such gossamer light material as to make it mere artifice.

As though to remind him of their mission, Caiaphas and Annas started to make loud complaint against their prisoner, Caiaphas in particular staring indignantly at Herod. Enough time had already been wasted. The longer the matter was protracted, the more dangerous the situation could become. He had paid his Temple staff well, to make as much tumult as possible before Pilate, and again now outside the Citadel. Others also amongst the citizenry had accepted the Temple silver, to join in the massive outcry to crucify the Nazarene! Herod Antipas craved Jesus death. So why did he sit like a statue when time was so important. As many supporters as Caiaphas now had, he knew the fickleness of crowds, how little it took to sway them. Jesus had thousands of supporters. They must not be allowed to know what was happening until it was too late!

'So, you are the one who terms himself the King of the Jews,' exclaimed Herod, with expression of contempt. He looked disparagingly at Jesus, trying to evade looking into his eyes. Then his face grew thoughtful. 'We have heard that you are a performer of miracles, Rabbi. Perform one for us here, so that we may judge of your powers!' He looked at Jesus curiously. 'Come, Rabbi, just one miracle that is all we ask! Do you wish to have one blind or crippled brought here for your demonstration, or would you prefer one smitten of the palsy?' He stopped talking and waited on Jesus answer. But the stately figure before him spoke nothing. He merely lowered his eyes momentarily, as though in distaste.

'How is this? Herod frowned angrily. He badly wanted to see proof of the miraculous powers that so many of his subjects proclaimed. Why was this fellow being so stubborn?

'So then, you have no miracle to show your Tetrarch?'

'My Lord, why waste time on this blasphemer? Will you not just pass sentence?' the High Priest frowned impatiently, as his colleagues began to murmur at the delay. Herod scowled. Although he wanted Jesus death, knew that Caiaphas was relying on him, yet something about the quiet man standing before him worried him and of course, there was also Pilate's reluctance to execute the so called Messiah. He looked pathetic in that torn and bloodstained robe. What would he look like in the robes of a king? Herod glanced about him, his eyes lighting on Tetrarch Phillip, who was wearing a particularly regal purple velvet cloak. He beckoned him.

'Phillip, should not a king be correctly dressed?' Phillip fixed his mild stare on his brother. 'That fine cloak of yours, place it about the Nazarene's shoulders! I am wishful to see, whether it will produce the right effect on Jesus. Who knows, he may then be prepared to produce a miracle for us!'

Phillip hesitated. His cloak was new and he was proud of it, nevertheless, if it would please Antipas! He could buy many more such. He detached the cloak and handed it to the royal guard. The man walked over to Jesus, and draped the lustrous velvet about his battered form. Antipas closed one eye and considered the man standing so serenely before him. Yes, he had the bearing of a king! As he glanced briefly into the shimmering gold eyes, Herod suddenly shivered. He had a flash of insight. This man, with the bruised face and beaten shoulders—was indeed, the Christ!

'I cannot sentence him,' he muttered soundlessly. But he had to do something, it was expected of him. He commenced to mock Jesus. He rose up from his golden throne, and walked about the velvet clad figure, crying out jeering remarks, calling to his guards to join in. They did, with utmost enthusiasm. Soon the whole court were shouting out abuse and ridicule.

Caiaphas was delighted. Surely Herod would act now. But he didn't. Caiaphas could hardly believe his ears, for Herod was saying, 'I find no ill, in this fellow! The desert sun has touched his wits—that is all that is amiss here. Return him to Pilate, and say that Herod Antipas finds no fault, in Jesus of Nazareth!'

There was a gasp of fury from the priests! Caiaphas moved a few steps forward, looking as though he would attack Herod physically. Then he glanced at the royal guards, who had placed their hands on the hilts of their swords. He calmed down. He did not bother to address Herod. He did not trust himself.

'Bring the prisoner forth, guards,' he cried! His own Temple guards now came forward. They made to remove the velvet cloak, but Phillip shook his head. It would be bloodstained now, anyway. The Nazarene could keep it.

'Yes, take Jesus back to Pilate wearing this robe! I think the humour of it will appeal to the Prefect!' And Caiaphas had no option but to obey Herod. Jesus gave one last quiet look at Herod, who quailed uneasily beneath it, turning his head away. Then the guards marched their prisoner out and the half maniple of Roman legionaries fell in about the party, as the enraged High Priests Caiaphas and Annas and chief priests, made their way from the palace. The mob waiting outside gave voice to a furious howl when they saw their prey before them again and this time dressed in a royal robe. Their shouts and insults jarred his ears, as he walked wearily between the guards, back to the Antonia. Then his eyes widened slightly. Amongst the crowd he had seen John, son of Zebedee together with his mother and the other women who followed him so devotedly. Then these dear ones were swallowed up in the seething mass of people.

The sound of the crowd alerted the legionaries within the Antonia, long before the party came in sight. The Centurion commanding the half maniple, now took over of proceedings. He called on his men, to take charge of Jesus, and cried to those within the fortress palace to open the gates. Caiaphas was furious, but dared not object as he knew the fortress contained at least six thousand armed men.

Pilate was again summoned to the lithostratos. To his annoyance, he found that Jesus had been returned by Herod. One of his men handed him a note. He scanned it. Herod thanked the Prefect for his courtesy in presenting the prisoner. He like Pilate could find no fault in the man. Pilate smiled triumphantly! He almost liked Herod at that moment, and from that time on treated him with grudging respect.

'Summon the High Priests, Caiaphas and Annas,' he said, standing boldly at the gate. The boisterous mob became subdued, as they saw it was the powerful representative of the Emperor, standing before them. Caiaphas strode up to Pilate, his torn robe fluttering in the slight breeze. Pilate thought he had never seen a man look so furious. He glanced at those flanking Caiaphas, the Sadducees and leading Pharisees, members of the Great Sanhedrin. Every face was distorted by bloodlust.

Pilate indicated Jesus, standing calmly in his purple robe.

'You brought this man as one inciting the people to rebellion! I have examined him in your presence and have found no basis for your charges against him.' He looked at them disparagingly. 'Neither has Herod, for he has sent him back to us. As you can see, he has done nothing to deserve death. Therefore I will punish him and then release him!'

The roar that erupted from their throats was like that of angry wolves, denied their prey.

'He is a blasphemer! Crucify him! We demand his death!'

Pilate looked at them a slight spark of indecision in his eyes. The matter was getting out of hand. He glanced at the weary figure, between two of his men. Then an idea came into his head—Barabbas! He was supposed to sentence the Zealot leader today, and knew that this would be one troublemaker the less! Now it was traditional, as a mark of goodwill towards the Jews, for the Prefect to release a prisoner to them at Passover. Surely if given the choice between a murderer, especially one who might have brought severe reprisals on his people because of his constant insurrection, and Jesus of Nazareth, who for all their animosity towards him, had done nothing worthy of death, surely faced with this choice even this mob would choose to have Jesus released and Barabbas crucified!

'I will today release one prisoner to you,' said Pilate in gracious tones. 'Now, shall it be the murderer Barabbas or do you want me to release to you this Jesus, King of the Jews?'

'No—not him,' the crowd bellowed, shaking their fists at Jesus. 'Give us Barabbas! Barabbas—Release Barabbas!' Caiaphas and Annas were almost dancing with rage, screaming words in Hebrew which Pilate did not understand. But he did understand the potential insurrection brewing outside the Antonia and with the extra million people within the city precincts, come for this most sacred feast of Passover, the position could explode all too easily into massive uprising. Pilate could surely deal with this, but with complaints against his rigid rule constantly being sent by the Jews to Emperor Tiberius, he could not afford at this time to risk a major incident. He ordered his men to bring Jesus back into the fortress and to close the gates.

He walked over to the judgment seat, and had Jesus brought over to stand before him. Pilate looked at him, perplexed. He turned to Marcus.

'This man is innocent of wrong doing. But to placate the mob, I will have him flogged and then release him. He was just about to give the order, when he saw Centurion Claudius approaching with a silver salver. There was a letter on it, which he proffered to Pilate, with a bow.

'My Lord Prefect—the Lady Claudia sends this letter to you!' Pilate was doubly amazed. Firstly that a man who but yesterday had been at death's door, should be standing before him in the full vigour of manhood and that his lady wife, should try to contact him whilst attending his official business. He lifted the letter from the salver, turning it over in his hands

'Centurion Claudius—welcome back to your duties! I will give libation to the gods, for your miraculous healing!' He turned to Marcus, 'Yet I feel that it is too early for the Centurion to be burdened with undue responsibility! See to it, Marcus, that Claudius has ample time to recover his full strength!' He nodded to Claudius to take his position beside Marcus amongst the tribunes, honour indeed!

Then Pilate broke the seal, and commenced to read the brief note from his wife. So it was that he did not see the appalled glance that Claudius shot upon the noble figure, whose bruised countenance was grey with tiredness and pain, the livid marks of the savage beating he had received standing out, mute legacy of the Sanhedrin's hatred. Claudius looked into the sad eyes, of the Holy Son of God and the pity and distress on his face, as he realized his own inability to change or halt the course of events was noted by that still figure. Jesus looked at him and that look of love, bent on Roman soldier, poured like healing balm of Claudius soul. For that look spoke of forgiveness, of understanding.

Pilate read the letter through a second time. He was shocked to receive such communication from his wife, for never before, had she attempted to interfere in matters of state.

'Don't have anything to do, with that innocent man,' Claudia had written, 'for I have suffered a great deal today in a dream, because of him!' Pilate snorted! Claudia and her dreams! Yet, if the prisoner was the unwitting cause of her dreams, all the more reason why Pilate should set him free. There was something very strange about the Nazarene, those eyes of his for instance, that seemed to look deep into a man's soul, the lack of fear that he showed. All men feared death! Every man that Pilate had ever sentenced had shown the same signs of horror of his approaching fate, the stupefied look of terror. Men and women alike would plead and cry out. Jesus merely stood serene. Perhaps he did not fully understand the facts of crucifixion, the pain and torture of it, the degradation! Pilate would spare him this, if it were possible.

The mob without the gates, were hammering upon them now, their roar for blood, vibrating around the lithostratos, seeming to bounce off the walls of the four huge towers.

'Have the prisoner flogged,' said Pilate. He did not look at Jesus, as he was led away and marched up to a post some two hundred yards away. Here he was stripped first of the velvet cloak, then of his other garments. He was chained to the posts. Marcus had walked over to take command of proceedings. His eyes swept pityingly, at the purple contusions, already criss-crossing Jesus back. Marcus feared that the Holy man might not be able to sustain the flogging that was to follow. But he was a soldier of Rome. No human emotions were allowed to interfere with duty.

The Tribune nodded to the huge guard, massive muscles bulging, who had marched across the paved courtyard in reply to a centurion's summons.

'Commence the punishment, soldier!' He moved slightly towards the fellow, who stank of garlic and stale perspiration. 'Pilate wants him alive,' he murmured. Then he stepped back to a distance. He wished to look away, but could not. The guard swished the flagellum through the air, as though working up his stroke. Then the first blow fell upon Jesus shoulders, splitting the skin, sending spray of blood onto the sand which surrounded the post. Again and again the whip lashed into Jesus body, ripping the flesh, as the sharp pieces of metal and bone, which projected from the leather thongs, did their deadly work. And still the whip rose and fell, even circling Jesus neck. At last the guard lowered the flagellum. He bowed to Marcus and saluted. Then he turned and cast wondering look at the prisoner, who had not cried out, only given a soft moan, and who now had murmured something. It had been forgiveness! As he looked at the sickening mess of bruised broken skin, of the man who hung half fainting from the post, something cracked in the guard's tough soul. He marched away, blinking quick tears from his eyes.

Tribune Marcus approached the post. 'Release him,' he ordered. If he were shocked at the appearance Jesus now presented, he tried not to show it.

'Clothe him,' he said. One of the guards threw a bucket of brine, over Jesus torn and bleeding back, then with his fellows, pulled their victim's clothes roughly back upon him. A young centurion gave a harsh laugh, as he ordered the velvet robe to be placed once again about the prisoner. One of the soldiers had been busily plaiting a makeshift crown, from twigs of a sharp barbed thorn bush that smothered one of the walls. He approached the centurion.

'A fitting crown for such a king, sir?'

'Excellently done! Place it on his majesty's head,' laughed the centurion. The soldier rose to his toes, and jammed the thorny wreath onto Jesus head. The soldiers surrounding Jesus now began to laugh and jeer! The incident was providing light relief to their day.

'Hail—king of the Jews,' they cried! One of them went as far as to smite Jesus on the face, but Tribune Marcus heard the commotion, and turned furious face upon them.

'Bring the prisoner here,' he exclaimed. He had been whispering words of caution to his friend Claudius, who had turned white, when he had heard the thudding blows, descending upon the innocent Son of the Almighty. His eyes were wild with pain and Marcus feared that Claudius might forget that he was in the presence of Pilate. So now, he pressed firm fingers on his arm.

'Steady, my friend,' he whispered. Then he commanded that Jesus be brought once more before the Governor. Pilate was beginning to tire of the whole situation. He looked with expression bordering on pity, at the swaying figure before him, who still managed to keep about him that strange dignity. Drops of blood from his cut neck and thorn pierced brow, were dripping onto his robe but the golden eyes were fixed questioningly on Pilate now and Pilate shivered beneath that gaze. He sprang to his feet.

'Open the gates and bring the prisoner out!' He himself walked before Jesus, his tribunes forming a protective flank about him, as a cohort, javelins poised, drew close about the group.

Caiaphas and Annas had now worked themselves up into a state of almost apoplectic fury. Nothing mattered to them now, but to accomplish the death of Jesus. For once, even their fawning respect of Pilate, was put aside.

'Look!' shouted Pilate, raising commanding voice to the crowd, who now slowly abated their screeching, to listen to him. 'Look—I am bringing him out to you, to let you know that I find no basis for a charge against him!' ' He gestured to the guards behind him, who now thrust Jesus forward. The crowd glared with pitiless eyes at the desperately hurt man, wearing the purple robe and crown of thorns.

'Behold—the man,' cried Pilate, and his cry was to vibrate through all centuries of time to come! But as soon as the chief priests and officials saw Jesus, they started to brandish their fists and to cry for his death—their paid underlings taking up the cry. 'Crucify, Crucify—Crucify!'

Pilate gave an exclamation of exasperation.

'You take him and crucify him,' he said, knowing full well, that it was without their authority. 'As for me,' he continued, 'I find no basis for a charge against him. I repeat it—no basis, whatsoever!'

'We have a law,' they insisted. 'And according to this law, he must die, for he claimed to be the Son of God!'

'The Son of God?' and Pilate suddenly paled. Already apprehensive of this almost deranged crowd of Jews, he realized that this was a situation beyond his normal understanding. He felt a real sense of fear now of that bruised yet regal figure before him.

'Bring him back within,' he muttered. He marched back to his judgement seat.

'Where do you come from,' he asked Jesus? To his annoyance, Jesus merely looked at him. Pilate sprang forward in his seat, hands outstretched, as though he would seize him, to shake the answer to his question from him.

'Do you refuse to speak to me? Don't you realize that I have the power to crucify—or to free you?' Pontius Pilate knew he was fast losing control of the situation! At last the prisoner opened battered lips, his face almost unrecognizable from his repeated beatings.

'You would have no power over me,' he said calmly, 'If it were not given to you from above. Therefore, the one who handed me over to you is guilty of a greater sin!' The golden eyes watched Pilate impassively.

Pilate's head was aching from the strain of all that was happening. He couldn't kill this man, did not want to! But the baying outside the gates was getting louder and louder. Pilate commanded his men to carry his judgement seat outside the gates. It was already noon, the sun blazing down with furious heat. The crowd were pushed roughly back by the legionaries, who now provided protective phalanx about their Governor. Pilate seated himself before them.

'Here is your king,' he said.

'Take him away, crucify him! Crucify him,' they howled.

'Shall I then crucify your king,' cried Pilate. It was Caiaphas who answered. He looked implacably at Pilate then shouted, at the top of a voice almost hoarse from his impassioned screams.

'We have no king, but Caesar!'

'We have no king but Caesar! Caesar!' The crowd took up the cry. 'If you do not crucify the one who pretends to be a king then you are no true friend of Caesars!'

It was the one thing they could have said to sway Pilate. How indeed, would Tiberius react, if he were told that Pilate had insisted on releasing a man pretending to the throne, even though Pilate knew this to be completely opposite to the truth?

'Shall I then release Barabbas to you,' he called to them, in placating tones, and they knew they had him.

'Barabbas! Bring out Barabbas,' they shouted. Pilate cursed under his breath, but whispered an order to a centurion. He saw Claudius eyes upon him, pleading mutely. But there was nothing he could do now. He couldn't risk report of all this, getting to Tiberius.

Barabbas was jerked roughly to his feet, straw clinging to his filthy tunic. His face was caked with dust, through which tears had runnelled. His jailer scowled at him. He could not be brought thus before the governor.

'You look a foul mess, Zealot,' he said. 'You stink!'

'What do you expect? Give me water to cleanse myself!' Anything to delay what lay ahead. The jailor cursed and turned to one of his assistants. 'Bring a bucket of water. He pointed to it. 'Now wash yourself,' he instructed. 'Comb your hair and beard man—and hurry, hurry!'

Barabbas paled, as he rubbed his hands dry on his torn tunic. Had it come then, the day of condemnation and execution? During the long days and longer nights of his captivity, he had tried to thrust the actuality of his eventual fate to the back of his mind. Now the fear so long kept at bay, leapt like a ravening jackal at his throat. The jailer indicated to his assistants, to unlock the prisoner's leg irons. The Zealot hardly noticed the open sores now exposed caused by the metal's cruel bite

'Hurry man—move!' The guard pushed him violently before him, handing him to the four soldiers, who stood waiting above at the top of the dungeon's steps. They secured Barabbas hands, commanding him to walk between them. He did as he was bid, trying to keep the fear out of his eyes. At least he would show them how a Zealot could die, with pride in the brotherhood and as a servant of his God. But how would he be able to sustain his courage under the hammer of the executioner? How could he bear the cross!

He looked about him. He was standing before Pontius Pilate, the most powerful, most hated figure in the land, representative of the Roman god emperor, Tiberius. The Zealot stared out of smouldering eyes at the Roman, glance now sweeping upwards from the man's white toga, fringed in purple, to his stern face, now obviously in the grip of strong emotion, seeing the thick, black brows drawn together in displeasure, corners of the petulant mouth drawn down. He risked a sideways glance at those other individuals around him. Saw before him, the High Priest, Caiaphas and that other High Priest, Annas. Here too, were the most important dignitaries of the Temple and the wealthy ruling class of Jerusalem. He looked perplexed at their infuriated faces, heard the partly stifled roar of the huge crowd, there must be thousands out there, but why? He could hear shouts of 'Crucify—crucify!' But surely, there could not be such hatred of him? What had he done to warrant this? Then his eyes travelled behind him slightly. He noticed Jesus of Nazareth for the first time. Almost he did not recognize him. He had obviously been tortured, for his face was, well—Barabbas shuddered! Yet Barabbas knew it was the Messiah. He had mingled with the crowds about Jesus too many times in the past not to recognize him even in this state. Barabbas eyes were filled with pity. His eyes met those of Jesus. Even as the two men stared at each other, he heard Pilate's cry,

'You wish me then to release Barabbas to you?'

'Yes! We want Barabbas! Give us Barabbas!' He looked away from Jesus, fixing unbelieving stare on Pilate. The Governor signed to his men, to remove the prisoners bonds, to set him free!

'You are free to leave,' said Pilate, but added menacingly, 'but should you offend again, it will mean instant execution! Go!' Barabbas didn't wait for a second bidding, yet before he moved he looked back at Jesus.

Sudden understanding dawned. The special concession at Passover, the release of a favoured prisoner to the crowd, this was why! And he knew it was the death of Jesus that they sought! If only there were something he could do, if only he had a few hundred Zealots at his back! Why, oh why had the Holy One not listened to reason? Why had he not allowed himself to be proclaimed king! Now he wore a royal robe, but indeed, his kingdom was not to be of this world. Tears started to Barabbas eyes. He gave one last glance at Jesus, imploring forgiveness that his life was being spared at the expense of the Messiah's own. For poignant moment, Jesus stared back at him and although he spoke no words, Barabbas knew that this man, whom he would have made king, understood and forgave. Then he hurried out into the crowd, who received him with joyful chanting, slapping him on the back and crying out his name.

'What shall I do then, with the one you call King of the Jews,' called Pilate, although he knew the answer.

'Crucify him!'

'Why, what crime has he committed!' Pilate made one last feeble attempt. But they knew they had won.

'Crucify him! Crucify him—crucify him!'

Wearily Pilate turned to one of his officers. 'Bring me a basin of water,' he said softly. Surprised, the soldier ran to do his bidding. He returned with a metal basin and a towel. Pilate then rinsed his hands dramatically before the people.

'I am innocent of this man's blood,' he said sombrely. 'It is your responsibility!'

At this, they cried out in triumph, as Caiaphas planted himself firmly before Pilate. 'Let his blood be upon us, and our children,' he cried. Pilate dried his hands. He called to Marcus. He did not look at Jesus as he said tonelessly,

'Take him—and crucify him! I am going to my apartments. I do not wish to see anyone else today!' His eyes fell upon Claudius. He saw the stricken horror on his centurion's face and he scowled at him. 'Do what you have to do,' ordered Pilate to his officers, indicating Jesus, 'And shut the gates on this rabble!' His eyes, as he strode away, were tormented.

Chapter Twenty-Three

John caught Mary of Nazareth to him as she collapsed. Mary of Magdala clasped onto his other arm. Joanna and Susannah held onto each other, faces white with shock! For they had all of them pushed their way between the crowds, until they were close to the front. They had just seen Barabbas released. He had indeed cast an uneasy look at John as he picked his way swiftly between the supportive crowds. They heard Pilate's final words on Jesus.

'Take him and crucify him!'

'No—Oh, no!' moaned Mary, his mother, while the other Mary's face was ravaged by tears. Then the mother of Jesus took a deep, trembling breath. She looked pleadingly at her Son's favourite disciple, 'John—I want to be there. I want him to have the comfort of my presence—when they....!' Her voice broke on a choking sob.

'Are you sure,' asked John gently?

'I am his mother' she replied!

'Lady, we will come too,' sighed Mary Magdalene, placing her strong your arms about the stricken woman. 'John, we all look to you,' she said steadily. She heard her name being called and saw the brothers David and Simeon, who had become separated from them in the crowd. The boys spoke no word, just looked protectively at the women. John signed to them to stay close.

An order rang out! Centurion Lucius appeared from the fortress, leading sixty men. He was mounted, his horse snorting impatiently. The plumes of his helmet stirred slightly, for a chill breeze was arising. Behind him, walked a soldier carrying a placard, bearing the name of the prisoner and his crime. It read 'Jesus of Nazareth—King of the Jews.'

It was the only statement Pilate had allowed, not wishing to give the crowd the satisfaction of his agreeing that Jesus was guilty of any crime.

Behind the man bearing the placard, marched the first ten soldiers, in two's. Then came a figure bent beneath the heavy cross bar of the cross.

The royal robe had been removed from his shoulders, and his tunic was soaked through with his blood and blood dripped from his forehead which still bore the crown of thorns. A hiss of rage rose from the crowd, who shook their fists menacingly, howling expletives at the stumbling figure who could barely manage to bear the weight of the heavy piece of wood on his shoulders. Pain attended every step, as the solid wood opened up his stripes, tearing the shredded flesh even further. It was proving too much for one who had already endured such cruelty. As he staggered along the narrow road leading out of the city to the place of execution, Golgotha, he fell several times, almost fainting with fatigue and throbbing agony. John Mark was amongst those who lined the street. He looked on horrified, staring at the once majestically serene face of the Holy One, now marred by man's malevolence, as he saw Jesus fall to his knees, obviously unable to continue.

'Halt!' The centurion had turned. Lucius quickly sized up the situation. There was no way in which the prisoner could manage to carry the heavy wood cross piece to his destination. Nor did Lucius fancy such slow progress amongst this volatile crowd. Even now, they were shouting out curses and threats to the Nazarene. He saw a tall, muscular figure standing passively at the side of the road. He had two youngsters with him. The man was staring at Jesus with sympathy.

'What is your name, fellow?'

'Simon of Cyrene, so please you sir and these are my sons, Alexander and Rufus.' The handsome, dark skinned man bowed respectfully. He followed the centurion's pointing finger.

'Take it up,' said Centurion Lucius, pointing to the cross piece, glancing uneasily around, his tone brooking no refusal.

Simon did so, gently lifting the heavy plank of wood beneath which the poor man whose painful progress he had stopped to watch was pinned. He lifted it easily to his great shoulders, putting one hand down, to help Jesus to his feet. Then he walked slowly at Jesus side, his two young lads attempting to keep pace with him between the malevolent, struggling crowd. Jesus eyes met his for a brief second with look of gratitude.

Many curious glances were turned upon Jesus in his journey to the city gates. Others now were following the noisy throng of priests, who accompanied the legionaries guarding Jesus. Some were the very men and women who had shouted psalms of praise in his honour a few days ago. At first they did not recognize him. Then they read the notice carried before him, and a heavy murmuring arose. How dare the Romans lay hands on their Messiah, but then, surely if he were the true Messiah, he would not have allowed this to have happened to him? They attached themselves to the crowds, who had accepted the temple gold and who still cried 'Crucify him! Crucify Jesus—crucify the blasphemer!'

Jesus heard their cruel chanting, through the pain, through the soul weariness. No longer did he feel his Father's love about him, for now he bore his burden of the sin of the world, and being deprived of that love, blackness of despair enveloped him. But he knew he must endure all things, for this he had been born.

Claudius and Miriam followed too amongst the crowd. Claudius had insisted to Marcus, that he was going, unofficially if needs be but going he was and nor did the Tribune seek to stop him. Claudius had sent for Miriam, knowing that she must be there, despite the fact that it would cause her great distress, to see what inevitably must happen. His men looked in surprise, as their respected Centurion demanded to be let out of the gates, the graceful form of his wife, clinging to his arm.

Miriam looked about her, terrified by the howling, bloodthirsty mob. She held tightly onto her husband as he made passage for her, men falling back before the dignity of his uniform.

'Is there nothing you can do, Claudius,' cried Miriam, her face wet with tears, for now they had drawn level with the death party. She saw Jesus and she screamed as she saw the Holy Son of God, in such piteous state. Another heard her scream. The disciple John called to them and Claudius recognized Jesus mother and Mary Magdalene and in front of them, Joanna and Susannah, and his adopted son Simeon, together with David. They closed the gap between them, unable to talk because of the shouting, taunting crowd. Mary of Nazareth glanced pathetically at the tall Centurion, a desperate gleam of hope in her eyes, but he shook his head sadly. There was nothing that he could do, would that there were!

The women were close to collapse, as they climbed the steep slopes of the small hill bordering the quarry. This was the place of execution, Golgotha. The soldiers had formed a protective circle around the condemned man, not out of any consideration for him, but because all things had to be done in order, with true Roman efficiency. No attempt must be made to rescue the prisoner, not that he would get far in the state he was in. They ordered the crowd to stand back. It had already thinned out a great deal, much to the soldiers' relief. Caiaphas and Annas, and most of the Temple hierarchy had returned triumphantly either to their homes or to the Temple to rest after their battle of wills with Pilate. They sensed that they might have to face eventual retribution from the Governor, and felt uneasy at the thought. At least, Jesus was being dealt with! 'Praise be to Jehovah,' they murmured self righteously, yet slight apprehension began to stir within their breasts. Pilate could be ferocious in his rages.

But some of the chief priests had come the complete distance in order to keep Caiaphas informed of the end of this man who dared to call himself, the son of the Living God! They peered as best they could between the soldiers, who faced outwards, swords at the ready. Now they had recovered their breath from their climb, they started to shout jibes again, staring upwards at two crosses, which already bore victims, thieves it was said. They craned their necks forward, as they glimpsed Jesus being stripped of his garments. Simon of Cyrene had already released the heavy plank of wood into the hands of a legionary and stepped back sadly. He went to his to young sons, shielding their eyes. He did not want them to see the horror which was to follow. Suddenly the crowd became silent. They heard a faint cry of agony, as heavy nails were hammered, one into each arm, slightly above the wrist. Then the prone figure was hoisted erect, for they had lain him flat on his back, hands extended over the heavy cross piece, upon which they had forced him to rest his shoulders, whilst a soldier with heavy hammer, had driven the huge nails in, with practised stroke.

The gaping crowd saw Jesus form being held above the waist, as the soldiers manhandled him upwards, inching the crossbeam into the slot prepared to receive it, so that he was a few feet above the ground. Then another nail was hammered through the crossed ankles, smashing through the bones. Another wail escaped Jesus lips, as the weight of his body, suspended from his arms had jerked the body downwards, causing the nails to lodge at the wrists, leaving gaping wounds. Above his head, the placard which had been carried before him, stated 'Jesus of Nazareth—King of the Jews.' His lips moved. They heard these incredible words,

'Father—forgive them—for they know not what they do!'

The priests ignored his words. They craned their necks to read the placard. Then some of their number kilted their robes to return to Pilate. Furiously he came down to the gates at their repeated summons.

'The sign above Jesus head, it is wrong!' so exclaimed a chief priest, staring defiantly at the Prefect.

'Wrong, what do you mean, wrong?' scowled Pilate! Really, he had had as much as he could endure today with this stiff necked people.

'You should have had it written, this man claimed to be the King of the Jews—not that he is the King of the Jews!' They waited expectantly, waiting for him to issue another order, to redress this obvious mistake.

'What I have written, I have written,' blazed Pilate, and seeing the fury in his eyes, they backed away nervously and thwarted in their aims, returned to Golgotha, the Place of the Skull. Claudius and the apostle John eased their way as near as possible to the base of the cross which was still surrounded by a strong barrier of legionaries. Claudius noted with contempt that a few of them had drawn to one side, as crouching down they were casting lots for their victim's clothes. True it was the custom, one of the perks of an execution party, but not for this prisoner! Yet there was nothing he could do. Centurion Lucius was in command of the crucifixion and Marcus had only allowed his friend to attend in a private capacity, for he knew the anguish of soul, Claudius was enduring and had readily agreed that he would bring his friend's petition for immediate resignation before the Prefect.

The four men who formed the official execution squad had divided up his few articles of clothing, but now they held up the blood stained robe, the seamless garment of Galilean weave which he constantly wore, woven in one piece from top to bottom. It was a pity to tear it. It was this they were now casting lots for.

'Let's not tear it,' they cried. 'Let's decide by lot, who will get it!'

'This is in fulfilment of scripture,' said a deep voice, and Centurion Claudius glanced curiously at John. 'It is written so in the psalms.' John's face was contorted by agony, yet there was strange look of acceptance also.

'I wish to be nearer to my son,' said a voice, suddenly firm and Mary of Nazareth, head held high, demanded of the soldier in front of her to allow her access. She was followed by the other women, Mary Magdalene close at her side. Centurion Claudius nodded to Lucius, who saw his commander for the first time.

'Let them through,' said Claudius quietly. Lucius nodded. If it was Claudius wish well, it could do no harm at this stage. John offered Mary his arm, and now that she was to have her wish, she suddenly clung to it. Above her head, in utmost agony, hung her beloved son, his lacerated body barely clinging to life. She gave a moan. Then she raised her head slightly, as she heard the two thieves, one on each side of him, calling breathlessly to each other. What was it they were saying? She realized that one was trying to hurl insults at her son.

'Aren't you the Christ? Then save yourself—and us,' he sneered! Then the other criminal rebuked him. He had once heard Jesus preach. He gasped out an indignant protest.

'Don't you fear God, since you are under the same sentence? We are punished justly, for we are getting what our deeds deserve.' He jerked his head feebly. 'But this man has done nothing wrong!' Then he called softly to Jesus, and John leaned forward, barely making out the words.

'Jesus, remember me, when you come into your kingdom!' But Jesus heard that cry. These comforting words came clearly between the broken lips of the Son of God.

'I tell you the truth. Today—you will be with me—in Paradise!' As he spoke, a strange darkness seemed to be falling around them and men started to moan in sudden fear, for it was only the sixth hour! Darker it grew and darker and many started to hurry home, for surely a great storm must be brewing!

Mary tried to draw nearer to the cross and he became aware of her. With great effort, trying to ignore the screaming agony of damaged nerves and his raging thirst, he bent his head slightly. He saw Mary, his gentle mother and John, his beloved disciple. He called to Mary.

'Dear Woman,' he whispered. His eyes turned towards John, 'Here is your son,' he said, then still looking at John, the quiet voice continued, 'Here is your mother!' His voice faltered to a halt, as a moan escaped him. Did John understand the commission he had just laid on him? He did. From that moment on, John, son of Zebedee took Mary of Nazareth into his home. The mother of the Messiah was now to be treated as his own.

Now darkness encroached entirely upon the scene and the Roman soldiers muttered uneasily. It was said that the crucified man possessed magical powers—even that he was the son of the Jewish God. A chill wind arose, moaning in from the desert, stinging sand in its furious breath.

Three hours passed. The women had retreated a hundred yards, not able to bear to be too close, nor wishing to intrude on his silent agony. All they could do in the semi blackness was to pray through shaking lips. But Claudius remained there, standing stiffly at Lucius side.

'What do you think is happening, sir,' asked Lucius uneasily? 'I had thought at first, that this was an eclipse of the sun. But an eclipse never lasts for this period of time!'

Then, from above their heads, the dying man gave an anguished cry, 'Eloi—Eloi--lama sabachthani!'

One of the onlookers, a Jew who had but imperfectly caught the words exclaimed, 'He is calling for Elijah!' Nor did any know that the faltering voice had really cried,

'Father! Father—why have you forsaken me?'

Before the nails had been hammered into his hands, the soldiers had offered Jesus wine drugged with myrrh which he had refused, giving them cause for respect. Now one of them got up and took a sponge. He filled it with sour wine, put it on a stick and raised it, offering it to Jesus to drink. Perhaps the Holy man wished to say something more.

'Now leave him alone. Let's see if Elijah comes,' they muttered. In the strange blackness, illumined only by the fire which the Romans had lit to throw some light on the scene, men began to fear what would happen next.

Jesus slowly bowed his head, in acceptance of the fulfilment of the burden he so cruelly bore for those present—and for those yet to come.

'It is finished,' he said, the words echoing through the forecourts of time! Then as his head drooped upon his breast, he gave one last piercing cry, which rang out loudly in the silence.

'Father—into your hands—I commit my spirit!'

When he had said this, he breathed his last. There was an immense flash of lightning! It zigzagged across the sky, followed by a low growl of thunder which reverberated amongst the hills. Then a sound, a terrible rumbling shook the ground on which the soldiers and spectators were standing, and a rift opened, men screaming and just managing to draw away in time. In the Temple, Caiaphas stood in terror as the heavy veil, shielding the Holy Place, was rent from top to bottom. In the rest of

Jerusalem, buildings trembled and some fell.

Lucius turned to Claudius, his young face wild with fear. He glanced up at the still figure above his head.

'Surely this man was the Son of God,' he breathed in awe!

'Lucius, he was! Never will there be such again, and we killed him!' Claudius voice was strangely muffled. At last, the few priests still present noticed with some relief that Jesus seemed to have expired. Stumbling and with much trepidation, for fear of another earth tremor, they made their way to the Antonia. A deputation was sent to Pilate. He had been sitting alone, acutely aware of the weird atmospheric conditions, the strange darkness and the earthquake and knew it to be connected to the Nazarene. Now he came downstairs to their summons.

'We want the bodies taken down, before sunset,' they demanded. 'We ask that you have their legs broken to speed death, that the Sabbath be not profaned!'

'Let it be done,' muttered Pilate. So the order went to the soldiers, to break the legs of the dying men. They smashed the bones of the two thieves, ignoring their screams of agony, which soon ceased, as the men asphyxiated, unable to support themselves longer, on the small peg seat of their crosses, as their breathing was cut off.

'This one is already dead, sir,' said a legionary to Lucius. 'But I suppose I had better make sure.' Without waiting for confirmation, he drew his shoulder back, then reached up violently with his spear, thrusting it deep into Jesus side, making gaping hole in the rib cage. Blood and water slowly welled. The Son of God was surely dead.

'Not one of his bones will be broken,' said a trembling voice! 'And again, as it says in scripture, they will look upon the one they have pierced.' Then Joseph of Arimathea placed shaking hand upon his colleague Nicodemus.

'Come, my friend, we have work to do! The last service we can now afford the Messiah!' They hurried together to the Antonia, asking admittance, no thoughts of defilement worrying them. Pilate received them.

'My Lord Prefect,' said Nicodemus, with quiet courtesy. 'We have come to ask your gracious permission to take down the body of Jesus of

Nazareth and to give it burial.'

'I have my own tomb in which I wish to lay him,' said Joseph of Arimathea boldly. 'It is newly cut out of the rock, we will lay him there.' He bowed his head before Pilate, but there was no fear in his eyes, indeed, his grey beard jutted out firmly before him as he raised his glance to the Prefect's face

'What! Is he dead already then,' asked Pilate, seemingly surprised. But secretly he was glad. The strange blackness, which was only now lifting, combined with the earthquake, had badly scared him. He felt it was reprisal from the strange man from Galilee, whom he would have saved had he been able. His wife Claudia was completely distraught, refusing to speak with him. She had thrown herself upon her bed, prostrate with grief. So Pilate nodded absently, wondering how best to placate his wife.

'I wish first to speak with the centurion in charge of the execution. Have him brought to me!' A soldier hurried to do his bidding. They waited.

'Centurion Lucius is the King of the Jews dead,' he inquired? Jesus had indeed earned that title he thought grimly and in his own mind continued to think of the Galilean so.

'Yes, my Lord. He died bravely, I have never met such a man before,' blurted out Lucius. Pilate nodded thoughtfully.

'Then yes, Joseph of Arimathea, and you Lord Nicodemus, I give you permission to take down the body, and to give it burial according to your custom.' Pilate dismissed them with a nod. He looked at Lucius.

'You look tired, centurion. Not a pleasant duty, crucifixion. Get yourself down with the other officers and drink deeply of some wine, boy! Off with you, no, wait! Did you see Centurion Claudius?'

'Yes, sir,' replied Lucius. 'He stood with me at Golgotha. 'Without his presence, I would have found matters trying. It was my first crucifixion.'

'It will probably not be your last,' said Pilate ironically. 'Now go, get that wine!'

Nicodemus and one of his servants staggered under the weight of the seventy five pounds of myrrh and aloes. The Pharisee was unused to such labour, yet somehow he seemed to receive strength to carry the heavy bag. Joseph of Arimathea bore a bundle of strips of clean linen. They set their faces towards Golgotha. Nicodemus sank panting onto the ground, at the base of the central cross. Joseph and the servant looked down at him anxiously.

'Are you unwell, my friend?'

'I'm just a little weary and wondering how we are going to be able to take the body down unaided!' Nicodemus placed hands over his eyes, grieving.

'I will help you,' said a low voice. Startled, they glanced around, there were indeed some few people still lingering, unable to believe that now at the end of the traumatic day all was as they thought, finished. Now one by one, they started to make return to the city for the Passover celebration. But it was none of these who had spoken, but a Roman centurion, who bowed gravely before them.

'We have permission from Pilate, to remove the body of Jesus for burial,' said Joseph authoritatively. Then with very human look of consternation, he added 'But we had not thought how to lift him down.' Joseph cast considering eyes at the stalwart Roman, but it was more than he dared to hope, that a high ranking Roman officer would so demean himself, as to handle a corpse. But this Roman did! He showed them what to do to help him and at last, they straightened the stiffening limbs, shuddering as they saw the ghastly wounds left now that Claudius had withdrawn the nails, and that huge gash in his riven side. The violent wind that had arisen in the storm, when the face of the sun had been masked for three hours, and darkness had covered the land, had swept fine covering of dust and sand over peoples clothing, and the crucified bodies alike. Jesus bruised and broken body was covered with a grey dust that had swirled from the neighbouring quarry.

'Will you help us further, Centurion,' asked Nicodemus. 'We need help to carry him to the tomb, but first, we will cover him.' As he looked at the officer, he saw his face was swollen with weeping and wondered at the cause. Then he removed his cloak from his shoulders, covering that battered body now almost unrecognizable as that of the gracious figure, who had told him that sacred truth of being born again, when Nicodemus had sought the Holy One on the Mount of Olives, and learned that which had turned his life around.

'Did you know Jesus of Nazareth,' he asked Claudius gently, as he straightened?

'I know him to be the Son of the Living God,' replied Claudius, in a choking voice. 'Come, let me help you. I will carry him for you.' Claudius mighty arms carried his precious burden. He hardly looked where he walked, merely following the two members of the Sanhedrin, the only two, who had loved and tried to protect Jesus.

'It is here, Centurion,' said Joseph of Arimathea, 'Do you wish to wait while we do what we Jews traditionally do? You might perhaps like to sit on that rock over there.'

Claudius realized that they didn't want a Gentile watching their preparation of the body for burial. He very gently laid Jesus body before them and departed some twenty yards. He did not see the gentle cleansing of the corpse, each of those stripes and terrible wounds, bearing witness of the cruelty of men, did not see the body carefully covered with mixture of Myrrh and aloes, the limbs wrapped about with linen bandages. At last, the thing was done, just his face remained exposed, bruised, a mass of cuts which stood out lividly against the deathly pallor. With utmost gentleness, his chest heaving with grief, Nicodemus wrapped the face and head with a fine linen cloth.

Joseph of Arimathea helped him lift the still figure, the white robe of whose ministry was exchanged for the white wrappings of the tomb. They stooped and entered that new cut place of the dead. And now they laid him on that narrow shelf of rock, within the tomb which Nicodemus had ordered built against his own death. The two men knelt in prayer, then the words of mourning over, they bent and came out of the narrow entrance of the rock tomb—now to seal it. A huge boulder needed to be pushed in the groove prepared for it, to block the entrance, sealing it against wild beasts. They looked about for the Centurion to aid them. Where had he gone? They called, softly, urgently. They did not want any to see where they had laid Jesus. Claudius was coming towards them accompanied by a small group of women.

'My name is Mary Magdalene,' said one woman, whose heavily veiled face, was bent low. 'We are followers of the Messiah, have been with him, through most of his ministry. We wished to see where you have laid him.' Her voice was rough from weeping.

'Lady, he is here in my own tomb. I am a member of the council, Joseph of Arimathea, but I did not consent to this crime.' He watched, as Mary looked within the tomb, stretching her hands out then dropping them to her sides.

'Tomorrow is the Sabbath,' she whispered. 'But on the day following it, I would like to bring spices, if you permit?'

'Lady, you know now where he lies. Surely you and your companions may come as you please. But now, I think it would be wise if we were to all return to our homes.' Joseph of Arimathea made courtly bow to this unknown woman, acknowledging the small group about her. Then he remembered the Centurion.

'I do not even know your name. Will you not tell me who you are, that I may know who to thank, and to pray for, when.....?'

'My name is Claudius,' replied the centurion, voice gruff with emotion. 'This lady,' he pointed to one of the veiled women, 'Is Miriam, my wife. We both loved Jesus of Nazareth, even as I see, you did also.'

'Are you that Claudius, who holds high position in the Antonia,' asked Nicodemus in amazement. He had thought the officer looked familiar. 'You have an adopted son, Simeon?'

'Yes, I am he. But I intend to resign my commission,' replied Claudius, 'and to return to Galilee.' He held out his hand to Miriam, who had waited those weary hours with the other women. Jesus mother had been led away hours since, by John, son of Zebedee. Now Claudius must conduct these exhausted women back into the city. He raised a hand in farewell salute to Joseph and Nicodemus.

'My friend,' said Nicodemus quietly, 'If ever I can do anything to help you in return, know that I am indebted to you.'

'I make this same pledge,' added Joseph, and watched as the Roman officer, guided the distraught group of women away from the place of death. Surely it must be the strange power of Jesus of Nazareth that had caused enemy of the Jews, to behave with such graciousness. What was it that Nicodemus had explained to him of Jesus words—about being born again!

Caiaphas tossed upon his bed that night, unable to sleep. Every time he closed his eyes, that face of the Nazarene, was imprinted on his inner vision—the shimmering gold gaze, stripping through the sanctimonious mask which Caiaphas wore to deceive the world. Time and again, he sat up in bed, terrified. Suppose Jesus had indeed been more than mere man!

Even Pilate had been affected by him, as had that master of cruelty Herod Antipas! He clambered out of bed, walking restlessly up and down, pacing his chamber biting his lips in agitation. Suddenly he stood rock still. What was it that Jesus had said, that he would arise on the third day? No, but that was thing impossible, wasn't it? But supposing Jesus disciples decided to remove the body from the tomb, then gave out false reports of his having risen! Why, this could cause even worse unrest than had gone before. He pulled at his hair in agitation. There was so much that was inexplicable in this affair!

What of the informer, Judas Iscariot! He who without blenching in the slightest at betraying the Rabbi whose chosen disciple he was, yet as soon as he heard Jesus sentenced had returned to the Temple, throwing the thirty silver coins he had received as payment for his treachery at the feet of the chief priests! Caiaphas remembered that high pitched voice screaming, screaming, hands upraised above his head, eyes wild with shame and sorrow. He had looked haunted, gaunt, seemed to be demented with fear.

'I have sinned,' he had wept, 'for I have betrayed innocent blood!'

'What is that to us,' the chief priests had cried. 'That is your responsibility!' He had made a gesture of despair, before rushing out of their presence. They had looked in perplexity at the silver coins. One of them bent, and commenced to pick up the scattered money. He held it towards Caiaphas.

'It is against the law, to put this in the treasury, since it is blood money!' After hurried conversation, they decided to use the money to purchase a piece of land known as the 'Potter's field' to be used as a future burial ground for foreigners. Nor did they know that while they yet wrangled, whilst still in a state of nervous exhaustion after the protracted trial of the Nazarene, that even while they decided on the eventual use of Iscariot's money, that man had rushed out beyond the city gates and hanged himself. The tree from which his twitching body hung suspended, creaked under the weight until at last, the rotten branch snapped and the mortal remains of Judas Iscariot, plunged down the steep slope, rupturing his abdomen. The place was to be named, Akeldama— the field of blood.

But Caiaphas heard of it later that night, with cynical amusement. Yet now, as he paced his cold marble floor it rose again in his mind, together with other details brought to him by the priests who had followed Jesus to the place of execution. He had heard of the crowd of Jesus supporters, who had joined in the death procession and of large numbers of women weeping for him and of Jesus addressing them.

'Daughters of Jerusalem—do not weep for me! Weep for yourselves and your children. For the time will come, when you will say—Blessed are the barren women, the wombs that never bore and the breasts that never nursed.' He had then quoted from the Prophet Hosea, saying 'Then they will say to the mountains, fall on us and to the hills cover us. For if men do these things when the tree is green, what will they do when it is dry?'

Caiaphas pondered these words, seeking their meaning. He also marvelled that Jesus had refused the pain killing drug offered to him at the point of execution. Why had he done that? Why too, when he had nothing to gain, had he breathed forgiveness to his executioners? The whole business was spiked with mystery. Caiaphas did not believe in an afterlife. The Sadducees did not, although the Pharisees did, but now a strange unease flooded his mind. What if one day, he should be held accountable for the death of Jesus, who had indeed possessed strange powers! Suppose the incredible were possible, that Jesus had been the promised one, and that he, Caiaphas had killed him! Suppose the Almighty God of Israel should demand answer for his treatment of His Son!

Caiaphas shuddered, forcing the thought back to the further recesses of his mind. But what must be attended to, was to place guards about the tomb. He already knew where Jesus had been entombed. One of his spies had lingered by the cross, and had seen the two members of the Sanhedrin, who had dared to oppose the High Priest, remove the body, with the help of a Roman officer and followed the small party to the garden tomb, had taken careful note of the cave so used.

Pontius Pilate ground his teeth together in exasperation, as he was told that a deputation of chief priests and Pharisees were asking to speak with him. He was still furious at their having got the better of him yesterday and that against his better judgement, he should have had to crucify the man who claimed to be king of a spiritual kingdom, who despite his wounds and blood spattered robe, had been the most regal figure Pilate had ever met. But it was done and Pilate would always hold Caiaphas responsible, for his wife's nervous collapse. Claudia was steadfastly refusing to speak with him, and nor according to her slaves was she eating.

'Well, my Lord High Priest, what would you have with me today? Another king you want crucified?' He bent his most autocratic look on Caiaphas.

'Lord!' It was Annas who replied, seeing his son-in-law's face darken at being spoken to in such fashion. 'We remember that while he was still alive, that deceiver said, "After three days I will rise again." So give the order for the tomb to be made secure until the third day. Otherwise his disciples may come and steal the body and tell the people, he has been raised from the dead! This last deception,' he added hastily, will be worse than the first!' His eyes rested on Plate's face, trying to get the Prefect to understand the urgency of the situation.

Pilate looked as though he were about to explode. He controlled himself with difficulty.

'Take a guard, your Temple guards, and make the tomb as secure as you know how!' They hurried from his presence, bowing respectfully, aware that his ire was rising. So it was that four guards were set about the tomb, to be replaced every four hours by another shift. They bore javelins and wore swords, their uniforms paralleling those of the Romans and their training was almost as rigorous. They laughed together somewhat nervously, as they stared about the empty garden, fragrant with wild jasmine and bright with scarlet and purple bougainvillaea. It was obvious that a gardener had been trying to cultivate this wild spot, in order to soften the bleak appearance of the sealed rock cavern, where many interlocking chambers had been prepared to take at least several bodies. Joseph of Arimathea had gone to trouble and expense to provide himself with a final resting-place suitable to one of his rank and for future generations of his family. One of the soldiers spat reflectively.

'Uri, I do not like this place! To guard a tomb is eerie commission, especially one housing remains of one as mysterious as this Jesus of Nazareth! I will be glad when we are relieved!'

'Can't say I care much for it myself, Michael. I am glad we are not taking either of the night watches!' The speaker leaned back against the huge stone sealing the tomb in slight gesture of bravado. 'But then, the dead can't hurt us! And the troublesome Rabbi from Galilee is most certainly dead!' He picked up a wineskin, for there were none to see, and took a deep gulp. 'Well, after this duty, we are off until early tomorrow morning, we come on again, two hours before dawn.'

'But that is still dark--I cannot say I fancy it! However, we are only to guard the tomb for a few days. The Strategios says, it is because Jesus announced, that he would be crucified and rise from the dead on the third day!'

'Well, I hardly think that is likely to happen,' joked a third man, stroking his chin in amusement. 'I am surprised that the High Priest took such nonsense seriously!'

'You know we are not here because of any thought of that!' It was their sergeant who spoke. 'We are here, to prevent his disciples attempting to steal the body away, and thereby spreading rumours of his pretended resurrection. So keep a sharp eye out men. It would go ill with us, if we allowed anyone to tamper with the tomb.' At this, the others straightened up, each one staring in different direction, whilst the sergeant explored the perimeter of the garden.

It was evening. John Mark stood before the sad eyed women, in Lady Joanna's villa. All were exhausted from grief, Mary of Nazareth's face so ravaged by sorrow, that he was hard put to recognize her, before she lowered her veil.

'Lady,' he said gently, 'I am come to invite all in the household to leave this place, which is too close to Herod's palace for safety. Many know that you are here and although it is most unlikely that Caiaphas will take action against those who followed Jesus, there is slight danger! Therefore, I have consulted with my mother and as we have many rooms in our villa, I suggest that you all slip out quietly and come with me. The disciples are already there and Lazarus.'

'If you think it is best,' said Mary listlessly,' then of course we will come with you.' She glanced around at the others, particularly at Joanna, whose guests they were. Joanna's grief stricken violet eyes fixed anxiously on John Mark's face.

'But will it be safe to go out of the main gates? The Herodian guards are always patrolling the neighbourhood of the palace! Chuza, my husband, knows that we are here. He is aware of all that happens in Jerusalem.'

'He will not know this! Now listen carefully. Take just a few possessions such as you can easily carry, and do as I say.'

So it was, that with the help of David and Simeon that John Mark managed to help the women to scale the six foot wall that enclosed the garden at the back of the villa. As they jumped the last few feet, with David to steady them, they found themselves in a narrow, stepped walkway. Even their servants had not seen them leave. Soon, Mark's mother, also named Mary, welcomed her grieving guests. The little huddle of scared, dispirited disciples waiting to greet them, merely muttered few words and stole away to their own rooms. Sorrow filled the house.

Mary Magdalene placed a restraining hand on Peter's arm, as he was about to follow the other men.

'Peter, in the morning, I am going to the tomb to pray and to bring spices and sweet herbs.'

'You should be careful, Mary.' He shook his head disapprovingly. 'I would advise against it and yet, if you feel that you wish to pay this last service to the Master then who am I to dissuade you.' He, who had lacked courage to confess his Lord, knew he had not the authority to prevent brave action by one who had followed him to the cross.

'Where is Miriam,' asked Lazarus, who had just realized that the women had arrived.

'I can tell you that,' replied Lady Joanna. 'Miriam sent word today, that her husband, the Centurion, has resigned his commission. It seems that Pilate has given permission for Claudius to retire to the villa at Capernaum. He is to be given property there and is to retain the honorary title of Centurion.' She sighed softly. 'We shall all of us miss Miriam! She has left with her husband and even now, they are on their way to Galilee!'

'So Simeon, what will you do, and Sarah? Join them there?' Lazarus eyed them protectively. They were so young, this couple who had shared his home.

'Not yet. We will stay here with the rest of you,' said Simeon firmly. 'Something more has to happen.' They all looked at him, not knowing what he meant. Then the servants came to show the weary Galileans to their bedchambers. John, son of Zebedee, bowed before Mary of Nazareth, before the young slave girl led her above. He had left the distressed mother at Joanna's villa yesterday whilst he went to visit John Mark, at whose house he heard the other disciples had assembled. He had to make a decision as to where to take Mary, for it had been Jesus last dying commission to him to care for his mother. To John, it would remain a sacred duty to take Mary of Nazareth, as his own mother.

'Honoured Lady,' said John softly. 'I ask that you remain safe within doors here, until the time comes for return to Galilee.' She nodded apathetically, then managed faintest smile tinged with gratitude to this man, whom her own dearest son, had instructed her to regard as her own son. What would she have done yesterday, without his strong courage to strengthen her? She looked at his weary, worried face and saw behind the tiredness, to the inner strength and spirituality, that would cause this man, once in filled with the Holy Spirit to write down as gospel, all that he had learned of Jesus and his doctrine in such a way that the shining truth and love, would blaze through his writings, bearing his Master's message to those in distant centuries yet to come.

It was two hours to dawn, on the first day of the week, it being the start of the third day that Jesus had been laid to rest in the stone cold tomb. The watch had just changed; those who had taken the night duty, glad to be relieved of an unusual and distasteful break from their normal Temple policing. Guards Uri, Michael and Arah arranged themselves about the tomb. Their sergeant stared after the departing night guards. According to them, nothing untoward had happened, no single person intruding into that place of death. Even the gardener, had been forbidden yesterday to perform his normal duties, not at least until the third day had passed. A chill mist hung about the place. They gave perfunctory examination to the seal that had previously been placed on the tomb. It was still intact! Two hours to wait now, until the sun's rays brought warmth and light and lifted their spirits. The sergeant bent his hands down, to the glowing embers of the small fire their predecessors had built against the cold, as his eyes searched the perimeter of the garden, but no intruders moved in the stillness. All was peaceful and he and his men who stood so vigilantly in front of the boulder sealing the tomb, relaxed slightly.

'Here lads, I've a skin of wine!' He beckoned them forwards, with a grin, and nothing loathe they came towards him. The sergeant held the wine-skin, taking a deep gulp, before offering it first to Uri. He wiped his lips with the back of his hand, then his mouth opened slackly and his eyes bulged. For at this very moment the earth started to shudder, and a brilliant light suddenly shone about them. Terrified, the guards glanced behind them, at the mouth of the tomb! A figure, throbbing with light, light brighter than lightning flash and wearing clothes whiter than driven snow, was approaching the tomb entrance. The four men cried out aloud in their terror, for the angel gave slight touch to the huge stone and pushed it aside. He seated himself upon it.

'Mercy—mercy Great One!' cried Uri, his face pale as death. The men held onto each other, too frightened even to run. Their limbs shook! What was this? What was happening? They thought they saw movement in the tomb, but after briefest glance looked away, hearts pounding with fear. The Angel of the Lord made a slight gesture, which the sergeant partly glimpsed. On legs that seemed turned to water, he started towards the bushes lining one wall of the garden, his men stumbling after him. There was another noise, like thunder shaking between the hills, and the men collapsed in frightened heap and remained thus, almost paralysed.

Chapter Twenty-Four

Mary Magdalene and Joanna picked their way carefully down the steep sides of the hill, until they reached the wall bordering the garden where the cave tomb was situated, which had been prepared for Joseph of Arimathea and his family. Hewn out of the rock by skilled masons, it now housed instead all that remained of the mortal form of their beloved Lord Jesus, Son of the Living God. Alas, he was dead and the women wept as they opened the small gate, nor saw the huddled figures of the guards some thirty feet from them. Joanna paused, her violet eyes trying to pierce the gloom, which was dramatically dispelled as she rounded a rocky buttress. She gasped and placed sudden shocked hand on Mary's arm, lowering her eyes, before the sudden pulsing, throbbing unearthly radiance.

'Mary---over there! What is that light?'

'I don't know,' whispered Mary, through shaking lips. 'Come, we must go on, to anoint his body with these spices and perfumes. But there is going to be a problem, we have not considered how will we be able to move that enormous stone!'

'Mary, look, the light's getting even brighter—nor is it yet dawn! Oh and see, the great stone has been removed! The light is coming from within the tomb itself!' Suddenly Joanna pulled her veil over her eyes in terror, and flung herself prostrate on the ground. But Mary, eyes smarting from the unceasing tears she had been shedding, since her Lord died, moved forward on trembling legs. She was too distraught even to fear the wondrous being that stood before her at the tomb, raising a hand in movement of peace.

'Do not be afraid,' intoned the Angel in deeply resonating voice. 'I know you are looking for Jesus who was crucified. But he is not here! He has risen, as he said he would!' He beckoned to Mary and to Joanna who had clambered to her feet.

'Come and see the place where He lay,' continued the Angel, and Mary stared into the tomb, looking at the shelf on which Jesus had been laid. It was empty!

'He is not there,' cried Mary, calling distractedly to Joanna

'Go quickly,' the angel continued, 'And tell his disciples He has risen from the dead! He is going before you into Galilee. There you will see Him!' intoned the Angel.

With a moan of terror Mary fled, catching at Joanna's hand. The two women ran until their chests burned from lack of breath. Afterwards, they had little memory of that rush through early sunlight, along still deserted streets. At last they reached the villa where the others waited.

'Peter! John!' the women cried, to the first disciples they saw. 'The tomb is empty—we saw an Angel!' Each one tried to present her own story, then Mary came out with the only fact she could really assimilate.

'They have taken the Lord out of the tomb and we don't know where they have put him—only the Angel said that he has risen, will look for you in Galilee!'

Peter and John looked at each other in amazement. Mary was usually so calm, so reliable. But this story—it was incredible! Her grief must have destroyed her reason. Yet, Joanna was telling the same tale. They must go for themselves and see what this portended.

They hurried out of the city gate, the women following behind more slowly. The sun had now fully risen, pulsing over the top of the city, burnishing the gold crested Temple whose priests had rejected and sentenced the Son of the Mighty, Living God whom they purported to serve. Its radiance polished the white marble colonnades under which the Holy One had loved to teach, licking over the villas of the rich, the palace of Herod Antipas and warming the old stone of the crumbling buildings of the lower city. Now the sun shot high, its rays penetrating and dispersing the mists veiling the garden at the bottom of the hill of the skull, Golgotha, the garden where lay the tomb of Jesus of Nazareth.

John had thoughts too awesome even to frame, bursting through his head. He reached the tomb slightly ahead of Peter, but could hardly bring himself to enter, to confirm that which he was daring to believe. For he had remembered the Lord's words, so often spoken, 'The Son of Man will be lifted up—but will rise again on the third day!' He stooped his head, and stared inside.

There, neatly folded on the shelf where the body would obviously have lain were the folded grave clothes, the fine linen which had so recently encased their Lord's lifeless form! John withdrew his head, his heart pounding with the turbulence of his emotions. Peter had now arrived. He pushed past John, going right inside the tomb.

'Look!' shouted Peter, in utter amazement, 'Here are the strips of linen, folded! John, I don't understand! Yes, and look here! It's the cloth that would have covered his head, lying separately. What does it all mean?'

Then John stilled the tumult in his breast sufficiently, to completely enter the tomb himself. As he stared at the pile of folded linen and the cloth that had covered the dear face of his Lord, he now believed, even though for the last three days he had not quite understood that which Jesus had so often and so patiently told them. He looked into Peter's troubled eyes, seeing his friends black bearded face contorted with worry. He raised a shaking hand.

'He had risen—Peter, he has risen!'

'Let us go,' cried Peter, plainly deeply distressed, unable to comprehend. So they went, nor tried to prevent the women, who had now caught up with them, from remaining. Joanna watched them go, seeing the amazement on their faces.

'I will stay here,' said Joanna softly, for she was unable emotionally to approach the tomb a second time. But Mary Magdalene did. She stood outside it, crying as though her heart would break. Had she dreamt the vision of the angel whom she had encountered on her first visit that morning? She had to know, she had to try to understand the supernatural happenings almost beyond her powers of belief. She bent her head, and looked in, placing hands in front of her face, dazzled by the brilliant light, for now two angels clothed in white, were sitting where once Jesus body had lain.

'Woman?' and their voices sounded like the chime of deep bells. 'Woman, why are you crying?

'They have taken my Lord away,' she wept. 'And I don't know where they have put him!' She shrank away from these awesome beings, sent from the courts of God, remembering all that the first angel had said to her of the Lord having risen! But how could she believe this? No, someone had stolen his body. But then, what of those strips of linen that had shrouded his form, the neatly folded face covering? She blundered back into the garden, her eyes welling with bitter tears. She would never see him again, the wonderful Son of God, who had changed her life, filled it with joy, but was gone forever.

The sun was streaming brightly in the garden now, the early mist steaming as it evaporated, the flowers making vivid patches of colour and the few trees rustling in the slight puff of wind. Mary saw all through glitter of tears, but sudden movement made her look up. A figure stood before her. It wasn't Joanna but a man. Who was he? Her swollen eyelids lifted, as she tried to focus through blur of tears. Surely the only person likely to be in this garden of death would be the man who tended the flowers, the gardener! Then—a strangely familiar voice asked gently,

'Woman—why are you crying? Who is it that you are looking for?'

It must be the gardener. Mary drew her veil over her face. It was not seemly for him to see her grief.

'Sir, if you have carried him away tell me where you have put him,' her voice broke on a sob, as she continued with determination, 'And I will get him!' She stood still before the man, her bosom heaving.

'Mary!' The voice fell like healing balm.

She raised her head incredulously. It was his voice, it was the Lords!

'Rabboni!' it was her favourite word for him, 'Teacher?' She tossed back her veil, and now at last she knew! It was true. He had risen! Jesus of Nazareth, Son of Almighty God, had risen from the dead! She fell before him, laughing and crying all at once, as she tried to hold onto his feet, watering them with tears as once she had before, only now the tears were of joy! Praise be to God—he was alive!

Jesus smiled down on her, expression of utmost tenderness in his eyes, as he gently stepped back from her clasp He could not stay now, must make her understand this.

'Do not hold onto me, for I have not yet returned to the Father!' She looked up and arose on trembling legs. 'Go instead to my brothers, and tell them,' and his voice rose prophetically, 'I am returning to my Father and to your Father! To my God and your God!' As she stared at him, realization dawned on Mary, of the magnitude of the event she had witnessed, as she accepted that Jesus was supernatural being as well as man. He was, he really was, Son of the Living God, from whom he had come and to whom he was now to return! Death had not been able to hold him. Dimly she began to realize what this knowledge would mean to centuries of men yet unborn.

She turned to take his message, looking back once. He smiled. When she looked a second time, she saw him no more. But her heart was now bursting with sheer happiness. She found Joanna sitting dejectedly on the other side of the garden wall, on a flat topped rock.

'Joanna! I've seen him! He is alive! Jesus is alive!'

'Mary, what can you mean?' Joanna's eyes opened in wonder. A glimmer of hope was dawning in her eyes, as she stared at Mary.

'Jesus was in the garden but now. At first, I hardly recognized him through my tears. Then he spoke my name. He said 'Mary'! You know his dear voice! He goes soon to God his Father, but wants to meet with the disciples first!'

'Well, let us go swiftly, Mary. How greatly blessed are you of all mankind, that the Holy One should show himself first to you, give you the commission to tell his apostles. Mary, I cannot wait to see their faces!'

The two young women hurried back towards the city, faces once stiff with weeping, now soft with joy!

The disciples heard Mary's words with disbelief. Only one man smiled, his joy matching hers! John raised his hands in praise, as he whispered, 'Alleluia---Glory and honour to the Messiah, the wondrous Son of God!' Peter looked at John sadly, shaking his head. He would liked to have believed, after all, there had been the folded linen bandages, the face cloth, but for Jesus to be wandering about in the garden? Peter shook his head, obviously bewildered, his brown eyes troubled. Then he remembered something that he had meant to have remarked on earlier.

'John, those temple guards we passed on our way to the tomb, they looked as though they had seen a ghost. They were terrified, ran past me without a sideways glance. I was sure they would have recognized me from that night in the High Priest's courtyard, but they didn't!'

'I saw them too,' said John thoughtfully. 'At the time, my attention was only on the tomb, but you are right! They were just coming away from the garden!'

The door opened and Simon the Zealot walked in. He tossed off the disguising Phoenician cloak he wore. He had just returned from the

Temple courts, where he had been listening to those who spoke of the Rabbi from Galilee, who had been crucified. Whilst many had used sarcastic remarks about Jesus, hundreds amongst the crowds were deeply upset, obviously mourning one whom they had loved. Simon too had noted the distraught party of Temple guards, pushing people roughly out of their path, as they hurried to find their captain, the Strategios. He had watched the door they had entered by, saw them come out again, this time accompanied by their officer, who marched them towards that part of the Temple, private to the High Priest. Simon had sidled up to some uniformed guards coming out of their office. He overheard their words.

'They said there was an earthquake! The ground shook, and a heavenly being appeared frightening them out of their wits!'

'Huh! They were probably drunk! It will go hard with them, if they tell that tale to Caiaphas. He made a point of placing his most experienced men on guard duty at the Nazarene's tomb.'

Simon listened closely, his curiosity aroused despite his sorrow. Now he repeated all this to the other disciples, as he wondered why Caiaphas had thought it necessary to guard the tomb, it made no sense. Then Mary's jubilant voice rang out.

'Jesus has risen! I have spoken with him,' cried Mary Magdalene. 'Do not look at me like that, Simon! I speak truth!'

'Hush, Mary,' said Simon soothingly.

'I tell you that it is true!' Hearing that voice ringing out across the room, the other disciples paused to listen to Mary once again. But what she said was incredible. They shook their heads. But another did believe. Mary of Nazareth had entered. She had been resting in her chamber, trying to come to terms with her sorrow. She had heard Mary's joyful cries, and stood transfixed, holding on to the doorway.

'Mary, my daughter! Is this true?'

'Lady—it is. The Holy One is alive again, has conquered even death itself!' The mother's eyes lit up with joy! There was instant belief, for had he not said that on the third day he would rise! How foolish they had all been, to forget this! She fell into Mary's strong young arms.

'Mary, tell me all!'

'Shall we go into the courtyard by the fountain? I fear that the men do not believe yet, but it is most wonderfully true!' So the women who had followed Jesus, gathered about the two Mary's, faces radiant with hope and ecstatic joy.

Two of Jesus followers, were walking the seven mile road, to the little village of Emmaus, the hoods of their cloaks, shielding their sorrowful, frustrated faces, chattering sadly of all that had recently happened. Nor did they immediately recognize the tall stranger who joined them, walking quietly at their side.

He questioned them about recent events in Jerusalem, seeming to know nothing of the wonderful prophet whom they described to him as being powerful in word and deed before God. Amazed at his seeming ignorance, they told him of the trial before Caiaphas, of his agonizing death by crucifixion. Nor was this all, for now, on the third day following his execution, some of the women who were of their party, had visited the tomb where he had been laid and seen a vision of angels, who had told them that the Lord had risen. The disciples had gone to investigate, found an empty tomb and of the Holy One, no sign!

The two men listened to the stranger in surprise, as he said,

'How foolish you are and how slow of heart to believe all that the prophets have spoken! Did not the Christ have to suffer these things and then, to enter into his glory!'

When they arrived at Emmaus, the stranger agreed to join them at table. He broke bread with them after first giving thanks! Suddenly, they looked him full in the face. Before, their thoughts had been so distracted, that they barely registered him as a person. But now they saw—that it was he! It was Jesus! How could they have been so blind? But even as they looked at him in utter amazement, he disappeared from their sight. One of the men, Cleopas, leapt to his feet! They must return at once to Jerusalem—to the house of John Mark, to tell the apostles of this most marvellous happening!

Cleopas and his friend Simon, burst into the presence of the disciples, who were still discussing the mystery of the empty tomb and Mary Magdalene's vehemently repeated story. The apostles looked up, as these two who had so often followed Jesus and who like scores of other followers, would eventually join them from time to time in this spacious villa, were now almost jumping up and down in their impatience to be heard.

'It is true,' cried Cleopas! 'The Lord has risen and has appeared to Simon and to me!'

They were surrounded by the incredulous apostles, who questioned them, demanding to know exactly what had happened? They explained.

'We only really recognized him, when he broke bread with us!' The babble of conversation that followed filled the room and soon all others in the house, joined them.

David and Simeon listened, faces tense with growing excitement. Already, they had heard Mary's account several times, and had believed! Now this other testimony! Their eyes shone with excitement. The women stood somewhat apart, whispering together at the far side of the room, indignant that Mary's words had not been believed earlier, except by John. Mary of Nazareth stared toward the disciple tenderly.

'Peace be with you!'

The men sprang back in amazement at the voice of the one suddenly standing in their midst! It was—Jesus!

They started to tremble violently, muttering that it must be a ghost! How else had he suddenly appeared thus? Yet as they raised frightened eyes to his face, they saw the familiar shimmering gold gaze upon them, the gentle smile about his lips. But it couldn't be true! He had been crucified, dead and buried! So how could he be here, standing before them? It must be some ghostly manifestation. Peter's face was white with shock, but his brother Andrew had dawning hope in his eyes. Simon the Zealot stood rock still, eyes dilated and the others registered various forms of incomprehension—only John, son of Zebedee had tears of joy flooding in his eyes.

'Why are you troubled,' said the dear, familiar voice of the Holy One. He lifted his arms, drawing back the sleeves of his robe, displaying the terrible marks above the wrists; the wounds inflicted by the Romans when they hammered their cruel nails between the radius and ulna, the holes so made greatly enlarged, by the full weight of the body suspended from them. He lowered his arms, after giving them time for inspection, and raised the hem of his gown. They cried out in horror, at the savage wounds in his ankles.

'Why are you troubled,' he repeated. 'And why do doubts rise in your minds? Look at my hands and feet! It is I, myself!' He held his hands out towards them now, watching them compassionately, as at first they tried to back away.

'A ghost doesn't have flesh and bones, as you see I have!'

First one and then another reached out timid hands to touch him. He was real! It was true, only now they were so overcome with joy that they hardly knew what to do or say. Jesus eyes held slight flicker of amusement as he asked plaintively, 'Do you have anything to eat here?' He waited, while Peter rushed to the kitchen, coming back with a piece of broiled fish, the first food he had found. He held it out.

'Here,' he cried.

'Glory be to God,' breathed all in the room, as Jesus calmly ate the fish in front of them, after all a ghost couldn't eat fish!

'This is what I told you, while I was still with you! Everything must be fulfilled that is written about me in the Law of Moses, the Prophets and the Psalms!' He gestured that all should sit and took his place among them as he had in the past, opening their eyes to all those passages in scripture, which foretold his coming and the reason for his death and now they listened with bated breath, eyes shining.

'This is what is written,' he told them, in vibrant, ringing tones! 'The Christ will suffer and rise from the dead on the third day and repentance and forgiveness of sins will be preached in his name to all nations, beginning at Jerusalem!' He looked at them, eyes glowing with the fervency of his message.

'You are witnesses of these things! I am going to send you what my Father has promised! But stay in the city, until you have been clothed with power from on high!' Now slowly, the women came forward, kneeling about him, at last daring to lift their eyes. The love that shimmered from his gaze brought joy to every breast—especially to that of his mother, Mary of Nazareth. The whole room resounded to cries of praise, and then they lowered their voices, for Jesus had raised his hands in blessing.

'Peace be with you! As the Father has sent me—I am sending you! Receive the Holy Spirit,' and he breathed on them. 'If you forgive anyone their sins, they are forgiven, if you do not forgive them, they are not forgiven!'

Then suddenly, Jesus was gone. For a week, they discussed what had happened. What was this power from on high, they were to receive? They remembered how at Gethsemane, Jesus had spoken of the Holy Spirit, the Comforter, that he would send to them. But what form would this take? He had told them to remain in Jerusalem until then, but would it matter if they returned briefly to their homes in Galilee?

A week later, they were still in the house of John Mark's mother. One of the eleven, Thomas, had not been present at that exultant reunion with their risen Lord. Thomas, ever a difficult man to convince, had listened to their wonderful news with skepticism.

'Unless I see the nail marks in his hands and put my fingers where the nails were, put my hand into his side, I will not believe it!' Nor would he deviate from this stance. Day by day, the disciples were growing more uneasy. Fear burgeoned, that they might be rounded up by Caiaphas Temple guards—or the Romans and face possible death for having been friends of one accused and condemned for insurrection.

So now the outer door of the house was firmly bolted, as also was the door of the upper room where they all assembled for prayer and discussion. During the week that passed since Jesus appearance amongst them, doubts for the future and worry for their safety had arisen.

Now, despite that locked door, they all stepped back in amazement, as Jesus once more stood serenely next to them. As Thomas saw him, his jaw dropped open in shock!

'Peace be with you,' said Jesus softly, his eyes turning towards Thomas. He walked over to his doubting disciple. He held out his wrists.

'See my hands!' He made movement with his garments. 'Reach out your hand and put it into my side! Stop doubting, and believe!'

Thomas fell to his knees, eyes filled with tears, as his exploring fingers had told him the truth he had refused to believe. He clasped his hands before him, crying out 'My Lord and my God!'

Jesus looked at him, a quizzical smile at the corner of his mouth. He knew what this lesson was to do to the soul of Thomas, removing doubt for all time, replacing it with the confidence of a shining faith that was to reach out to all with whom he came into contact.

'Because you have seen me, you have believed Thomas. Blessed are they who have not seen, and who yet have believed!' And Thomas never forgot the shame with which he lowered his head nor the confidence with which he lifted it again.

While these things were happening in Jerusalem, Centurion Claudius, no longer member of the Imperial army but retired, honoured citizen of Rome, wandered in the gardens of his magnificent villa, now permanently his by the will of Pilate, together with large tract of land. He heard Miriam singing softly in her favourite arbour. It was a plaintive, Jewish psalm, full of grief and longing. Claudius sighed deeply, for he knew his wife was mourning the death of Jesus of Nazareth. His own heart was overcharged with latent emotion, bitterly reproaching himself because he had not thrown himself in front of the Prefect during the course of the trial, begging for the life of Jesus, defending the Holy One who had stood defenceless as sacrificial lamb, before the raging hatred of Caiaphas and his minions screaming for his death to Pilate. He remembered Pilate's obvious wish to release Jesus, his sardonic expression as he questioned the Holy One, his gathering unease, as he heard Jesus spoken of not only as a king, but as the Son of the Living God! He remembered too, the almost angry look that Pilate had cast at Claudius, when the Roman Governor had sentenced Jesus to crucifixion.

'He was angry, because he knew he had come to the wrong decision,' muttered Claudius to himself. 'He knew that he was condemning not only one completely innocent of all wrong, but whom even Pilate suspected was no ordinary man.' Again and again, his thoughts went back over the events of that terrible day. Pilate was aware the Claudius respected Jesus, as did his beautiful wife Claudia, whose message born of her terrifying dream, the Centurion had borne to Pilate, hoping it would soften the Prefect's heart. It had not! But Pilate resented Claudius, because even his cruel heart was smitten with guilt at giving in to Caiaphas merely as matter of political expediency.

Could he have done more to help? He remembered the scene at the cross, the patient figure stripped, revealing the terrible beatings he had undergone, yet turning his head away, when the soldier offered him drugged drink, which had to be done according to Jewish law, before nails were driven through his wrists with efficient mallet. He had chosen to bear crucifixion, in all its utter cruelty, this most barbaric of all deaths which no Roman was allowed to suffer.

He remembered again, the strange darkness as the sun's face was frighteningly masked, the mighty wind that had arisen, the earthquake and the Son of God crying out that—'It was finished!'

He remembered also, helping Nicodemus and Joseph of Arimathea to reverently lower the lifeless body to the ground, closing the eyelids over blank eyes, where once had been that strange luminous stare and bearing Jesus to his last resting place, the tomb in the garden.

'If only, oh, if only I had been able to do something more,' cried Claudius aloud, placing hands over his smarting eyes.

'My dear Lord,' said a sweet voice. 'You did all you were able. Nothing could have prevented his death. It was ordained to happen, for this he was born, to be lifted up. He said so many times.' Miriam paused, and looked along the length of Galilee's sea, as though she could see far beyond, past Galilee and Samaria, to distant Judea where stood the cradle of her race, Jerusalem. 'I remember also the words that Jesus spoke, when speaking of his death. That on the third day, he would rise again! I often spoke of this when I was with the other women. His mother I am sure believed his promise, even as I want to.' She looked at Claudius questioningly. 'How many days have sped by since that terrible day, husband?'

'Why, this is the first day of the week, so some two and a half weeks my dear.'

'I would that we could have received word of the disciples. They must have remained in Jerusalem, as well as Mary Magdalene and the other women. Then again, we have had no communication from Simeon or David. I just hope that they are all safe! But Claudius, it is more than concern for all of them. I want to know if anything happened on that third day?' Her eyes filled with tears, as the small bubble of hope which kept rising in her breast, did so again.

Claudius slipped an arm about her shoulders, cradling her to him. She had lost much weight he realized, for she had not been eating properly. How wonderful though it was to wake in the morning and see her beautiful black hair stretched over the pillows. True she had not shared her body with him yet, but Claudius knew this had nothing to do with the terrible experience she had once undergone, when raped by the Sicarii. No. Her with-holding herself was thing born of her deep sorrow for the Holy One and as Claudius himself held the same grief, he had not pressed her. Enough that their marriage had survived, their love deepened as never before. Claudius lifted one of her slim hands to his lips.

'Wife—as to Jesus surviving crucifixion—what can I say? Only that the man I carried to the tomb was completely without the breath of life. He was dead, my dearest, would that it were otherwise!' He walked her back to the villa, breaking off a scarlet blossom and giving it to her. Once she would have placed it in her hair. Now, she turned it over absently in her hands.

'Mencius! Mencius, come here,' cried Claudius. 'Look after your mistress, see that she is given appetizing meal. I am going riding!' He bent and kissed Miriam, who stared at him surprised. She would have questioned him, but with his usual swiftness of action, he was gone.

As he stroked his horse's neck, he looked around for a place to tether it. Yes, this was the place he sought, the charred remains of the miserable hut where his wife's defiler had yielded up the ghost, mocking Claudius, even as he had died. What had he expected to find here? He stood hand still holding the reins, as he glanced around. The place looked peaceful, sheep grazed the green pasture, and Claudius saw a shepherd standing staring at him curiously. Above him, the sun burned down, casting glittering net upon the waters of Galilee's inland sea far below. But yes, it was here that his soldiers had searched feverishly for the fiend who had ravished their Centurion's wife and not far away, the ravine where his men had been ambushed and where they had captured Barabbas! Barabbas? Where was he now?

He looked at the blackened ruin of the little hut and doing so, remembered the old couple who at his command had lost their home. Why did he think of them now? What affair of his, their eventual destiny? But now his conscience rose to prick him. They had been so old, so weary and so frightened! They had obviously been living like paupers. Where could such as these have gone? He looked up startled, as the shepherd approached him.

'Sir!' said the man, recognizing the Centurion, even without his uniform, for he had seen this imposing Roman many times in the past. 'What seek you? May I be of assistance?' He smiled gently at Claudius.

'I wonder if you know what became of the old couple, who used to live here?' The Centurion indicated the burned out hovel.

'Why, yes, my family took them in,' replied the shepherd in surprise.

'I would like to see them,' said Claudius. 'No! Never fear. I do not wish them ill! But tell me, why did you take them into your care? Are you related to them?' He looked into the shepherd's warm brown eyes, seeing the kindliness there.

'No. They are not kin of mine, but then He would have wished it,' said the man slowly. He looked as though he would have said more, but stopped.

'Who would have wished it, their dead son,' forced out the Centurion?'

'Not so. I speak of Jesus of Nazareth. He told us that we should invite the stranger in, that if we did this we were doing it to him, and would be blessed of God!'

'Did you know him, did you know the Holy One,' asked Claudius eagerly.

'I heard him preach many times! Lord,' he hesitated. 'It is strange to hear a Roman refer to Jesus as the Holy One!' He looked into Claudius handsome face wonderingly.

'I believe him to have been the Son of God.' The words hung quivering upon the silence of the place. Claudius blue eyes shone with deep sadness. The shepherd laid comforting hand upon his arm. His face softened to exultant smile.

'Not to have been, the Son of God. He is the Son of God, sir! He is alive! He has risen, and has been seen several times by his disciples and by others.'

Claudius gasped in stupefaction. Was it possible? His eyes bored into those of the shepherd. He read truth there and deep happiness.

'How can you know this? Who told you?'

'I had it from Peter himself, the Lord's chief disciple. He is here in Galilee, has come on brief visit but returns to Jerusalem in a few days time. I do not know why I am telling this to you, to a Roman. But I feel that you are one of us?'

Claudius looked at him. He wanted to believe, was frightened to. But obviously this shepherd did. If only he could see Peter. But yes, he was one of them now, one of those who loved Jesus of Nazareth. A strange excitement sent the blood tingling through his veins. He must tell Miriam! But wait, first he must see Peter, to be sure that this wonder of resurrection had indeed come to pass. But there was something to put right, even before this!

Claudius looked around him at the idyllic loveliness of the lush, Galilean countryside, each blade of fresh grass, each quivering bright yellow flower that decked the pasture, every shining green leaf of wind tossed bush translucent in the sunlight, as upsurge of new life, the springtime revival of this wild and beautiful land, echoed promise from God to man of renewal and rebirth. The promise of the Christ, the now risen Christ, to bring eternal life to all those who followed him! Claudius looked deep into his soul, seeing flashing before him, those innumerable men he had either wounded or slain in battle, heard the screams of those in sacked villages, saw the flames of towns rising in memory, belching black smoke. He saw the battlefields of the years, where once victory was won he had then wandered among the dead and dying. But what had it all been for? What had it accomplished?

'I have merely been pandering to the greed of Rome and of an Emperor who sought power even beyond this world, naming himself Dominus et Deus, lord and god! By what right, have we Romans despoiled the many countries of the world, robbing them of their resources, their people, selling them into slavery! It is wrong, I want no more of it,' cried Claudius and the shepherd heard his impassioned words with joy. How wonderful, that the Son of God had been able to touch the heart of this Gentile, bringing even fierce Roman Centurion, into his fold of love.

'May I see the couple we were speaking of,' said Claudius at last. The final pictures that had floated before his eyes, had been the flogging of Barabbas and his own journey to Jerusalem, full of hate and deepest hurt, trying to assuage his pain by seeking power in all its trappings—and its emptiness.

'Their names are Samuel and Elizabeth. They have grieved deeply for the terrible wrong that their only son, Zeke did to your Lady. This boy grew up amongst cruelty saw the crosses of those thousands crucified by you Romans, following the uprising of the Zealots at Sephoris. Heard their screams, heard the weeping of their widows and mothers. Hate was born in his heart. He had only one thought, to kill those who had brought such terrible grief to his nation.'

'I can understand a man standing openly in battle against those who have ravished his country, but to spend that hatred, in the defilement of an innocent woman, whose only crime was to marry the man she loved! Can you understand what I went through, shepherd?'

'I can. But I also know that you have to forgive Zeke, lay your hatred aside, leave it here on this hillside, so that when you descend you will know that Almighty God has dealt with it, for if we seek His forgiveness for our own sin—then we must forgive others first!' The shepherd's open, weather-beaten face glowed with zeal. He placed his hand on Claudius shoulder, staring into the Roman's distracted blue eyes.

'Do you forgive?' The question reverberated through Claudius soul. He turned his head to look again at the blackened hut, seeing there now, a man whose spirit had been suffused by hatred, whose life had been warped because of it. This was what hatred did, caused division between man and God. It was a sickness driving men insane. But look what Zeke had done to his beloved Miriam. Then another picture shone before his eyes, of a man innocent of all sin, the gentle Son of the Living God, nails ripping through his flesh, as he was hoisted upwards upon the barbarity of the cross. He heard those wonderful words issuing between broken lips.

"Father—forgive them—for they know not what they do!" He bowed his head. When he lifted his face, the shepherd saw his blue eyes were full of tears.

'I do—forgive Zeke,' said the choking voice and as he said it, a great burden was lifted from his soul. There was peace—peace, still and beautiful, as buds of love towards his fellow men started to unfurl in his heart.

The shepherd raised his hands in praise, murmuring Hebrew words that Claudius did not know, yet he understood them to be a cry of gratitude to the One God. Then the shepherd walked with him to the top of the hill. He pointed to a small farmstead in the valley.

'That is my home, Centurion. There you will find Samuel and Elizabeth.'

'My name is Claudius, friend!'

'And mine, is Nathaniel,' They clasped hands and the shepherd shaded his eyes with his hand, as he watched the tall figure mount his horse and gallop down the hillside.

The couple shrank from him in fear as they recognized him. Then fear turned to wonder, as Claudius leaned hands upon the oaken table and smiled at them encouragingly.

'I have come to ask your forgiveness for my cruelty to you in destroying your home, and to tell you that for my part, I have forgiven Zeke.'

They looked at each other, the woman's face aged beyond her years through hardship, her husband tired, beaten by life. Then they looked back at the Centurion. Samuel asked a simple question.

'Did you ever meet Jesus of Nazareth, sir?'

'Yes and I know him to be the Messiah—the Son of Almighty God!'

'Then this explains all. Sir, we do willingly forgive your actions, for we understood and grieved for the cause, felt shame for our son. We will always remember that you could have killed us and did not.' His quavering voice grew stronger, as he said. 'Will you tell us what you know of Jesus, for we have heard that you are newly from Jerusalem?'

Claudius seated himself, accepting the goats' milk and fresh bread Elizabeth set before him, and after eating made himself speak of all that had occurred just over two weeks ago.

'Thank you for sharing these things with us, Lord. It cannot have been easy to have been there, to have seen his sufferings. But now he has risen from the grave! All of Capernaum is bursting with rumour that he may even come back here!' The old man's face was radiant with joy. He believed it was obvious! Claudius told them he would arrange for them to be given new home of their own, would ensure that it was built close to the house of their benefactor, Nathaniel. Then he rose to his feet, drawing gold coins from his purse. He placed them on the table then he was gone. They watched from the doorway, as his horse bore him back towards Capernaum.

He rode into the streets of Capernaum, dismounting before the house of Peter. Yes, he was told, Peter was indeed back. But he had left early that morning, had not been seen since. Frustrated, Claudius remounted his horse and as sunset stroked crimson fingers across the water, burning the sky to smouldering purple cinders, he went wearily back to the villa, to Miriam. He had wanted to bring her proof! But did he need proof? Was it not enough merely to believe!

He held her in his arms, trying to quieten her, for she had been uttering wild ecstatic cries of happiness, as she heard his news.

'Where are the women? Where are Mary and Joanna?'

'I do not know yet,' replied Claudius. 'Now come to bed. You are overwrought with joy!'

When she lay asleep, Claudius slipped out of bed, and looked out upon the still, Galilean night. Stars twinkled in the cold immensity of the black, velvet sky, the half hooped moon, suspended over the expanse of serene waters, tiny wavelets, crested in silver, lapping the shore. Claudius dressed himself, and stole quietly out of the room. He went below, leaving his wife and sleeping slaves behind him, as his feet bore him down the many steps leading from terraced gardens to the beach. The two guards posted about the house saw him go and drew themselves erect, but he did not seem to notice them. The cold night air was fresh with the scent of the honeysuckle, which clung to the wall bordering access to the pebbled shore, and he breathed deeply.

'What now,' mused Claudius? 'I believe—yes, I believe that he has risen, that he is looking up at these stars even as I am, more, that he was present with his Father when this earth of ours, the stars, planets sun and moon were created. That Almighty God, who always was, who is and always will be, sent this wondrous Son of His to teach us of himself and to die for our sins, like the unblemished lamb of the Jewish Passover feast. But how could God, loving his Son as He surely must, have allowed Jesus to suffer so terribly? Surely God must bear immense tenderness for sinful man, to have permitted this. But would people change now that it had happened? Would the killing stop, the greed, the wish for power that some men exercised over other men's lives?

He thought of Emperor Tiberius, of Pilate, of Caiaphas and of Herod Antipas. Would men such as these, change? He bent and picked up a stone, swishing it across the waters, watching the ripples, ever expanding, as it sank.

Was his answer there? Would these, the great and powerful of this world, sink into abyss prepared for those who would not learn, would not listen to the impassioned cry of Jesus, to all men, 'I am the light of the world. Whoever follows me, will never walk in darkness—but will have the light of life!'

But the others who would listen to that message as it spread ever outwards, like the ripples on Galilee's sea, they would find complete change in their lives, learn to forgive and to love, even as Claudius himself had, but also how to bring the words of Jesus to all mankind?

How could this be accomplished? If Jesus did return to his Father, as he had always said he would, then surely that only left a collection of for the most part, frightened fishermen and a few helpless women to carry the news of all that had happened to the world! It needed something more, but what?

All night he paced along the shore, walking many miles away from Capernaum, the thoughts surging through his head, negating all tiredness. At last he turned and started back along the wet shingle. An hour later, the stars suddenly dimmed, a slight breeze pulsed—and the sun rose above snow capped Mount Hermon flooding flame down the flank of the hills, blazing across the waters, touching the timbers of the fishing boat coming in to shore, with vermilion glow.

Claudius stared at the fishing boat and at the figure of the man in the prow. Surely it couldn't be—but it was, Simon Peter and the sons of Zebedee, and Thomas! There were a few others whom he couldn't identify from this distance. Then a voice rang out across the waters, carrying clearly to those in the boat.

'Friends—have you caught any fish?'

Claudius stiffened in shock. That voice—could it be? He glanced ahead, could see a figure standing there, but such was the brilliance of the sun that he could not make out the man's features.

'No, we have caught nothing,' the men in the boat replied.

'Throw your net on the right side of the boat and you will find some!'

The men in the boat responded in obedience, too tired to remonstrate with this stranger. Suddenly the net was full to bursting point, the weight of the catch so heavy, that the disciples could hardly land it. Then the disciple Jesus loved, John, Son of Zebedee, called to Peter in throbbing tones,

'It is the Lord!'

Peter looked at John, eyes wide in amazement and joy. He wrapped his cloak about him, and as Claudius watched, Peter jumped out of the boat that was now towing the heavy net full of fish. It was only a hundred yards through the shallows. Claudius climbed the bank above the approaching boat, seeing a fire burning beneath him on the shingle. The flame of dawn was turning to gold, the water hazed with mist rising on its surface, sky and sea silver blue. Claudius did not need to see his face to know the man who faced the dripping figure of Peter, was Jesus of Nazareth! Claudius trembled.

Peter approached his Lord then stood rooted to the ground. He looked into those shimmering gold eyes that seemed brighter now even than the golden dawn and remembered, even as he had all night long, that terrible night when he had denied the Holy One. As he stood there, a sob burst from his breast and he turned running back to his friends, helping them to pull the heavy weight of fish ashore. He could not face Jesus. During those first meetings at Jerusalem, he had been too amazed, too overjoyed, to think of anything but that the impossible had happened. Jesus had risen from the grave even as he had said he would.

But since then worry had set in of his cowardly behaviour, which he had now compounded by persuading most of the disciples to make this trip back to Galilee, leaving the women with John Mark's family in Jerusalem. For fear had arisen in Peter's mind, just as it had at the house of the High Priest, fear of the future, fear of arrest, fear of death! Like deadly infection this fear had festered, passing from one man's spirit to another's. They had made the four-day trip from Judea, back to the safety and familiarity of Galilee. Here, on the water which they had fished since boyhood, they forgot Jesus instruction, 'To go, and to become fishers of men!'

They looked at each other sheepishly. What would he say to them? He had told them to remain in Jerusalem until they had been clothed with power from on high, leaving them unsure as to what form this was meant to take.

'Bring some of the fish you have caught,' called that much loved voice. There was no condemnation in it, no displeasure. Peter gave a final furious tug on the net and the slippery, heavy burden was ashore. Later they were to count the catch and find that they had one hundred and fifty three large fish! Now one of them handed him some of the catch.

'Come and have breakfast!' How often they had heard this warm invitation in the past. The question, 'Who are you?' had at no point arisen, for there was no doubt! It was their dearest teacher, who had conquered even death. They gathered about him in awe, then as they started to relax, seated themselves in a circle about him. That fish smelt good, thought Claudius. He was aware that he was hungry. How strange that presented with this most amazing sight, that of the risen Christ, he should look on it as so entirely natural that he should think of his stomach!

'Come,' said that familiar voice, which Claudius had heard so many times amongst the sick and maimed in Galilee, and under the colonnades in the Temple, and he realized that his hiding place was discovered. His face flushed scarlet, as he rose to his feet, and scrambled awkwardly down the bank. One of the disciples offered him fish and bread and he ate it joyfully, as he listened to the words of that figure who he now loved above all things, even above his own beloved Miriam. He saw Jesus rise at the conclusion of the meal, raising his hands in blessing before he summoned Simon Peter to walk a little apart with him.

'Simon, Son of John. Do you truly love me, more than these?' Jesus had not used his favourite name for Simon, had not called him Peter—his rock! Hurt spread across Peter's face, as he blurted out confirmation of what he was asked.

'Yes Lord, you know that I love you.'

'Feed my lambs,' said Jesus. Then he repeated the question.

'Simon, Son of John—do you truly love me?'

Peter's face crumpled with grief at the repeated question. Surely Jesus knew that he did, even though he had let him down so badly.

'Yes, Lord,' came the broken tones. 'You know I love you!'

'Take care of my sheep,' said Jesus, making sweeping movement of his hand, encompassing the horizon. Peter nodded. He knew the sheep of whom Jesus spoke, that vast army of men and women who rejected God's love, as demonstrated in His Son, the Christ.

'Simon—son of John, do you love me?' probed the gentle voice and Peter was never to forget this thrice repeated question. Tears sprang into his eyes as he turned his face to Jesus, beseeching forgiveness for his cowardice, knowing that his Lord's words were warranted, wishing to be sure that Peter would never let him down again. Peter never did. He raised brown eyes, brimming with tears to Jesus.

'Lord, you know all things—you know that I love you!'

'Feed my sheep!' Other words he spoke to Peter, then added the familiar, 'Follow me!'

Claudius bent over Miriam, shaking her shoulder, his face though he did not know it, shining with supernatural joy. She sat up rubbing her eyes, looking endearingly young. Then, as she looked at the dear head bending over here, saw his face, his radiant expression, she knew.

'You have seen him, haven't you? You have seen the Holy One!' Her eyes begged his answer.

'Yes wife, he truly lives! I knew this, believed! But oh, what wonder to sit close enough to touch his robe, to see the crumbs about his mouth as he ate! Dearest Miriam, life will never be the same again. Now, I want you to get dressed. We are returning to Jerusalem.'

She slipped out of bed into his arms and Claudius knew that the warm, breathless embrace, told him that his wife had become so again in very truth! An hour passed, and with it all traces of the hurt and bitterness that had kept them apart. Now she sang, as she called to the servants to help her pack the few clothes they would take with them.

How strange it felt, to be back in Jerusalem without his uniform, and not to be making for his luxurious apartment in the Antonia. He was now an ordinary citizen, he mused, and would have to accustom himself to the fact that men no longer treated him with respect for his rank, his authority. True, he was wealthy enough, could live comfortably for the rest of his life. But that which had sustained him for so many years, the confidence born of having the men he commanded rely on his judgement and obeying his orders without question; showing instant obedience, as he took his own small niche in the enormous fighting machine that was the Roman army, all this was now gone, and he would have to accept that a great change had come over his life.

But that change had also brought release. Now he was only answerable to the rules of God, as laid down by His Son, the Lord Jesus.

If called upon to decide, between obedience to Emperor Tiberius and following the Way shown by the Christ, well he knew now what course he would take, however dear it might cost him.

Miriam looked about her with slight unease as they rode through crowded streets, where camels swayed in stately path, where rich merchants were carried in litters by sweating slaves and men dragged donkeys bowed down under heavy loads. Where as always, the poor shrank back against the walls of the narrow streets, while grubby urchins watchful for dropped coin, waited to dart dangerously between relentless stream of pack animals. The high pitched, ever present tension that was Jerusalem, glimpsed in the faces of its citizens, all of this brought back the horror of that fearful day when Jesus had faced the howling mob, and had been sentenced by Pilate to the pain and humiliation of the Cross.

Suddenly their horses were forced to halt and draw to one side, as a maniple of troops from the Antonia marched by, their officer recognizing Claudius, gave him salute, but proceeded without stopping. It was now that Miriam heard a small group of men beside them discussing Jesus, as they tugged at their beards in spirited discussion.

'It is said that he has risen, that the Nazarene has been seen by his disciples!'

'But that is thing impossible,' scoffed an elderly man in a long fringed robe. A younger man wagged his finger at him.

'Yet, did he not say that he would rise again?'

Then the men realized that Claudius could overhear their words. His clothes, his bearing, announced him as a Roman and they drew back. To Miriam's amazement, she heard Claudius say softly, 'Yes, my friends. It is true! He has risen. Jesus of Nazareth lives!'

Then they continued their progress, as the blockage caused by the legionaries was relieved. Miriam reached out a hand and touched his. Claudius looked at the veiled figure who rode at his side, followed by the one servant they had brought and he smiled gaily. He had said it, proclaimed the truth which was the Way!

'I am so proud of you, dearest husband,' came the whispered words and Claudius squeezed her hand, heart full to overflowing. But where were they to stay? The disciples had said that Lady Joanna was no longer at her villa. Perhaps they should seek a good hostelry. They were passing through the wealthier area of the city now, where perfumed gardens scented the air from behind high walls, and palm trees hung motionless in the noon day heat. Suddenly they heard a shout!

'Father!'

Claudius turned his head, reining his horse. Then he saw the slim youth, waving at him from a gateway. It was Simeon! Claudius sprang down from his horse and embraced his adopted son, holding him to his breast, slapping his back.

'I have missed you, boy,' he said huskily. 'Where are you staying?'

'Here, sir, at the house of John Mark. Mary and Joanna are within as well, and many others!' Then he noticed Miriam sitting quietly upon the mare and seeing her thus together with Claudius, knew that reconciliation had taken place. His earnest young face glowed with relief. 'I am so happy for you both,' he breathed, his dark eyes damp with emotion. Then he noticed that Claudius was not in uniform.

'You are not wearing your armour sir?'

'Simeon, I am no longer officer of Rome. I have another master, Jesus of Nazareth!'

'I heard it rumoured! Why, but this is thing most wonderful,' blurted out the young man. 'But come within, for surely this house is your home now, as it is to all who follow the lord!' He opened the gate to the courtyard, showing Mencius where to take the beasts, as he escorted Claudius and his wife. There was tremendous welcome for these two, once the disciples who remained there together with the women, heard the amazing news that Claudius had indeed resigned his commission in order to follow Jesus. How wonderful that a Gentile should believe, to have given up all he had stood for, to become one with them!

Mary Magdalene embraced Miriam, laughing and crying all at once. Then Mary stood back, staring shrewdly at Claudius, then at Miriam's face, as the young wife smiled tenderly at her husband, whose hair Mary noticed had silvered during the pain of their separation. She knew that what they had all prayed for had happened these two were reunited in love. Joanna's lovely violet eyes were bright with unshed tears, as she too threw her arms about Miriam.

'Remember, how you cried out in the night for him and I told you, that one day you would be together again,' said Joanna softly.

'Yes, dearest Joanna.' Then she smiled, as Claudius also was embraced.

'Sarah, child, come here!'

Claudius had seen Simeon's betrothed enter the room. He looked at her, puzzling at slight difference in the dusky skinned Samaritan girl, soon to be his daughter. When last they had all been together, she had still been a child on the verge of womanhood. Now she possessed a new maturity. He looked around at them all, at the dark, glowing face of Susannah,

David, smiling at him, no longer bristling with resentment towards Rome. Then Claudius bowed in greeting to the woman whose lustrous hair was winged with silver, and whose face still bore signs of the suffering she had undergone when her son had suffered such cruel death, but whose eyes were now radiant with love. She smiled at him.

'Greetings, Claudius. I will no longer call you Centurion, as I did when first we met. Welcome. I have been told of all you did, your help to Nicodemus and Joseph!'

'Lady, I would have protected your son with my life! But I stood by and let it all happen.' Claudius sank his chin upon his breast, remembering with an all consuming sorrow.

'Claudius, we were worse! We ran away,' cried Phillip, one of the twelve. 'And now sadly some of our friends have returned to Galilee for we fear reprisals by the authorities. I myself am fearful to leave this villa even for short walk, in case of arrest!'

'I saw your friends in Capernaum,' said Claudius gently.

'You saw them?' They looked at him in questioningly.

'Yes. Even now they should be upon the road returning to you. They were fishing. Jesus came, cooked breakfast for them and talked. They are coming back!'

John Mark's mother, Mary of Cyprus, took the couple with her, showing them to a chamber they could use in this overflowing villa. She confided to her new guests that altogether and including the missing disciples there were approaching a hundred people now based at the house. Some returned to their own dwellings at night, but most slept here.

'Are your resources such, that you can afford to keep all of these,' asked Claudius in amazement?

'All contribute as they are able and if they are unable to, then surely the Lord told us to share our goods one with another!'

The eleven apostles were reunited, for the party led by Peter, had returned from Galilee strengthened by that wonderful morning when their risen Lord had once again shown them where to cast their net upon the waters, His words whirled repeatedly through their minds.

'All authority in heaven and earth is given to me! Therefore—go, and make disciples of all nations, baptising them in the name of the Father and of the Son and of the Holy Spirit and teaching them to obey everything I have commanded you. And surely, I am with you, even to the very end of the age!'

Now all of them met together in the upper room of the villa, the only room large enough to hold so large a gathering. They sat long into the night, discussing the Lord's instruction. How could such as they, ordinary men, not well educated, nor gifted with eloquence, speaking only their own Aramaic tongue, together with Hebrew, how could they possibly instruct even the thousands in Israel, never mind the teeming millions in the outside world! Why, they even risked arrest here, if discovered by Caiaphas spies, could end up in prison for the rest of their days, or maybe dead with a knife between their shoulders! How could this mighty work laid upon them, be accomplished?

It was David who spoke.

'Said he not, to wait until you should have been clothed with power from on high?' They looked at the youth, remembering. Yes—he was right!

But what was this power? When would it come and what form would it take?

Chapter Twenty-Five

For a further week the disciples waited, always discussing the problem uppermost in their minds, how were they to bring Jesus teaching to all nations as he had instructed? They tried not to panic, as they heard the sound of the heavy marching steps of patrolling legionaries clattering past the villa, iron shod feet resounding on the cobbled street. Would those fierce legionaries stop one day, the door pound with urgent demand, as the disciples were rounded up, imprisoned, executed? The Romans gave short shrift to any concerned in insurrection, and Jesus had been crucified as King of the Jews, and they were his followers. Again and again, fear reached creeping tendrils into their breasts.

Only when Jesus suddenly appeared again, teaching them as so often in the past of the Kingdom of God, would the fear abate and a spirit of jubilation once more enfold them. It was now forty days since he had risen from the darkness of the tomb, into eternal life. He stood amongst them today, speaking with an urgency that made them realize that this occasion was different to all others.

'We are going outside the city with Jesus, onto the Mount of Olives,' said John, calling for his brother James. The other disciples looked at each other questioningly. Was it not dangerous to walk out together, in full daylight? But they looked at the gracious figure in their midst, saw the love shining in his eyes, the encouragement—and fear subsided.

It was good to be outside the city. Tension drained away, as they scrambled up the steep hillside behind their beloved master. As they reached the summit, Jesus stopped and faced them. His eyes shone with an unearthly light and they started to tremble. The change that was coming upon him, the pulsing brightness, the radiance around him, what did this portend? His eyes searched their faces, one by one and they sank to their knees before that shimmering, golden gaze and the blinding whiteness of light, shining round his head.

'Do not leave Jerusalem, but wait for the gift that my Father promised, which you have heard me speak of. For John baptised with water, but in a few days you will be baptised with the Holy Spirit!'

'Lord, are you at this time, going to restore the kingdom to Israel?' Peter waited his answer with bated breath. Surely the glory surrounding Jesus must indicate this. Peter could hardly raise his eyes, such was his awe.

'It is not for you, to know the times or dates the Father has set, by His own authority!' Jesus raised his arms, turning his hands towards them in blessing and when his voice rang out again, it was with the resonance of a golden bell.

'But you will receive power, when the Holy Spirit comes upon you—and you will be my witnesses, in Jerusalem—and in Judea—and Samaria—and to the Ends of the Earth!'

The glow about him intensified. The disciples dared one last look at him, felt sensation like throbbing current surging through them, sensed a love flowing towards them that bathed them in its power and tenderness. Then a white cloud started to form and descend upon Jesus hiding him from their view.

The cloud rose, brilliant with incandescent light, higher it rose and higher, ever upwards. The disciples stared up at it, tears in their eyes, knowing that their master, the Son of Almighty God had disappeared from their earthly sight.

Another light burst like lightning across their vision, as two with the appearance of men, in shining white, stood before them, eyes aflame, wings sparkling like sun on ice. The disciples stepped back in fright.

'Men of Galilee,' the angels said. 'Why do you stand here, looking up into the sky? This same Jesus, who has been taken from you into heaven, will come back, in the same way you have seen him go into heaven!' The light faded. The angels had gone. All that remained was dusty hillside. Drawn by common instinct, they climbed the last few yards, to that place where Jesus had once stood. To the East, sombre ranges of mountains encircled the Judean desert, and lying like huge turquoise, they could just make out the distant waters of the Dead Sea. Beyond it the violet mountains of Moab, to the North lay Samaria and beyond it, their own fair Galilee. They turned westward again and there across the Kidron valley, Jerusalem crouched in all its menace, like hostile beast. Further westward still was the coast of the Great Sea that men would one day name the Mediterranean and bordering this, the mysterious world ruled by Tiberius, whose subjects acclaimed him as god Emperor. It was this world, ruled by the mightiest kingdom on earth, where men worshipped statues of heathen gods and practiced strange rites, that had to be explored, its people told of the One true God, Jehovah and of His Son, the Lord Jesus Christ, and of that other kingdom, which could exist within men's hearts—the Kingdom of God!

Only they could bear this message to all men and they were so few, their task possible only through the power of Almighty God, which Jesus had promised them. So now they turned their feet back towards Jerusalem. There to await the coming of the Holy Spirit, which he, their dear Lord, had promised.

'He has gone, hasn't he?'

The disciples glanced about them and saw the two brothers standing seriously beside the slow waters of the Kidron Brook. David and Simeon had followed the disciples out of Jerusalem, not quite daring to accompany them onto the hill. But they had seen the shining cloud and knew that the Holy One had finally left them to return to God his Father. A great sadness came upon their young hearts, for they loved him dearly, worshipping him with all their being. How would they manage without him? Life would be so empty.

Simon Peter read their thoughts, and placed a great arm about each young man's shoulders. He had indeed become, Peter, the Rock.

'Yes, he has gone in his physical form. But he'll always be with each one of us, in our hearts. His words forever reign in our souls and those words have to be brought to all men, even as he has said, to the Ends of the Earth!' They looked up at Peter trustingly. Instinctively they now looked on him as leader, for Peter was remembering his Lord's command, to feed his sheep.

Their faces as they returned to the villa were rapt in wonder at the manner of Jesus departure. They climbed the stairs to the large upper room, and began to tell the others assembled there, that Jesus had now returned to place of glory at the right side of the throne of his Father.

'We will never see him again then,' cried Mary Magdalene, eyes wet with tears. Then she smiled softly, for she remembered his words to them; knew that one day they would all of them be with him again. Now their own task was to begin, the task for which he had been preparing them.

Mary of Nazareth fell to her knees, her lips murmuring in prayer. Her face was bright with joy, even though her mother's eyes were damp. All things had been accomplished, as he said they would and now the wondrous being whom she had carried under her heart, seed born of the Holy Spirit, whose boyhood she had watched over, cherishing this child she knew to be the Son of the Most High, who had now returned to his Father and rightful position of majesty and power, leaving behind his teaching and memory of miracles performed upon countless people healed of both physical and mental afflictions, their sins forgiven!

'His teaching will endure unto the end of time,' whispered Mary prophetically. 'How favoured are we, to have known him, to be his ambassadors, his envoys!'

A spontaneous hymn of praise arose from all their throats, led by the glorious voice of Susannah, dark face glowing with emotion. Claudius did not know the words, but the beauty of the song touched his heart. They were filled by sense of elation as they broke bread together that night, while they discussed what was to happen next.

When was the Holy Spirit to come? How would they recognize him? When finally they retired to toss upon their sleeping mats, for there were not beds enough to meet the needs of all, the eleven apostles and the other disciples searched in their hearts, wondering how they would achieve the courage to begin to spread the words of Jesus.

The following day, fear began to afflict them once more. Simon the Zealot made one of his many visits to the Temple. There he had witnessed a distressing incident. The crowds assembling as usual in the Court of the Gentiles had been discussing Jesus, and his crucifixion, with many pouring scorn on the words of two elderly men. These were maintaining that it was widely believed that Jesus had risen from the grave on the third day, even as he had said that he would.

'No, you are mistaken,' cried the crowd angrily. 'Have not the guards who stood outside the tomb sworn they fell asleep on duty, and that Jesus disciples came while they slept and bore his body away!'

'But he said he would rise again,' said one old man passionately, 'and I believe that he has! The guards were probably paid to spread that rumour in order to confuse our minds. Caiaphas would not want the truth to be known. For if Jesus has risen, proving that he has power even over death, then this proves as nothing else, that he is indeed the Messiah!!' He paused then his voice rang out challengingly.

'Think you that our High Priest and the Sanhedrin, wish it to be known that they have caused the Holy One of God to be tortured, crucified?'

A spy heard the man's words and hurried to the guardroom to alert the temple guards. The Strategios gave an order and the man and his companion were arrested, leaving the crowd troubled in their minds. If what the man had said was true, then what would be the outcome of all this? Some of them had accompanied the howling mob who had cried for Jesus death. Suppose he had indeed been the Messiah? They ignored the flowing words of the Pharisees, teaching under Solomon's porch where once that gracious figure whose eyes had searched their souls, had once stood and preached. The court of the Gentiles began to empty as men made their way back to their homes, pouring into the streets.

Some lingered, among them Simon the Zealot. As evening fell, he saw four guards come out of the guardroom bearing two inert figures between them. They left by the Golden Gate and Simon followed. He heard two thuds, as the bodies of the old men tumbled down the steep slope, bumping amongst the rocks. Simon shrank into a crevice between some stunted bushes, as the guards walked past him, laughing, as they returned to the Temple.

'After that beating, they will never survive,' said one.

'Shouldn't we have disposed of the bodies better, hidden them?'

'Not so, if they are recognized it will be lesson for others who might otherwise decide to repeat their words. None will dare to speak of a risen Messiah again!'

He spat, as he passed within two feet of Simon. When he was sure they had gone, Simon leapt swiftly down the slope and found them. Both old men bore terrible evidence of their treatment at the hands of the guards. Their backs were bloody mess of stripes. He felt their hearts. One man was dead. The other still seemed to have slight spark of life about him.

Simon lifted the old man's head onto his lap, stroking the grey hair, matted with blood where the whip had risen high. He watched, as the man's eyes opened, and stared uncomprehendingly into his face.

'Have no fear,' comforted Simon. 'I am a friend.' He moved slightly, withdrawing a small flask of wine from his clothing. He raised it to the old man's cracked lips. 'Drink,' he said gently. The man did, focussing his eyes upon Simon's face.

'God bless you, my son, for your care of a stranger.'

'I know the cause for which you suffered,' blurted out Simon wretchedly. He felt that he should have been the one telling the crowds in the Temple Courts of his Lord's wondrous resurrection, not leaving this task to two brave old men, who had paid the ultimate penalty for their courage.

'I just want to tell you, that the words you spoke are true! Jesus of Nazareth lives! We his disciples, have seen him many times since his resurrection and but yesterday he ascended into heaven, to be with his Father, taken from us in a cloud of light!'

The man struggled upright. His face shone with happiness.

'I believe,' he cried! 'Glory be to God and to His Son, Jesus!' Then his head sank down onto his breast, and he was dead. Simon felt great choke rise in his throat, as his tears fell down onto the old man's battered face. He buried them both. The Temple guards should not have the satisfaction of having their victim found by the curious. When it was finished, the stars were shining and the city gates locked. But Simon knew point at which those walls could be scaled, for the Zealots always needed secret ways in and out of the city.

Those disciples who were still awake heard his story in dismay. If this fate had overcome the two old men, who merely repeated what they believed, what would happen to them, when they began to preach the Messiah's message? Their hearts quailed. Fear once again reigned in the house.

Morning dawned and Peter came to a decision. He called the whole assembly together. All were present now, the eleven, the other many disciples, the women and Mary of Nazareth, joined now by Jesus brothers, who at last believed. Peter led them in prayer. Then he came out with that matter, which had been on his mind.

'Brothers, the scripture had to be fulfilled, which the Holy Spirit spoke long ago through the mouth of David, concerning Judas, who served as guide for those who arrested Jesus, he who was one of our number and shared in this ministry!'

Then Peter reminded them of Judas fate—that place where his intestines had spilled out, and which had been named, Akeldama, the field of blood. They listened to him, faces puzzled. Why trouble to talk of these things?

They were of the past, Jesus had risen.

'For it is written in the psalms,' continued Peter, and he quoted, "May his place be deserted—let there be no one to dwell in it" and again "May another take his place of leadership!"

Peter paused, looking over the roomful of intent faces. 'Therefore it is necessary to choose one of the men who have been with us beginning from John's baptism, to that time when Jesus was taken up from us. For one of these must become a witness with us of his resurrection.'

They had to be twelve again!

The room buzzed with conversation, as first one name and then another was put forward to replace the one who had betrayed. Peter was right someone must take the place of Judas Iscariot.

They finally put forward two names. One was Joseph, called Barsabbas. The other was Matthias. Not the same Matthias who was a Zealot. They began to pray aloud, calling on God for guidance in Jesus name.

'Lord, you know everyone's heart. Show us which one of these two, you have chosen to take over this apostolic ministry, which Judas left to go where he belongs!'

Then lots were cast and Matthias became member of the twelve. He looked from quiet eyes upon his comrade's face, rejoicing in his own selection, but sad for the disappointment which Joseph must feel. But Joseph bowed meekly, the only expression on his face one of joy for Matthias. The hearts of all within this room had changed. Worldly ambition no longer held sway.

It was the Eve of the Feast of Pentecost. Tribune Marcus sat with Pontius Pilate, enjoying the superb meal, his plate piled high with delicacies. It was only when the Prefect came to the Antonia, that Marcus had this welcome change from the garrison's normal fare. Lady Claudia sat at her husband's side, staring absently before her, plate untouched. She had asked Pilate to invite Marcus to this private dinner for specific purpose, to inquire of those rumours that had even reached Caesarea, at their palace home on the coast.

'Tribune,' she began quietly. 'My husband and I have heard some talk that Jesus of Nazareth arose from the tomb?'

'My dear, I have told you that this is arrant nonsense,' reproved Pilate, frowning slightly. He had thought that his wife had put aside all gloomy thoughts regarding the Nazarene. The nightmares had stopped and he hoped that Claudia would eventually forget the strange man he had tried and sentenced, even if he, Pilate, was unable to forget! Again and again that face would rise to haunt his sleep, the face of an innocent man, who was perhaps more than just—man?

'But he said to many that he would rise on the third day!' cried Claudia, slim hands gripping the edge of the table, as she raised imperious face to her husband.

'I have already told you, that the guards set to watch his tomb fell asleep on duty, woke up to find the body gone! Obviously, the disciples of the Holy One had taken opportunity to steal the corpse. I believe Caiaphas let his men off with mere dressing down and that I suppose is strange reaction from the High Priest. It would have been more in character, if he called for their execution, a whipping at least. How say you, Marcus?'

'I agree that there is mystery in the matter,' replied Marcus thoughtfully. 'It has been reported to me, that a certain young woman, Mary Magdalene, one of Jesus followers whom I believe is known to you Lady, did herself behold the risen Jesus. It seems she was the first person to see him. Found him walking in the garden at Gethsemane where he had been laid to rest in Joseph of Arimathea's tomb.' Marcus tucked delicate morsel into his mouth, his face thoughtful, as he pondered the strange events surrounding Jesus, which had not even ended with his death.

'Why then, if Mary saw him, then it's true for she would never lie!' Claudia's face brightened with joy. Pilate shook his head. They were both mad!

'Surely, Marcus, you do not believe in such absurdity,' he said stridently! He tossed off a goblet of wine with undue haste, coughing irritably. 'Well, Tribune?'

'If this woman truly believes it, whether it was hallucination born of grief or not, then her words will be accepted, as she was one of the small select band that Jesus kept about him.' Marcus knew he must proceed with caution. If Pilate had reason to think that his Tribune, in charge of the garrison here at Jerusalem believed the apparently impossible, then he might decide to replace him with more responsible soldier. Marcus loved his position, had worked towards place of authority all of his many years in the army. What if strange thoughts had come to him following the crucifixion of the Holy man from Galilee, such thoughts must not be allowed to stand in the way of ambition.

'All this talk of Jesus appearing to different disciples will fade in memory when the next wandering preacher comes to Jerusalem, or the Zealots give us more trouble,' continued Marcus lightly, and saw Pilate relax..

'So, it was not just Mary who saw the risen Jesus,' probed Claudia, not letting the matter drop. A touch of colour now warmed her pale cheeks. 'Tell me, Marcus?'

'Well, certainly it is rumoured that many people have seen and spoken with him, in different places, both here and in Galilee.' The Tribune gave sideways glance at Pilate. The Prefect banged his hand down on the table, the slaves jerking nervously behind him.

'Marcus! Don't encourage her! You and I both know that when a man dies of crucifixion, then he is truly dead! Centurion Lucius assured me that Jesus had most definitely expired and to make sure, a spear was thrust upwards into his chest cavity, entering the heart. No man can live after that!' Pilate snorted in frustration. He wanted no more of this conversation, but a slight thought perplexed him. Why had Caiaphas not shown more annoyance when his men had fallen asleep on duty? After all, he had come seeking Pilate's permission to make the tomb secure with extreme urgency. It would also have seemed more natural if Caiaphas had returned to Pilate, to ask his help in recovering the missing body. But he hadn't! Just allowed it to be known that his men had slept at their task and Pilate was convinced that the High Priest would have ensured only his most experienced men were put on guard!

'Where are Jesus disciples now?' asked Pilate finally.

'They are staying in the villa of a wealthy Cypriot woman and her son, a young man named John Mark. They rarely venture out of the villa and have caused no trouble. I have spies watching the place. They report that all those residing there have an air of nervousness about them. The servants have let slip, that Jesus was often seen there after his death.'

'There you go again,' howled Pilate! Then he glanced at Marcus mortified face and he started to laugh. 'Never mind, my friend. I imagine that if I had to remain here in this tension filled city as you do, I might also be affected by the strangeness of the place. I always experience a sense of brooding unease permeating the very walls, feel it every time my horse bears me through the city gates and that heaviness of spirit remains until I retire again to Caesarea.'

'They say,' dared Marcus, with quick glance at Claudia, 'that Jesus has now left this earth was taken up in a cloud!'

'Delighted to hear it,' exploded Pilate, 'Gone I suppose, to find his heavenly kingdom!' As he cried this out, a sudden spasm shook him, and he rose nervously from his couch. A film of sweat glistened on his forehead, for deep in his own soul, Pilate believed that the Galilean Rabbi who had claimed to be King of the Jews, was supernatural being and he, Pilate, had sentenced him to cruel and quite unjustified death. If Jesus had risen from the dead, then might he not seek vengeance on Pilate? Perhaps Marcus had inkling of the thoughts seething through Pilate's brain, for he stood up and faced him.

'My soldiers tell me that he refused the pain killing drug, which by Jewish custom is offered to those undergoing crucifixion.' He paused, looking deep into Pilate's eyes. 'They also tell me, that he said of the soldiers who crucified him these words, "Father, forgive them—for they know not what they are doing!'

'He said that?' Pilate looked at Marcus in amazement. Then his hands clenched. For Pilate knew, believed now, that Jesus had indeed been the Messiah! A great hatred for Caiaphas seized him. If it hadn't been for that pestilential priest, he would never have given the order, would have released Jesus. One day, he would get even with Caiaphas.

As for Jesus disciples, providing they caused no trouble in the city, then they had nothing to fear from him.

'More wine,' called Pilate. 'There is nothing we can do now about Jesus of Nazareth. As you yourself say Marcus, other matters will arise in the near future which will cause the fate of the Holy man to be forgotten, even as a dream disappears at the dawning of day.'

But he will never be forgotten,' said Lady Claudia. 'His words will pass down through centuries of time, when even great Rome is spoken of no more.' The men stared bemused, at her lovely face, rapt with expression of mysticism, as she stood slim and straight, in sombre black tunic, the colour she had insisted on wearing since Jesus death, but which she knew she would wear no longer.

'Lady, I have had word, that Claudius and his wife Miriam are in Jerusalem,' said Marcus, trying to distract her. Claudia uttered an exclamation of delight and Pilate relaxed. He signed that they should reseat themselves. More wine. He needed more wine! He would only stay for brief days here, until the Jewish Feast of Pentecost, when hopefully, there would be no disturbances, and then back to Caesarea, modern city with its theatres, games and hippodrome and sweet breeze from the sea! Perhaps Emperor Tiberius would recall him one day to Rome, to announce new assignment away from this turbulent, rebellious land. He was unable to look into the future, to see his own eventual disgrace and suicide.

The day of Pentecost dawned, the feast which traditionally took place on the anniversary of Moses receiving the sacred law from Almighty God, on Mount Sinai. On this day, two wave loaves of leavened bread, made from newly ripened grain, were offered to God. It was now fifty days from Passover.

The hundred and twenty men and women who assembled today in the upper room of the house, listened as first Peter and then John son of Zebedee, offered praise to God.

Then the whole room was quiet, as people prayed fervently that the power Jesus had promised them would soon be sent from on high. Then a complete stillness came upon the place. Peter was the first to sense that something was about to happen. He sank to his knees, murmuring Jesus name.

Suddenly, there came a rushing sound, as of a mighty wind! The room shook! The floor beneath them rocked. People knelt in fear as the whole house started to vibrate! And then it was as though a shock wave entered each form, as the power promised by the Son of God came upon them, and the Holy Spirit filled them.

Flames of celestial fire, incandescent bright, appeared above their heads, separating into darting tongues of light, which settled upon each one of them. Power coursed through their bodies, fear was swept away and now they rose to their feet, crying aloud, praising God in torrent of sound, speaking in different tongues! Praising! Praising! Glory—to God in the Highest! Amen and Amen! Louder and louder their cries of exultation arose, as new and wonderful confidence was born in them and with it, urgent need to spread the news of their risen Lord, to all mankind.

They rushed down to the busy street, and into the square beyond, still crying the name of Jesus at the top of their voices, shouting to all of what had recently happened. Telling of the wonders wrought by their mighty God, through His most precious Son, born as a man, who had taught and healed all who came to him, forgiving their sins and whom the people had crucified in their hate and disbelief. Who had now returned to God his Father in heaven! Now, it was their commission to spread his teaching of repentance, love and forgiveness to all men!

The passersby stood listening thunderstruck! Were these men drunk? Peter heard the sniggers and refuted the accusation. But still some insisted that these Galileans had drunk too much wine.

Then a sense of amazement, of awe came upon the crowd, for at last they began to realize that these men and women, although obviously Galilean, were speaking in such way that every person listening, heard their words in their own tongue, for there were present in Jerusalem, God fearing Jews from every nation under heaven.

Men looked at each other bewildered, crying out to each other— 'Are not these men who are speaking, Galileans? Then, how is it, that each one of us hears them in his own language? Parthians, Medes and Elamites— residents of Mesopotamia, Judea and Cappadocia, Pontus and Asia, Phrygia and Pamphylia, Egypt and parts of Libya near Cyrene, yes, and visitors from Rome, both Jews and converts to Judaism, Cretans and Arabs! We hear them declaring the wonders of God, in our own tongues!' They looked at each other, perplexed. 'What can all of this mean?'

Isolated voices still called out that the disciples were drunk. Then Peter and the rest of the twelve called upon the people to be still. Peter started to address them.

'Fellow Jews, and all of you who live in Jerusalem, let me explain this to you! Listen carefully to what I say!'

The crowd, which was growing every minute, quietened, hearing the authority in the tones of the tall, black bearded, bushy haired Galilean. Those at the back of the square pushed forward, struggling to get a better view of what was happening. Peter held up his hands for absolute silence and got it. He pointed to the eleven.

'These men are not drunk as you suppose. After all, it's only nine o'clock in the morning!'

The people smiled at this, for it was right.

'No,' Peter continued. 'This is what was spoken by the Prophet Joel' and he quoted, "In the last days, God says, I will pour out my Spirit on all people. Your sons and daughters will prophecy. Your young men will see visions—your old men will dream dreams. Even on my servants, both men and women, I will pour out my Spirit in those days and they will prophecy! I will show wonders in the heaven above and signs on the earth below, blood and fire and billows of smoke!"

The crowd breathed sighs of awe.

"The sun will be turned to darkness and the moon to blood, before the coming of the great and glorious day of the Lord!" His voice rose deeper and ever louder, "And everyone—everyone who calls on the name of the Lord, will be saved!"

He had their attention now. David and Simeon edged nearer to Peter, eyes shining as they listened to his fearless speech. For this square was near Herod's palace, and some of his guards were amongst the crowd, but Peter ignored them! Claudius with Miriam holding tight to his arm came to flank the disciples, even the women of the group, standing boldly before the people. Again Peter held up hands for silence.

'Men of Israel, listen to this! Jesus of Nazareth was a man accredited by God, to show you miracles, wonders and signs, which God did among you through him, as you yourselves know!'

'Jesus of Nazareth? He speaks of Jesus of Nazareth—these men must be his disciples, for they are of Galilee,' murmured the crowd, straining their ears. 'But Jesus is dead! So why do they speak of him now?' They were perplexed. What was the big fellow saying now? They pushed closer. Peter's voice rose strongly again.

'This man Jesus was handed over to you, by God's set purpose and foreknowledge and you, with the help of wicked men, put him to death, by nailing him to the cross! But God raised him from the dead, freeing him from the agony of death, because it was impossible for death to keep its hold on him!'

Now he held the attention of every man and woman there, for he spoke of that which had been but faint rumour in the city, and not believed. But here was one of Jesus disciples stating it freely, in front of all men. Could it then be true? And if so, what manner of man was this Jesus of Nazareth, that he had been raised from the jaws of death! Rich merchants, shopkeepers, poor folk in from the country, Zealots and

Pharisees, soldiers and beggars, men from all nations, listened amazed and understanding that which was spoken in their own tongue.

Mary of Nazareth stood there too, listening as Peter spoke of her son, her Lord. She heard Peter quoting from the psalms, speaking in the words of King David, reminding the people of the promise God had made to David, to raise up one of his descendants to sit upon his throne. How David had foreseen that the Christ would come and that he would not be abandoned to the grave, nor his body see decay and the crowd with their knowledge of the scriptures, knew of what he spoke, for this was well known passage.

"The Lord said to my Lord, sit at my right hand until I make your enemies a footstool to your feet!"

Mary heard the people repeating these words with Peter. Their faces were upturned as their minds opened to the truth.

'Therefore, let all Israel be assured of this,' thundered Peter. 'God has made this Jesus, whom you crucified, both Lord and Christ!' His accusing finger swung over all. The people began to cry out in fear and agitation, as they realized the enormity of the sin they had jointly condoned, the death of the Holy One of God. They crowded about Peter and the apostles their hands raised in pleading. Mary heard their desperate cry,

'Brothers—what shall we do?'

Peter raised his hands in exhortation. His face glowed with the power of his message.

'Repent and be baptised, every one of you—in the name of Jesus Christ—for the forgiveness of your sins. And you will receive the gift of the Holy Spirit! The promise is for you and your children and for all who are afar off, for all whom the Lord will call!'

Mary raised her own arms in praise, as the power of the Holy Spirit flooded through her, as it had done over thirty years ago. She remembered how the Angel had announced to her as a young virgin that she was to bear God's own son, who was to be the Saviour of the World. Her whole being was vibrating with feeling of love towards those who now sank to their knees in the square, even the soldiers. She saw three thousand people coming forward that day, saying that they wished baptism, would become followers of the Christ—of Jesus of Nazareth,

Son of God!

All of the disciples were preaching now, as groups formed about them, and so it went on, until night fell and at last people dispersed to their homes, here they too spoke to their families, starting to spread the word that was one day to encircle the whole world.

Herod heard of it in his palace and trembled in the quiet of his bedchamber. Pilate and Tribune Marcus stared at each other in troubled amazement, Lady Claudia heard it from the lips of her slave women, and wept from sheer joy and Caiaphas heard it from members of the Temple guards, and his face darkened with rage and fear. They must be stopped, these disciples of the Nazarene!

A young physician also heard the story and wondered at this tale of Jesus the Nazarene, who had taught his people of Almighty God and of His heart of love. How he had forgiven their sins, healed the sick in way impossible even to most skilful doctor, and he, Luke should know this, for was he not one of the most famed physicians of his day! No-one but God could heal the crazed madman, or one ravaged by leprosy. So this Jesus, who had been raised by God from the blackness of the tomb was indeed the son of the Most High, and Luke wished to know more, knew that this teaching must reach the ears of all beyond the shores of Palestine.

And so the story spread! Claudius and Miriam brought it back to Galilee with them, opening doors of their villa, to any who wished to learn of all that had recently happened in Jerusalem! No longer did armed guards prevent entry to the house of Claudius, but rather, small crowds of people led by old Zebedee, father of the disciples James and John, came to sit in the elegant, marble floored reception room, where Miriam herself brought food and drink to them and Claudius reached out hands in greeting.

'So, he really was the Christ,' breathed a stranger, who had come from Nazareth and followed the procession of people to the villa by the shore. 'But he grew up with us, was member of our community and we rejected him.' The man's head drooped in sorrow. Claudius looked at him, judged him to be the same age as Jesus.

'You knew Jesus well, friend?'

'We sat together at the feet of the same teacher, in the school run by the synagogue, in the way that all Jewish boys are educated,' said the man, concentrating on his memories. 'But there was always something different about Jesus, although we didn't know what it was. All in my village refused to believe that he was the Messiah. Will he ever forgive us, we tried to throw him off the hill on which our town is built, could have killed him!'

'How are you called, my friend,' asked Claudius gently?

'My name is Jonathan.'

'Well, Jonathan, as you are probably aware, I was until recently a Centurion in high authority at the Antonia fortress and was present when Jesus was brought to trial. I just stood there, did nothing to help him! And you see, I believed in him, knew him to be the Son of God! I was there when he was scourged, his back torn to pieces by the flagellum and I was there, when he was nailed to the cross.'

Claudius swallowed painfully, as he continued,' And Jonathan, I was there when he opened broken lips, blood streaking his face from cruel crown of thorns, placed in mockery upon his head by one of the soldiers, and I heard these words uttered.' He paused, almost unable to go on.

'What did he say,' prompted Jonathan?

'He said, "Father—forgive them—for they know not what they do!" So in the same way, my brother, he forgives all those who repent and confess their sins and believe in him, will intercede with His Father in heaven, Almighty God, on our behalf. And that includes all men and women—you who rejected him, and I who stood by and let them crucify him, and all others who will put their lives in his hands.'

Miriam smiled wonderingly as she heard her husband teaching the people, standing before them in simple brown tunic, instead of polished armour and scarlet plumes. She had seen many miracles, yet was this not also miracle, the miracle that could be wrought in the everyday life of all who would receive Jesus message of repentance and love.

The people had departed, inviting Claudius and Miriam to visit them whenever they wished and Claudius knew that they had forgiven him for his roughness when he had swept through Capernaum with his men, seeking the ravisher of his wife. They no longer held this against him. He was one of them now.

He told Miriam he felt like a walk.

'But it is late, husband. See, the sun is already low in the sky!' He smiled at her, and pulled her to him in the old familiar gesture.

'Dear Miriam.' He loosed the hair she had swept high on dainty head, letting the black masses of it cloak her shoulders. Love and trust shone out of her green eyes and a new, deeper happiness. She raised her face to his kiss.

'I will not be long,' he murmured. 'I'm going up on the hill behind the villa. It is the one he used to climb,' he explained. He panted as he mounted the steep slope, breathing in the rich spiced fragrance of the luxuriant vegetation, which grew sparser as he reached the summit. He stood there, looking down on Galilee, seeing the waters suddenly flood with crimson, as the sun hung poised, painting the western sky in torrid red and magenta before sinking to rest. His eyes dampened, as he thought of the times that Jesus must have stood so, looking down on the world he had created.

Now he looked down from heavenly heights, from the right hand of his Father's throne, from whence, in time to come, he would judge that world.

'You!'

'Barabbas!'

They stood staring at each other, wary, unbelieving.

The Zealot chieftain wore a sword at his belt, Claudius was unarmed. Barabbas stared at Claudius curiously.

'Where is your uniform, Centurion?'

'I gave it up. I have resigned from the Legion.'

'Huh—did you get tired of ordering men beaten, Roman offal!' Barabbas spat out the words, staring evilly at Claudius, as his hand went to the hilt of his sword. Claudius stared back. But there was no aggression in his blue eyes.

'I did my duty as Roman officer, just as you were acting according to your principals. But I think you cannot complain too much of Roman justice, for you should have been crucified some weeks ago—instead of another!' He threw out the challenge quietly, as his eyes searched the heavily bearded face before him in the last of the fading sunset. Saw the expression change, the hatred turn to uncertainty.

'It was not my fault that they chose me, instead of Jesus!' His eyes were full of torment. 'I deserved death. I have robbed, killed, will probably do the same again to rid my country of you Roman scum. But he, the Holy One, had done nothing wrong. Pilate knew it. I could see it on his face. He gave in only because Caiaphas had inflamed his sycophantic priests and an unstable crowd.' Suddenly Barabbas sank down on the ground, clamping his hands over his face, rocking backwards and forwards in agony of remorse. For the Zealot leader had been in torment for the last few weeks.

If only he hadn't kept up his constant pressure on the Zealots, to keep the name of Jesus ever before the crowds as political leader, a future king, then perhaps they would not have turned against the Holy One when he disappointed them in this, proving to be man of peace, and now as Barabbas truly believed—Son of God!

'Why did he let it happen,' whispered Barabbas? 'You were there, Centurion!'

'My name is Claudius!' He sank down beside the Zealot. 'Yes, I was there. I also stood below the cross. He forgave them, the soldiers who drove in the nails and lifted him up! In his agony, he forgave them.'

'But, why?'

'For the same reason that I have now forgiven the man who raped my wife, even though he is dead. Jesus taught us to forgive, Barabbas! He said that with the same judgement we mete out to men, we ourselves will one day be judged by Almighty God!'

'He forgave me too. I know he did. He looked into my eyes, before I slunk out of the gates into the crowd! I will never forget that expression! He was the Messiah, wasn't he, Claudius?'

Claudius rose to his feet and threw his arms wide.

'Not was but is, for he has risen from the grave!'

The Zealot scrambled to his own feet and stood staring at his former enemy with puzzled, uncertain expression. Claudius reached out a hand and placed it on Barabbas shoulder. The other did not pull away.

'I heard rumours, we all have,' muttered Barabbas. 'But it is not possible!'

Claudius smiled triumphantly, as he cried out, 'Barabbas, I've seen him with my own eyes, heard him speak, seen him as he cooked a meal for his disciples, eating fish fresh caught from the lake. They are all in Jerusalem now, preaching his message to thousands, yes, thousands, who are also becoming believers. Nothing can stop it now, Barabbas!'

'But where is he? Where has he gone, the Holy One?'

'He was taken up in a cloud on the Mount of Olives. His departure from this earth was witnessed by the disciples. He has returned to heaven, from whence he came.'

Claudius voice rose, and the power of the Holy Spirit came upon him, as he reached out to the corrupt soul of Barabbas. And Barabbas wept. They were healing tears. Claudius set his arm about him and Barabbas, his back scarred from Roman whip, clasped his enemy to his breast.

They stood together as brothers, watching the stars twinkling out of the young night, the lights of Capernaum glittering below them.

'So, what happens now, Claudius?'

'Why, we carry out his great commission, Barabbas! These are his instructions!' And Claudius repeated words that floated prophetically on the winds of time. "You will be my witnesses in Jerusalem—and in Judea—and Samaria—and to the Ends of the Earth!"

This story is continued in book two - TO THE ENDS OF THE EARTH and in book three - ROAD TO ROME.

Printed in Great Britain
by Amazon